One with the Land

by Preston L. Gorbett

To Rebecca,
    Enjoy the Adventure!

Preston L. Gorbett

PublishAmerica

Baltimore

First printing

ISBN: 1-4137-1298-3
PUBLISHED BY PUBLISHAMERICA, LLLP
www.publishamerica.com
Baltimore

Printed in the United States of America

In memory of my father
Emery W. Gorbett
for taking me to the wild places
and allowing me to learn to love what I found there.

Nettie Stein made this book a possibility;
for that, I will be eternally grateful.

I would also like to thank Jaci Presely
for the time and effort she put into editing this story.

Cover art by Lissette Gillespie.

To learn more about Preston L. Gorbett, go to
www.crookedfingerproductionsllc.com.

Part One

Chapter One

His lungs ached. His legs were weary. Blood trickled from two small cuts on his face. He had been running through rugged terrain for hours, and now exhaustion forced him into a shuffling, stumbling gait.

His name was Scott Walker, and he was running because he had killed his best friend.

As he ran, he swung his head and glanced over his shoulder. He saw nothing that indicated he was being pursued, but before he could look forward again, his left foot became entangled in a vine and he fell heavily to the ground.

He was too exhausted to rise from where he had fallen. He accepted his need for rest, but when he closed his eyes and laid his head on the soft moss that carpeted the forest floor, his mind suffered a flood of memories from earlier that day.

Scott had been hunting with Falling Feather, the only real friend he had in this New World.

They had been tracking a deer and as they did so, they came upon the tracks of a much larger deer. The larger tracks had turned and followed the original tracks. Falling Feather motioned to Scott, indicating they should split up and parallel the tracks.

A half-mile after they split up, the open timber gave way to a dense stand of younger timber. Experience had taught Scott the two deer were probably bedded down in the thick forest. He increased his efforts to walk quietly.

When he was just a few yards into the younger forest he heard the unmistakable *twang* of a bowstring. There was a small opening ahead so he quickly moved toward it. After a quick look at the thick forest, he knew he would not have a shot unless the deer ran through the opening.

As Scott got himself into position, he heard one of the deer running in his direction, but as he nocked his arrow, he also heard two successive bow *twangs*.

He tried to concentrate on the rapidly approaching deer, but something in the back of his mind was trying to warn him. Something was wrong!

Falling Feather was a very good hunter and the best bow shot Scott had ever seen; but it was physically impossible to shoot two arrows as rapidly as the two shots Scott had just heard.

The two shots could mean only one thing: He and Falling Feather were no longer alone.

When the implications of this thought sank into Scott's brain, the deer became unimportant.

He immediately crouched down into a more concealed position. As he did so, he heard another bowstring. This one was much closer. As he searched for the source of the sound, an arrow struck the tree by which he was standing. If he had not crouched down when he had, the arrow would have pierced his heart.

Scott quickly rolled behind the tree and used it for cover as he tried to think of a course of action. He had been involved in skirmishes in the past and was fully aware of the difficulties involved with the task before him. He was also aware of his own capabilities and knew his new enemy faced a formidable foe.

Scott quickly peeked around the tree, but did not see any sign of his antagonist. He rolled to the other side of the tree and peeked again. This time he did see movement. The Indian was hiding behind two trees, which had nearly grown together. He was about thirty yards from Scott, on the other side of the small clearing.

Scott was also concerned about Falling Feather. He had not heard another bow *twang* for several minutes; he was worried that his friend had been ambushed. His immediate concern, however, was the unknown Indian across the clearing from him. It occurred to Scott that if Falling Feather had been ambushed, he would have to watch his backside to prevent being surprised by his friend's killer.

Scott stood up, keeping the tree between himself and the Indian. When he was fully erect he stepped from behind the tree. The Indian was ready and quickly launched an arrow toward him. Scott ducked back behind the tree. When he saw the arrow fly by, he ran to another tree, closer to the Indian. Another arrow flew over his head as he slid to the ground. This Indian was very fast at reloading his bow; Scott was going to have to be very cautious.

The tree he was now using for cover was much smaller than the first one; he would have to be careful not to expose himself. He didn't think the same trick would work twice, but he didn't know what else to do and he didn't have time to think up another plan.

Scott stepped from behind the tree; to his horror, he saw the Indian was also standing – with his bow at full draw and pointed directly at him.

2

(present)

Scott pushed himself to his knees and stood up. He looked around and noticed he would soon be out of daylight. He had rested longer than he had intended.

It was late winter and though much of the snow had melted, the weather was still unpredictable. He would have to make camp before dark so he could make the necessary preparations. At this time of year, the weather could kill a man as surely as an enemy's arrow.

Resting had helped to clear Scott's head and he now jogged rather than running full out. He was well conditioned to jogging through the forest and could cover many miles in a day.

As Scott jogged, he watched for a suitable place to camp. He knew he would need a fire; he also knew he would have to build it so it wouldn't be seen by anyone who might be following him.

As dusk was gathering, Scott found a suitable camping spot. Off to his right a giant old tree had blown over. The roots of the tree jutted ten feet into the air. Most of the roots were still covered with dirt and grass. Near the base of the old tree was a small rock outcropping. It was ideally located for Scott's needs. If he camped between the tree and the rock outcropping, he would be sheltered on three sides.

Scott checked his back trail one more time before he went to his campsite. He dropped his pack near the upturned roots and went in search of firewood. Limbs from the fallen tree provided him with an ample supply of wood. After he dropped the last armful into the pile, he opened his pack and withdrew his hatchet, flint and steel. He soon had a small, cozy fire burning. He got up and gathered wood until it was too dark to see.

As the warmth of the fire began to soak into his tired body, his stomach grumbled. He realized he had not eaten all day. He took a small piece of jerked venison from his pack and began to eat. After a few bites, he realized he had no appetite. He knew, however, he would have to eat to keep his strength. Strength and courage were two things he was going to be calling on regularly for quite some time.

When Scott finished the piece of meat, he tried to go to sleep but when he closed his eyes he saw Falling Feather lying on the ground, with his arrow in him. The memories flooded back once again.

3

(flashback)

Scott watched in disbelief as the Indian let his bow off to about half-draw. Scott was looking directly into the eyes of the Indian. The man appeared to be surprised or confused about something; though he obviously had the upper hand.

It occurred to Scott this Indian had never seen a white man before. Scott, himself, was an imposing figure at over six feet tall and one-hundred-ninety pounds. His unruly, shoulder-length, blond hair had drawn curious looks from many Indians, but his bushy, light-colored beard had always been a source of immense fascination.

As Scott watched, the Indian seemed to overcome his shock. The Indian pulled his bow back to full draw. Scott knew he didn't have time to take cover, so he charged the Indian.

Scott had taken one step toward the Indian when the Indian reached full draw on his bow.

When he took his second step, he saw the Indian's eyes get bigger.

When he took his third step, the Indian's bow broke in half. The Indian took his eyes off Scott and looked in disbelief at his bow. When he looked back at Scott, it was too late. Scott was too close – and he had his knife in his hand.

Scott hit the Indian at a full run and knocked him sprawling. Scott was on him before he could react. As the Indian struggled to get away, Scott stabbed the knife into his belly and ripped upward with all of his strength.

Scott rolled off the Indian. He watched in revulsion as the other man looked at his belly and then began to try to put his entrails back into his stomach.

Scott wiped the blood off his knife and hands, and then went in search of Falling Feather.

As he approached where he thought Falling Feather would be, he slowed his pace and moved with utmost caution. He made use of all available cover, crawling when cover was scarce. He moved a few feet then scanned the visible terrain before moving on.

He stopped when he came to a small rise. From his location he could see the thick stand of timber giving way to a large meadow, spotted intermittently with scrubby trees and bushes.

As he watched the meadow, he saw the grass moving in a peculiar manner about forty yards in front of him. There was no wind blowing; it had to be a man crawling in the grass.

With the fever of the battle still pumping wildly through his veins, Scott pulled his bow back to full draw, took careful aim and launched his arrow.

He heard a soft thud and a muffled groan; he knew his shot was true.

He watched for half an hour, without moving. In all that time, he heard no sound, nor did he see any movement.

With his senses alert, Scott began to crawl slowly toward the Indian in the grass. He considered trying to signal Falling Feather but knew that if his friend was involved in a skirmish he would not answer back.

As Scott approached the body in the grass, he saw his shot had indeed been a good one. The arrow had gone through the man's rib cage, probably hitting the heart and lungs.

"Wait!!! NO…NO…NOOOOOOOOO."

Scott sprang to his feet and ran to the body, a sinking feeling churning in his guts.

He rolled the body over and looked at the dead face of Falling Feather.

4

(present)

Scott awoke with a start. He hadn't realized he'd gone to sleep. He looked at his fire and realized he had been asleep for quite some time, for only a few embers remained. He moved quickly to rekindle the fire and every muscle in his body screamed at him. He could not remember ever being so painfully sore. When he considered he had probably covered thirty miles yesterday afternoon, he could understand why he ached.

Scott bent over the fire and gently blew on the coals. The coolness of the night caused a chill to run through his body. When the coals began to glow with red heat, he used his knife to make shavings from a bark-less limb. He placed the shavings on the coals and began to blow on them again. In a matter of minutes, he had a small fire going. A short time later, he was able to put larger wood on the flame.

He looked to the eastern sky and noticed it would soon be dawn. There was no need to build a long-lasting fire.

As he drew warmth from the flames, he chewed another piece of meat. He had enough meat for one more day then he would have to hunt again. He had been too distraught to look for deer signs yesterday; he had no idea how plentiful game was in this area.

He ate another piece of meat as the fire died and the eastern sky grew lighter. When he finished the meat, he repacked his gear and shouldered his pack. He kicked the fire apart and walked to the dim trail he had been following the day before.

Sadly, he looked to the east and knew death and shame awaited him there. He looked to the west, knowing not what awaited him in that direction, but it seemed his only option.

Chapter Two

As Scott turned his back on the rising sun, and ventured deeper into the uncharted wilderness, he reflected on his dream. The death of Falling Feather had not been a dream; it was all too real. The means of his death were real, too. Scott wondered if he would be plagued by the nightmare for the rest of his days?

The trail he followed showed no sign of recent use by game or Indians. In places, it was very easy to follow; in others, it became nearly invisible. Scott's thoughts were miles away, on the settlers at James Fort, as well as Falling Feather's family in their village. His lack of concentration caused him to lose the trail several times.

Scott's father had arrived in the New World *via The Godspeed* in 1607. Together, with the other settlers, they had established James Fort. In 1620, the investors of the colony sent a ship with an unusual cargo to the New World. The cargo was a shipload of women who were to serve as prospective wives for the colonists.

The years had been long and lonely for the colonists and most of them were married within a week of the arrival of the women.

Scott Walker was born in 1622.

That same year, Powhaten, the local Indian chief, led an attack against the settlement. Three hundred fifty people were killed in the attack; Scott's mother was one of the victims. She had been caught unaware in an open field near the fort. As she ran for the protection of the fort, she twisted an ankle and fell to the ground. Before she could get back to her feet, an Indian rushed by and bashed her head with a war club. She was carrying Scott in her arms when she fell. Fortunately, she had had time to cover him with her body before she had been overtaken.

Scott's father, Ezra, had been deeply in love with his wife. He took her death very hard. In fact, he never got over her. Many of the settlers thought he was never quite right after her death. In some unexplainable way, Ezra Walker blamed Scott for his wife's death, as if, perhaps, she could have run faster without him in her arms.

Scott was raised by various families within the settlement. As he grew older, he learned who his father was, but the man would have nothing to do with him. This treatment by his father troubled Scott a great deal; he wanted a real father like the other children in the settlement.

When Scott reached his early teens, he spent his days working for anyone who had work. When day's end arrived, he would eat at the table of that settler and sleep in his house or barn.

When he was fifteen, a man he had often worked for died of the fever. The man's wife gave Scott his long bow and a quiver of arrows.

Scott was overjoyed by the gift and began to practice immediately. As time went by, the only thing that stopped him from practicing with the bow was the necessity to work to have a place to eat and sleep.

One day a small group of Indians approached the fort. They carried heavy packs of furs and had come to trade. The steel tools of the colonists were the envy of all the Indians.

The group of Indians gathered in an apprehensive knot outside the gates of the fort.

There wasn't any particular trouble between the Indians and the settlers at that time, but it seemed there was always a certain amount of tension between the two factions.

Several men, who had traded regularly with the Indians, went outside the fort to participate in the ceremonies before the trading began. Men with muskets climbed to platforms on the interior walls of the fort and covered the men while they conversed with the Indians.

When it was determined there was no danger of attack, the gates of the fort were opened and the trading began. The Indians proved to be shrewd traders, but in the end, everyone got what they wanted.

Scott leaned against the exterior wall of the fort and watched the trading. His interest was more in the Indians, themselves, rather than the trading. He was fascinated by their clothing and their demeanor. He could not understand their words and he made little sense of the hand gesturing.

Scott's attention shifted to a young brave who appeared to be a couple of years older than himself. The young brave was not involved in the trading but he paid close attention to the actions of his elders.

The young brave must have sensed Scott looking at him. He looked away from the trading and directly into Scott's eyes. His piercing eyes made Scott extremely uncomfortable but he did not look away. After a few moments, the Indian returned his attention to the trading.

When the sun reached its zenith, the trading came to a close. The Indians were gathering their new belongings and preparing to leave. Unbeknownst to the rest of the settlement, or the Indians, Scott Walker was loading his own pack.

2

(*present*)

Two hours passed before Scott realized he was traveling north. He now stood on top of a high hill, trying to decide what to do. He did not wish to leave the trail; it had become a source of security to him in a time of need. However, it was more important to him to travel west rather than north.

Apprehensively, Scott left the trail and turned west, once again.

Much of the terrain was covered with oak and maple trees, interspersed with conifers and brush thickets. The ground was covered with deer tracks and droppings but Scott did not want to kill a deer yet. It had been instilled in him by Falling Feather and his people not to waste meat. He assumed that Falling Feather's people were after him for what he had done. They would catch him for sure if he took the time to cure an entire deer.

As luck would have it, he saw a flock of turkeys before he saw a deer, and with a little more luck, he soon had a fine young tom roasting over a fire.

Scott had been so preoccupied with his recent past that he had not been paying attention to his surroundings or the weather. Before the turkey finished cooking, the dark, ominous clouds that had been threatening all day opened up and dumped a downpour on Scott and his fire.

Scott hastily erected a rough shelter of limbs and bark, and prepared to wait out the storm. Experience had taught him that such heavy rainstorms seldom lasted very long; this one lasted throughout the night.

Scott tried, without success, to build another fire. He was drenched to the skin and his shelter was barely adequate. As darkness fell, he ate his fill of half-cooked turkey and then shivered himself to sleep.

The next morning, Scott awoke stiff and sore again. He ate more of the turkey and stored the rest in his pack. He shivered uncontrollably until there was adequate light to travel.

Once on the move, Scott began to feel better; when his muscles were sufficiently warmed up, he began to jog. As the miles melted away, Scott took consolation in knowing the rain was going to make his trail extremely difficult to follow.

3

After a week on the trail, Scott had not been overtaken by Falling Feather's people. He had no idea how far ahead of them he was. At present, however, he was confronted with another problem. He was on a prominent ridge and he could see smoke rising from an Indian village in the valley below him.

If he remained on the ridge he could avoid the village, but he was concerned about inadvertently being discovered by a villager.

Scott followed the ridge, which ran in a south-westerly direction. There was enough brush cover on the ridge that he didn't have to worry about sky lining himself as he traveled.

He had killed a small deer the day before so meat was not an immediate problem. The deer had been a small doe, crippled in a fall or some other serious mishap. Both of the doe's front legs had been broken. She had been unable to run from Scott as he approached her. Scott killed her with his hatchet, preventing him from having to waste an arrow. Much of the meat had been bloodshot and as such, was unusable. He had stripped and smoked enough meat to last him for about two weeks.

Scott followed the ridge until it disappeared near a small river. He crossed the river and continued southwest for another day before turning west and entering a mountain range. In an attempt to maintain as fast a pace as possible, he refrained from climbing the ridges to cross the mountains. Instead, he located a river and followed it upstream. It was a winding course but he made good time.

He followed the river for three days until it turned due north. He was deep in the mountains now and decided to climb the slopes rather than follow the river in a northerly direction.

By the time he reached the crest of the first ridge, after leaving the river, it began to rain again. Scott wished he had taken the hide from the crippled doe; it had not been cured but it would have offered some protection from the rain.

Scott considered stopping and building a shelter until the storm passed but he knew the rain was his only hope of losing Falling Feather's people; he should keep moving as long as he could.

The ridge that Scott was on ran north and south. He didn't want to go in either direction. If he dropped off where he was, he might leave tracks on the steep slope; tracks the rain probably wouldn't wash out. Scott turned south on the ridge-top and traveled for several hours before he found a game trail that contoured into the canyon. The rain was so heavy and the clouds so thick that Scott could not determine the extent of the mountain range.

Scott followed the game trail off the ridge until it ended in a narrow valley. Darkness came early that night and he was unable to locate a suitable shelter before the light faded completely from the sky. He crawled under a fallen tree and tried to build a fire. He was soaked to the skin and all of the available fuel was wet, as well. Despite his best efforts, he was unable to get a fire going and spent the night shivering under the log.

Two hours before sunup the storm passed and the skies cleared. Scott rolled out from under the log and walked through the valley. By the time the sun finally began to peek over the ridge he had crossed yesterday, he came to a fork in the valley. He took the western fork but it was taking him farther north than he wanted to go. He turned west and began climbing the slope of another ridge.

Walking warmed Scott and made him feel better, but he was tired. Soon he would have to stop to rest. The days of hard, fast travel were taking their toll on him. Climbing the steep ridges wasn't helping either. He decided to watch for a good place to camp and rest for a couple of days.

Scott topped out on a long, narrow feeder ridge that made a sweeping turn to the west where it joined with the main body of the north and south mountains. He stayed on the feeder ridge until he gained the crest of the main ridge. The ridges joined in a large saddle with long, gentle slopes in either direction. The middle of the saddle was relatively flat; it contained a stand of timber that would provide shelter and firewood.

Upon exploring the stand of timber, Scott found several deadfalls of various sizes. Though he was exhausted, he immediately began constructing a lean-to shelter. By nightfall, he had a secure campsite that would protect him from detection and the elements. He had built a small fire earlier and then huddled close to it, adding fuel as he ate more deer meat. He stripped off his wet clothing and hung them near the fire, careful not to get them too close. He sat down near the fire and leaned against a tree; he was asleep in a matter of seconds.

The next morning, Scott was awakened by the sun as it shone it's life-giving light into his eyes. The sunlight was warm but the air was cool; he quickly dressed and rekindled his fire. When he was thoroughly warmed, he went in search of a deer to replenish his food supply.

When he had gone a few hundred yards, he came upon a young buck feeding on the grassy ridge top. The deer was north of him; the wind was from the east. He didn't have to worry about the deer getting his scent. He approached slowly and carefully for there was very little cover. The deer was so intent upon his meal he probably wouldn't have noticed the man even if he had been less careful.

When Scott was within thirty yards, the deer raised its head and looked directly at him, but it was too late for the arrow was already on its way. The deer probably saw the arrow coming but it didn't have time to react. The arrow struck the deer in the rib cage; he bucked and kicked before he ran up the ridge.

Going to the edge of the ridge, Scott hunkered down beside a bushy tree, waiting for the arrow to do its work. He waited for an hour before he began to track the deer. He knew his shot was good and the deer would die soon. He also knew, if he pushed it too soon, it could run a long way before it finally collapsed.

The deer had bled well; it was an easy trail to follow. The buck had gone less than two hundred yards. He had lain down to rest and had not gotten back to his feet.

Scott quickly removed the entrails and then carried the animal back to his camp. He spitted the heart of the deer over the fire to cook while he skinned the carcass. He staked the hide in the sun and then began to cut thin slices of meat from the body of the deer.

While the meat cured, Scott scouted the terrain and found that the ridge he was on was the tallest one in the mountain range. At last, he was near the other side. There would be more ridges to cross, but the worst of the climbing was behind him.

By the third day, Scott was fully rested. He had a pack full of freshly smoked meat and a green hide to work. He left his cozy camp and descended from the ridge.

Chapter Three

Dawn was breaking over a distant ridge as a hundred pair of hostile eyes watched the sleeping Indian village.

They were Seneca of the powerful Iroquois league. They had come a long way to punish the insolent Shawnee. The Seneca expected compensation from any tribe living in an area that might be deemed as *their* hunting grounds.

The Shawnee assumed there would be safety in distance. They had assumed incorrectly. They had not heeded the stories told around campfires of the stamina of the Seneca. It was said the Seneca could run for days without rest, win a battle, and return home without fatigue.

The Seneca awaited the signal of their war chief. They were anxious for the fight to begin, but they were well trained in battle and even the young warriors were cautious to make no sound lest they alert the Shawnee before the trap was sprung. Such an error would be an unbearable disgrace.

Suddenly, the gobble of a turkey could be heard throughout the sleepy village. It was the signal! The Seneca warriors jumped to their feet and issued war cries as they attacked the village. They shot arrows and threw spears into the hide-covered lodges of the unsuspecting Shawnee.

The Shawnee were taken completely by surprise. They were thrown into a panic that even the most experienced warriors were unable to bring under control. With their women and children crying and screaming, the warriors did what they could to ward off the attack.

Some of the Shawnee warriors circled the women and children, facing the Seneca, putting a defensive wall between the attackers and their vulnerable families. Their efforts were in vain.

The Seneca were interested in taking slaves. They were very discriminate in selecting who would survive. If a person appeared to be unfit to make the return trip, they were put to death. Of course, in the heat of battle some potential slaves were accidentally killed. No Shawnee warrior was spared.

The Seneca soon overwhelmed the surprised Shawnee. Several warriors had escaped, leaving their loved ones behind.

The Seneca were led by a fierce war chief named Man-who-has-killed-many-bear. He had earned his name the hard way and was very proud of his accomplishments. He feared nothing on the face of the earth.

With a faint smile that is allowed the victor, Man-who-has-killed-many-bear appraised his captives. Most of the prisoners appeared to be between ten and twenty years of age; perfect for his intentions. They would be slaves until they accepted the ways of the Seneca.

The shocked survivors were herded into a circle. As they were being bound together, several braves were sent in pursuit of the escaped Shawnee warriors. The captives were bound around the wrists with rawhide thongs. The thongs were then tied together with a long piece of rawhide rope. They were tied about three feet apart, giving them enough room to walk in single file.

When the Shawnee were bound, they were forced out of the village. They barely got a backward glance at what was once their home.

One middle-aged squaw fell to her knees and began to wail as she was forced to walk by her slain husband. A warrior quickly came forward and bashed in her skull with a tomahawk. The woman was cut from the group of prisoners, her twitching body left where it fell. A clear message was sent to the remaining Shawnee.

The Indians marched through the forest until dusk. They made no stops for food or rest. When darkness fell, the frightened captives slept on the ground, with no fire or blankets for warmth.

Shortly after dark, the Seneca warriors who had remained behind to search out the escaped Shawnee returned. There were no survivors. They celebrated when they rejoined their brothers, casting menacing glances at the prisoners. Man-who-has-killed-many-bear and his warriors were elated with the results of the day.

2

Deer-with-one-antler was sixteen summers old. He had great skill for a young man. His father had taught him well the ways of battle and manhood. When the Seneca walked by him or looked in his direction, he masked the seething hatred that threatened to overwhelm him. He knew he could not help his people if he were dead, which he surely would be if he displayed his feelings.

There were five of his people behind Deer-with-one-antler: two boys and two girls of about ten summers of age, and a young squaw. The young squaw was Dew-on-the-grass-in-the-moon-when-the-leaves-fall. She was entering her eighteenth summer and was the only one behind him he could count on for assistance. Their eyes met, and with a simple nod of his head, Deer-with-one-antler conveyed the message that he would do what he could to escape and she should be ready.

Sleep was not to come easily to the Shawnee. There were muffled sobs from the young girls. Their reward was a beating with a stout stick.

A rock protruded from the ground near where Deer-with-one-antler lay. It did not have a sharp edge, but with enough time, it would serve as a tool to fray the ties that bound his wrists.

Moving carefully, to avoid drawing attention to himself, Deer-with-one-antler leaned forward and began to slide the thongs over the edge of the rock. Bending and rubbing was torturous. His face was beaded with perspiration, his shoulder and arms ached, but he worked through the pain.

Moving so slowly that it was barely perceptible, Dew-on-the-grass-in-the-moon-when-the-leaves-fall reached into a fold in her dress and removed an awl. The awl was made from a splintered leg bone of a deer. She had been using it the day before and had neglected to put it away when she finished her task. She now put the large end of the awl on top of her thigh and pierced her bindings with the needle sharp tip. It was tedious work but the bindings soon began to tear.

Dew-on-the-grass-in-the-moon-when-the-leaves-fall saw Deer-with-one-antler's body jerk slightly and heard his bindings part. At the same time, they saw a sentinel walking along the line of prisoners, moving toward them. Dew-on-the-grass-in-the-moon-when-the-leaves-fall placed her arm on top of the awl. They both lay motionless as the sentinel passed by.

The warrior seated himself above the trail at the end of the line of captives. Unless she did something soon, they would be unable to continue their efforts to escape.

Dew-on-the-grass-in-the-moon-when-the-leaves-fall moaned softly and rolled onto her back. The warrior was on his feet in an instant. She turned her head toward him and their eyes met. She looked at him shyly and sat up. Even in the darkness, the warrior could tell she was beautiful. He went to her and squatted down in front of her. Dew-on-the-grass-in-the-moon-when-the-leaves-fall had to look away from his leering eyes. He reached out with his left hand and grabbed a handful of hair from the side of her head. He twisted his hand slightly and pulled her head closer to his.

He was about to speak when Deer-with-one-antler rolled over. The instant the brave looked away, Dew-on-the-grass-in-the-moon-when-the-leaves-fall grasped the awl in her hands and thrust it into his sternum. The brave issued a gasp but he did not cry out. He fell forward, on top of her, and then rolled onto his side. He was dead before he rolled off of her, but she wore the stain of his blood on her dress.

Quickly, Deer-with-one-antler and Dew-on-the-grass-in-the-moon-when-the-leaves-fall were on their feet, squatting low, to avoid detection. Deer-with-one-antler went to the dead brave and took his knife. He cut the bindings from the captives who were behind him and then those from the youth in front of him.

He gave the knife to the youth and motioned him to pass it forward. With hand signals, Deer-with-one-antler instructed the released prisoners to scatter in all directions to avoid recapture. They all knew there were more Shawnee, far to the south, on the banks of the great river.

With that done, Deer-with-one-antler disappeared into the night. Dew-on-the-grass-in-the-moon-when-the-leaves-fall also left the trail and ran into the darkness. She moved slowly for a time and then she began to move faster. She heard a warning cry behind her, and then the shrieks of her people. She knew many of them would not see the next sunrise.

Dew-on-the-grass-in-the-moon-when-the-leaves-fall began to sprint. She did not stop until the sunlight began to streak across the eastern horizon. She knew she would have to conceal the signs of her passing or die. And die she surely would, for she bore the blood of the slain sentinel.

She broke out of the forest into a small meadow. The meadow contained a grove of ancient maple trees. There was a large, fallen conifer that reached from the edge of the forest to the grove of maples. She went to the fallen tree, climbed on top of it, and walked its back. When she was near enough, she jumped to a maple limb. She looked up toward the top of the maple tree and saw two massive limbs stretching out toward the next tree in the grove.

Dew-on-the-grass-in-the-moon-when-the-leaves-fall climbed to the two limbs. One was far enough above the other that she could walk on one as she held onto the upper one. Cautiously, she walked out the limbs. When she reached a limb in the next tree that would support her weight, she jumped again. She grasped the limb with her hands as her feet dangled far from the ground. With little effort, she pulled herself onto the limb and scooted to the trunk of the tree. There were not sufficient limbs in this tree to allow her to get to the next tree. Risking a fall, she climbed and shinnied down the trunk until she came to the last limb. She was still high up the tree – too far to jump. She walked out on the long sweeping limb until it became unstable. Bending down, she grasped the limb in her hands and lowered herself. Moving hand over hand, she worked her way toward the end of the branch. The farther she got from the trunk, the more her weight bent the limb, until it lowered her gently to the ground.

The instant her feet touched the ground, she squatted low and ran through the meadow as fast as possible. When she reached the forest, she straightened up and continued to run. She ran on deadfalls and rocks when possible. She crossed a game trail and resisted the urge to use it. Using the trail would be much faster and easier, but her tracks would be more easily detected.

At about mid-day, Dew-on-the-grass-in-the-moon-when-the-leaves-fall saw a pine tree that had blown over and fallen into an oak tree. The top of the conifer was hung in the oak, where it had fallen several years earlier. With the utmost care to leave no sign, she worked her way through the brush to the pine. Once there, she carefully ascended the leaning trunk. As she walked, the tree swayed, nearly causing her to lose her balance.

The conifer was rotten and it broke quickly and quietly and without warning.

With the reflexes of a cat, she sprang for the nearest oak limb and held on for her life. The limb was not very big, but it was green and did not break. She pulled herself hand over hand until she reached the trunk of the tree.

A few feet above her, there was a huge bowl in the tree with four massive limbs spreading out in as many directions. She climbed to the bowl and found the limbs had created a pocket in which she could hide without fear of being seen or falling while she slept.

Some time later, Dew-on-the-grass-in-the-moon-when-the-leaves-fall awoke with a start. It took several moments for her to remember where she was and why she was there.

Slowly, she raised her head far enough to scan the forest around the tree. A careful survey revealed no one on her back trail. She settled back in her nest to rest until dark. She couldn't move as quickly at night, but it would be easier to avoid detection.

Finally, as the last rays of sunlight were disappearing, she climbed down the tree. Dew-on-the-grass-in-the-moon-when-the-leaves-fall took the lowest limb in both hands and swung down, still high in the air. Releasing the limb, she hit the ground hard, lost her balance, and had to reach for the tree trunk to keep from falling.

She had just stopped moving when a crashing blow to the back of her head caused her to see stars. Dew-on-the-grass-in-the-moon-when-the-leaves-fall did not completely lose consciousness, but nonetheless felt faint and nauseated. Instinctively, she reached for the awl as she fell to the ground.

The brave was on her quickly – too quickly. He grabbed her shoulder and spun her around.

With her last conscious will to survive, Dew-on-the-grass-in-the-moon-when-the-leaves-fall stabbed with the awl as she was spun around.

The awl went into the brave, its needle-sharp point exiting his back, near the spine. With a look of shock and disbelief on his face, the brave fell in a crumpled heap, on top of Dew-on-the-grass-in-the-moon-when-the-leaves-fall.

3

Bright…Bright…Why so bright? Dew-on-the-grass-in-the-moon-when-the-leaves-fall thought to herself as she squinted at the brightness of the sun. Squinting made her head hurt worse. She put her arm on her forehead, but the pain remained. She opened her eyes. The pain increased, if that were possible.

Dew-on-the-grass-in-the-moon-when-the-leaves-fall squirmed out from under the brave's body and rolled to her stomach, feeling a wave of nausea. After a few moments, the feeling passed. She got to her hands and knees. With considerable difficulty, she managed to gain her feet. Dew-on-the-grass-in-the-moon-when-the-leaves-fall stumbled away from the dead brave and into the forest.

Chapter Four

Ten days after Scott left the temporary camp, he was out of the mountains. He had seen a large river to the northeast during the descent and he searched for that river now.

Scott alternated from trotting to walking throughout the course of each day. He covered many miles from daylight to dark. Though he had seen no sign of Falling Feather's people, he was constantly looking over his shoulder for sign of pursuit.

Scott stood on the bank of a small river. He had been following the watercourse for several hours, looking for a safe place to cross. The water was extremely swift. At last, he came upon a shallow place at the end of a long, slow, deep hole. Unfortunately, others had found the crossing before him; the trail on either side of the river was filled with moccasin tracks.

Not knowing how often the trail was used, or where it went, Scott backtracked several hundred yards and took cover in a brushy thicket. He had not been walking on a trail when he found the tracks and felt confident he had left no sign of his passing.

As Scott sat in the brush, trying to plan a strategy to get safely to the large river, his thoughts returned to the tracks in the trail. They reminded him of the tracks he had followed out of James Fort so long ago.

2
(flashback)

Scott had spent the night in the wilderness on many occasions. It had always been by design and not necessity, for he had never been far from the settlement. He was not adequately prepared for the trip he was now taking because he did not know the location of the Indian village.

The trail of the Indians was extremely difficult to follow in the thick underbrush and dark, dark forest. He could not get too close to the Indians for fear of being discovered.

When darkness began to fall, Scott stopped to make camp. He had no idea where he was but he was not lost. If he lost the trail of the Indians, he had only to walk east to the coast and follow the shoreline to the settlement.

The next morning, he was on the trail again. It seemed the farther the Indians got from the settlement, the harder their trail was to follow.

Late that afternoon, Scott began to feel uncomfortable. He had lost the trail an hour earlier. As he searched for it, he had the feeling he was being watched.

He stopped looking for the trail and scanned the forest, but saw nothing out of the ordinary. However, the feeling would not go away. He looked about again, more carefully. As his eyes searched through the forest, they fell upon a human face concealed in the leaves of a bushy tree. The Indian was so well camouflaged, Scott continued to search the forest for several seconds before he realized what he had seen.

His eyes returned to where he had seen the face. The Indian immediately realized he had been discovered. He left his cover and began to move toward Scott. Scott was painfully aware that the Indian made no sound as he slipped through the forest.

Scott instantly recognized him as the younger brave who had accompanied the trading Indians to James Fort.

The young Indian approached slowly and stopped several yards from Scott. He looked at Scott curiously, obviously wondering why he was in that part of the forest.

With a slight tilt of his head, the Indian indicated that Scott should follow him. The movement was so subtle Scott missed it. The Indian began to walk away but stopped when he realized Scott was not following. He turned toward Scott, and with a scant smile, waved his arm in a sweeping arc.

Scott suddenly comprehended what the Indian wanted and followed him when he turned and led the way. Scott proceeded with some reluctance, for he knew not where the brave was leading him. On the other hand, he didn't know what the Indian would do if he refused to follow.

They traveled through the forest at a fast pace and Scott was hard put to keep up. He was also embarrassed by the amount of noise he made compared to the young Indian.

Shortly after dark, Scott was led into the Indian village. He was apprehensive about entering the village, but felt he had little choice.

Most of the villagers had retired to their lodges by the time Scott was led through the village, but those who remained outside looked curiously at him.

He was taken to a thatched lodge on the northern edge of the village. The young Indian opened a hide flap that served as a door. He indicated Scott should enter the lodge; he followed immediately behind.

There were five other Indians in the lodge: a very old woman, a middle-aged man and woman, and two young girls. Scott found out later the young brave's name was Falling Feather. The other occupants of the lodge were his grandmother, father, mother and sisters.

Falling Feather's father quickly rose to his feet as Scott entered the lodge. The older man and Falling Feather began a discussion but Scott could not understand their words. The older man's eyes kept returning to Scott as the conversation continued; Scott was certain they were talking about him. Falling Feather's father did not seem hostile, but Scott could tell he was uncomfortable with a strange white man in his lodge.

Scott felt uncomfortable himself, like an unwanted intruder. He could not speak their language, nor they his. The language barrier alone seemed to drive a wedge into the gap that existed between the two races.

Finally, the conversation ended. The patriarch of the home motioned for Scott to be seated.

Falling Feather's mother began to pass out a stew of sorts that was served in hewn wooden bowls. Scott was served first but did not partake of the food until Falling Feather's father began to eat. The older man took that as a gesture of respect, when in fact, Scott was waiting to see how they fed themselves from the bowls. They simply turned them up and drank from them.

Falling Feather's father tried several times to communicate with Scott but Scott could not understand his words. When the older man tried sign language, his hands moved so quickly and with such fluidity, Scott could not determine his meaning. The older man finally gave up in frustration. Scott was angry with himself for his inability to understand.

Scott was provided with a sleeping mat and a fur robe with which to cover himself. Shortly thereafter, the lodge was filled with sounds of sleeping people. Despite his uneasiness, Scott was soon asleep, as well.

The next morning, Scott was awakened by the sounds of people moving about. He had slept well and felt he could have slept longer, but quickly rolled out of his bed. By the time he had rolled up the sleeping mat and robe, the morning meal was ready to eat.

Falling Feather was eating quickly so Scott followed his lead. When they finished eating, Falling Feather got to his feet and motioned for Scott to follow him.

Falling Feather went through the hide doorway and let it drop back into place. At the doorway, as an afterthought, Scott turned to Falling Feather's family and nodded to them. It was the only way he knew to thank them for their hospitality.

Scott followed Falling Feather into the forest. He knew immediately he was being taken back to James Fort. He found himself wishing he could remain in the village, with Falling Feather and his family.

If only he could communicate with them, he could ask them about the possibility of living in the village. There were many things Scott would like to discuss with the Indians. However, foremost in his mind were questions about Indian life.

As Scott and Falling Feather walked through the forest, Scott became overwrought with his inability to communicate with these people.

"I say," said Scott, much too loudly.

Falling Feather whirled around and went into a crouching, defensive posture so quickly it was barely perceptible. His eyes scanned the surrounding forest, seeming to see everything all at once.

Scott suddenly felt threatened. He dropped his bow and raised his open hands to chest level in front of himself. He also took a couple of involuntary steps backward. Scott felt foolish that he had allowed himself to back away; his face reddened deeply.

Falling Feather came out of his defensive stance the instant he realized there was no danger. He looked at Scott quizzically, with a slight frown on his face.

Scott placed his hand on the base of a large tree and said, "Tree."

Falling Feather's questioning look told him he didn't understand what he meant. Scott patted the tree, stepped away, and pointed at it and repeated, "Tree."

Falling Feather said something Scott didn't understand. Scott placed a cupped hand behind his ear. Falling Feather repeated what he had said. Scott could say the words in his mind but his tongue refused to cooperate.

Falling Feather turned and started through the forest again. As Scott followed, he said the words over and over again in his mind. Under his breath, he practiced saying the words until he thought he had them right.

Scott hissed at Falling Feather, hoping not to startle him again. When Falling Feather turned around, Scott patted another tree and said the words he had been practicing.

Falling Feather shook his head slightly and said different words. Scott looked at the tree. Perhaps it was a different kind of tree, he didn't know. It was frustrating to want something so badly and not know how to acquire it.

Scott pointed to the tree and moved his hands and fingers. Falling Feather immediately understood what he was asking. He pointed to the tree and gestured with his hands but his movements were so smooth and fluid, Scott had difficulty following them. Falling Feather saw that Scott was having trouble and repeated the movements more slowly. When Falling Feather finished, Scott tried to make the same movements and did very well.

During the trip back to the settlement, Scott learned how to say several things with his hands. Much of what he learned to say described inanimate objects such as rocks, bows, arrows and the like, but it was a start and he was excited about his progress. Scott was anxious to learn more but his time had run out for they were within sight of the settlement.

Falling Feather nodded to Scott, turned and disappeared into the forest. Once again Scott was impressed with the Indian's ability to move soundlessly through the forest. When Scott had been following him, and not fumbling around with the sign language, he watched how he walked and where he stepped. This too, would take much practice, for even when Scott walked where the Indian had, he still made noise, when the other had not.

When Scott walked into the settlement, a cry went out that he was back. He was quickly surrounded by a group of worried settlers. They all expressed their relief in finding that he was safe. Some of the settlers thought he had been taken captive by the Indians, others thought he had wandered into the wilderness and had suffered some unthinkable fate.

As Scott imparted his story to the anxious settlers, he saw his father standing by a nearby cabin. When he realized Scott had noticed him, he turned and walked away. Scott continued telling his story. He and his father did not speak that day, nor would they ever do so again.

3

Now, the wilderness seemed to have a stronger attraction to Scott than ever before. He had watched Falling Feather make camp and by applying what he had learned, he was able to make himself more comfortable when he slept under the forest canopy. His self-confidence grew daily, as did his abilities, and soon he was venturing farther and farther from the settlement. Eventually, it was not uncommon for Scott to be gone four or five days at a time; the settlers soon stopped worrying about him.

The first snow of winter was silently covering the open meadows and clearings of the wilderness when Scott walked into Falling Feather's village for the second time. It had been several months since Falling Feather had returned him to the settlement. He was feeling quite proud of his accomplishment, despite the fact that Falling Feather was standing at the edge of the village waiting for him.

Scott did not know there were scouts spread in a protective circle around the village and his approach had been reported several hours earlier.

Falling Feather seemed angry as Scott drew near him. A quick glance at the village told Scott something important was going on. The activity in the village was brought on by more than the snowstorm that was blanketing the area.

Falling Feather motioned Scott to follow him. As they walked through the village, two dozen warriors ran by them. They disappeared into the forest on the eastern edge of the village. The warriors were naked to the waist, despite the cold. Their bodies were streaked with various colors of paint.

Scott followed Falling Feather to the same thatched house he had stayed in on his first visit to the village. Once inside, Falling Feather removed his buckskin shirt and quickly painted his chest and arms. His family was present, with the exception of his father. Falling Feather motioned for Scott to remain in the lodge, then he stepped through the flap and was gone. Scott attempted to follow, but Falling Feather's mother gently grabbed his arm and motioned him to sit.

Scott had no way of knowing that in the past few days a great deal of tension had arisen between these Powhatans and the neighboring Pamunkey. A warrior of another Powhatan village had encountered a Pamunkey in the forest. Each accused the other of trespassing on the other's hunting grounds. The argument turned violent and the Powhatan killed the Pamunkey in the ensuing struggle. The Pamunkey were incensed and threatened to attack the Powhatan village unless the culprit was handed over to them. Unfortunately for the Powhatan, the incident had occurred in Pamunkey domain. The chief of the Powhatan village sent runners to all of the Powhatan villages asking for support, in the event a compromise could not be reached. As it ultimately turned out, the offending warrior was turned over to the Pamunkey. No one ever spoke of him again and Scott never learned what fate befell the unlucky warrior.

Scott waited three days for Falling Feather to return. In the interim, the snow melted off and returned again to an accumulation of several inches.

There was little to occupy Scott as he waited. He walked through the village and studied the construction of the thatch houses. The only men left in the village were old and he had no way of communicating with them. Besides, they showed little interest in developing a relationship with him.

On the fourth day, Falling Feather returned. His father gave Scott a questioning look as he entered the house. Falling Feather, himself, seemed surprised that Scott was still in the village. It was late afternoon when the warriors returned to the village. Falling Feather's mother quickly began to prepare a meal. The family conversed among themselves, they laughed and smiled as they spoke. Even with Scott's inability to understand their language, there was no doubt there was love in this family. Even the savages seemed to have attained something that was not within his reach and, once again, he was envious of them.

4

During the time the warriors had been gone, the remaining villagers had continued to eat on a regular basis, however, no one had hunted to replenish the food supply.

The next morning, Scott was rudely awakened by Falling Feather as he nudged him with his foot. As Scott quickly got to his feet, he saw that Falling Feather was holding his bow and quiver of arrows.

Scott had gotten more arrows from one of the settlers and had spent many hours practicing in a meadow near the fort. His skill had improved quickly and more often than not, he would return to the settlement with fresh venison.

Falling Feather motioned for Scott to gather his weapons. When he had done so, they stepped out of the lodge into the cold morning air.

A group of young men had gathered near the center of the village. Falling Feather and Scott walked toward them. Scott noticed the braves all seemed to be about the same age as Falling Feather. The warriors gave Scott a curious glance before turning their attention to the business at hand. There was much talking and pointing, in this direction, and that. After a few minutes, the discussion ended and the group broke up into parties of two or three. They went into the forest in different directions. Falling Feather and Scott went north.

The sky was filled with massive black clouds and an hour after the hunting parties had left the village, the snow once again began to fall.

Falling Feather looked often to the dark sky as they continued to hunt in a northerly direction. They began to trot so they could cover more ground as they searched for fresh deer tracks. It was late morning before they found deer tracks that weren't filled with snow. Upon discovering the tracks, Falling Feather turned in the direction the tracks had gone and increased his pace.

Scott was gasping for breath when Falling Feather finally slowed to a walk. Scott had been so intent upon keeping up with Falling Feather that he hadn't noticed there were now several sets of fresh tracks.

Scott was dismayed to see that Falling Feather wasn't breathing any harder than if he had walked to where they now stood.

Scott and Falling Feather were in a large flat area, but the timber was thick and visibility was poor. The snow and the darkness of the day made it seem later than it was.

Falling Feather motioned for Scott to move off to the right. He pointed to his eye and then in the direction he wanted Scott to go and then back at himself. Scott assumed that he was telling him to stay within sight of each other. When Scott was thirty yards away, he found that he was spending as much effort watching for Falling Feather as for the deer.

Suddenly, there was an especially thick stand of trees separating the hunters, and Scott completely lost sight of Falling Feather. Scott increased his pace until he had gone by the thick timber. When he saw Falling Feather again, he was standing stalk still with his bow drawn back. Scott let his eyes drift from the Indian, in the direction he was pointing his arrow. He could see nothing, but nocked an arrow anyway. Scott heard the *twang* of the bowstring as Falling Feather released his arrow. He also heard the hollow thud and knew from his own experience that the arrow had buried itself in a tree. Scott heard the deer bounding through the forest; it was coming toward him.

Scott suddenly felt as if the weight of the world had just dropped onto his shoulders. It wasn't as if his capabilities were being tested and he *had* to do well. He *wanted* to do well. He *wanted* to be accepted by these people. No, he *needed* to be accepted by these people. He had friends among the settlers, but he felt that he was different from them, and had different needs. What he wanted more than anything was to be Falling Feather's friend and companion.

Scott saw a flash of movement between the trees and drew back his bow. He saw the deer clearly on two occasions but it was moving too quickly and did not offer a clean shot. However, he was able to determine the route it would be taking. Scott picked an opening in the timber and waited. The deer was running from left to right; when Scott's left eye detected movement, he released the arrow. Though Scott would never admit it, he had just made the luckiest shot of his life. The arrow broke the deer's neck and it fell to the ground, dead.

Scott looked to Falling Feather, for approval, but he had disappeared into the forest.

Scott walked to the deer and saw that it was a fine buck. He withdrew his knife from the scabbard on his belt and field dressed the animal. Just as Scott finished dressing the deer, he heard footsteps crunching in the snow. He turned to make certain it was Falling Feather and saw his friend walking toward him with a doe slung over his shoulder. Scott loaded the buck on his back, and together, they began the return trip to the village.

Scott had packed many deer out of the wilderness, but he had always done so at his own pace. Now, he was in a position that required him to keep up with someone else. He had too much pride to ask Falling Feather to slow down. He matched the other's pace until he thought his knees would buckle, and his legs would refuse to continue. Scott shrugged the deer from his back and leaned against a tree.

Upon hearing the deer fall to the ground, Falling Feather stopped and turned around. A slight frown furrowed the Indian's brow for a moment and then he returned to where Scott rested. Falling Feather stood waiting for Scott, refusing to drop his burden.

They were about half way back to the village when Scott had stopped to rest. The already dim light of day was beginning to fail quickly.

Scott knew it was going to be dark before he got to the village, but he was nearing exhaustion.

Scott sat in the snow to get the deer on his back and then struggled to his feet. Falling Feather was anxious to be underway; he displayed his eagerness by leaving before Scott had gotten to his feet. Falling Feather slowed his pace but Scott still had to struggle to keep up with him.

Weariness was overtaking Scott. He had to reach into the depths of his very existence to maintain the pace, but he had already determined that he would not put the deer down again until he was in the village.

When Scott was within two hundred yards of the village he was numb with exhaustion. Each step required a direct order from his brain to his legs. His knees trembled and shook uncontrollably. He reached out to a sapling for support and dropped his bow in the process. He didn't have the strength or coordination to bend over and pick up the bow. He took a few staggering steps to the next sapling. Absently, Scott wondered what the Indians would think when he entered the village without his bow. He was too tired to worry about that.

It was too far to the next sapling and Scott stumbled and fell but managed to keep the deer on his back. He crawled to the next sapling and used it to pull himself to his feet. In his agony, he was thankful Falling Feather had not seen him fall.

Scott was not trying to impress Falling Feather or his people; however, he did want to be accepted by them. He knew he would have to earn their respect before he was accepted. He also knew they had nothing but disdain for weakness.

Darkness had long since surrounded Scott and he could see the twinkle of campfires through the thick timber. He heard excited voices from the village and knew Falling Feather had made his entrance. Scott tried to hurry, but it was of no use; it was all he could do to get from one tree to the next.

Finally, he was at the perimeter of the village! He took a few tottering steps and stopped to rest. He took two more steps and stopped again. The weight was becoming unbearable. Scott couldn't lift his head to see where he was going. All he could see was the ground around his feet…HIS FEET…MOVE FOOT!…MOVE! His mind screamed the command and the foot shuffled forward a few inches. The ground was flat but he was so bent over with exhaustion that his hands were on his legs, just above his knees. He grabbed his pant leg and pulled on the material to help his leg muscles pick up the foot.

If Scott could have seen the faces of the villagers, he would have been uncertain of how to interpret the way they looked at him. No one spoke or moved, they just watched; perhaps each was reliving some personal struggle they had encountered in their own lives.

No one came forward to assist Scott. This was his struggle, his attempt to prove himself. He did not realize at the time that it mattered not that one individual could out perform another, as long as everyone did the very best they could do.

That cold, snowy night, in the light of many flickering campfires, Scott became accepted by Falling Feather's people. He dropped the deer next to the one Falling Feather had carried. He slowly straightened his back, turned, and walked into the forest to retrieve his bow.

By the time Scott returned to the village, both deer had been skinned. Large pieces of meat were being sliced from the bone and placed over the fires. As it turned out, Scott and Falling Feather had been the only ones to return to the village with meat.

A large piece of meat was presented to Scott. He was very hungry but he had to eat slowly because he wasn't sure he could keep the food down.

When Scott finally finished the piece of meat, he went to the lodge of Falling Feather's family. He fell onto the sleeping mat and barely had time to cover himself before he was sound asleep. He slept until late the next morning.

5

Over the course of the next five years, Scott spent much time in the Powhatan village. He had the freedom to come and go as he pleased. Falling Feather came to the settlement several times; however, Scott was more welcome in the Indian village than Falling Feather in the fort. The whites, though not openly hostile, were suspicious of Falling Feather. There was no mistrust directed at Scott within the Indian village.

There were times when the relations between the settlers and the Indians were strained. During those times Scott avoided the Indian village but the settlers were somewhat suspicious of him. He supposed that he didn't help to alleviate those suspicions when he refused to spy on the Indians.

In 1641, Scott's father died. He died a poor and lonely man. Scott was in the wilderness at the time of his death, but he wouldn't have attended the funeral had he been in the settlement.

In 1642, Scott turned twenty years of age. He had reached his full adult height of six feet several years ago. Now, however, he was no longer skinny. He had filled out a great deal and possessed a body that was built for strength as well as endurance. He could whip Falling Feather in a wrestling match; however, his friend could leave him far behind in a race through the forest.

On the eve of that fateful day, in late winter, Scott went to the Powhatan village. Tension was building between the settlers and the Indians again, but Scott hadn't seen his friend for several weeks and decided to go anyway.

Scott was warmly received in the village, as usual, but he did notice a few hostile glances from some of the warriors. Perhaps there was some suspicion in the village after all.

Scott was in the mood to hunt and it took little effort to convince Falling Feather to join him. Scott had never completely mastered the Indian language. He often wondered if he had a physical problem with his tongue; he just couldn't say some of the words the Indians used. However, he had gotten very good at sign language and used it as his primary source of communication.

After a short discussion, Falling Feather and Scott decided to go west from the village. There was no immediate need for food, so their venture into the forest would be dedicated as much to exploring as hunting.

Scott and Falling Feather traveled in a westerly direction all day. That night they camped in the wilderness. They were on their way again at first light. Scott had not been in this particular area before, in fact, he had never been this far west; he was excited about entering new territory

Before noon, they discovered the deer tracks that led to the death of Falling Feather.

Chapter Five

From his hiding place, Scott considered the moccasin tracks. He had no idea how far inland Indians existed and he had never thought to ask Falling Feather. For all he knew, the tracks were made by Falling Feather's people.

Scott had been watching the crossing for several hours without seeing any Indians. He slowly got to his feet, and, as quietly as possible, made his way back to the small river. He jumped into the river from hard packed earth, hoping not to leave tracks, and landed in the shallow water as it rushed over the gravel bar. He ran across the river, getting himself considerably wetter than if he had walked. When he reached the opposite bank, he searched for and found a place to exit the river without leaving any tracks.

It occurred to Scott that if the moccasin tracks weren't made by Falling Feather's people, there could be an Indian village nearby.

After he got out of the river, he immediately moved away from the trail. When he was several hundred yards into the forest, large drops of rain began to splatter loudly all around him. Scott looked at the foreboding sky with relief and regret. He could look forward to another cold, wet night but if the rain washed out his tracks, he could look forward to waking up the next morning.

The rain fell for two days, and for two days and nights Scott was wet and cold. He had no idea where the Indians were who had made the tracks at the river crossing, and was too fearful of being discovered to build a fire, even at night.

On the third day, a cold north wind began to blow. Scott was numb with cold and he had to stop and build a fire. He came upon a large conifer that had died but had not fallen down. The tree had shed its bark in large sections. The sections lay scattered about near its base.

Scott gathered some of the large pieces of bark and leaned them against a nearby tree that was much smaller than the one that had died. He filled in gaps and holes with smaller pieces of bark. From the underside of a fallen tree, he gathered dry twigs and soon had a cozy fire going in his hastily built, yet cozy, shelter.

Scott leaned his back against the tree that he had piled bark around. The fire in front of him was small but little wind entered the shelter. The warmth quickly surrounded Scott and he soon began to nod off. He slept fitfully throughout the remainder of the day. He awoke several times and ate, and added fuel to the fire during the night.

Scott's sleep would have been more peaceful had he known that Falling Feather's father had long ago discovered the scene of the bloody battle. He had wept for his lost son and then disposed of the body in Powhatan tradition. Falling Feather had killed one of the other Indians, that Indian's body, along with the body of the Indian Scott had killed, were hacked to pieces and scattered throughout the forest. They found no sign of Scott and assumed he had been taken prisoner. Falling Feather's father led a battle against the offending Indians but Scott was not found. They assumed he too, had been killed. No one from Falling Feather's village ever went in search of Scott.

2

Dew-on-the-grass-in-the-moon-when-the-leaves-fall was barely able keep her feet under her. She was dizzy and disoriented. She fell many times and it took all of her strength to get back to her feet.

As she staggered along, she came to a small stream. She inadvertently got to close to the bank and fell into the water. She only fell a short distance, but the water was not deep and she bruised her knees on the submerged rocks. She sat back on her heels and tried to make sense of where she was. She leaned forward and splashed water on her face. The water made her feel better but she soon began to shiver. She rose to a squatting position and then stood up. She wrapped her arms around herself in an attempt to stop the shivers. She stepped out of the small stream and walked into the forest. She had regained some of her equilibrium.

As night began to fall, she searched for a place to sleep. She found a moss-covered rock near another stream. She peeled the moss from the rock and covered herself with it, and then she fell into a deep, deep, sleep.

Rain drops falling on her face woke her the next morning. She blinked the sleep from her eyes. Her head ached and she felt miserable. She threw off her moss blanket and rolled to her hands and knees; with great effort she got to her feet.

She stumbled through the forest all day. She fell many times and each time it took all of her strength to get back to her feet.

By nightfall, Dew-on-the-grass-in-the-moon-when-the-leaves-fall had stood about all she could stand. She was soaked to the skin, she was tired and she was hungry. She knew if she stopped to rest, she would fall asleep and probably die of exposure. She had no food and was not capable of building a fire. She continued to walk, or stagger, throughout the night and the next day. She hoped the rain would wash out her trail or at least make it more difficult to follow. It would have made her ill to learn how little distance she had covered since the day she had been injured, and killed the Seneca warrior.

As dusk approached, she tripped over a small limb. She reached for a tree to keep from falling. She missed the tree and fell heavily to the ground. The fall knocked the wind out of her in a gush. She moaned and tried to push herself to her feet. She got to her hands and knees but fell again. The lack of food was taking a toll on her. She rested a moment and tried again. This time she got to her feet but only made a few steps before she fell again. It was hard, so hard. She had to rest – she couldn't rest. She got to her hands and knees again and looked for some shelter from the rain. She discovered that she was in a small meadow. If she could get back into the forest she might be able to find some sort of shelter. She began to crawl across the meadow on her hands and knees. She was almost to the edge of the meadow when she became extremely dizzy. She stopped and shook her head. The feeling would not pass. As she started to crawl again, darkness overtook her and she fell unconscious on the wet grass of the meadow.

3

Scott awoke an hour before dawn. The rainstorm had passed but he could hear water dripping from the sodden forest canopy. He warmed some meat over the coals of the fire as he awaited the dawn.

Scott reckoned he had enough meat for two more days. Running out of food could be risky business, so as he traveled, he remained alert for any sign of game, as well as the Indians.

After several hours on the trail, Scott saw an opening in the forest. It appeared to be a meadow. He had often seen deer gather in the small forest meadows; Indians also gathered in the meadows. He approached with utmost caution.

As he drew nearer to the meadow, he studied it thoroughly from concealment. There was no sign of visitation by Indians; there were no deer in the meadow either. He began to work his way around the perimeter of the clearing, hoping to discover a hidden branch of the meadow that couldn't be seen from his present location.

Scott had walked nearly half way around the meadow without seeing any deer or fresh sign thereof. He was about ready to turn away from the meadow when his eyes detected a strange colored object in the nearby grass. He was unsure what he was seeing; he watched the object closely, from concealment, for several minutes. When he was satisfied the object presented no threat, he began to walk slowly toward it.

Scott was suddenly overwhelmed by the memories of Falling Feather lying dead in the grass, and he now knew what he was seeing. With great effort, he pushed the past aside and moved closer to the fallen Indian.

He knelt beside the Indian and suddenly realized she was a woman. He saw a nasty cut on the back of her head. He gently rolled her over and saw her chest rise and fall as she breathed. Scott took her by the shoulders and pulled her into a sitting position. He wrapped his left arm around her back and and his right arm under her legs. He was going to carry her to a safer location. Just before he stood up, he looked at her lovely face and saw her dark eyes upon him.

Slowly, Dew-on-the-grass-in-the-moon-when-the-leaves-fall moved her hand toward a fold in her dress. Her hand came out empty; she had lost her deadly awl. She suddenly felt a wave of panic from being captured by this strange, hairy-faced man. She tried to fight free from him, but she was too weak, and his arms were too powerful.

Scott picked the woman up. Just before she passed out, she pointed toward her back trail and mumbled words he didn't understand. He looked in the direction she pointed, but saw nothing.

As he carried the woman into the forest in search of adequate shelter, he was flooded with mixed emotions. He did not consider himself a murderer, yet he had killed men in the wilderness. If he did not kill this woman or leave her to die, would she put her people on his trail? If he stopped until she was healthy, would he be captured and killed for his trouble? Looking upon the innocent face of the beautiful young woman in his arms, he knew in his heart she would not die by his hand. Suddenly, Scott rationalized that by saving this life, that had already come perilously close to being snuffed out, he might, in some way, make up for the wasted life of Falling Feather.

Scott carried the woman for nearly a mile before he found a location that suited his needs. He had come upon two wind-felled conifers that were lying parallel to each other. The two trees were less than fifteen feet apart; their massive root systems were interconnected, providing an excellent windbreak. Scott had to go to the tops of the fallen trees to get between them. When he reached the root systems, he placed Dew-on-the-grass-in-the-moon-when-the-leaves-fall on the deer hide he had been working, and went in search of firewood.

Scott built a small fire and then went to a nearby stream and filled a tin cup he had taken from his pack. When he returned to the fire he took a piece of venison from his pack and sliced small slivers of meat into the water. He placed the cup next to the fire to let it warm.

Scott rolled the girl over and looked more closely at the wound on the back of her head. It was indeed a nasty wound; it was a wonder she had survived the blow. He cleaned the wound as best he could, knowing his medical skills were pitifully deficient.

He gently rolled the girl onto her back and studied her face thoughtfully. He had been around many Indian women in Falling Feather's village, but he had never encountered as lovely a woman as the one that lay before him now.

Scott went about the tasks of making the camp as comfortable and convenient as possible. As he did so, he talked to the young woman in quiet tones that would not carry beyond their shelter. At first, he was startled by the sound of his own voice; it had been a long time since he had heard himself speak. As he was adding sticks to the fire, talking softly, he looked across the fire into the eyes of the woman.

Though perhaps a bit apprehensive, the woman displayed no outward sign of fear.

Scott dipped a finger into the broth, found it to be warm but not hot and handed the cup to her. She looked at the cup curiously and then looked back at Scott. He cupped his hands and motioned her to drink. Dew-on-the-grass-in-the-moon-when-the-leaves-fall placed her lips on the cup and took a small sip of the liquid. She found it acceptable, and drank more.

Scott spitted a piece of meat over the fire and let it warm as the girl drank the broth. He noticed her looking hungrily at the meat, over the top of the cup. When she had finished the broth, Scott took the meat off the fire. He cut it into thin slices and handed them to her. When she had eaten her fill, Scott took the cup to the stream and refilled it with water. Upon returning, he handed the cup to the girl, which she took thankfully. After she had drunk the water, the warm food and fire began to have a narcotic effect on her. Her eyelids began to get heavy and soon she was in a deep sleep.

In the remaining daylight, Scott went about the business of making the shelter as weatherproof as possible. Other than a few brief showers, the night passed with no major rainfall.

Scott woke before dawn and stirred the fire to life. He made more broth for the woman and spitted another piece of meat. Dew-on-the-grass-in-the-moon-when-the-leaves-fall was awakened by the sound of Scott moving about the camp. When Scott noticed she was awake, he gave her the broth and some of the meat.

When the woman finished eating, Scott shrugged into his pack and slung his bow over his shoulder. He then bent over and picked up the woman.

This time Dew-on-the-grass-in-the-moon-when-the-leaves-fall offered no resistance to being carried; she knew this strange looking man meant her no harm. However, when she realized that he was going west, she motioned to the south and told him that her people were in that direction. The man looked in the direction she pointed and then continued toward the west.

Scott was once again confronted with the stigma of not being able to communicate with the Indians. When the woman pointed to the south, she didn't sound frightened, but he didn't know whether she feared that direction or wanted to go that way. Scott hesitated momentarily and then continued moving west.

Dew-on-the-grass-in-the-moon-when-the-leaves-fall didn't try to argue; at this point, she had no other options.

When Scott had carried the woman for two hours, she indicated she could walk. He gently put her on her feet and held her so she wouldn't fall. Though she was somewhat unsteady, she was able to stand. After a few moments, Scott took a couple of steps and waited. The girl hesitantly looked to the south and then turned and followed Scott. The girl walked too unsteadily for Scott to release her. He held her by the upper arm as they walked side by side through the forest.

Scott was relieved not to carry the girl. He was not growing weary; he could have carried her all day. It was difficult to watch for Indian sign with her in his arms. It also restricted his movements and made it difficult to watch his back trail.

As they walked on, Scott watched the face of the woman for signs of fatigue. He was impressed by her recuperative powers. As he looked at her, he wondered where she came from and where her people were. He also thought back to the good camp they had left that morning. He would liked to have stayed for at least another day to let the woman regain more of her strength.

He grew anxious when he stayed in one place for too long.

By mid-afternoon, they had covered less than half the ground Scott would have covered by himself. He was, nonetheless, pleased with the woman's progress.

Several hours before nightfall, Scott stopped when they came upon a likely spot for a safe campsite.

Scott took his flint and steel from his pack and prepared to build a fire. The woman watched curiously, and gasped involuntarily as Scott struck a spark into the small pile of tender. Scott glanced at her and then returned his attention to the tiny ember that glowed softly in the tender. Scott soon had a small fire hungrily consuming the small pieces of wood he placed on it. When he was satisfied the fire was going to burn, he went in search of larger wood. After he had collected an adequate supply of wood to sustain them through the night, he motioned the woman to stay where she was. Scott took up his bow and quiver and went in search of a deer.

An hour after Scott had left the camp, he saw a doe and yearling buck feeding toward him through the forest. He quietly concealed himself and waited patiently for the deer to feed into arrow range. He had already decided to take the yearling. He would have preferred taking the doe, which would provide more meat. However, he didn't want to carry extra meat in case he had to carry the woman, too.

Shortly before dark, Scott returned to the camp with the small deer slung over his shoulder. Working quickly, he soon had the deer skinned and fresh meat cooking over the fire.

The woman spoke to Scott when he handed her a piece of meat.

"I don't understand your words," Scott said.

The woman looked at him blankly.

Instinctively, Scott attempted to communicate with sign language. The woman's look did not change.

Scott said a few words in Powhatan. The woman displayed no sign of comprehension.

Sadly, Scott realized he would have to begin at a basic level to learn to communicate with her. Not knowing what she would decide to do when she was healthy, he wondered if it would be worth the trouble.

"Fire," Scott said, pointing at the small blaze. She opened her mouth and looked at him questioningly. Scott repeated the word more slowly. "FIRE."

"Fi...Fi," she said cautiously.

"FIRE," Scott said, leaning forward with excitement.

"Fire," the woman said softly.

"Yes!" Scott said happily.

"Yes," she repeated with an abrupt nod of her head.

Pleased with their sudden progress, Scott decided to continue.

"Scott," he said pointing to himself.

"Sco...Sco...Sco..." she looked at him for assistance.

"SCOTT," he repeated for her.

"Sco...Sco...tt. Scott," she said with heavy emphasis on the "T."

"Yes! yes, that's it!" Scott said even more excitedly.

"What is your name?" Scott asked pointing at the woman.

Once again she looked at him questioningly.

He pointed to himself and said, "Scott." He then pointed at her.

Comprehension suddenly brightened the woman's face. Speaking softly, and much too quickly, she spoke her name to Scott.

Scott exhaled a slight moan of disappointment. Though her language seemed to be more fluid than Powhatan, it was still very difficult for him to make the sounds the girl had spoken.

With the woman's help, and many attempts, Scott finally repeated the words she had said. Desiring to commit the words to memory, Scott said the words over and over under his breath.

Scott was so engrossed in the lessons, he completely forgot about the cooking meat until the woman got up and removed it from the fire. She handed the spitted chunk of venison to Scott. He allowed the meat to cool before cutting it in two and giving her an equal share.

"Meat. Good meat," Scott said with a mouthful of venison.

"Meat," Dew-on-the-grass-in-the-moon-when-the-leaves-fall said, once again over-emphasizing the "T." Hungrily, she continued to devour the meat without further comment.

The difficult day of traveling had taken its toll on both people. Scott would have liked to spend more time exchanging words with the woman but they were both tired. Moving slowly, so he wouldn't frighten her, Scott moved to the woman's side. He slipped his hand under her hair and gently lifted it away from the wound on her head. She offered no resistance as he examined the injury. Satisfied that the wound was healing well, with no sign of infection, Scott returned to his side of the fire, stretched out and was soon asleep.

As was becoming a habit, Scott awoke at least an hour before dawn. He had awakened several times during the night and added fuel to the fire. He had fallen back to sleep watching the sleeping woman across the fire from him. He was surprised at the comfort he gleaned from her presence.

He now rekindled the fire. Suddenly the woman rolled over and got to her feet. Without hesitation, she walked around the fire, picked up Scott's knife and sliced another chunk of meat from the carcass of the young deer. When Scott had an adequate fire going, she spitted the meat over the flames. Without a word, she walked away from the campsite, into the gloomy predawn forest.

Apprehensively, Scott watched her go. He was shocked at the amount of regret he would feel if she did not return. He considered following her, but immediately discarded the idea. He would not hold her against her will.

Presently, the woman reappeared. Scott was barely able to contain his emotional relief.

As he watched her, he saw that she was carrying several sticks. She walked into the campsite and went directly to the carcass of the deer. With Scott's knife, she cut the remaining meat from the bone, spitted it on the sticks and placed them over the fire. They ate their morning meal as they waited for the rest of the meat to cook.

By the time Dew-on-the-grass-in-the-moon-when-the-leaves-fall finished eating, the day was brightening. Once again she walked into the forest. This time she stayed within sight of the campsite. Scott watched her as she walked around with her head bent down, apparently searching the forest floor for something. Finally, he turned to his own business and began to repack his belongings into his pack. When the meat finished cooking, Scott removed it from the fire and kicked the remaining fuel away from the flames. The meat had cooled by the time the woman returned; Scott placed it into the pack and shrugged the pack onto his back.

The woman returned with a stout stick of about two inches in diameter. It was straight and barkless, and about five feet long. When Scott turned to leave the campsite, he saw that the woman intended to use the limb as a walking stick.

As the two travelers moved through the forest, Dew-on-the-grass-in-the-moon-when-the-leaves-fall stopped often to dig roots and gather grasses and herbs.

Because they had encountered no Indian sign, Scott felt reasonably comfortable attempting to communicate with Dew-on-the-grass-in-the-moon-when-the-leaves-fall; though he spoke softly. He employed the same method he had used to break the communication barrier with Falling Feather.

Late in the afternoon, Scott and Dew-on-the-grass-in-the-moon-when-the-leaves-fall came upon a small river. Scott decided not to attempt a crossing until the next morning. With little effort, they found a suitable campsite. Scott immediately set about gathering fuel for the evening fire. Dew-on-the-grass-in-the-moon-when-the-leaves-fall arranged their meager belongings around the fire and then began to prepare a meal. She baked some of the roots and tubers she had gathered. Scott's stomach grumbled with anticipation when he smelled the cooking food, as he dropped an armload of wood near the fire.

Scott loved the taste of venison and he knew it would sustain him for a long time. However, he had also learned, by observing the diet of Falling Feather's people, that he would need more than just meat to maintain his health and strength.

Much to Dew-on-the-grass-in-the-moon-when-the-leaves-fall's satisfaction, Scott ate hungrily of the vegetables she had prepared.

4

The morning sun warmed their backs as they stood on the bank of the small river. The stream was about one hundred yards wide and did not appear to be very deep. Scott was certain that this was not the river he had seen from the crest of the mountains.

Cautiously, Scott led Dew-on-the-grass-in-the-moon-when-the-leaves-fall into the river. Fortunately, the water was not swift for it was somewhat deeper than Scott had thought it would be. He had removed his pack and carried it on his right shoulder. He helped Dew-on-the-grass-in-the-moon-when-the-leaves-fall with his left arm. The water reached his armpits at its deepest point.

Scott was ten inches taller than Dew-on-the-grass-in-the-moon-when-the-leaves-fall. Had he not pulled her to him and supported her she would have been forced to swim. Scott was acutely aware of her closeness, and though somewhat embarrassed, he regretted releasing her when they reached shallow water.

The warm sunshine felt especially good when the dripping pair of travelers stepped out of the river. They wrung as much water as possible out of their clothing, but it would be several hours before they were completely dry.

As they walked away from the riverbank, they came upon a large meadow. Scott had no desire to expose them to danger by crossing the meadow. As they skirted around the perimeter of the meadow, Scott's hand inadvertently touched a blade of tall grass. His hand came away wet with morning dew, and he absently wiped his hand on his pant leg.

In a move that startled him, Dew-on-the-grass-in-the-moon-when-the-leaves-fall grabbed his arm to get his attention.

When he turned to face her, he saw that she was very excited. She touched a blade of dew-laden grass and patted her self on the chest.

Bewildered, Scott tried to imagine what she was trying to tell him.

The woman spoke to him in her language. Wait. She had said the words that were her name. Now he knew what she was trying to convey, but he didn't know what she meant.

Patiently, Dew-on-the-grass-in-the-moon-when-the-leaves-fall dropped the blade of grass and gently grasped another one. She broke the blade off. Holding the blade in her right hand, she shook the moisture off into her left palm. She dropped the blade and pointed to the drops of moisture in her hand.

Scott's first impression was that she was indicating 'water' but had that been the case, she would have attempted to communicate her name at one of the streams, or the river they had crossed.

The only explanation could be the dew she had shaken off of the grass.

"Dew?" he asked, questioningly.

She touched the moisture with her fingertips and then patted her chest.

"Dew," Scott repeated, more sure of his conclusion.

She then motioned to all of the surrounding grass.

As if a blindfold had been removed, meaning finally dawned on Scott. "Dew-on-the-grass," he said. After the time he had spent in Falling Feather's village he was accustomed to Indian names that other whites would consider unusual. Though he wondered about the origin of her name, he did not think it peculiar.

To let her know he understood, he patted himself on the chest and said, "Scott." To his surprise, she said his name in unison with him. He reached out, and touching her gently, said her Indian name and then said, "Dew-on-the-grass."

She placed her hand over his and said, "Dew," with a smile that made her even more beautiful, if that were possible.

Scott was overjoyed, but he suddenly felt vulnerable. They had been standing near the edge of the meadow. There was some brush between them and the meadow but they would have been visible from any part of the clearing.

Dew-on-the-grass-in-the-moon-when-the-leaves-fall was saddened when he turned away from her and looked across the meadow. She immediately understood why he had acted as he had. She scanned the meadow herself. They saw no movement. Scott turned away from the meadow and melted deeper into the surrounding timber. Dew-on-the-grass-in-the-moon-when-the-leaves-fall followed closely behind, both watching their back trail carefully.

Scott noticed Dew-on-the-grass-in-the-moon-when-the-leaves-fall's alertness and was thankful for the extra help. Being on continuous alert, ready to fight or run at a moment's notice, could wear a man down after a while.

5

As the days slipped by, Dew-on-the-grass-in-the-moon-when-the-leaves-fall regained more and more of her strength. When she was completely recovered, she helped Scott hunt. She proved to be a skilled hunter and a very good tracker. Several times, as they traveled, Scott had seen her stop long enough to conceal some signs of their passing. Though Scott was a good tracker, he failed to see the sign until she pointed it out to him. When they camped near streams that were large enough to support fish, she showed him how to make fish traps. The fish were a delicious variation from their normal diet.

Finally, they came to a very large river. Scott was certain it was the one he had seen from the top of the mountains. Now, he was appalled at the size of the river before them. It appeared to be over a half-mile wide and very swift. He was not sure what he had expected to find when he was looking for the river, but this certainly wasn't it.

When Scott recovered from the shock of the size of the river, he began to formulate a plan to reach the other side. He did not have the material to build a raft. He did not have the time or the knowledge to build a canoe.

They still had several hours before dark, but he was not going to attempt a crossing without carefully considering all of his options. Any number of things could go wrong during a crossing of this magnitude; he hadn't come this far to drown in a river.

That night, Scott and Dew-on-the-grass-in-the-moon-when-the-leaves-fall camped in a grove of trees above the high water line of the river. Wood was plentiful, but spring was making its presence felt; the days were warm and the nights were not too uncomfortable without a fire. They only built a fire to cook raw food. There were fresh tracks of various animals close to the camp, but if Scott killed an animal, he would have an extra burden to carry across the river.

Scott lay down in the camp and tried to think of a way to cross the river. He watched Dew-on-the-grass-in-the-moon-when-the-leaves-fall as she staked out and worked the hides of the animals he had killed for food. She had seemed agitated since they had come upon the river. He wondered what troubled her.

Disgruntled by the formidable task before him, Scott got to his feet, picked up his bow and quiver and walked to the edge of the river. As he stood watching the water flow by, he wondered about the river: where did such a river come from, where did it go, how big did it get?

His eyes watched a short log float down the river as his mind asked questions he had no answer for. Slowly, his attention was drawn back to the log. Suddenly, he realized that with a little luck, he could float himself and Dew-on-the-grass-in-the-moon-when-the-leaves-fall across the river on a log such as the one that had just floated by.

Scott turned and walked upstream, looking for a log that had been deposited by high water. When he had gone nearly a mile he came to a bend in the river. There was an eddy on his side of the river. There were several sticks and pieces of bark floating in the eddy, but nothing big enough to float them to the other side. Higher up on the bank, however, was a broken log about two feet in diameter and six feet long. It looked perfect for his needs.

Scott returned to the camp in somewhat better humor. He was certain he could get them across the river with the use of the log, but it would still be very dangerous. If there was another solution, it escaped him.

Scott also realized that once they crossed the river, their trail would be very difficult to locate. However, watching their back trail had become a habit they would not discard simply because they felt relative safety.

When Scott walked into the camp, Dew-on-the-grass-in-the-moon-when-the-leaves-fall looked up from her work. The look on her face disturbed Scott a great deal.

As they had traveled through the forest, they had each learned many words in the others language, but Scott didn't have the words to ask Dew-on-the-grass-in-the-moon-when-the-leaves-fall what troubled her.

As dusk closed in on them, Dew-on-the-grass-in-the-moon-when-the-leaves-fall rolled up the hides and tied them together. She was making Scott a new pair of leggings; his old ones had many holes and were too far gone to repair. She had hoped to have them completed by the time they reached the river, but she had not had the time.

Scott opened the pack and withdrew a large chunk of meat. He sliced off a piece and handed it to Dew-on-the-grass-in-the-moon-when-the-leaves-fall. She accepted the meat and watched him as he sliced a portion for himself. They ate in silence. When they finished eating, they rolled into their furs and went to sleep.

Scott was sitting at the edge of the camp, looking toward the river, when Dew-on-the-grass-in-the-moon-when-the-leaves-fall woke up.

"Scott," she whispered.

Though she had spoken softly, he had heard her. He got to his feet and stepped into the camp area. As Dew-on-the-grass-in-the-moon-when-the-leaves-fall sat up, Scott began to stuff his belongings into the pack.

As the stars faded, and the eastern sky became lighter, they walked to the edge of the river. Dew-on-the-grass-in-the-moon-when-the-leaves-fall was so agitated she was shaking. Scott couldn't imagine what troubled her.

Scott turned to go upstream.

Dew-on-the-grass-in-the-moon-when-the-leaves-fall reached out and touched his arm. She patted her chest and said: "Dew-on-the-grass-in-the-moon-when-the-leaves-fall," and pointed downstream.

Scott pointed upstream and tried to tell her that he had come up with a plan to get them across the river.

Dew-on-the-grass-in-the-moon-when-the-leaves-fall started speaking her language excitedly, using hand language to emphasize the seriousness of what she said. Scott had no idea what she was trying to tell him.

He patted his own chest and said his name, and then pointed upstream.

Dew-on-the-grass-in-the-moon-when-the-leaves-fall clenched her fists in exasperation. She turned and took two steps downstream. She turned back to Scott and motioned for him to come with her. He shook his head and motioned for her to follow him.

Sadly, Dew-on-the-grass-in-the-moon-when-the-leaves-fall turned and began to walk downriver.

Scott's mouth dropped open in pure shock as Dew-on-the-grass-in-the-moon-when-the-leaves-fall walked away from him. He didn't know what she wanted. He felt that in order to survive, he must cross the river and continue going west. He had grown very fond of her in the short time they had been together, but until she disappeared in the willows along the riverbank, he didn't know just how much she had come to mean to him. Broken hearted, he turned and walked upriver.

Chapter Six

"Dew-on-the-grass-in-the-moon-when-the-leaves-fall, what is the matter with you, woman?" she asked herself, as she walked along the edge of the river. "Why are you walking away from the man, Scott? Have you forgotten that he cared for you when you were injured? Have you forgotten that he shared his food with you when you were too weak and hungry to find your own? What Shawnee brave would have done the same? What will become of you if you are fortunate enough to find a Shawnee village? Will you become the slave of some brave who will never care for you? You will be abused by the other women of the village. What of Scott? What will become of him if you are not there to guide him? You foolish girl, have you forgotten how you feel about him?"

Dew-on-the-grass-in-the-moon-when-the-leaves-fall stopped walking. She looked up river but she could not see Scott. He had not followed her. He was a gentle man; he would not force her to go where she did not wish to go. Did he care for her? Why hadn't he followed her? She had seen the hurt in his face when she did not follow him. What was she to do? She looked down the river.

2

Scott walked along the riverbank as if he were within the safety of the walls of a fort, and he had nothing in the world to fear. When his head cleared and he became aware of his precarious situation, he found that he was sitting on the very log he intended to use to float across the river.

Sullenly, Scott stood up and removed his pack. He leaned his bow and quiver against the pack and then began the work of getting the log into the water. The log was very heavy and slightly embedded in rocks and gravel. The bank to the river was steep and washed clean. If he could dislodge the log, it would roll into the water.

Assuming a nearly prone position, Scott placed his hands and right shoulder against the log and pushed. The side of the log away from the river lifted an inch and no more. Scott took a deep breath and tried again. The log moved a little more and stopped.

Scott was good-natured and very slow to anger. But now, faced with the loss of Dew-on-the-grass-in-the-moon-when-the-leaves-fall and the stubborn log that refused to roll, his anger surfaced. He kicked the log, which hurt his foot and added to his anger. He pushed the log again, cursing under his breath and straining every muscle in his body. The log rose again. It stopped, rose a little more and stopped again. The log would rise no more.

Suddenly, from out of nowhere, Dew-on-the-grass-in-the-moon-when-the-leaves-fall was beside him, pushing on the log. With strength renewed by powerful emotions, Scott reached deeper within himself, and together, they lifted the log out of its bed and watched it roll into the river.

"Dew-on-the-grass!" Scott said in a hoarse-croaking voice, as he stood up and faced her. "You came back!"

Dew-on-the-grass-in-the-moon-when-the-leaves-fall said, "Scott…" but before she could say more, he stepped toward her and took her into his arms.

After several moments, Dew-on-the-grass-in-the-moon-when-the-leaves-fall began to speak excitedly. Scott released her and looked where she pointed. The log was floating into deeper water. Scott rushed down the bank and into the river. When he was waist deep in water, he reached out and grasped the log. With little effort he pulled it back to the shore. When he turned away from the log, he saw that Dew-on-the-grass-in-the-moon-when-the-leaves-fall had carried all of their belongings to the edge of the river.

Holding on to all of their belongings, as well as the log, would be very difficult, especially in the swift current. Scott pushed the log into deeper water. He motioned Dew-on-the-grass-in-the-moon-when-the-leaves-fall to join him and then had her lean over the log. Scott did the same and then pushed the log away from the bank.

With both people kicking their feet, the log quickly moved through the gentle water of the eddy. The swifter water of the main current was another matter completely. The log was too large and they had virtually no control over it. All they could do was to keep it moving toward the far shore, though very slowly. On several occasions, the log started to roll. They were fortunate, in that they both realized it at the same time and lunged out of the water and leaned heavily over the log. In this position, they were unable to kick their feet effectively.

The swift current of the river had carried them more than three miles downstream by the time the log struck a rock and grounded itself near the far shore.

Scott and Dew-on-the-grass-in-the-moon-when-the-leaves-fall were almost too exhausted to wade ashore. Scott carried their belongings; Dew-on-the-grass-in-the-moon-when-the-leaves-fall followed, supporting herself by holding onto Scott's shirt with both hands. When they stepped out of the water, they both fell heavily onto a small, sandy beach.

The sun warmed their backs and seemed to assist their recuperative powers. They got to their feet and slowly moved away from the river, in search of a safe place to stop.

After eating and resting, they continued west. As they traveled, Scott reflected on the river crossing and the danger he had put both of them in. He vowed to himself, he would never cross a river in that fashion again. He wasn't sure what he would do, but that way was too dangerous.

As they walked away from the river they both noticed very many deer tracks. Scott was about to comment on the number of tracks when Dew-on-the-grass-in-the-moon-when-the-leaves-fall spotted a young buck. Scott removed his pack and began to stalk the deer. When he was within range, he took careful aim and released his arrow. The shot was good, hitting the buck in the lungs.

Scott and Dew-on-the-grass-in-the-moon-when-the-leaves-fall hunkered down, in relative concealment, for half an hour as they waited for the deer to die. When enough time had passed, they began to track the young buck.

The deer had bled well, and they had no trouble following him. The buck was quite dead when they found him. Together, they made short work of butchering the animal.

Scott decided to risk a fire as they cured the meat. It was indeed a risk, but because the weather was warming, the meat could spoil if it were not properly cared for.

As Scott prepared to build a fire, Dew-on-the-grass-in-the-moon-when-the-leaves-fall borrowed his knife and went off to a clump of willow bushes. From his location, Scott could see the tops of the slender trees shaking violently. When Dew-on-the-grass-in-the-moon-when-the-leaves-fall returned, she dragged an arm full of the vegetation behind her.

Scott watched, without speaking, as Dew-on-the-grass-in-the-moon-when-the-leaves-fall began to strip the bark off the long, thin pieces of wood. Methodically, she cut the willows into various lengths and then tied them together. In a matter of minutes Dew-on-the-grass-in-the-moon-when-the-leaves-fall had constructed enough drying racks to dry half of the fresh meat.

Scott was impressed with how quickly Dew-on-the-grass-in-the-moon-when-the-leaves-fall worked. He was also impressed with the drying racks. They could now dry more meat, more quickly, lessening the time they would have to spend in the area after building a smoky fire.

Scott spent the rest of the day gathering wood and searching for any signs of Indians. Dew-on-the-grass-in-the-moon-when-the-leaves-fall stretched and fleshed the fresh hide. She also spent some time searching for edible vegetation.

Scott returned with an armload of wood and told Dew-on-the-grass-in-the-moon-when-the-leaves-fall he had found an old campfire, but there were no fresh tracks. The discovery of the campfire was upsetting to both of them. Though she couldn't express it to Scott, Dew-on-the-grass-in-the-moon-when-the-leaves-fall was not sure which Indians had built the fire.

The next morning, they were on the trail an hour before dawn, moving cautiously, but quickly, out of the area.

There was too much meat to fit into Scott's pack. They had bundled much of it into one of the older hides Dew-on-the-grass-in-the-moon-when-the-leaves-fall had been working. She carried the bundle, slung over her shoulder.

3

For two weeks the terrain had remained relatively flat. They encountered countless deer tracks everyday. They had been rained on twice, but the showers were brief and because of the rising temperature, felt rather good. They had crossed Indian tracks on several occasions but none of the tracks were fresh. Each time they encountered an Indian sign, Dew-on-the-grass-in-the-moon-when-the-leaves-fall became extremely nervous. She was always anxious to be on the way. She walked closer to Scott after such an encounter.

Late in the afternoon, they came upon a well-used Indian trail. Once again the tracks were not fresh but there were many of them. They quickly moved away from the trail but soon found themselves on the bank of another large river.

Scott felt trapped, and became extremely anxious, himself. Though this river was not as wide as the one they had floated across, it was large nonetheless. There was not enough daylight to attempt a river crossing of any kind.

The proximity of the river lowered the surrounding temperature considerably. Wrapped in the soft hides and cuddling together, Scott and

Dew-on-the-grass-in-the-moon-when-the-leaves-fall spent a chilly night hidden in a nearby thicket.

Dawn found them creeping silently through the brush at the edge of the river. When they had traveled upstream, north, for an hour, Dew-on-the-grass-in-the-moon-when-the-leaves-fall suddenly stopped in her tracks. She crouched down and pulled Scott down beside her. She motioned for Scott to wait, wiggled around him, and disappeared through some tall grass.

As quickly as she had disappeared, she reappeared. She crawled back through the same grass she had vanished into. Her head popped out of the grass and by the look of the smile on her face, the situation had improved drastically.

Scott had wanted to follow her. He had crawled forward two steps, on his hands and knees, but he had enough respect for her judgment to do as she asked.

When Dew-on-the-grass-in-the-moon-when-the-leaves-fall's head popped out of the grass, her face was just a few inches from Scott's. She leaned forward and gently touched Scott's nose with her own. She back away, giggled softly, and motioned Scott to follow her.

It took Scott several moments to regain his composure before he could follow Dew-on-the-grass-in-the-moon-when-the-leaves-fall through the grass. When he caught up with her, she was peering at a small cove from a dense thicket.

There were signs that people had spent a lot of time here. There was a fire pit and many chips of wood. No one was at the camp now. Cautiously, Scott and Dew-on-the-grass-in-the-moon-when-the-leaves-fall slipped through the thicket and walked to the campsite.

As Scott stood, looking about the camp, wishing to be away from it, he wondered why Dew-on-the-grass had brought him here. From behind him, he heard her hiss. When he turned, he saw her removing bushy limbs from a pile of limbs. By the time he got to her side he saw that she was uncovering a canoe.

Scott was dumbfounded by the discovery. Dew-on-the-grass-in-the-moon-when-the-leaves-fall nudged him with her elbow and brought him back to his senses. He quickly began to help uncover the canoe. When all of the limbs were cleared away, Dew-on-the-grass-in-the-moon-when-the-leaves-fall ran to the other side of the canoe, and together, they pushed it into the river. There was only one paddle, but Scott soon had them going toward the far shore. The current was too swift to allow them to go directly across the river. However, they hadn't drifted very far downstream when Scott beached the craft on the opposite bank.

When their belongings had been removed from the canoe, Scott shoved the vessel into the current. There was no sense in showing anyone where they had disembarked. Scott watched the canoe until it had drifted out of sight.

They traveled hard and fast for the rest of the day. Scott decided not to build a fire when they stopped for the night. They ate cold meat for supper. When it was too dark to perform any more tasks around the camp, Scott lay down to sleep.

Dew-on-the-grass-in-the-moon-when-the-leaves-fall did not sleep. She had a difficult problem to work out; however, there was no one to ask for guidance. Usually, when a man and woman decided to become mates, there was a ceremony. There could be no ceremony for her and Scott. She would be Scott's mate if he would have her. How could he let her know without a ceremony?

She watched as Scott moved about the camp in the gathering darkness.

When it was completely dark he went to his side of the camp, lay down on his furs, and prepared to go to sleep.

Several minutes later, Dew-on-the-grass-in-the-moon-when-the-leaves-fall decided on a course of action. She pulled her dress over her head and dropped it on the ground – on her side of the fire.

Scott was just about to fall asleep when he heard Dew-on-the-grass moving. He heard a soft footfall in the dust, near his furs. Slowly raising himself on his elbow, he felt his blankets being pulled away. Before he knew what was going on, Dew-on-the-grass-in-the-moon-when-the-leaves-fall's naked body was under his blankets, lying beside him.

"Dew-on-the-grass-in-the-moon-when-the-leaves-fall Scott's woman," she said softly, as she pulled the blankets on top of them.

4

After several days of hard traveling since the last river crossing, Scott began to notice distinct changes in the terrain. The timber seemed to be thinning, the grass was tall and thick. Game was plentiful.

Scott stopped to examine some strange tracks. The tracks were similar to deer tracks but much larger. Dew-on-the-grass-in-the-moon-when-the-leaves-fall knelt beside him and upon seeing the tracks, became very excited.

"Wapiti. Wapiti, much meat," Dew-on-the-grass-in-the-moon-when-the-leaves-fall said quietly. "Good hide," she added.

They still had at least three days worth of meat, and with all of the signs they had been seeing, there was little chance of running out. However, Scott had never heard Dew-on-the-grass make a special reference to an animal's hide before. He felt it must be important to her.

As they followed the tracks, Scott noticed there were twelve to fifteen animals traveling together. The sign was becoming fresher with each step.

Two hundred yards after he had first seen the tracks, Scott spotted the elk in a grove of trees. Some of the animals were lying down, while others were feeding nearby.

Scott and Dew-on-the-grass-in-the-moon-when-the-leaves-fall squatted low in the tall grass and removed their packs. Dew-on-the-grass-in-the-moon-when-the-leaves-fall waited with their gear as Scott began to stalk the elk.

There was little breeze, but when it blew, it was in their favor. Using the tall grass for cover, and moving slowly, Scott was soon close enough for a shot.

A huge, antler-less bull walked within twenty yards of him, but the animal was so big, Scott was afraid his arrow would not kill it. A much smaller cow walked several steps behind the bull. The cow was quartering away from Scott. He drew back his bow, stood up and released the arrow.

The cow heard the bow, and a moment later saw Scott. She bolted from the herd. The rest of the herd scattered after being startled by the wounded cow. They made a great deal of noise, breaking limbs and crashing through the brush. In just a few moments, the elk had passed out of hearing range and all was quiet.

For a very long time, Scott had been traveling in relative silence. Even after he had found Dew-on-the-grass and they began traveling together, they spoke very little when on the trail. When they did speak, it was always in lowered voices.

The elk had moved so noisily, Scott was sure someone else would have heard them. He stood in the tall grass looking at Dew-on-the-grass with a look on his face that asked 'What have I done?'

Scott crouched down. With only his head showing above the top of the grass, he scanned the surrounding terrain. He noticed Dew-on-the-grass doing the same thing. They saw no movement.

Scott returned to Dew-on-the-grass-in-the-moon-when-the-leaves-fall, and together, they waited for about an hour before they started tracking the elk.

Scott and Dew-on-the-grass-in-the-moon-when-the-leaves-fall followed the blood trail until they came upon the downed elk. The cow was down but not dead. When she saw Scott and Dew-on-the-grass-in-the-moon-when-the-leaves-fall she sprang to her feet and ran a few steps. She was weak from loss of blood, and fell to the ground.

Scott shrugged out of the pack and withdrew his hand axe. As the elk struggled to regain her feet, he ran to her side and split her skull with the axe. The cow died instantly.

Dew-on-the-grass-in-the-moon-when-the-leaves-fall began to butcher the elk while Scott went in search of a suitable campsite.

The elk had died at the bottom of short ridge. Scott walked along the bottom of that ridge, until he came to a flat area about an acre in size. There were a few conifers in the area. On the left side of the area, a trickle of water bubbled from a small spring. The place was relatively well protected; it also offered an ample supply wood and water. Satisfied with what he had found, Scott returned to help Dew-on-the-grass.

By the time Scott rejoined her, Dew-on-the-grass-in-the-moon-when-the-leaves-fall had the animal gutted. Working together, they quickly skinned the carcass. The elk was much too large for Scott to pack in the same manner he had packed deer. Using the hand axe he cut the carcass in half. Dew-on-the-grass-in-the-moon-when-the-leaves-fall carried both packs as Scott carried the hind half of the cow to the new camp. While Scott returned for the front half of the elk, Dew-on-the-grass-in-the-moon-when-the-leaves-fall went in search of material to make new drying racks. When Scott returned with the last of the elk, Dew-on-the-grass-in-the-moon-when-the-leaves-fall was about to finish the first drying rack. Scott began to gather material for a fire.

By nightfall, they had stretched and fleshed the fresh elk hide. They had cooked some of the meat during the day. After the sun went down and the smoke couldn't be seen they smoked as much as they could. They decided to sleep in shifts, hoping to process more meat in the time they had.

In her spare time, Dew-on-the-grass-in-the-moon-when-the-leaves-fall finished the leggings she had been making for Scott. She also presented him with a new pair of knee-high moccasins.

After five days of resting and eating their fill of elk meat, they had reduced the meat supply to an amount that they could carry without restricting their movements.

Scott felt a little regret at leaving the camp. It was a good site. However, when he stayed in a place very long he became overly anxious and fearful of being detected. He had scouted around the camp and found no Indian signs. He supposed he had not quite gotten over being spooked on the day he had killed the cow elk.

Surprisingly, it felt good to be on the move again.

After two days on the trail, Scott noticed a marked decrease in the number of trees. The land was opening up and he was growing concerned about the lack of concealment. Two days later they went by the last conifer and looked upon a vast, grass covered plain of rolling hills.

Chapter Seven

They tried to keep to high ground when the entered the plains. The grass was high enough in most places to adequately conceal them. From high ground they had a very good view of the surrounding area.

From one hilltop, Dew-on-the-grass-in-the-moon-when-the-leaves-fall stopped Scott and pointed out what appeared to be a thousand black dots on the valley floor. The black dots were about two miles away and at first appeared to be part of the landscape. However, under closer observation, one could definitely detect movement. Scott was concerned and somewhat worried about what he was seeing. He didn't know what they were; thus, he didn't know if they represented a threat to their safety.

Some of Scott's questions would soon be answered.

When they crossed the next rise, they came upon a smaller herd of the shaggy beasts. Scott was surprised at how much they resembled cattle. The great beasts watched, unconcerned, as Scott and Dew-on-the-grass-in-the-moon-when-the-leaves-fall circled around them.

Scott had confidence in his ability to provide food for himself and Dew-on-the-grass, but he was not anxious to tackle one of the buffalo.

They were on top of a high hill when it began to grow dark. There was a small stream and a few trees in the valley below them. Not wishing to build a fire on the ridge-top, they hurried down the hill.

They reached the stream and quickly set up their camp in the last remaining minutes of daylight.

After they had eaten, Scott put the small fire out and then walked back to the top of the hill, above their camp. There was no moon, but the sky was clear and full of stars. Far off, to the south, he could see the twinkle of a campfire. Suddenly, Dew-on-the-grass was standing beside him. She sat down and leaned against him, both of them comfortable with the closeness of the other. Together, they sat on the grassy hilltop looking into the night, wondering about the distant fire.

The next morning, they were on their way an hour before the sun came up. Around noon, from the top of a gently sloping hill, they looked down upon an Indian village. Scott and Dew-on-the-grass-in-the-moon-when-the-leaves-fall were well concealed as they watched the village. Their location formed the northern wall of a rather large basin. The village was in the basin.

Without warning, five braves came from the south and rode into the village. When Scott saw the horses, he was so shocked he nearly stood and revealed their location. He hadn't seen a horse since he had left James Fort. Dew-on-the-grass-in-the-moon-when-the-leaves-fall was equally amazed; never in her life had she seen a horse.

Scott also noticed the Indians lived in cone shaped tents, unlike the thatched lodges of the Powhatan.

After they had watched the village for more than an hour, Scott and Dew-on-the-grass-in-the-moon-when-the-leaves-fall dropped off the backside of hill and traveled north for the remainder of the day. They stopped and ate at dusk and then turned west and walked throughout the night.

They discovered that they could cover nearly as much ground traveling under the starlit sky as they could during the day. They decided not to travel during the daylight hours for the next couple of days, until they were well away from the village.

As soon as dawn began breaking, they started looking for a safe place to spend the day. They could see no trees, but the shallow draw ahead of them contained some large boulders. The boulders would not provide as good a shelter as Scott would have liked, but under the circumstances, they would have to do.

As Scott drew near the rocks, he heard a buzzing sound. A frown furrowed his brow as he listened to the sound, trying to determine what it was.

With no warning, Scott was hit from the backside, and fell face first to the ground, with Dew-on-the-grass-in-the-moon-when-the-leaves-fall on top of him. She rolled over him and helped him to his feet. Scott was about to ask her why she had knocked him down when he saw her pointing to the snake.

Scott was appalled. He had never seen such a large snake. The creature was beautiful, but judging by Dew-on-the-grass's actions, it was also deadly.

The snake was coiled under one of the rocks they were going to use for shelter. Cautiously, they walked toward it. Dew-on-the-grass-in-the-moon-when-the-leaves-fall picked up a rock that was about half the size of Scott's head. Without warning, she threw the rock at the snake, crushing part of its body but not its head. The snake started to slither away. Scott shed his pack and drew his knife. Dew-on-the-grass-in-the-moon-when-the-leaves-fall moved more quickly. She sprang at the snake and grabbed it just behind the head. She let her other hand slide down it's body, which was longer than she was tall, until she had a hold of its middle. She dropped the head of the snake and whirled it above her head. After several revolutions, she stepped toward one of the boulders, bashing the snake's head.

Dew-on-the-grass-in-the-moon-when-the-leaves-fall watched the snake until she was sure it was dead, then turned to look at Scott.

The incident had happened so quickly, Scott had not had time to react. Dew-on-the-grass-in-the-moon-when-the-leaves-fall had taken control of the situation leaving Scott to watch, with eyes bulging and mouth agape.

Together, they turned from the snake and walked to their packs. When they turned toward the boulders, they saw sixteen mounted warriors watching them.

2

The Indians were on a ridge-top about two hundred yards away; they had witnessed the snake-killing incident.

Scott and Dew-on-the-grass-in-the-moon-when-the-leaves-fall had been so occupied with the snake, they had not seen the approaching Indians.

There was nowhere to run. The boulders would not provide adequate protection, had they decided to make a fight of it. All Scott and Dew-on-the-grass-in-the-moon-when-the-leaves-fall could do was stand and watch as the Indians rode toward them.

When the Indians were several yards away, they stopped their horses. They all looked at Scott curiously. One of the Indians spoke to Scott.

Scott didn't understand the Indian's words and was about to try to communicate with him through sign language when Dew-on-the-grass-in-the-moon-when-the-leaves-fall began to speak.

Another brave turned his horse toward them and answered Dew-on-the-grass-in-the-moon-when-the-leaves-fall. She and the brave talked for several minutes and then the brave turned to his companions and spoke to them.

Scott realized then, that Dew-on-the-grass and the brave she had spoken to, spoke a different language than the rest of the Indians. He found this to be a bit curious and was interested in learning the reason.

When the interpreter stopped speaking, the other Indians nodded their heads and spoke among themselves. Some of them were smiling and they did not seem unfriendly.

The interpreter spoke to Dew-on-the-grass-in-the-moon-when-the-leaves-fall. Before she answered, she looked briefly at Scott. After she answered, she tried to explain to Scott what they wanted. She was unable to make him understand.

Scott took a step back as the Indians came nearer. The interpreter extended an arm to Dew-on-the-grass-in-the-moon-when-the-leaves-fall. She took his arm and swung onto the horse's back. She motioned for Scott to do the same. Apprehensively, Scott clasped arms with the offering brave and swung on behind him.

Scott knew they were being taken to the Indian village. As it turned out, it was the same village he and Dew-on-the-grass-in-the-moon-when-the-leaves-fall had observed earlier, from the ridge-top. Scott knew that if the Indians had meant them harm, they would be dead now. However, he was still uncomfortable with being forcefully taken to the village. As far as he knew, they would hold a council and dispose of them later. There were too many unanswered questions.

Meanwhile, Dew-on-the-grass-in-the-moon-when-the-leaves-fall and the brave she rode behind, conversed continuously.

They rode into the village late that afternoon. Several of the younger braves split from the party and galloped their horses through the village, whooping and hollering. Some of the squaws chattered and shook their fists at the young men, which only served to make them more rowdy.

The remainder of the party drew their horses up in front of one of the cone-shaped tents, near the center of the village. The braves dismounted; Scott and Dew-on-the-grass-in-the-moon-when-the-leaves-fall did likewise. Scott's legs ached from spending the day on the horse's back; he knew better than to openly display his discomfort.

A man, whose face looked like wrinkled parchment, stepped out of the tepee. His black hair was long and streaked with white. When he walked, he looked as though the two old squaws who assisted him were a necessity, rather than a luxury. The old man glanced briefly at Scott and then addressed the interpreter. The interpreter spoke at great length; the old man looked at Scott several times as he listened to the brave.

When the brave finished speaking, the old man nodded his head, said a few words, and then hobbled toward Scott.

Scott got a strange feeling as the old man approached, not fear exactly, but a feeling you get when you are in the presence of a great man – a feeling of respect.

The old man motioned for Dew-on-the-grass-in-the-moon-when-the-leaves-fall to stand beside Scott. When she joined him, the old man spoke to the interpreter, while looking at Scott and Dew-on-the-grass-in-the-moon-when-the-leaves-fall. When the old man finished speaking, the interpreter translated to Dew-on-the-grass-in-the-moon-when-the-leaves-fall.

Scott could tell by her reaction to the translation that they were safe. When the interpretation was complete, the old man returned to his tepee. The interpreter motioned for Scott and Dew-on-the-grass-in-the-moon-when-the-leaves-fall to follow him. As they walked, she tried to explain what had transpired but the language barrier was still too significant. All she could manage was, "Hurt not. Hurt not here."

It wasn't much but it was enough and though Scott still wasn't happy with the situation, he could relax a little.

The interpreter stopped at an apparently empty tepee at the edge of the village. He motioned toward the tepee and then spoke to Dew-on-the-grass-in-the-moon-when-the-leaves-fall. He looked from Dew-on-the-grass-in-the-moon-when-the-leaves-fall to Scott and then turned and walked away.

"We stay," Dew-on-the-grass-in-the-moon-when-the-leaves-fall said, pointing at the tepee.

"How can you talk to him?" he asked.

"He Shawnee. Dew-on-the-grass-in-the-moon-when-the-leaves-fall Shawnee. He is Man-with-no-hair," she explained.

That explained a lot but it also created more questions. Scott wondered why one of Dew-on-the-grass's people was in this village.

They unpacked their packs and unrolled their blankets. When Dew-on-the-grass-in-the-moon-when-the-leaves-fall was satisfied with the arrangement of their belongings, she led Scott out of the tepee. They sat cross-legged, in front of the tepee, watching the village as the sun disappeared over the western horizon.

Scott had to stifle a chuckle as he watched the inhabitants of the village. The villagers were very curious about the new visitors and went out of their way to put themselves in a position to observe them. They were very polite however, and did not stare, which only added to the humor.

Scott heard horses neighing and turned to see six teenage boys pushing the herd closer to the village for the night. There were over thirty horses in the herd.

In the last moments before nightfall, Scott prepared to make a fire to warm their evening meal.

Dew-on-the-grass-in-the-moon-when-the-leaves-fall went to him and said,

"No. Not eat now. Eat with people."

Scott wasn't sure he understood what she meant, but he knew she knew what he had been about to do. She was as hungry as he was. He would wait. When she was ready to eat, she would say so.

Scott was about to reseat himself when he heard a commotion near the center of the village. He noticed a large fire burning there. He could see silhouetted people dragging wood and others throwing it on the fire. Many other people were standing around the perimeter of the fire.

From out of nowhere, the interpreter, Man-with-no-hair, was standing before them. Scott was taken aback by the silence with which the man moved.

Man-with-no-hair motioned for them to follow him. Scott assisted Dew-on-the-grass to her feet and together they followed the man toward the fire.

Scott and Dew-on-the-grass-in-the-moon-when-the-leaves-fall were led to where the old man was seated. He spryly got to his feet and greeted them. He motioned for them to be seated and then sat down himself.

Shortly after Scott and Dew-on-the-grass-in-the-moon-when-the-leaves-fall were seated, several women came out of a nearby tepee and presented them and the chief with bowls of steaming stew. Now Scott understood why Dew-on-the-grass had insisted they not eat earlier. Scott found the stew, if that was what it was, to be very good and he ate it hungrily. When their bowls were empty, they were given large pieces of freshly cooked meat.

Before they had finished eating, a drum began to beat a slow, methodical beat, from somewhere on the other side of the huge fire. A young brave sprang to his feet with a whoop, and danced to the rhythm of the drum. Soon another drum began to beat and more young braves joined in.

After nearly an hour, the drums suddenly stopped and the braves seated themselves. Once again, the drums started, but now they beat at a much slower tempo. Slowly, the young women of the village approached the fire and began to dance. The women did not cry out as the men had; instead, they moved slowly, sweeping and arching their bodies.

When the drums stopped again, the women took their seats and the children jumped to their feet and began to frolic around the fire. There was no hidden meaning in the dance of the children. They danced for pleasure, as they jumped and ran and rolled, some issuing as fierce a war cry as their small bodies could manage. The entire village smiled with pleasure as they watched the dancing children.

When the children finished dancing, more meat was passed around. As the villagers ate, an old man wearing a buffalo robe and a hollowed-out buffalo head, advanced to the fire. As the drums started again, the old man began to chant and dance jerkily. He opened his arms to the heavens as he chanted and wailed. When the old man had danced and sung for what seemed an eternity, he gasped and fell to the ground. The villagers cheered and whooped until the drums stopped. The only sound was the snapping and crackling of the fire as two old squaws came forward and gently helped the old man to his feet and then led him away.

When the old man was out of sight, the villagers began to disperse. As Scott and Dew-on-the-grass-in-the-moon-when-the-leaves-fall walked toward their tepee, they noticed the sun breaking over a distant ridge.

As Scott lay in his blankets, with Dew-on-the-grass snuggled close to him, he considered their situation. He was no longer fearful that harm would come to them at the hands of these people; in fact, he felt safe for the first time in a long time. However, he wondered what would happen if he and Dew-on-the-grass decided to leave the village.

He also considered the young woman beside him. His affection for her seemed to grow stronger every day, which, in a way, concerned him a great deal. The only other Indian he had cared for had died at his hand. The loss of Dew-on-the-grass would be more than he could stand.

The woman moaned in her sleep and snuggled closer to him. He wrapped his arm around her shoulder and held her close until he fell asleep.

Scott awakened at mid-morning. He could have gone back to sleep, but rolled out of the blankets instead. He sat in the sun outside the tepee, watching the quiet village. There was very little activity and the peacefulness of the village was relaxing and soothing. After a few minutes, Dew-on-the-grass joined him and together they sat and absorbed the tranquility.

After a time, more of the villagers began to stir, and soon the village was bustling with activity.

Suddenly a shadow was cast over Scott and Dew-on-the-grass-in-the-moon-when-the-leaves-fall. Startled, Scott looked up and saw Man-with-no-hair standing over them. Shaken by the man's sudden appearance, Scott hastily got to his feet, joined by Dew-on-the-grass-in-the-moon-when-the-leaves-fall. Scott was unnerved by the man's ability to move so quietly; this was the second time he had come upon Scott unobserved.

Man-with-no-hair spoke to Dew-on-the-grass-in-the-moon-when-the-leaves-fall. She went into the tepee and came back out with Scott's quiver and one of her beautifully worked hides. Scott was unsure what was taking place but said nothing. With a tilt of his head, Man-with-no-hair indicated for them to follow him. They walked through the center of the village to a tepee on the other side. Man-with-no-hair sat cross-legged outside the tepee, Scott and Dew-on-the-grass-in-the-moon-when-the-leaves-fall followed his example. A short time later, a middle-aged man stepped out of the tepee. Man-with-no-hair spoke to the man, who also sat cross-legged, facing the trio. Man-with-no-hair spoke to Dew-on-the-grass-in-the-moon-when-the-leaves-fall and she handed the hide to the man facing them. The man unrolled the hide, examining it closely. The man turned toward the tepee and summoned his wife. A woman stepped out of the tepee, came forward and examined the hide. She spoke excitedly to the man and then returned to the tepee. The man spoke to Man-with-no-hair, who nodded his head, as if in agreement. The man went into the tepee and returned with about two dozen arrows, he handed the arrows to Dew-on-the-grass-in-the-moon-when-the-leaves-fall, and kept the tanned deer hide.

Scott was overwhelmed by the transaction. He had been concerned about his dwindling arrow supply for some time. If necessary, he could have made serviceable arrows, but they would not have been as dependable as arrows made by a skilled arrow maker.

A couple of days later, Scott noticed a group of people gathering near the center of the village. When he began to hear shouting and laughing, he and Dew-on-the-grass-in-the-moon-when-the-leaves-fall walked over to see what was going on. He was surprised to see two young men rolling around on the ground; they appeared to fighting. Suddenly, one of the men got the upper hand and the other conceded. The two men got to their feet and clasped hands. The man who had yielded, stepped aside; the winner stood with his arms folded across his chest. Another man stepped forward and faced the winner. The two men began to circle each other, crouching low, arms spread wide, watching for a window of opportunity. Suddenly, the challenger lunged forward, attempting to grab the legs of the winner. The winner quickly sidestepped, causing the other man to miss him completely. The winner fell upon the challenger and put him in a painful hold; the match was quickly over. Once again, the winner stood stoically, waiting for another challenge. He waited for several minutes but no one came forward. He issued a dare to the jovial crowd but still no one came forward.

The man began to search the crowd, hoping to see someone he could intimidate into coming forward. His eyes fell upon Scott and a smile of anticipation crossed his face. The man spread his arms and motioned for Scott to come forward.

At the sound of a gentle voice behind him, Scott turned to see Man-with-no-hair standing there. Man-with-no-hair was speaking to Dew-on-the-grass-in-the-moon-when-the-leaves-fall. When he finished, Dew-on-the-grass-in-the-moon-when-the-leaves-fall tried to translate to Scott.

"Scott can go if want, if not, don't," she said.

Scott knew what the wrestler had wanted; he had wrestled in Falling Feather's village. Now, however, he felt as if he had been put into a no-win situation. If he whipped the Indian, it may cause the other man shame; if he refused to step forward he may shame himself. There was one other scenario, if Scott lost, there would be no risk of shame to anyone. Scott didn't even consider the latter.

Scott took one step forward, stopped, pulled his buckskin shirt over his head and handed it to Dew-on-the-grass. Scott's hairy, muscular, upper body caused an apprehensive look to cross the face of the wrestler. The crowd of people talked excitedly among themselves as Scott stepped into the circle.

Scott's opponent was several inches shorter and twenty pounds lighter than he. Scott had seen the man wrestle, and knew he was strong as well as extremely quick.

The wrestler went into a moving, crouching position as Scott drew near. Scott crouched too, and the two men began to circle each other. The Indian feigned a lunge at Scott's legs, but Scott didn't fall for the deception. After several minutes of circling, with neither man presenting an opportunity to the other, Scott reached out with snake-like quickness and grasped the wrestlers wrist. Just as quickly, Scott shifted his weight and dragged the man to the ground. The wrestler tried to escape as Scott landed beside him, but Scott's hold on his wrist did not lessen, and the man was unable to escape. Scott threw his other arm over the Indian's back, released the wrist and slipped that arm under the wrestler. When Scott's hands came together at the Indian's breastbone, they clasped, and with his powerful arms, Scott squeezed the air out of the Indians lungs. The Indian struggled fiercely, but could not escape the bear hug.

When the Indian could struggle no more, he said some words and the crowd whooped and hollered excitedly. Scott released the man and sprang to his feet, assuming a defensive posture, in case he had misinterpreted the man's meaning. Before the defeated warrior could get to his feet, Man-with-no-hair and Dew-on-the-grass-in-the-moon-when-the-leaves-fall were at Scott's side. Man-with-no-hair was clapping Scott on the back. Dew-on-the-grass-in-the-moon-when-the-leaves-fall held her head high, with a look of pride on her face.

Scott stepped away from the congratulating crowd and went to the fallen, opponent. He extended a hand to the man, who had just achieved a sitting position. Scott had wished no ill will on the man and hoped he was not injured.

Reluctantly, the man accepted Scott's hand and was pulled to his feet. The man was obviously embarrassed and Scott had no desire to worsen the situation. He clapped the man on the back, turned, and went back to Dew-on-the-grass and Man-with-no-hair.

After most of the onlookers had congratulated Scott, the crowd began to disperse. Man-with-no-hair accompanied Scott and Dew-on-the-grass-in-the-moon-when-the-leaves-fall back to their tepee. Scott put his shirt on as they walked.

When they reached the tepee, Man-with-no-hair stayed for a few minutes as he talked with Dew-on-the-grass-in-the-moon-when-the-leaves-fall. He clapped Scott on the back again and then left.

"He want you go hunt," Dew-on-the-grass-in-the-moon-when-the-leaves-fall said, as they watched their new friend walk away.

Scott suffered a rush of mixed emotions. He loved to hunt, and he was anxious to learn new methods of hunting. He knew, by their geographical location, these Indians would employ different methods of hunting than the Powhatan. He was also concerned about the well being of these friendly people; he could not forget what had happened when he had hunted with Falling Feather.

Dew-on-the-grass-in-the-moon-when-the-leaves-fall saw the look of consternation on his face, and questioned him about it, but their communication had not developed to a point that he could explain the shameful deed to her.

He brushed her question aside as if nothing were wrong. He picked up his bow and began to examine it, in case it needed repairs.

3

The next morning, Scott was awakened by voices outside the tepee. He quickly got out of blankets and dressed. When he stepped out of the tepee, no one was there, but he heard the footfalls of horse hooves. A few moments later, a group of braves appeared, as they led their horses in the pre-dawn gloom. Man-with-no-hair led the group of braves; he also led two horses. Man-with-no-hair indicated for Scott to take one of the horses.

Scott took the reins of the horse and mounted when the rest of the hunters did. As they slowly rode out of the village, Scott remembered James Fort and was thankful for the few horses that had been there. Those horses had been slow, plodding, plow horses but Scott had ridden them occasionally and had developed some horsemanship skills. He was however, unprepared for the ride he was about to take.

When the hunters were outside the perimeter of the village, they kicked their mounts into a slow gallop. Two hours after leaving the village, Man-with-no-hair slowed his horse to a walk; the rest of the group followed his lead. A few minutes later, they came to the edge of a long, sloping hill. From the top of the hill, they looked down upon a herd of buffalo.

Scott was taken aback by the size of the herd. He was unaccustomed to using large numbers, but if had to guess, he would have placed their number at twenty thousand.

Man-with-no-hair spoke to one of the hunters, who then turned his horse and raced in the direction they had come. He then tested the wind and found it to be unacceptable, though not completely against them. The group of hunters moved to a more favorable location and dismounted.

Scott was puzzled by the decision of Man-with-no-hair not to attack the buffalo herd; however, he was unable to communicate with him, so he sat in the grass, and waited, along with the rest of the hunters.

They didn't have to wait too long, for a short time later, the hunter Man-with-no-hair had sent back, returned. The hunter spoke excitedly to Man-with-no-hair and the hunters were instructed to remount.

Man-with-no-hair led the hunters over the top of the ridge, toward the herd. They rode slowly, preparing their bows as they rode. Some of the buffalo looked up and watched the hunters descend the hill, but displayed little concern as they continued to eat.

As the hunters drew near, the buffalo grunted and trotted a few steps, and then resumed eating.

Scott held back somewhat, unsure of the technique used by the Indians. He watched closely as one of the hunters broke away from the group, and kicked his horse into a gallop. When the hunter's horse came alongside a buffalo, the hunter drew his bow, leaned over the side of his horse, and shot the buffalo behind the shoulder. When the buffalo fell to the ground, the brave whooped with joy and went after another animal. The rest of the hunters began to spread out and move in on targets they had singled out.

Scott was having some difficulty, for his horse kept trying to gallop. He wasn't sure he could remain mounted, on a running horse, while trying to shoot his bow. As Scott squeezed his legs tightly, he noticed the horse turned in response to leg pressure.

Scott finally picked a target and began to pursue it. When he was close enough for a shot, the buffalo turned. Scott turned his horse and resumed the chase. When he was alongside the massive beast, he reluctantly released the reins and drew his arrow back. He released his arrow just as the buffalo turned again. The arrow hit the buffalo behind the last rib; it was a lethal hit, but it would take the animal quite some time to die. Scott turned his horse and pursued the buffalo again. When once again he came alongside the running animal, he was more comfortable when he released the reins. When he unloosed his next arrow, the buffalo fell to the ground; however, by the time he turned his horse, the beast had regained its feet. As he watched, from horseback, the buffalo took two steps, fell to the ground, then struggled back to its feet.

Scott swung his right leg over the horse's neck and slid to the ground. With his bow in his left hand, he drew the hand axe with his right and approached the buffalo on foot.

Scott was intent upon the wounded animal and had not noticed the rest of the hunters had stopped chasing the herd. They had gathered on a nearby rise and watched as Scott walked toward the wounded buffalo.

When Scott was a few yards from the buffalo, he could see its sides heaving rapidly, blowing blood from its nostrils with each exhale. The beast grunted and tried to paw the earth, which nearly caused it to topple over again. The buffalo took two shaky steps toward Scott and lowered its head. Scott was just a few yards away; he rushed forward. Before the buffalo could respond, Scott buried the hand axe in the animal's skull, bruising his forearm on a horn in the process.

The watching Indians whooped and hollered as the buffalo fell to the ground. Scott looked from the dead animal to the cheering Indians. He was discomfited when he learned that he was being observed without his knowing about it, but quickly put it behind him, as he prepared to butcher the buffalo. Before he did so, he gave in to a sudden urge. He raised his arms and issued his best imitation of a fierce war cry. The watching Indians whooped and cheered in response.

As he drew his knife, he heard more cheering. He turned to see many of the women of the village descending the hill, leading horses that were dragging travois behind them. Scott spotted Dew-on-the-grass immediately. He watched as she left the group of women and led her horse toward him.

When Dew-on-the-grass arrived, she tried to shoo Scott away so she could butcher the buffalo. Scott looked toward the other hunters and noticed they were sitting on their horses, watching the women, as they worked over the dead animals.

Scott understood what he was expected to do; however, he was of no mind to do so. Since Dew-on-the-grass had recovered from her injuries, they had worked together. Side by side they had taken whatever nature had thrown at them – and they had won. Not because of any particular strength or prowess, but because they had worked in concert, as one.

In Scott's mind, nothing had changed. They resided safely in a village of people who treated them as friends. If he or Dew-on-the-grass were to become threatened, or be in danger, those people would assist in their protection, without question. But, he and Dew-on-the-grass were still outsiders. In a way, Scott and Dew-on-the-grass-in-the-moon-when-the-leaves-fall were a village unto themselves; with their own habits and customs.

Scott helped Dew-on-the-grass-in-the-moon-when-the-leaves-fall butcher the buffalo and load the meat and hide on the travois. Scott noticed some of the Indians returning to the village, others were still butchering. Scott and Dew-on-the-grass-in-the-moon-when-the-leaves-fall assisted those who still had work to do.

As Scott worked, he noticed Man-with-no-hair watching him closely, but he did not come forward, so Scott continued to work. When the last of the meat was loaded onto the travois, Scott and Dew-on-the-grass-in-the-moon-when-the-leaves-fall mounted their horses and rode, side by side, to the village.

It was late afternoon when the last of the buffalo hunters returned to the village. The weather was warm; in order to protect the meat, it would have to be processed quickly. Scott and Dew-on-the-grass-in-the-moon-when-the-leaves-fall, and many of the villagers, worked throughout the night, stripping the meat from the bone and smoking it. It was near noon of the next day when the task was finally completed.

The last chore was to stake out the massive hide. As they worked together on the project, Scott was distracted by the sound of excited voices near the center of the village. Looking up, Scott saw one of the hunters putting on an animated display. As he watched, he suddenly became aware that the brave was imitating the way he had killed the buffalo with the hand axe. The onlookers looked in Scott's direction. One of them indicated to the storyteller that Scott was watching the show. The storyteller turned toward Scott, raised his arms, and issued a war cry.

Scott simply nodded his head and returned to his work.

"Scott good," Dew-on-the-grass-in-the-moon-when-the-leaves-fall said proudly.

"I just killed a buffalo," he answered, a bit embarrassed.

When the last stake was driven into the ground, they rose to their feet and walked to the tepee. Their blankets beckoned them. After the difficulties involved with processing all of their meat, they were ready to get some much deserved rest.

Before Scott drifted off to sleep, he thought of the brave who had been imitating him. He had spent enough time with Indians to know they were not teasing or making fun of him. In a way, they were honoring him, and with honor, came acceptance. After the long lonely hours on the trail, never knowing if he would see the next sunrise, it felt good to be accepted once again. Very good indeed.

Scott did not wake up until the next morning. Dew-on-the-grass was not in the tepee. He quickly dressed and stepped through the hide-covered hole that served as a door. He immediately spotted Dew-on-the-grass. She was visiting with several women near another tepee.

Scott had no plans for the day, but an idea occurred to him, as he picked a piece of meat from the rack and ate it.

He walked through the village until he came to the tepee of the arrow maker. When he arrived, the man was sorting through some previously gathered shafts of wood. The man looked up as Scott approached, and then continued his task as Scott seated himself nearby.

Scott had nearly run out of arrows before he and Dew-on-the-grass-in-the-moon-when-the-leaves-fall had been brought to the village. If he could learn to make arrows from a master, he would not have to worry about that problem again.

A short time later, Dew-on-the-grass-in-the-moon-when-the-leaves-fall joined him. Together, they watched in silence as the man attached arrowheads and feathers to the shafts. When one arrow was completed, the man immediately began work on another.

Later in the day, when the man felt Scott was genuinely interested in making arrows, he showed him how to choose a good shaft. He then helped

Scott attach feathers and arrowheads.

Scott was pleased with what he had learned, and as he walked back to his tepee, he decided he would devote the next day to making arrows on his own.

Chapter Eight

As time passed, Scott learned to speak Shawnee well enough to communicate thoughts and ideas with Man-with-no-hair and Dew-on-the-grass. In the process, he learned that he had been calling Dew-on-the-grass-in-the-moon-when-the-leaves-fall by Dew-on-the-grass. Now he called her by her full name

Scott felt at ease in the village. Dew-on-the-grass-in-the-moon-when-the-leaves-fall was getting on well with the other women. They had both learned a great deal about life and survival on the open plains. However, Scott felt an unexplainable desire to move on. He no longer felt threatened by Falling Feather's people – if they were still coming, they would have found him by now. He didn't know why he wanted to leave; he simply felt an urge to see what was beyond the vast plains.

Scott and Dew-on-the-grass-in-the-moon-when-the-leaves-fall had been in the village for a month and a half when the urge came upon him. When he brought the subject up to her, she did not seem at all surprised. In fact, she acted as if that had been the plan all along. When he asked if she was anxious to leave, she said, "No. Scott Dew-on-the-grass-in-the-moon-when-the-leaves-fall's man. Where Scott go, Dew-on-the-grass-in-the-moon-when-the-leaves-fall go."

He knew she would miss the company of the other women, but she was smiling pleasantly when she told Scott she would go with him. He was thankful for her acceptance of his decision.

Together, they sought out Man-with-no-hair, to inform him of their decision. He acted disturbed when Dew-on-the-grass-in-the-moon-when-the-leaves-fall told him, but he told her he would assist them in telling the chief of the village.

The old man was very disappointed when he learned the two newcomers were going to leave, but he told them he knew of the wanderlust shared by all young people. He also told them they had a home in his village, whenever they wished to return.

The news of Scott and Dew-on-the-grass-in-the-moon-when-the-leaves-fall's departure soon spread throughout the village. Many of the villagers brought gifts of food, robes and weapons, and well wishes. Man-with-no-hair watched from a short distance until the last of the villagers had departed. When Scott and Dew-on-the-grass-in-the-moon-when-the-leaves-fall were alone, he approached and spoke to them.

"Man-with-no-hair would go with Scott and Dew-on-the-grass-in-the-moon-when-the-leaves-fall if they say he go," he said solemnly.

Scott was shocked that the man would want to leave the village and go with them. He was also excited about the prospect of having the extra help and knowledge that Man-with-no-hair would provide.

"Yes, you can go with us," Scott answered, smiling broadly.

"I have many horses," Man-with-no-hair added, though he had already been accepted.

Scott had not considered the use of horses. They already had all they could carry, not to mention the new gifts they had just received. Horses would be a godsend.

2

At dawn the following morning, Man-with-no-hair led six horses to the tepee shared by Scott and Dew-on-the-grass-in-the-moon-when-the-leaves-fall. The three worked together loading their belongings on the backs of three horses, leaving three to ride.

When the pack-horses were loaded, they swung up on the backs of the remaining horses and rode out of the village.

Scott glanced at their new companion and wondered what he was leaving behind. Dew-on-the-grass-in-the-moon-when-the-leaves-fall had told him that Man-with-no-hair was a Shawnee. He was born a bastard child and had been called Boy-with-no-father. He had to live with constant shame and humiliation. Hoping to gain the respect of his people, he had worked hard to master the methods of hunting and fighting, but to no avail. His mother died when he was twenty leaving no one in the village to miss him when he left. The elders of the Shawnee village had shaved his head to remind him of his shame. His hair had not grown back when he came to this village, thus his name: Man-with-no-hair. Scott did not know how old Man-with-no-hair was but he looked to be about thirty. He must have been in this village for ten years.

The season was late spring or early summer, a good time to be on the move. Scott's spirits were high and his excitement soon spread to Dew-on-the-grass-in-the-moon-when-the-leaves-fall and Man-with-no-hair. They had enough meat to last for more than a month. Man-with-no-hair had brought his tepee and many buffalo robes. Protection from the elements was always an issue and the things Man-with-no-hair had brought would serve them well while they traveled and when they reached their destination, wherever that happened to be.

A month and a half after leaving the village, they came upon a river that flowed from the northwest. They could see a massive mountain range on the western horizon. They had crossed numerous streams but as summer progressed, fresh water was becoming more difficult to find. Man-with-no-hair had killed an antelope the day before; game was plentiful, not so with water.

Scott suggested they follow the river up stream; Man-with-no-hair agreed.

Apparently, the water attracted others too, for as they traveled upstream, they saw fresh pony tracks daily.

Scott wasn't as apprehensive about being discovered by other Indians as he once had been, but their presence still made him nervous. It was his decision to leave the village; he felt responsible for the safety and well being of his companions.

Man-with-no-hair saw the pony tracks too, but made no comment. Scott could only assume that he felt no immediate danger.

In most places, the brush was thick along the river; there were scattered cottonwood trees as well. There was very little brush away from the river except in the bottoms of the draws.

On the third morning of following the river, they broke camp and mounted their horses. They had ridden but a few yards when they saw a dozen Indians. They were on a ridge top, about four hundred yards away. Scott, Dew-on-the-grass-in-the-moon-when-the-leaves-fall and Man-with-no-hair stopped and waited as the Indians began to ride toward them.

The Indians approached rapidly until they were close enough to see that Scott was not an Indian. They gathered together and talked among themselves, pointing and looking at Scott.

Finally, one of the Indians rode forward and Man-with-no-hair rode out to meet him. After several minutes, the brave rode back to the group of warriors and Man-with-no-hair rode back to Scott and Dew-on-the-grass-in-the-moon-when-the-leaves-fall.

"What did they say?" Scott asked, when Man-with-no-hair stopped beside him.

They had spent the evenings on the trail learning each other's language. They had made good progress and could communicate very well with each other.

"Fear you. Think you…ah…ah…spirit man. They not see man with hair on face before. They say we come near their village, they hurt us much," answered Man-with-no-hair.

Scott was somewhat angered by the implied threat. What right did they have to threaten him and his friends just because he was different? He had thought he had left such narrow-minded attitudes behind him, in James Fort. However, there was also a certain amount of relief in knowing that those Indians feared him. Perhaps he could use that fear against them, to avoid a confrontation in the future.

Scott did not want trouble with these Indians, but he didn't want to leave the river either. Within a short distance of the previous night's camp, they found a safe place to cross the river. There was little consolation in crossing the river; they did not know the location of the village.

Scott considered shaving his beard off and quickly discarded the idea. He couldn't change the color of his hair, which was as noticeable as his beard. He would rather be accepted by these people than feared by them; if acceptance was not forthcoming, fear might keep him alive.

Late that afternoon, they saw the village. It was more than a mile away in the bottom of a large bowl that was created by a large sweeping ridge. From their location, the village looked similar to the one Man-with-no-hair had resided in.

As they rode on, they lost sight of the village. Dew-on-the-grass-in-the-moon-when-the-leaves-fall noticed a frown on Scott's face.

"Scott not happy?" she asked.

Scott didn't think he could explain how he felt. Why was it so easy to be accepted by some people, and just as easily, rejected by others? As far as he knew, there were still some Indians who wanted to kill him, and not because they were afraid of him. The next strange Indian he saw, he wouldn't know whether to shoot him or scare him. Even worse, he might not know the Indian's intentions until it was too late.

In considering Dew-on-the-grass-in-the-moon-when-the-leaves-fall's question, he could only think of the Indian's outlook on life. He had seen very few Indians get angry, and when they did, they didn't stay that way for long.

So when he answered her, he simply said, "No," and gave her a halfhearted grin.

With Man-with-no-hair leading the way, they turned away from the river, attempting to give the village as wide a berth as possible. When nightfall was growing near, they made a dry camp in the bottom of a brushy, little draw.

They made no fire that night, or the next morning, but as they were breaking camp, they saw a band of Indians on the ridge above them. The Indians did not come toward the camp. Scott, Dew-on-the-grass-in-the-moon-when-the-leaves-fall and Man-with-no-hair rode out of the camp as if they hadn't seen the Indians.

When they left the camp, they rode to the ridge-top and followed it back to the river. They were well upstream of the village, but they were still being followed. They turned upstream when they reached the river and followed the watercourse for the remainder of the day. As dusk was gathering around them, they noticed that their escort was gone.

3

As they continued to travel upriver, the vegetation changed noticeably. The grass was much shorter and grew more sparsely; sagebrush and juniper became the dominant species. Thick stands of pine grew in the draws and canyons. They saw herds of buffalo, elk and antelope every day.

One morning they woke up to a light frost. Scott had noticed the change in the color of some of the leaves, but was surprised by the sudden drop in temperature. Scott suddenly realized that he didn't know what to expect from winter in this area.

"What will winter be like here?" Scott asked Man-with-no-hair, as they loaded their gear on the pack-horses.

"Much cold. Much snow. Much wind," he answered.

"How long do we have?" Scott asked.

"Not know. One moon. Maybe two," Man-with-no-hair answered.

"Should we make a winter camp now, or go farther upstream?" Scott asked.

"Have plenty meat. Plenty meat all around," Man-with-no-hair said, referring to the herds of game they saw daily. "We see good camp, we stop."

Scott had learned to trust Man-with-no-hair's judgment. They continued to follow the river.

The terrain was becoming more rugged and they couldn't travel as far as they had on the open plains. They were two weeks up river from the Indian village. For the last week, the river had been leading them in a westerly direction, rather than northwest.

That night as they sat around the fire, Scott's mind was filled with questions about the coming winter. How much was 'Much snow' and how long would it last?

Because of his lack of knowledge of winter in this area, he was more concerned about the snow than the wind and cold. He would soon know better.

The next day they came to a rockslide that hadn't closed the river but the route was impassable for the horses. The north bank of the river had been undercut by a rushing current, which made a river crossing far too dangerous, and thus, out of the question.

They turned around and rode a half-mile downstream before they found a game trail leading up a ridge. Their plan had been to cross the ridge and return to the river; however, when they reached the ridge top, they could see a very large Indian village. The village was on the north side of the river. It was several miles upstream and appeared to be at least three times as large as the village Man-with-no-hair had come from.

Scott preferred to avoid contact with the villagers; however, the lay of the land reduced their options. A river, flowing from the south, joined the river they had been following. Across this new river was a large flat area that offered very little cover; they would pass in plain view of the village.

The ridge they were on joined another ridge that appeared to follow the new, smaller river, into the mountains.

Man-with-no-hair suggested following the smaller river and Scott readily agreed.

They followed the ridge until it joined the main ridge. The main ridge had little cover, so they decided to descend to the river. The wall of the ridge was steep and they had to choose their route carefully. It took them an hour to reach the river. At this point they were on the edge of the large flat area opposite the village. From here they could see the forested canyon from which the river flowed. They rode their horses into the water and soon disappeared into the thick stand of pines.

As they rode up the river, the canyon walls surrounded them on both sides. By nightfall, the canyon walls were so steep they had no choice but to ride in the river.

Fortunately, they came upon a small flat just before dusk. The proximity of the river dropped the temperature by at least ten degrees. That night they were especially thankful for the robes Man-with-no-hair had provided, for they had once again decided not to build a fire.

The camp was peaceful; the chuckling sound of the river had an anesthetic affect, as if they needed it, after the long hours on horseback. They slept so well that even Man-with-no-hair didn't hear the wolves howling on the distant ridge tops.

The next morning, camp was broken and they were ready to travel before there was enough light to do so safely. In the deep canyon, the sun would shine on them for only a few hours each day.

As they rode upstream, Scott realized how fortunate they had been in locating last night's camp site, for he saw no other such place until around mid-day.

The next day, the ridges began to decease in size and the near sheer walls on either side of the stream gave way to gentle slopes. For the first time in two days they were able to ride their horses alongside the river, instead of in it.

Man-with-no-hair stopped and studied the terrain ahead of them. After a few moments, he pointed out the obvious: a great sweeping ridge indicating the river was flowing out of a box canyon.

They turned east and rode to the top of the first ridge. When they reached the ridge top they turned south again and rode deeper into the mountains.

The scenery, from the ridge top, was as spectacular as any they had seen. The slopes on either side of the river rose gently up and away from the watercourse. The slopes were covered with various grasses, sagebrush and juniper. The draws were full of pine, poplar and aspen. There was a small herd of buffalo feeding on a distant slope.

There was a game trail on the ridge top; it was crossed by other game trails that contoured off the ridge.

That night, they camped alongside a small stream that flowed toward the river they had left behind. They had heard elk bugling throughout the day and now that eerie sound filled the forest around their camp.

Their meat supply was not dangerously low, but the camp was a good one and game was in the vicinity. The next morning, Scott and Man-with-no-hair hunted in a timbered draw, in the direction of the elk they had heard the night before. Dew-on-the-grass-in-the-moon-when-the-leaves-fall went in search of edible greens.

Scott and Man-with-no-hair had gone less than half a mile when Man-with-no-hair spotted a large bull elk feeding through the forest.

Man-with-no-hair signaled for Scott to move off to the right.

Suddenly, Scott was overwhelmed with the horror of what he had done to Falling Feather. If the same thing happened to Man-with-no-hair...

This was neither the time nor the place to explain his clouded past to his new friend. He simply shook his head and motioned that he would follow Man-with-no-hair.

Man-with-no-hair looked at him quizzically, but only shrugged his shoulders and led the way toward the bull.

Once again, Scott was shocked by the silence with which Man-with-no-hair moved. He seemed to drift through the forest like smoke. Scott couldn't keep up without making too much noise. He was certain he was going to startle the elk.

Scott stepped on a small, dead limb. The limb cracked and another elk, a smaller bull, stood up from its bed. The wind was in Scott and Man-with-no-hair's favor; the elk were startled by the sound, but were unable to smell the hunters.

Scott and Man-with-no-hair both had an open shot at the smaller bull. Man-with-no-hair released his arrow an instant before Scott. Man-with-no-hair's arrow hit the elk behind the shoulder, piercing the lungs. When Man-with-no-hair's arrow hit, the bull lunged forward, causing Scott's arrow to hit in the guts. When Scott's arrow hit, the bull stopped running, hunched his back and took several unsteady steps backward. As the elk was backing up, Man-with-no-hair shot him in the neck. The arrow severed the bull's spine, and he fell to the ground dead. The sound of the falling elk caused several more elk to rise from their beds and crash through the underbrush, as they quickly moved away.

Scott wasn't aware of Man-with-no-hair's sense of humor until all of the elk had left the area. Man-with-no-hair imitated the gut-shot elk by hunching up and walking backward. He laughed heartily and clapped Scott on the back – he also made Scott remove the damaged entrails from the bull, while he went after two horses.

Scott took the kidding well. He had a sense of humor too; someday he would get even.

Scott had the elk gutted and had nearly finished skinning it by the time Man-with-no-hair returned. Dew-on-the-grass-in-the-moon-when-the-leaves-fall had come with him. Scott looked from his work to Dew-on-the-grass-in-the-moon-when-the-leaves-fall. She stifled a laugh and looked away. Scott looked at Man-with-no-hair and knew he had told her the whole story, including mimicry.

Scott mumbled to himself as he returned to his work. He would get even, yes indeed. A thought occurred to him: what if he had missed the bull completely? The harassment would have been intolerable.

Dew-on-the-grass-in-the-moon-when-the-leaves-fall and Man-with-no-hair came to his aid, and together, they made short work of the butchering.

When they got back to the camp, Scott and Man-with-no-hair rigged a ridge pole and tied the quarters to it. Dew-on-the-grass-in-the-moon-when-the-leaves-fall made a drying rack while Scott and Man-with-no-hair cut the meat into strips. When the rack was completed and covered with meat, Dew-on-the-grass-in-the-moon-when-the-leaves-fall took the undamaged intestines to the stream and washed them out. When the meat finished cooking she stuffed it into the gut and sealed both ends.

Late that afternoon they had cooked the last of the meat and were now broiling the liver over the fire. Man-with-no-hair had eaten some of the liver raw, while they were cutting and cooking the meat. Scott had tried a bite, but found he preferred it cooked.

As the last rays of sunlight faded from the sky, Scott decided it was time to unburden himself of his guilt. With his two companions sitting around the fire with him, he told them of Falling Feather's fate, explaining why he would not leave Man-with-no-hair's side while they had been hunting. His voice was choked with emotion by the time he finished the story. Man-with-no-hair and Dew-on-the-grass-in-the-moon-when-the-leaves-fall did not interrupt as he spoke.

When he finished the story, he looked directly into the dark eyes of Man-with-no-hair. "When we get where we are going, you can leave if you want to. It may be safer for you, if you go".

Man-with-no-hair maintained eye contact when he spoke. "Sometimes our quivers are full of bad arrows. Your heart is good. I am your friend and I do not wish to leave your camp. We will not speak of this again."

As they prepared to turn in that night, they heard wolves howling in the forest. The proximity of the howling indicated they had located the remains of the butchered elk. They weren't aware of how close the wolves had come, until they rode out of camp the next morning. Some of the tracks were closer than a hundred yards. Scott had seen many wolves, he had also seen the remains of their kill; he found their closeness a little unnerving. Man-with-no-hair seemed unaffected by the tracks.

4

When they rode the narrow trail out of the camp, Man-with-no-hair was in the lead, Dew-on-the-grass-in-the-moon-when-the-leaves-fall rode in the middle and Scott brought up the rear.

Scott took some time to consider his future. He had no idea where he was going, or what he was going to do when he got there. He was in the company of good friends, and he cared very much for them. He also loved this new country they were traveling through. It was a place where a man could be the master of his own destiny. After enjoying the freedom of the wide open land, he had no desire to return to the east. Punishment notwithstanding, it was all too likely he would become subservient to some unimaginative lord or squire and their confining, prohibitive laws. This is where he wanted to be, this is where he would stay. With Man-with-no-hair and Dew-on-the-grass-in-the-moon-when-the-leaves-fall, the three of them, working together, they could protect and feed themselves, and do whatever else was necessary to survive.

Man-with-no-hair stopped his horse in the trail; Dew-on-the-grass-in-the-moon-when-the-leaves-fall swung around his pack-horse and stopped beside him. Scott rode his horse into the rump of Man-with-no-hair's horse. Man-with-no-hair gave Scott a "Why don't you watch where you are going" look, as Scott was abruptly awakened from his daydream.

Scott gave Man-with-no-hair a sheepish look before he noticed the object that had caused him to stop so abruptly.

Across the canyon, on an open hillside, was a monstrous bear. It was brown, not black, like the bears Scott had encountered in the east. The bear was feeding on an unidentifiable dead animal. And though the distance was great, it was easy to discern that the bear was larger than a small horse.

"Good him there, us here," said Man-with-no-hair with noticeable awe in his voice.

"Yes it is," replied Scott as he imagined what a bear like that could do to a man. His thoughts flashed back to the muskets in James Fort. He quickly discarded the thought: even a well-placed musket shot probably would not stop that brute.

"I hope all bears are not that big out here," Scott mumbled.

"Not know," said Man-with-no-hair as he touched his heels to the flanks of his horse.

Man-with-no-hair's comment did nothing to make Scott feel better about the prospect of running into such a creature.

Scott did not sleep well that night. The camp was in a good location among the trees, against the wall of a bluff. The bluff deterred predation from that direction. Nonetheless, Scott woke at the slightest sound from the forest. When he finally fell into exhausted sleep, it was time to get up.

Scott rolled out of his blankets groggy and sleepy-eyed. Man-with-no-hair smiled then stood up and imitated a giant bear, standing on its hind legs, arms raised and spread apart. Then he imitated the bear after it had taken an arrow in the guts, hunching up and stepping backwards. Then he started to laugh. He laughed so hard he fell to his knees, eyes watering. Scott had never seen him laugh so much or so hard.

Dew-on-the-grass-in-the-moon-when-the-leaves-fall was not quite sure how to respond. She was trying not to laugh, for Scott's sake, but when she saw him laughing too, she quickly joined in.

They traveled on the ridge top for the entire day. They saw no more bears or signs thereof. That suited Scott just fine.

The ridge they followed wound farther and farther away from the small river, leading them in a southwesterly direction. For the most part, the ridge was open, with timber in the draws on either side. There were many rock outcroppings, but none expansive enough to cause them to leave the ridge or change direction.

As nightfall approached, they were unable to locate a sheltered campsite. They had come upon a bench that was about an acre in size. The bench was flat but there were no trees for shelter. The timbered slopes on either side of the ridge were too steep to camp on. The bench extended on both sides of the ridge until it finally gave way to the steep slopes.

A strong, cold wind began to blow out of the north. They dismounted and lead their horses to the southern most part of the flat, using the ridge as a windbreak.

They quickly unpacked the horses. Man-with-no-hair and Scott piled rocks against the side of the ridge and across the flat to assist in breaking the wind. Dew-on-the-grass-in-the-moon-when-the-leaves-fall gathered scraps of wood that were scattered about the bench.

Their location was exposed for many miles from the south, and despite the bitter cold, they were forced to keep the fire small, hoping to avoid detection.

The wind blew all night and the temperature fell well below freezing.

They awoke to the coldest morning of their journey. There was little frost however, for the wind had dried the moisture from the plants. The sky was clear and the promise of warm sunshine was encouraging.

They broke camp quickly, wanting to be on the move. Wrapped in the warm buffalo robes, they ate cold pieces of elk meat as they rode.

After a couple of hours, the wind died down and eventually stopped, with the exception of occasional breezes.

Late that afternoon, they camped near the top of the mountain the ridge had led them to. They were still too far from the top of the mountain to see what was on the other side. That would have to wait until the next day. All three of them were anxious for the night to be over. The journey had been long and the season was growing late; they needed to find a place to camp for the winter.

The next morning they were up and about long before dawn. They had eaten and packed the horses an hour before there was enough light to allow them to travel safely.

When, at last, there was enough light, they rode out of the camp only to find that it was farther to the top then they had thought. An hour before mid-day they rode onto the rounded knob that served as the mountaintop.

Scott, Man-with-no-hair and Dew-on-the-grass-in-the-moon-when-the-leaves-fall sat on their horses, mouths agape, as they looked upon the vast panorama before them. The valleys to the north were choked with timber. To the west was the majestic mountain range with serrated, snow-covered peaks they had been seeing for so many days. In looking south, they saw open rolling grassy hills with timber in all of the draws. Directly below them was a long, narrow, winding meadow of varied width. A small, slow stream wound its way gently through the middle of the meadow.

Man-with-no-hair was the first one to overcome the intoxication of the view. It would take more than a day to reach the valley floor; they should be on their way. With a grunt, he led the others in search of a route off the mountain.

Chapter Nine

There were many ridges leading into the meadow but most of them were too steep for the horses. They were anxious to reach the valley floor but they were not going to become careless at this point. Finally, Man-with-no-hair pointed to a ridge that didn't appear to be as steep as the others. All three riders looked the ridge over closely before deciding to try it.

Following a game trail, they reached the ridge they were going to descend. They had crossed other game trails that contoured the mountain and eventually led to the valley floor but Man-with-no-hair was afraid they might end, or lead them into an area that was unsafe for the horses; this slope of the mountain was very steep.

It took them an hour to reach the ridge they were going to follow to the valley floor. An hour after that, they came to the top of a bench. From the top edge of the bench to the bench itself was nearly twenty feet – straight down. They had to dismount and lead the horses as they contoured around the drop off.

The bench was over a hundred yards long and twenty yards wide, it would have been an excellent place to camp but there were still several hours of daylight left and they wanted to be sure to reach the valley the next day.

As it turned out, the ridge consisted of a series of benches and they came upon another one shortly before dark. The bench they camped on was smaller than the first one they had encountered, but it was more than large enough to suit their needs. There was a small seep in the grass-covered rock wall of the bench, but it was inadequate for watering the horses; Dew-on-the-grass-in-the-moon-when-the-leaves-fall had water bags for herself and the men.

The night was cold but they did not build a fire; they didn't know if the valley was inhabited. If they discovered people living in the valley, they could avoid them only if they, themselves, remained undetected. Once again, Scott and Dew-on-the-grass-in-the-moon-when-the-leaves-fall were thankful for the buffalo robes Man-with-no-hair had provided.

The next morning they were under way as soon as there was adequate light. The thick timber often blocked their view of the mountains but when they rode through occasional small openings, they were able to see the sunlight glistening off the towering, snow-covered peaks.

They had but a few minutes to make camp before darkness surrounded them when they finally reached the valley floor. The day had slipped away from them as they stopped and looked upon the majestic mountain range, during the descent.

They did not camp in the open when they reached the valley floor. Both sides of the valley was fringed in timber. They camped in the timber. Once again, they did not build a fire.

Scott had watched the meadow closely for signs of habitation but his view was often obscured by the timber. He had been growing more and more agitated as they neared the valley floor. He could not imagine people not living in a place of such incredible beauty. He imagined himself waking every morning, walking through the meadow and looking upon those spectacular mountains. Fulfillment of the dream would be prevented if people already lived here. If the valley was not inhabited, and there was adequate shelter and food supply, Scott could see no reason to go elsewhere.

The next morning they decided to leave the three pack-horses in camp, while they scouted the valley. It was a risky move but they felt they would be able to move more freely without them.

They rode along the edge of the meadow for more than five miles and saw no pony tracks or any other sign of habitation. Reluctantly, slowly, they rode across the meadow and returned toward their camp from the other side of the valley floor.

When they were within a mile of the previous night's camp, they came upon a narrow finger of the meadow that wound toward the base of a massive ridge. There were steep walls on either side of the finger, created by two feeder ridges that ran into the valley floor. Both ridges were covered with thick timber. The finger ended against a solid rock wall.

"This would be a good place to stay," said Scott. "The walls would protect us from the wind. We could keep the horses back here. They would be safe here," he added.

Scott could tell by the look on Man-with-no-hair's face that he, too, appreciated the qualities of the small finger.

"Good camp," said Man-with-no-hair. "We look other way first," he added.

Scott had been so excited about finding such a good location to live, he had almost forgotten they hadn't looked for signs of habitation in the other direction.

They spent the remainder of the day searching the west end of the valley. Happily, they discovered they were alone in the valley.

They had ridden approximately five miles in either direction. They had seen some horse tracks but they were very old and did not present an immediate threat. At the east end of the valley they had come upon a series of short ridges that wound their way to the valley floor. The ridges created somewhat of a maze and Scott was anxious to explore them, when time allowed.

They had an hour of daylight left when they returned to the pack-horses, and last night's camp. There was not enough time to move to the finger, where they had decided to live. Scott built a fire, while Man-with-no-hair staked the horses in the grass of the meadow.

Before dawn of the next morning, they mounted their horses and rode toward the hidden finger that would be their new home. The thought of settling down was appealing to Scott; he had been on the move for a long time, and he was tired. Winter was well on its way, and it was already obvious that winter was not a good time to be traveling in this country. Besides, there was no hope of crossing those towering mountains before snow began to fall.

An hour later, they rode between the two ridges and entered the small hidden meadow. The first order of business was to erect Man-with-no-hair's tepee. Scott had studied the tepees while in the village that Man-with-no-hair had come from, but this was the first time he had been involved with putting one up. Scott was surprised at how quickly they accomplished the feat.

As they worked on the tepee, Scott's mind wandered back to James Fort and he realized there were wooden structures he could build, as time allowed. For the time being, there were other, more important things to worry about.

The horses would be a major concern. If they weren't properly cared for, they would die. Scott had been afoot once and did not relish the thought of returning to that mode of transportation, especially in this country.

There were deadfalls scattered throughout the timber that bordered the valley. With his hand axe, Scott bumped knots and cut the deadfalls to desired lengths. He then dragged them to the back-end of the meadow. He used the deadfalls to build a fence across a narrow place between the two ridges. The back-end of the meadow was surrounded by sheer rock walls. The fence would impound about an acre of ground; a safe place for the horses.

The fence was within sight of the tepee. Man-with-no-hair and Dew-on-the-grass-in-the-moon-when-the-leaves-fall watched him curiously as he worked and they unpacked. Neither made a comment until the task was completed. Man-with-no-hair wasn't sure what Scott had built until he led the horses into the enclosure and slid the gate poles into place. There had been much horse thieving on the plains where Man-with-no-hair had lived; he had been one of the best at it. No one would steal their horses from them now.

Dew-on-the-grass-in-the-moon-when-the-leaves-fall was busy putting the camp in order, Man-with-no-hair went hunting and scouting and Scott went after wood.

2

By nightfall, Scott had a huge pile of wood stacked outside the tepee. It took very little fire to keep the tepee warm; he had enough wood for a month. Dew-on-the-grass-in-the-moon-when-the-leaves-fall had prepared a meal but Man-with-no-hair had not returned. It was cold and getting colder. Scott was beginning to worry about his friend.

Scott and Dew-on-the-grass-in-the-moon-when-the-leaves-fall ate in silence, both thinking the worst had happened to Man-with-no-hair. When Scott finished eating, he picked up a blanket and wrapped it around his shoulders.

"I am going to look for him," he told Dew-on-the-grass-in-the-moon-when-the-leaves-fall, from the door of the tepee.

"How you know where to look in the dark?" she asked, with concern in her voice.

"I don't know, but I have to look. I can't sit here and wait," he said.

"I understand. I don't want both of you missing," she insisted.

"I know," he said, as he stepped through the door.

Scott had just reached the gate of the corral when he heard the footfalls of Man-with-no-hair's horse approaching.

"I'm glad to see you," Scott said, as Man-with-no-hair slid from the horse's back. "I thought something had happened to you."

Dew-on-the-grass-in-the-moon-when-the-leaves-fall heard the horse walk by the tepee. She joined the two men at the corral gate. Man-with-no-hair watched her walking toward them. When she reached them, he turned to Scott.

"Tomorrow you ride with me. I find many pony tracks. Long way. Maybe far enough away. Maybe not."

Scott was deeply troubled by the presence of other people in this valley.

He wasn't bothered by the people themselves, but by the measures they could force him, and his friends, to take. If allowed to do so, they could peacefully coexist with other people, but if that possibility did not exist, they would be forced to fight and die, or leave. Scott was shocked when he realized how much he already loved this valley, and how willing he was to call it home. He didn't want to leave.

That night, Dew-on-the-grass-in-the-moon-when-the-leaves-fall made much of Scott's depression go away. He was amazed at her perception. He also realized that as long as he was with his two friends he would be happy, wherever he lived.

It seemed Scott had just closed his eyes when he felt Man-with-no-hair touch his shoulder.

"We go now," he said to Scott.

"Yes," said Scott, as he wiped the sleep from his eyes.

Dew-on-the-grass-in-the-moon-when-the-leaves-fall packed food for the men as they dressed. When they left the camp, they rode west for an hour before there was enough light to gallop the horses. They traveled at a slow gallop that made the miles fade away, without tiring the horses.

As they rode, Scott wondered how they could have missed the signs of "many horses." If they hadn't missed the signs, they had been made after they had scouted the valley.

Three hours after leaving camp, they came to a fork in the valley, one leading west, the other northeast. Scott remembered the place. It was where they had turned around while they were scouting the valley.

The tracks had come out of the western fork of the valley and gone into the northeastern fork. There appeared to be twelve to fifteen horses. The tracks were fresh.

Scott turned around and looked back up the valley. With a puzzled look on his face he rode back where they had just come from. When he had gone about a hundred yards he came to the tracks he and Man-with-no-hair and Dew-on-the-grass-in-the-moon-when-the-leaves-fall had made on the scouting trip. If they had ridden all the way to the forks of the valley, the Indians would have seen *their* tracks.

It wasn't enough to know the Indians had been here. Scott and Man-with-no-hair had to find where they lived. Of course, they had no way of knowing whether the tracks they followed were leading toward the village, or away from it. There was only one way to find out.

They followed the tracks at a slow walk for the remainder of the day.

Though Scott was growing concerned for Dew-on-the-grass-in-the-moon-when-the-leaves-fall, he paid close attention to the terrain ahead of them, not wanting to ride into an ambush.

That night, Scott and Man-with-no-hair camped in a dense thicket of pines. Once again they had no fire, but the buffalo robes kept them warm.

The next morning they awoke to a cloudy sky. The farther they rode, the narrower the valley became. By mid-day, the valley was less than ten yards wide. By late afternoon, the timber was becoming noticeably thinner, and the valley was beginning to spread out again.

An hour before dark, they were completely out of the timber and looking across a vast plain of rolling hills. As they looked across the plain, they saw the village. It was perhaps twenty miles away and barely perceptible at that distance.

"I think we not fear them much," said Man-with-no-hair, as he scrutinized the village.

"I agree, but it will bear watching," Scott replied.

As one, they turned their horses and galloped them toward the safety of the timber.

It was well after dark before they came to a small grove of trees. The sky had cleared and they were able to see by the light of the stars and the moon. With the loss of cloud cover, the temperature dropped into the low twenties.

3

Dew-on-the-grass-in-the-moon-when-the-leaves-fall was working near the outside fire when Scott and Man-with-no-hair rode into the narrow valley. She dropped her work and ran to them. Scott jumped from his horse and let her run into his arms. He explained what they had found as they walked the horses toward the corral.

The weather had changed again. Massive black clouds filled the sky and a strong wind was beginning to blow out of the north. It began to snow as they walked from the corral toward the tepee.

The next morning, Scott and Man-with-no-hair stepped out of the tepee and found an accumulation of eight inches of snow, and it was still snowing.

They led the horses to the main valley so they could eat. Using a long horsehair rope, they staked one of the horses, in case they needed it to round up the others.

The horses seemed content to stay nearby, but, much of the grass was covered by the snow, and they soon began to drift farther away in search of food.

Man-with-no-hair left Scott to watch the horses as he began a project of his own. Scott watched him as he went to a willow thicket and cut some of the long slender shoots.

Scott untied the staked horse, mounted it, and herded the rest of the horses closer together. He realized they would have to find another place to feed the horses, for soon all of the grass in the valley would be covered by snow.

As Scott sat on the horse, near the center of the valley floor, his eyes scanned the surrounding ridges. He noticed the wind had blown the snow from many of the ridge tops. When Man-with-no-hair finished his project, and could see to the horses, he would walk up to the exposed ridges to see if there was enough grass for them to eat.

Sitting on a horse in the snow and wind, Scott began to get cold. He rode into the sheltered camp to get a buffalo robe. Man-with-no-hair was sitting near the fire working with the willow he had cut. Dew-on-the-grass-in-the-moon-when-the-leaves-fall was adding meat and vegetables to the skin pot that hung over the fire.

Dew-on-the-grass-in-the-moon-when-the-leaves-fall greeted him with a smile and a hug when he slid off the horse. Man-with-no-hair was so intent upon his project, he didn't even look up.

Scott stepped into the tepee and came back with one of the robes.

"No. Not that. I make for you," said Dew-on-the-grass-in-the-moon-when-the-leaves-fall when she saw Scott with the robe.

She led him back into the tepee and handed him a pair of leggings and a shirt with the fur on the inside. She helped him out of his summer clothing and as he stood there naked, she threw his new clothing to the other side of the tepee.

Some time later Scott stepped out of the tepee. He was no longer cold, but it had little to do with the new clothing he was wearing.

Scott was very conscientious. He had thoroughly enjoyed the time he had spent with Dew-on-the-grass-in-the-moon-when-the-leaves-fall but he was concerned about the horses. He mounted the horse and rode out of camp. Man-with-no-hair hadn't looked away from his work but Scott could have sworn his friend was shaking his head as he rode by him.

The horses were safe and eating contentedly when Scott returned to them.

Sometime later, Scott saw Man-with-no-hair walking toward him. If walking was what you wanted to call it. He swung his legs out with each step. As Scott watched, he noticed Man-with-no-hair had something attached to his feet and he was walking on top of the snow.

"That's good!" Scott said excitedly, when Man-with-no-hair stopped beside him. Scott never ceased to be amazed by the ingenuity of his friends.

"You want, I make for you," said Man-with-no-hair, obviously pleased with his handiwork.

"Yes, I would like that," said Scott, as he considered that winter was just beginning and there was already a foot of snow on the ground.

Man-with-no-hair made a pair of snowshoes for Scott. When he saw Dew-on-the-grass-in-the-moon-when-the-leaves-fall looking at them longingly, he made a pair for her, too.

That night, as they sat around the small fire in the tepee, eating, Scott thanked God for allowing him to be a part of this life, with these people. There was never a display of temper, never an argument. He had awakened feeling out-of-sorts on occasion and had let it pass. Apparently, that was the accepted way of life among the Indians. If Dew-on-the-grass-in-the-moon-when-the-leaves-fall or Man-with-no-hair had ever been out-of-sorts, he had not been aware of it. No one refused to pitch in and help when asked, if they even had to be asked. During the time he had spent in Falling Feather's village and the village Man-with-no-hair had come from, he had noticed that gender determined the tasks one was expected to perform. Scott had done things, and he had seen Man-with-no-hair do things, to help Dew-on-the-grass-in-the-moon-when-the-leaves-fall that would have caused them to be ridiculed in a village. It made Scott feel good that Man-with-no-hair was the kind of man to put his pride aside for the good of the group. Scott appreciated him and attempted to show it by paying close attention when he was teaching him or by doing the best he could on the projects he chose or the ones Man-with-no-hair asked him to do. Everyday was a new adventure; there were new things to learn and beautiful things to see. It was an exciting time and place to live and he looked forward to each new day.

"Why do you not have a wife?" Scott asked Man-with-no-hair, thinking of how the quality of his life had improved since he had met Dew-on-the-grass-in-the-moon-when-the-leaves-fall.

Usually, that would have been an inappropriate question; if information was not volunteered, it was considered a personal matter. These were unusual circumstances however, for fate had thrown these three wanderers together in a unique environment. Man-with-no-hair did not take offense to the question.

"Woman die when baby born. Baby die, too," he answered sadly.

Scott was immediately sorry he had asked. The look of sadness on Man-with-no-hair's face made Scott feel even worse.

"Not feel bad," Man-with-no-hair said to Scott and Dew-on-the-grass-in-the-moon-when-the-leaves-fall. "Happen long ago."

"I'm sorry," said Scott.

"Why not take another woman?" asked Dew-on-the-grass-in-the-moon-when-the-leaves-fall.

"No woman like mine. Cared too much. Not want another woman," Man-with-no-hair replied.

"Man-with-no-hair is a good man. Should have many sons. They grow up strong and brave like father," said Dew-on-the-grass-in-the-moon-when-the-leaves-fall.

Man-with-no-hair appreciated the words of Dew-on-the-grass-in-the-moon-when-the-leaves-fall. He looked thoughtful for a moment and then said, "Maybe, someday."

4

The following morning, Scott wore his snowshoes as he slowly made his way to the corral. The snow had stopped falling but there were about sixteen inches on the ground. He wondered how deep it would get before winter was over.

He was about to slide the gate poles aside when Man-with-no-hair was suddenly at his side.

My God, thought Scott, *He can even move quietly in the snow.*

Man-with-no-hair was carrying both bows and quivers. He handed Scott's bow to him and said, "Come quick."

With much dread, Scott followed Man-with-no-hair. He knew they had been discovered and would now have to fight to keep their home.

As they hurried past the tepee, Scott was able to look out of the finger in which they lived and see the main valley floor. Much to his surprise, and relief, they had not been discovered; instead, a herd of elk was migrating through the valley.

Man-with-no-hair and Scott stopped at the mouth of the finger and looked on in awe. Dew-on-the-grass-in-the-moon-when-the-leaves-fall came up behind them and watched quietly. There were thousands of animals.

Occasionally, one of the elk would stop and eat some of the visible grass; for the most part however, they kept moving south. There were bulls with antlers so large one had to wonder how they were able to get through the forest.

Scott was surprised when Man-with-no-hair began to walk toward the elk. There was little cover but Man-with-no-hair didn't attempt to conceal his approach. Scott did likewise.

The elk on the outside of the herd tried to turn into the herd to avoid the approaching men but they ran into other bodies and were unable to escape. Some of the animals began to run but that only exposed animals that were, as of yet, unaware of the danger.

Scott and Man-with-no-hair each hit two elk. They had to wait for an hour for the remainder of the herd to pass by before they could butcher their kill.

Though they had just taken enough meat to last them through most of the winter; the horses still needed to be cared for. There was very little visible grass remaining on the valley floor. Scott remembered the open, grassy ridges and would have gladly taken the horses there, but that would mean Man-with-no-hair and Dew-on-the-grass-in-the-moon-when-the-leaves-fall would have to skin and butcher the four elk – a formidable task considering the weather conditions.

Unsure of which problem took precedence, Scott approached Man-with-no-hair.

"Should I take the horses to feed or help you butcher the elk?" asked Scott.

Unperturbed, Man-with-no-hair looked up from his work of disemboweling a fat cow. He looked at the sky and then scanned the meadow. The problem of keeping the horses fed had crossed his mind too, but to this point he had not considered a resolution to the issue. He was also sage enough to understand why Scott was asking for his advise.

"Where you feed horses?" asked Man-with-no-hair.

"There," said Scott, as he pointed to the snow-free ridge-tops.

Man-with-no-hair grunted and then said, "Horses must eat. You go. Man-with-no-hair do this." And then to add a bit of humor he said, "You would cut a gut if you helped."

Scott couldn't help but chuckle at the insinuation. He turned and walked to the corral.

Man-with-no-hair watched him go and was suddenly curious about white men. He wondered where they came from and how many there were. He also wondered if they were all like Scott. He had grown very close to Scott. The man had great strength and seemed to fear nothing, except the great bears. Despite his clumsiness in the forest he tried hard and listened well when he was spoken to.

Man-with-no-hair thought about the horses again. As a youth, there had been no horses in his Shawnee village. When he moved west and lived in a village that possessed horses, he was quick to understand their importance, though he was concerned that constant use of the animals would diminish his stalking skills. As if he were looking for a medium ground, Man-with-no-hair used the horses to locate his quarry and then stalked them on foot. Considering the ruggedness of this country, even he had no desire to be without horses.

He watched Scott riding one horse and leading the rest. He rode out of the finger and turn to follow the edge of the timber. Dew-on-the-grass-in-the-moon-when-the-leaves-fall dragged a hind quarter by him, and in passing, asked in Shawnee, "You think that cow will skin itself?"

His train of thought broken, Man-with-no-hair laughed heartily and returned to his work.

Scott rode until he came upon a place where the timber was sparse and the distance to the ridge was short. When he reached the clear ridge top, he untied the horses and let them spread out as they searched for food. He was disappointed when he found there wasn't as much grass as he had hoped.

Scott remained on the back of the horse as the animal fed. He had seen wolf tracks on the ridge and wanted to keep as high a vantage point as possible, to keep a lookout.

Late that afternoon, Scott led the horses off the ridge and back to the camp. As he rode by the tepee, he saw the carcasses of three elk. Man-with-no-hair and Dew-on-the-grass-in-the-moon-when-the-leaves-fall had accomplished a great deal; though much remained to be done. He turned the horses into the corral and walked to the tepee.

When Scott entered the tepee, he saw that Man-with-no-hair was gone. Dew-on-the-grass-in-the-moon-when-the-leaves-fall was tasting a stew she had made. Scott was about to ask her where Man-with-no-hair was when he entered the tepee with an armload of wood. He knelt down and placed it carefully near the small fire.

"Food ready," said Dew-on-the-grass-in-the-moon-when-the-leaves-fall as Man-with-no-hair rose and stood beside Scott.

Later, as they were eating, Scott asked a question that had been bothering him most of the day. "Why were there so many elk and where were they going?"

Man-with-no-hair frowned thoughtfully as he tried to think of a way to explain "migration" to Scott. "Elk go away from mountains. Too much snow. Not enough food. You saw geese fly south; elk do same."

Scott did remember the great flocks of geese and ducks they had seen flying overhead. He hadn't been completely sure why they were going south but he had spent enough time with the Indians to learn to watch nature. The season was changing when the birds began flying south.

Scott told Man-with-no-hair about the wolf tracks he had seen on the ridge. Man-with-no-hair took the information in stride. He was not surprised to learn there were wolves about, and he knew it was too early in the winter for them to be hungry enough to be a threat to the horses. He informed Scott that he would take the horses to feed tomorrow. Scott agreed taking turns would break the monotony of the task.

The next day, Scott and Dew-on-the-grass-in-the-moon-when-the-leaves-fall boned out the remaining carcasses. They had smoked most of the meat by the time Man-with-no-hair returned with the horses.

Man-with-no-hair nodded as he rode by Scott and Dew-on-the-grass-in-the-moon-when-the-leaves-fall. Scott detected something in his manner that disturbed him. He turned to Dew-on-the-grass-in-the-moon-when-the-leaves-fall and knew immediately she had felt the same thing.

Scott turned away from Dew-on-the-grass-in-the-moon-when-the-leaves-fall and walked to the corral. Man-with-no-hair was sliding the poles back into place when Scott arrived.

"What did you see today?" Scott asked.

"Man-with-no-hair see wolf tracks," he answered, as they walked back to the tepee. "Man-with-no-hair see tracks of big bear," he added hesitantly.

"Where did you see the tracks?" Scott asked.

"Come off mountain," said Man-with-no-hair. "Cross valley," he added pointing to the other side of the valley floor.

5

That night as they ate, Man-with-no-hair suggested Scott and Dew-on-the-grass-in-the-moon-when-the-leaves-fall take the horses to feed the next day. He would track the big bear to see where it was going.

Reluctantly, Scott agreed. He was dismayed to find that a bear had come so close to their camp, but the responsibility of protecting them did not fall on Man-with-no-hair's shoulders alone. Once again, the well-being of the horses took precedence over one's own desires. He knew Dew-on-the-grass-in-the-moon-when-the-leaves-fall was perfectly capable of leading the horses up the ridge, but what if she encountered the wolves, or worse, what if the bear circled back?

The next morning, Man-with-no-hair, Dew-on-the-grass-in-the-moon-when-the-leaves-fall and Scott each rode a horse and led another out of the finger. When they came to the bear track, Man-with-no-hair dismounted. Scott was unable to muffle a moan as he saw the size of the track.

Man-with-no-hair gave him a wry grin as he turned and began to follow the bear tracks. Scott suggested that he take a horse but Man-with-no-hair insisted that he was unsure of the terrain he would be going into and a horse could be more of a hindrance than a help.

When Man-with-no-hair entered the timber on the other side of the valley, Scott led the way along the edge of the timber, following the tracks Man-with-no-hair had made the day before.

Scott and Dew-on-the-grass-in-the-moon-when-the-leaves-fall spent the day on the ridge top. Scott was glad to spend the time with her, but he worried about Man-with-no-hair.

When they returned to camp that evening, Man-with-no-hair was not present. Dew-on-the-grass-in-the-moon-when-the-leaves-fall busied herself preparing a meal and Scott worked around the camp until darkness prohibited him from doing more.

When he stepped into the tepee, Dew-on-the-grass-in-the-moon-when-the-leaves-fall's concern was obvious on her face.

"Tomorrow I'll go look for him," stated Scott.

"Yes, I know," said Dew-on-the-grass-in-the-moon-when-the-leaves-fall. "But you must come back to me." she said, unable to keep her voice from breaking.

Scott's heart went out to her. What must it be like to be a woman and fear being left alone in these mountains? He took her in his arms and held her for a long time.

"I will come back to you," he told her just before they sat down to eat. "I will bring Man-with-no-hair back with me," he said, hoping he wasn't making a promise he couldn't keep.

The next morning, the dark sky threatened more snow. Scott knew he would have to hurry lest Man-with-no-hair's tracks be lost to the new powder. He had decided the night before to take a horse. If the route became impassable, he would leave the horse behind. He had asked Dew-on-the-grass-in-the-moon-when-the-leaves-fall to let the horses feed near camp. There wasn't much feed but it would have to suffice until they returned.

Scott held Dew-on-the-grass-in-the-moon-when-the-leaves-fall in his arms as he waited for enough light to track Man-with-no-hair.

"If I'm not back in a week, go to the village Man-with-no-hair and I told you about," he said to her.

She pushed him away to arms length and said, "This is my home. This is home for Scott and Man-with-no-hair. I will stay here."

"You should be safe in the village," Scott insisted.

"What matters 'safe' if you and Man-with-no-hair are not here?" she asked.

"But…"

She gently put her fingers on his mouth. "Go now, my man. Come back to me and bring our friend with you."

Scott could see that arguing would resolve nothing. He ducked out of the tepee, mounted the horse and rode out of the finger.

Man-with-no-hair's tracks were easy to follow. When Scott reached the timber on the other side of the valley he was unable run the horse, but he kept the animal at a fast pace, nonetheless. Man-with-no-hair's trail led Scott to a game trail that contoured up a ridge at a gentle grade. The snow was deep in places, causing the horse to struggle, and Scott to fret because he could not make as good time as he wanted

Scott suddenly realized he was pushing the horse too hard. He stopped for a few minutes to let the horse blow. As he waited, he surveyed the trail ahead of him and as he did so, it started to snow.

When the horse's breathing returned to normal, Scott clucked and touched his heels to its flanks.

Around mid-day, Scott crossed a main ridge and entered a large timbered basin. He was forced to dismount and lead the horse because the timber was so thick and there were many low-hanging limbs. Scott considered tying the horse and leaving it behind but quickly rejected the idea; a tied horse would be easy prey for a hungry predator.

There were many deer tracks in the timber and Scott could see where Man-with-no-hair had stopped to examine some of them.

Man-with-no-hair's tracks led to a ravine in the basin. The ravine was not wide. It was no more than thirty yards at its widest point, and varied in depth from twenty to fifty feet, with jagged rocky walls.

At the edge of the ravine, Man-with-no-hair's tracks turned to the left. On foot and leading the horse, Scott followed the tracks for a quarter of a mile. Had he had been on horseback, he would have dismounted as he followed the trail along the edge of the ravine. One slip, and horse and rider would be over the edge.

Scott went around a rock outcropping and saw Man-with-no-hair lying in the deep snow on the bottom of the ravine. He could also see broken pieces of a fallen tree scattered about on the floor of the ravine. There were scrape marks in the snow on both sides of the chasm. Scott could see that Man-with-no-hair had tried to cross the ravine on the back of the tree, which had fallen across its width. What he didn't know was why he would try such a risky thing?

Scott took the horse away from the ledge and tied it to a tree. He returned to the edge of the ravine and began to search for a way down. Had it not been for the snow, Scott may have been able to get to Man-with-no-hair from where he was. As it was, the snow made that descent too dangerous.

Though he was anxious to get to his friend, Scott kept his wits about him. He walked along the edge of the ravine, in the direction Man-with-no-hair had been going before he had fallen. A couple hundred yards farther, Scott found another deadfall. This dead fall was a large ponderosa pine. It was larger than the one that had broken under Man-with-no-hair. It had grown farther back in the stand of timber and had not reached across the ravine. It was close enough to the edge that when it fell, most of its weight was hanging over the edge, causing the entire tree to slide to the bottom of the ravine.

There was snow on the fallen tree and it would be slippery, dangerous business getting to the bottom; but this tree would not break.

Scott kicked the snow from the tree as he shinnied down. The limbs that remained on the trunk were pointed toward the natural top of the tree, and the bottom of the ravine, and offered little assistance in the descent.

The ravine was only about forty feet deep where Scott descended, but it took him twenty minutes to reach the bottom. As soon as his feet touched solid ground, he raced to where Man-with-no-hair lay in the snow.

Scott silently thanked God when he found that Man-with-no-hair was still alive. He carefully rolled his friend onto his back; there were no visible life-threatening injuries, no blood or protruding bones. Man-with-no-hair moaned and began to shiver; his eyes fluttered, but did not open.

Scott went to the fallen tree and gathered small pieces of wood. As he was returning to Man-with-no-hair, he noticed a small cleft in the wall of the ravine. It wasn't much, but it would provide some shelter from the wind and the rock wall would reflect the heat of a fire.

Scott carried the wood to the cleft and found that it was about three feet wide and three feet deep. He cleaned as much snow away from the wall as possible and then built a fire. When the wood was burning satisfactorily, Scott went to Man-with-no-hair and dragged him into the cleft. He leaned his friend against the stone wall before returning to the dead, broken tree for more wood.

The wood was dry and well seasoned and burned well, too well. There was not enough available wood from the broken log to sustain the fire for the entire night. Man-with-no-hair's buckskins were soaked from lying in the snow; without a fire he would freeze to death.

Scott was loathe to leave his friend but he had to go in search of more wood. He walked along the edge of the ravine, gathering sticks and twigs along the way. When he had an armload, he quickly returned to Man-with-no-hair.

Man-with-no-hair stirred when Scott dropped the load of wood. He opened his eyes and smiled thinly when he saw Scott.

Scott went to his side. "Are you hurt?" he asked.

"Not broke," Man-with-no-hair replied quietly, as he lifted both arms to show that his bones weren't broken. "Head go around," he added, as he shook his head in an effort to clear the cobwebs.

Scott hadn't considered a head injury and his concern for his friend was renewed.

Nightfall was less than an hour away and he still didn't have enough wood to last throughout the night.

"I have to go after more wood," Scott explained.

Man-with-no-hair answered by simply nodding his head. Scott turned and ran to where he had left off gathering wood.

There were no trees in the bottom of the ravine. This, in conjunction with snow on the ground, made wood gathering difficult. The wood that Scott was finding were limbs from the trees that lined the rim of the chasm. There were occasional blow downs that offered larger pieces of wood.

Scott took a second load of wood back to the hastily devised camp. Man-with-no-hair appeared to be sleeping. Scott dropped the load of wood as quietly as possible. The activity did not disturb him. Scott added more wood to the fire and then went after another load.

On each trip Scott made to gather wood, he ventured farther and farther from Man-with-no-hair and the camp. On the last trip, he came upon a game trail that appeared to lead out of the ravine. In the growing gloom of dusk, it was impossible to determine if the trail was adequate to lead them to safety. Hastily, Scott returned to the camp.

It was dark by the time Scott got back to the camp. He was guided by the small, twinkling light of the camp fire. Man-with-no-hair was awake and adding bits of wood to the fire when Scott arrived. Scott dropped the load of wood and made himself as comfortable as possible, leaning against the opposite wall of cleft.

As Scott offered Man-with-no-hair some of his smoked meat, he was glad to see that his friend seemed to be recovering from his mishap. Man-with-no-hair was getting warm and his buckskins were drying out well.

After he had eaten, Man-with-no-hair closed his eyes and was soon fast asleep. Scott dozed off but awakened an hour later and added more wood to the fire. Scott was worried about the horse but he knew there was nothing he could do for it now. He hoped the closeness of himself and Man-with-no-hair would be enough to deter predation.

Though Scott was concerned and worried, he was also very tired. Soon he dozed off again.

The next morning, Scott awakened before Man-with-no-hair. He added the last of the wood to the fire, left some meat for his friend, and went to examine the game trail he had discovered the night before.

When Scott reached the game trail, he found that it was a bit narrower than he had hoped, but he was sure the horse would be able to make the passage. Fortunately, the trail was on the same side of the ravine as the horse.

Scott used the trail to ascend to the upper edge of the ravine. Once on top, he quickly sought out his horse. When he reached the animal, he was relieved to find that it had made it through the night unscathed.

He untied the horse and led it to the game trail. The horse was reluctant to follow him into the ravine, but with a little patience and persistence, it soon allowed Scott to lead it down. Scott could hear the horse blanket rub against the rock wall as the horse walked down the trail. He hoped that Man-with-no-hair would be strong enough to stay on the horse's back without his assistance when they rode out of the ravine.

A gentle breeze was blowing down the ravine as Scott led the horse toward Man-with-no-hair. Scott could smell smoke from the fire. The horse began to prance about, acting nervous. Scott tightened his grip on the lead rope as he continued.

By the time Scott reached the cleft in the rock, the horse was nearing panic.

Man-with-no-hair rose and staggered to the outer edge of the cleft. He pointed across the ravine and Scott saw what he had overlooked in his haste to get to Man-with-no-hair.

The bear had apparently chased Man-with-no-hair onto the log, which had spanned the ravine. When the bear had tried to follow, the log had broken. The bear hadn't been so lucky as Man-with-no-hair for it had fallen onto the rocks and died immediately.

Scott went to the bear and stared in absolute amazement at the size of the creature. He looked back across the ravine and Man-with-no-hair was signaling him to skin the bear.

An hour and a half later, Scott had finished skinning the bear. The bear had fallen in an awkward position and it required all of Scott's strength to roll it over. The hide was wet and heavy; Scott was not sure how they were going to get it back to their valley.

While Scott had been skinning the bear, Man-with-no-hair had been stroking and talking to the horse. When Scott finished skinning the bear, Man-with-no-hair asked him to bring the hide to the horse. Every muscle in the horse's body quivered as Scott approached with the hide. But the horse did not panic. Man-with-no-hair had that kind of affect on animals, especially the horses.

After allowing the horse to become adjusted to the closeness of the bear hide, Man-with-no-hair asked Scott to place the hide on the horse's back.

Scott smiled, shaking his head. He expected the horse to go insane with panic. Instead, the horse allowed him to drape the hide over its back. The horse was nervous, to be sure, but it did not panic.

Unassisted, but with great effort, Man-with-no-hair mounted the horse. Scott took a step to help but stopped himself. If Man-with-no-hair needed help, he would ask.

When Man-with-no-hair was situated on the back of the horse, Scott led the way out of the ravine.

There was less than an hour of daylight left when Scott led the horse into the narrow finger of the valley. Dew-on-the-grass-in-the-moon-when-the-leaves-fall had been working around the outside fire. She had backed into the shadows at the sound of the approaching horse.

When she recognized Scott, she ran to him and threw her arms around him, hugging him fiercely. Scott was surprised and gladdened by the passion of the hug. When she finally released him, he saw that there were no tears on her cheeks but her eyes glistened in the dim light of the fire.

While Dew-on-the-grass-in-the-moon-when-the-leaves-fall was hugging Scott, Man-with-no-hair slid off of the horse's back. When Dew-on-the-grass-in-the-moon-when-the-leaves-fall released Scott, she went to Man-with-no-hair and hugged him, as well. She said something to him in Shawnee. Man-with-no-hair did not answer.

Dew-on-the-grass-in-the-moon-when-the-leaves-fall helped Man-with-no-hair into the tepee. Snow began to fall as Scott led the horse to the corral.

The next morning, Man-with-no-hair was able to walk around the camp. His muscles were sore from the fall and exposure, but he was resilient and would soon be himself again.

Scott led the horses out of the corral, through the camp and toward the ridges. Without leaving the valley floor, he could see there was no food available on the ridges. There had been no wind to blow the new snow from the backs of the ridges and the grass now lay under a foot of snow.

Scott returned to the camp and informed Dew-on-the-grass-in-the-moon-when-the-leaves-fall of what he had seen. He told her he was going to look for grass in the timber, along the edge of the meadow.

While Scott was talking to Dew-on-the-grass-in-the-moon-when-the-leaves-fall, Man-with-no-hair stepped out of the tepee and asked if he could go with Scott. Scott knew that he would not have asked if he hadn't felt up to the task.

"I would like that," Scott responded.

Man-with-no-hair untied the fourth horse from the third one and swung onto its back. He rode to Scott's side and together they rode toward the meadow.

Before they reached the stream, Scott handed the lead rope to Man-with-no-hair and said, "I'll be back." With that, Scott turned his horse and raced back to the camp.

Dew-on-the-grass-in-the-moon-when-the-leaves-fall was adding wood to the fire when Scott rode in.

"Would you like to go, too?" he asked.

"I have much…" she began before she saw the look on his face.

"I will go with you," she said, with a large smile.

It made Scott feel good to see her smile like that. He reached his arm down to her and she swung up behind him. Dew-on-the-grass-in-the-moon-when-the-leaves-fall wrapped her arms around him and held him tightly as they rode to where Man-with-no-hair waited. A knowing smile crossed Man-with-no-hair's face as he watched the pair ride toward him.

Together, the three friends rode in search of feed for the horses.

6

The snow had been on for more than three weeks when the temperature suddenly began to warm up. A warm wind was blowing and in less than a day, all of the snow melted.

Scott and Man-with-no-hair staked the horses near the stream. They would not put on weight with the new-found grass but they would get their bellies full.

Scott and Man-with-no-hair lounged around the camp during the warm spell. They had been so intent upon their own survival and the well being of the horses, that they had not had a respite from their daily responsibilities since they had left Man-with-no-hair's village.

Now, they were content to sit near a fire and watch the horses. Dew-on-the-grass-in-the-moon-when-the-leaves-fall, however, was not inclined to lie around camp. It seemed she always had some menial task to perform. Scott felt somewhat guilty but she would not allow either one of them to help her with her work. That particular week she was busy sewing new clothes; it was just as well they didn't get involved.

The warm weather lasted for a week and then the skies clouded up and the snow began to fall again. The morning after the change in the weather, they awoke to six inches of fresh snow, with the threat of more to come.

Scott and Man-with-no-hair were thrust back into the routine of devoting many hours a day to the survival of the horses. The grass near their camp was soon exhausted; they had to travel farther and farther afield to find an adequate supply of feed.

One night, the wind began to howl, blowing snow into deep drifts. The temperature became so cold that no one left the tepee except to relieve themselves. On such occasions, Scott or Man-with-no-hair checked on the horses, but there was nothing they could do to satisfy their hunger.

Three days after it had begun, the blizzard blew itself out. Though the wind and snow had stopped, the sky remained cloudy; and it was very, very cold.

Scott and Man-with-no-hair were thankful for Dew-on-the-grass-in-the-moon-when-the-leaves-fall's persistence during the week of nice weather, for they both had new jackets and mittens; without these they would not have been able to stay outside long enough to care for the horses.

Once again, the wind had blown the snow around. Generally, it was no more than a foot deep. The drifts, however, were several feet deep. They also realized that they had chosen their campsite well, for when the wind howled through the meadow, only occasional gusts burst into the protected finger.

7

Winter was long and tedious and it seemed as though it would last forever. It was a constant battle to keep the horses fed, but Scott and Man-with-no-hair managed to keep them alive and well. They survived two more blizzards, one lasting a week, but it was followed by another Chinook wind.

One day the moisture that fell from the sky, fell in the form of rain, rather than snow. The temperature began to rise, buds appeared on the willows along the stream, and the days were growing noticeably longer. Spring was coming to the mountains and the weary friends were thankful.

Chapter Ten

With spring came new life. The grass became tall and green. Shoots and flowers appeared as if by magic. Two of the mares were heavy with foal.

A new life had also begun within Dew-on-the-grass-in-the-moon-when-the-leaves-fall. She had known for some time that changes were taking place in her body, but had not associated them with pregnancy until the time of the last blizzard. She was unsure of what to tell Scott. She was surprised he had not already noticed her condition. In a few more weeks it would become impossible to conceal.

As spring progressed, all three occupants of the valley had more time on their hands. The demands of survival were lessened considerably.

Man-with-no-hair seemed to have a burning desire to see what lay over every hill and look into every valley in the area. He later tried to explain that he was learning the areas that were preferred by certain animals. Scott didn't doubt what Man-with-no-hair said, but he couldn't help but feel that Man-with-no-hair, as well as himself, was overwhelmed by the beauty and immensity of the mountains in which they lived. They both wanted to see it all.

One night, Man-with-no-hair and Scott discussed following their valley to the east, to learn how far it went and how big it was. In the morning, as they were making the final preparations, Dew-on-the-grass-in-the-moon-when-the-leaves-fall stated that she would prefer to remain in camp.

This struck Scott as odd, because she loved to explore as much as either one of the men.

Scott looked over the back of his horse and his eyes met Man-with-no-hair's. The look on his face told Scott that he was surprised by her words too, and maybe Scott should see if she was well.

"Are you not well?" Scott asked. Before the words were out of his mouth, he noticed that she seemed a little pale.

"I am well," she answered, without looking him in the eye.

"Do you want me to stay here with you?" Scott asked, in a concerned tone.

"No. You go with Man-with-no-hair," she said with a brief smile, still avoiding eye contact.

As Scott and Man-with-no-hair rode away from the camp, Scott turned and looked back at Dew-on-the-grass-in-the-moon-when-the-leaves-fall. She was busy and did not see him. Her behavior was uncharacteristic of her and it concerned Scott a great deal.

When they were away from the camp, Scott told Man-with-no-hair that he would prefer not to be gone too long. Man-with-no-hair readily agreed.

After Man-with-no-hair and Scott had ridden for several hours, they reached a point where the valley forked. It appeared that the main valley continued east. The branching valley entered from the south. Because they did not intend to be gone all day, they decided to explore the southern fork of the valley. They assumed it would be a smaller valley and would take less time to investigate.

When they were an hour into the southern valley, they realized it was much larger than they had anticipated. There were many smaller valleys branching into the main one and it would take many days, if not weeks, to fully understand the lay of the land.

"These valleys are beautiful and I would like to spend more time here, but I think we should turn back now," Scott said, as he and Man-with-no-hair looked at the surrounding country from a small rise.

Man-with-no-hair agreed with a grunt.

They turned their horses to the north and rode toward the main valley. They had seen much sign of game and would keep this place in mind for hunting. There was plenty of game near their camp but they felt it would be better to leave those animals undisturbed except in the case of emergency. Man-with-no-hair had told Scott that when animals in a certain area are hunted often, they tend to get flighty and it was harder to get close enough to them for a clean shot.

When Scott and Man-with-no-hair reached the main valley, they saw a small herd of buffalo in a thicket on the northern fringe of the valley. They stopped and watched the animals for a few minutes. Scott was fascinated by the great, shaggy beasts and would have watched longer, had he not been concerned about Dew-on-the-grass-in-the-moon-when-the-leaves-fall.

Near mid-afternoon, they rode into camp and found Dew-on-the-grass-in-the-moon-when-the-leaves-fall working on a hide. She seemed surprised that they were back so soon.

She got to her feet and went to the fire to warm some food for them. She was adding wood to the fire when the men returned from taking the horses to the corral.

"You are early," she said, without looking up.

"We thought you might not be well. We came back early because we were worried about you," Scott answered.

"I am well," she said, but the look on her face belied her words.

Dew-on-the-grass-in-the-moon-when-the-leaves-fall rose from a squatting position and reached for some larger pieces of wood. She fell to her knees, gripping her stomach. Scott was beside her in an instant, but she pushed him away. Retching, she got to her feet and staggered into the forest.

Scott looked at Man-with-no-hair, who was looking at him. Scott was genuinely concerned for Dew-on-the-grass-in-the-moon-when-the-leaves-fall, but he had no idea what was wrong with her or what to do for her. He had hoped for some insight from Man-with-no-hair, but got none.

Scott walked to where Dew-on-the-grass-in-the-moon-when-the-leaves-fall had gone into the forest. She saw him coming and waved him away. He could see her bending over, vomiting. He went back to the fire.

"She won't let me help her," Scott said forlornly. "What can I do?" he asked.

Suddenly, Man-with-no-hair jumped as if he had been startled out of his wits. He looked toward Dew-on-the-grass-in-the-moon-when-the-leaves-fall, at Scott, toward Dew-on-the-grass-in-the-moon-when-the-leaves-fall and back to Scott. He had noticed slight changes in her, both physical and emotional. The changes had been so subtle that he had overlooked them. Now, he knew what was the matter with her.

"She is carrying a child," Man-with-no-hair said flatly.

Scott, too, had noticed changes in Dew-on-the-grass-in-the-moon-when-the-leaves-fall, but he had no experience in such things and therefore, hadn't known what had caused the changes.

Scott was so taken aback by the news that he failed to notice Man-with-no-hair's lack of excitement.

Dew-on-the-grass-in-the-moon-when-the-leaves-fall returned to the fire and Scott went her side.

"Man-with-no-hair feels that you are with child. Is that true?" Scott asked, barely able to control his happiness.

"Yes, I am." Dew-on-the-grass-in-the-moon-when-the-leaves-fall answered.

"How long? Why didn't you tell me? Are you well?" Scott asked excitedly.

Dew-on-the-grass-in-the-moon-when-the-leaves-fall smiled sheepishly at Scott's questions.

"Baby come…three, maybe four moons. Dew-on-the-grass-in-the-moon-when-the-leaves-fall not sure what to say to Scott. Dew-on-the-grass-in-the-moon-when-the-leaves-fall not sure Scott want baby – not sure you still want Dew-on-the-grass-in-the-moon-when-the-leaves-fall."

Generally speaking, Scott was not overly emotional. At this moment, however, it was all he could do to fight back the tears.

He knelt beside Dew-on-the-grass-in-the-moon-when-the-leaves-fall and took her hand into his and held it tightly. She turned to face him and he looked deeply into her dark eyes as he spoke to her. "I want the baby that comes from Dew-on-the-grass-in-the-moon-when-the-leaves-fall and me. I will want all of the babies that come from you and me. As long as I live and breathe, as long as the sun shines and the snow falls, I will want you by my side."

Dew-on-the-grass-in-the-moon-when-the-leaves-fall was so relieved she was unable to stop the tears of joy that escaped from the corners of her eyes. She dropped to her knees and threw her arms around Scott. She held him for a long time.

When Dew-on-the-grass-in-the-moon-when-the-leaves-fall released Scott, they noticed that Man-with-no-hair was no longer by the fire. They thought that curious, but they didn't dwell on it.

"Baby not come for long time. Scott and Man-with-no-hair not have to be here all the time. I want you to go look…go hunt. Bring home much meat so baby will grow strong."

"I will do as you ask," Scott answered. "As long as you tell me when you don't feel well enough to be left alone."

"I will tell you," Dew-on-the-grass-in-the-moon-when-the-leaves-fall promised.

2

The next morning, Man-with-no-hair and Scott were on the trail early. They followed their tracks from the day before, but at a slightly faster pace. Man-with-no-hair seemed to be preoccupied, as if he had something to say but didn't know how to say it. Scott did not press him. He knew his friend would say what was on his mind, in his own time.

When they reached the junction of the two valleys, they rode into the southern fork, once again.

As they rode south, they explored the smaller valleys that fed into the larger one. Most of the feeder valleys were much the same: they started out narrow, widened in the middle and ended abruptly at the base of a massive ridge. The longest of the smaller valleys swept around the base of the ridge, spreading out to the south and west.

By the time they had explored the long winding valley, it was mid-afternoon and time to return to camp. They still had not seen all there was to see in the southern valley.

Scott and Man-with-no-hair rode into camp just before dark. Dew-on-the-grass-in-the-moon-when-the-leaves-fall seemed to be in high spirits, which made both men feel better. She began to prepare a meal as the two men tended to the horses.

Man-with-no-hair spent a little extra time examining the two pregnant mares. When the meal was ready to eat and the three were seated around the fire, Man-with-no-hair said, "Mare have young tomorrow. I will stay. You can stay or go back to the southern valley."

Scott looked toward Dew-on-the-grass-in-the-moon-when-the-leaves-fall but she gave no indication that she had been listening to the conversation. He knew that if he stayed in camp, he would be underfoot, trying to help her, until she shooed him away. Man-with-no-hair would not need his help either.

"I will go alone. I want to see more of that southern valley," Scott told them.

3

Two hours before dawn, Scott swung onto the back of his horse, and rode out of the camp. He had a long way to go and wanted to get an early start. He rode slowly at first, until there was enough light to safely increase the horse's pace.

Scott did not mind riding or exploring alone, but he much preferred to be in the company of his friends.

He rode into the southern valley an hour after sunrise. Two hours later, he had gone beyond where he and Man-with-no-hair had turned around and was seeing new country.

He stopped on a small rise and became lost in the beauty of the surrounding terrain. He could see the end of what they had come to call The Southern Valley. The valley ended at the base of a tall mountain. The northern boundary was the steep ridge that had been at the end of the smaller valleys he and Man-with-no-hair had explored earlier. The southeastern boundary was formed by the gentle slopes that branched off the massive mountain range. The valley ended in a circular basin that encompassed several thousand acres.

As Scott looked upon the vista, a sense of peacefulness overtook him. He thought of his friends and their peaceful, protected valley, and felt...at home.

The thought was so powerful, he said it out loud, "Home."

The horse raised its head and nickered at the sudden sound of Scott's voice. Scott chuckled and started to turn the horse around, but he was struck by a thought of James Fort. He hadn't thought of the fort for a long time, but the thought that was in his mind now was the difference between the people of the fort and himself. He had no knowledge of his lineage; if his people were farmers, those genes had not been passed to him. He had no desire to spend his life walking behind a plow. It was enough for Scott to travel the land and see it the way the hand of the Maker had left it. It saddened him to think that someday a plow would drag through the valley below him, ripping the soul from the land. Hopefully, he would not live to see that day.

The horse took a step, enabling it to reach more grass; the movement awakened Scott from his daydreams.

He was about to turn the horse around (he knew he didn't have time to go all the way around the end of the valley) when something about the massive ridge drew his attention. If that was the same ridge that was behind their camp, and he could find a saddle in it, he thought he could return to camp that way and save several hours of riding time. If he could not find a passage, he would have to spend the night alone in the wilderness.

Scott began to ride across the open meadow. He felt a little uncomfortable because he and Man-with-no-hair usually rode at the edge of the meadows, hoping the timber or brush would break up their outline, making them more difficult to see. The ridge was several miles away and there was much timber ahead of him; he would not have to be in the open all of the way.

Scott clucked the horse into a slow gallop and felt a little better about crossing the open ground. When he had gone about a mile, his horse shied violently, nearly unseating him. He grasped the mane and squeezed the horse's ribs with all of his strength. Scott quickly regained control, but the horse continued to prance, sidestepping and throwing its head about.

Unable to gain complete control of the animal, Scott jerked the reins and spun the horse around. When it was facing in the direction from which they had come, he jammed his heels into its flanks and raced the horse for one hundred yards. He pulled the horse to a skidding stop and spun it around, scanning the area ahead of him.

The extra distance seemed to make the horse feel more at ease; it seemed at least willing to stand still.

Scott watched the terrain ahead of him for quite sometime; he saw no movement whatsoever.

Scott was a cautious man, but, he was also a curious man. If there was danger, he should learn the source of the danger. A threat to him, was a threat to his friends.

Scott walked the horse slowly forward. He watched very closely for movement; he also relied on the horse to make him aware if something was amiss.

Scott saw the horse's ears twitch and felt its muscles tense.

Scott heard something. It sounded like splashing water. There was no stream nearby. He saw movement but could not discern what he had seen. He watched closely and saw it again. About one hundred yards beyond where his horse had shied, Scott saw mud flying ten feet into the air.

As Scott watched, puzzled, the wind changed directions. It had been in his face, now it was at his back. As suddenly as the wind had changed, a giant reddish-brown bear appeared from where the mud had been flying.

The bear was covered with mud, and water was dripping off its long, thick fur. It also had an arrow protruding from its chest.

The bear charged without warning. The horse nearly unseated Scott again as it spun and lunged into a full gallop. A man on foot would be doomed. Scott was determined to stay on the horse's back. When he regained his position, he turned to locate the bear. He was shocked to see the bear gaining on him. He had become accustomed to the security one gained by being mounted; he had never considered the possibility of being run down by a predator while on horseback.

Slowly, the horse began to outdistance the bear. Scott turned again and saw that the bear, having given up the chase, was standing on its hind legs. Its mouth was open wide, as it swung its massive head and forearms.

Scott reined in the horse. As he coaxed the animal to slow its pace, he saw a blur of movement off to his left. His first thought was that it was another bear; instead, it was another horse. He knew immediately it was not one of their horses. In fact, this was the most beautiful and unusual horse Scott had ever seen.

The horse had been spooked by the bear and it was seeking the company of another horse. As it drew nearer, Scott got a better look at the unusual markings. The horse was off-white, its hind quarters were covered with large black spots, the rest of the body was covered with smaller black dots.

Scott stopped his horse. He alternated his glances from the strange colored horse, to the bear.

Suddenly, the strange horse spun around in a peculiar manner. When it regained its footing, it seemed unable to move.

Scott clucked to his mount and moved in the direction of the strange horse. As he got nearer, he saw that the horse had a rawhide rope around its neck, which it had been dragging. The rope had been tied to a small log that the horse had broken when the bear startled it. The broken log was now lodged between two large, flat rocks. The horse was pulling directly against the way the log was snagged and would never be able to free himself.

Scott was about to dismount, to free the horse, when the bear charged again. Scott could not allow such a beautiful animal to fall prey to the bear.

Scott had been rash in his judgment before and most certainly would be so again, provided he lived long enough. He wondered what Man-with-no-hair would have thought, or done, as he raised his hand that held the reins and slapped his horse viciously on the rump.

For an instant, the horse was more afraid of Scott than the bear, and it leapt into a gallop. When the horse reached its stride, Scott took the reins in his teeth and nocked an arrow.

The horse was bearing down on the bear without realizing it. When it saw the bear, it veered to the right. The bear took an angle to intercept. When the bear was close enough, Scott took his shot. The arrow went deep into the bear's neck but seemed to have little affect on the animal. Scott's mount dug deep into its spirit and came up with enough speed to escape the bear's lunge.

The bear must have been tiring; it did not pursue them as far as it did before.

Scott turned his horse again and nocked another arrow. His horse seemed to be getting wise to what he was doing, and wanted no part of it. However, another sharp slap to the rump changed its mind. As they raced toward it, the bear rose onto its hind legs.

The horse's fear of the bear was instinctual. Nothing Scott could do to the horse would make it completely overcome that fear. As they drew nearer to the bear, the horse began to take an angle that would not allow the bear to reach it. Scott was disappointed, but he did get close enough for a shot before the horse carried him away from the bear.

His second arrow took the bear in the throat. The wounded creature swatted at the arrow until it broke the exposed shaft. The beast gave a mighty roar and tried to give chase. The horse, though it was becoming winded, easily outdistanced him.

When the bear broke off the chase, Scott stopped his horse. He was preparing to nock another arrow when the frustrated bear decided it had had enough. Issuing grunts and growls, the bear turned and loped toward the southern end of the valley.

Scott considered giving chase, his confidence having reached a new high, but thought better of it. He decided just to follow the bear to make sure it was really going away.

Scott waited for a few minutes to allow his trembling horse time to recuperate. He considered going to the strange horse but he did not want to dismount until he knew the bear had left the area.

He rode in the direction the bear had gone. There was blood on both sides of the trail and Scott had no trouble following in the bear's footsteps. When he had followed the trail for a mile, he stopped on a small rise and watched. Finally, he saw the bear cross another rise a half mile ahead of him. The bear had not changed direction. Scott was sure it would not return.

As Scott turned and began to ride back to the strangely colored horse, he went over the incident in his mind. The mud the bear had been throwing had obviously come from a buffalo or elk wallow; but what had the bear been doing in there? Where had the horse come from?

Scott was suddenly struck by a dreadful premonition that caused goose bumps to stand out over his entire body.

Instead of going to the snagged horse, Scott raced to the wallow. As they approached the wallow, the horse became agitated again; the scent of the bear was strong. Scott dismounted and tied the horse to a small bush.

The grass was tall on the south side of the wallow; he had to walk around to look into the hole.

What he saw caused his stomach to convulse. He struggled to keep his bile down as he looked at the ripped and torn body of a teenaged Indian boy. The youth had been completely disemboweled. His head and right arm had been mauled so badly, they barely remained attached to the body. The thigh bone of his right leg was protruding through his buck-skin leggings.

Scott felt he should do something, but he was unsure what. He couldn't leave the body where it was, but he didn't know what he would do with it when he had it out of the wallow. He could bury it, of course, but many

Indians were superstitious about burial rites. He had no idea where this Indian had come from or what their customs were. He did not wish to offend anyone. He decided he would drag the body from the wallow and conceal it. He would bring Man-with-no-hair here; he would know the right thing to do.

Scott attempted to walk into the wallow, but his stomach retched and he had to withdraw. The Indian was lying with his back against the south wall of the wallow. Scott walked around to that edge, got on his belly and reached down and got a hold of the youth's wrist. Scott pulled him far enough that he had to get to his knees. The Indian was halfway out and Scott had to get to his feet to pull him the rest of the way out. As Scott pulled-dragged the boy from the wallow, some part of the body hung up on something and the boy's right arm came off in Scott's hands.

"NOOOOOOO!" Scott screamed at the top of his voice. Scott dropped the arm and backed away from the body. Unable to stop the retching, Scott fell to his hands and knees and vomited in the tall, green grass that surrounded the wallow.

Heaving and retching, Scott crawled to his horse. The thought of that boy's arm coming off in his hands would remain with him for the rest of his life.

He crawled to his horse and used the animal's leg to assist him in getting to his feet. When standing, he found that he was unable to swing onto the horse's back. Taking up the reins, he led his horse toward the horse of the fallen Indian. Walking made Scott feel better but his head was numb; he seemed to be acting more from instinct than by thinking. He bent over to disentangle the horse and promptly fell to his hands and knees. Rather than risk falling again, Scott sat between the two horses until his head cleared and he was able to function again.

A half-hour later Scott untangled the Indian pony's lead rope, got to his feet and swung upon the back of his horse. The Indian pony was not accustomed to Scott. However, it was in the company of another horse and that seemed to be a comfort to him. He followed Scott without a problem.

All thought of the new route home was forgotten. Scott returned to camp the way he had come.

They had a new horse to add to their herd, and Scott had defeated one of the great bears. There should have been great joy. Instead, his heart was heavy with the news of death and sadness he would carry into camp.

It was dark when Scott rode into camp. Dew-on-the-grass-in-the-moon-when-the-leaves-fall was standing by the outside fire. He saw the relief wash over her face as he rode by. She started to run to his side. When she saw the look on his face and the strange horse he was leading, she stopped. She walked behind the horses, knowing the news he had was going to be bad.

Man-with-no-hair came from nowhere and opened the corral. As Dew-on-the-grass-in-the-moon-when-the-leaves-fall stepped into the corral, Man-with-no-hair slid the bars back into place. Scott swung off the horse's back; Man-with-no-hair and Dew-on-the-grass-in-the-moon-when-the-leaves-fall were beside him when his feet touched the ground.

Scott expected a barrage of questions; what he got was questioning looks. His friends were going to let him tell the story in his own way, in his own time.

Scott looked back and forth from Dew-on-the-grass-in-the-moon-when-the-leaves-fall's eyes to those of Man-with-no-hair. "One of the big bears killed an Indian boy today," he said, in a flat tone.

"Are you hurt?" asked Dew-on-the-grass-in-the-moon-when-the-leaves-fall.

"No," answered Scott, "I am not hurt."

Man-with-no-hair wanted to examine the new horse but the death of the young Indian shocked him. He stayed near to hear the rest of the story.

The three of them walked to the outside fire and stood in a circle around it, watching the small blaze turn the wood to ash.

Finally, with Dew-on-the-grass-in-the-moon-when-the-leaves-fall by his side, Scott began to talk. As he imparted the events of the day, no one interrupted. Man-with-no-hair grunted several times but said nothing.

When Scott finished his recitation, Man-with-no-hair asked, "Was there sign of more ponies?"

"Not that I saw," answered Scott.

"Maybe he alone, but somebody will miss him," stated Man-with-no-hair. "Tomorrow we will go there, care for boy, kill the bear," he added.

Dew-on-the-grass-in-the-moon-when-the-leaves-fall's closeness made Scott feel better; he was saddened when she moved away to begin preparing a meal.

Scott alternated his gaze from Dew-on-the-grass-in-the-moon-when-the-leaves-fall to the sparks that rose from the fire into the surrounding darkness. His thoughts kept returning to the unfortunate Indian boy. He felt no guilt. The incident had transpired before his arrival; he could have done nothing to prevent the death. He felt remorse that the boy had suffered such an agonizing death. He also knew it could have been any one of them instead of the young boy. Scott made a silent vow: he would kill any bear that came into or near their valley.

Scott wondered why the Indian boy had been on foot. He remembered the way his horse had shied. If the Indian boy's pony had shied too, causing him to fall, that would account for his broken leg. Scott had seen no weapons near the boy's body. Man-with-no-hair would be able to study the signs and formulate an opinion of what had transpired.

Dew-on-the-grass-in-the-moon-when-the-leaves-fall offered Scott stew in a wooden bowl she had hewn from a slab of wood. He looked at the bowl dumbly, thinking of life without her.

Scott suddenly realized Dew-on-the-grass-in-the-moon-when-the-leaves-fall and Man-with-no-hair were staring at him. He looked into their eyes and knew they were concerned about him.

Oftentimes, one does not realize what one has until it is lost. Today was an excellent reminder to Scott that a human life could be snuffed out in an instant, in this wild, beautiful, spectacular, *unforgiving* land. He wondered how long it had been since he had thanked Dew-on-the-grass-in-the-moon-when-the-leaves-fall for all she did, not just for him, but also for Man-with-no-hair and the well being of their camp.

He looked at the bowl. He looked at Dew-on-the-grass-in-the-moon-when-the-leaves-fall. He didn't know where to start. He felt his emotions coming to the surface.

"This bowl is beautiful," he said. "Thank you for making it," he added with a voice that was beginning to break. "Thank you both for everything you do." With that said, he had to look away from them. He ate what she had prepared, though he had no appetite.

Dew-on-the-grass-in-the-moon-when-the-leaves-fall was deeply concerned about Scott. They had all looked upon the face of death; they had all been touched by death. She knew why the death of the young Indian had such a profound affect on him. She walked to him, wrapped her arms gently around his stomach and leaned her head between his shoulder blades. "Make me happy to do for you," she said softly.

Scott ate little and slept even less. When he closed his eyes he saw the Indian boy running for his life with the great bear at his heels. His eyes would fly open and he would seek a new position, only to have the scene repeated.

He was relieved when he heard the birds begin to sing their morning songs. He quietly slipped from the tepee and knelt beside the ashes of the outside fire pit. A few stars remained in the clear sky and it promised to be a beautiful day. Scott was still suffering from what he had witnessed, but he felt somewhat better than he had the day before. His appetite had returned and he stirred the ashes and rekindled the fire to heat some meat for breakfast. He was anxious to be under way but would not disturb Man-with-no-hair or Dew-on-the-grass-in-the-moon-when-the-leaves-fall. He sat by the small fire he had created and enjoyed the sounds of the morning.

Before long, he heard stirring within the tepee. A moment later, Man-with-no-hair and Dew-on-the-grass-in-the-moon-when-the-leaves-fall burst out of the tepee. They were gladdened to see Scott sitting near the fire. Scott looked at them with a look on his face that asked, "What's the matter with you two?" And as strange as it seemed, the look told them they didn't have to worry about him.

Relieved, the three made preparations for the journey. Man-with-no-hair's mare had thrown a filly the day before. Dew-on-the-grass-in-the-moon-when-the-leaves-fall would have to remain behind to care for the horses. The two men would not return until the next day, at the earliest.

Man-with-no-hair asked Dew-on-the-grass-in-the-moon-when-the-leaves-fall to be especially watchful of the filly. She said she would and he thanked her.

Scott was thankful that Man-with-no-hair treated Dew-on-the-grass-in-the-moon-when-the-leaves-fall respectfully. In his experience, braves were usually less than cordial to some squaws. He wondered how many braves of Man-with-no-hair's status would even consider being kind to a squaw?

Dew-on-the-grass-in-the-moon-when-the-leaves-fall stuffed their packs with extra meat as the men readied their mounts.

Dew-on-the-grass-in-the-moon-when-the-leaves-fall spoke to Man-with-no-hair in Shawnee. Scott saw Man-with-no-hair glance at him as she spoke. She turned and threw her arms around Scott and held him tightly. Finally, she released her hold and he swung onto the back of the horse. As they rode out of the camp, Scott knew she had asked Man-with-no-hair to watch out for him; perhaps the time had come for him to start watching out for them instead.

Scott rode a different horse today. The one from yesterday needed and deserved a rest. The horse had performed well when Scott had needed it the most. He hadn't considered using the new pony; he would have to spend some time working with and getting to know it, before he could trust it on an extended excursion.

Scott and Man-with-no-hair rode at a fast pace; there was much to do and they had a long way to go.

When they arrived at the wallow, Man-with-no-hair studied the scene from horseback. He scanned the surrounding area thoroughly before he dismounted. He asked Scott to remain mounted and keep watch, in case the bear happened to return.

Man-with-no-hair waded across the wallow, bent down and picked up the young Indian. Struggling to keep his balance in the slick mud, Man-with-no-hair carried the boy out of the wallow and laid him down several yards away.

Man-with-no-hair looked closely at the boy's clothing and the designs that were sewn into them. He then got to his feet and walked around the wallow. When he found the tracks of the Indian boy, he backtracked them until he found where he had fallen from his horse; there he found the boy's bow and quiver. With these new items in hand, Man-with-no-hair walked back to the body. He examined the markings on the bow and the quiver; he looked thoughtfully at the six remaining arrows.

"We get wood, burn the body," said Man-with-no-hair as he placed the bow and quiver beside the boy. Scott was appalled but Man-with-no-hair quickly added: "If we not burn boy, animals come. Scatter bones across valley."

What Man-with-no-hair said made sense. But, Scott could not shake a strange feeling that washed over him when he thought of the boy's body being consumed by fire. He thought about it as he gathered wood and realized that it made no difference to the deceased how his body was disposed of. It was a matter of what the living were accustomed to and what they were willing to accept as a respectful means of disposing of a body.

There was not enough wood near the wallow to build an adequate fire and neither man was willing to carry the body closer to a more abundant wood supply. Consequently, they had to drag fallen trees and limbs from the nearby forest.

Scott and Man-with-no-hair gathered wood for several hours before they had enough to do what was needed. They piled the wood high, placed the body in the center and piled more wood on top. Together, they lighted opposite ends of the pile. As the fire licked the dry fuel it began to grow; within a few minutes they had to back away from the intense heat.

Despite having come to terms with what they had to do, Scott was not inclined to stand around and watch the fire burn. He walked to his horse and swung onto its back. Man-with-no-hair turned from the fire, looked at Scott and then strode to his own horse.

Man-with-no-hair looked at the fire again. He exhaled, shook his head and said, "We kill bear now."

As they rode away from the fire, Scott had a feeling they were being watched. Perhaps he was beginning to understand Indian superstition; he felt as if it were the spirit of the young Indian that was watching them. Though they were in the process of seeking revenge for the young man's death, Scott doubted the spirit was a happy one.

The trail of the bear was as easy to follow now as it was the day before. They followed at a rapid pace, stopping occasionally to survey the surrounding terrain.

Man-with-no-hair was surprised by the bear's ability to continue, considering the amount of blood it had lost. The trail finally turned out of the open meadow and into a timber-choked ravine. At the edge of the timber, Man-with-no-hair stopped and looked both ways. He turned right, off the bear's trail, and rode along the edge of the timber for about one hundred yards. At that point, he turned and rode his horse into the timber.

"Why did we go away from the trail?" Scott whispered.

"Trees thick. Can't see. Don't want bear to see us before we see him," answered Man-with-no-hair.

With Man-with-no-hair in the lead, they rode to the bottom of the ravine and up the other side. When they were a couple hundred yards up the other side, they turned left. When they came out of the timber, they turned left again. Shortly, they came back to where the tracks had disappeared into the thick forest.

"The bear is waiting for us," Man-with-no-hair said as he dismounted. "Don't tie horse. If bear come, they can run away."

Scott realized they had made a circle and had not seen any sign of the bear exiting the ravine. Scott wanted this bear dead, but he wasn't sure he wanted to tackle it on foot. On the other hand, he certainly wasn't going to let Man-with-no-hair go alone. He slid from the horse's back and followed his friend into the dense stand of timber.

The bear had torn up the thick, loose duff that covered the forest floor. In places it looked as though he had fallen and rolled down the gentle slope. The trail was very easy to follow, but the timber was so thick it could have concealed the bear if it were fifty feet away. Rather than walk in single file, Scott and Man-with-no-hair walked side by side – spread out. If one wasn't able to see something, the other probably would. Scott would take three or four steps and look all around, sometimes squatting down to look under a limb or between trees.

Near the bottom of the ravine, they began to encounter rock outcroppings. When they reached the bottom, both canyon walls were solid rock. There were no visible tracks, but the last sign they had seen was going up the bottom of the ravine. There was no timber growing in the rocks; their vision was not impaired, but they still moved slowly.

A short distance ahead, the ravine turned sharply to the left and ended in a boulder-strewn, circular basin, approximately two hundred yards in circumference.

Man-with-no-hair climbed atop the first boulder, to scan the basin. He saw a huge cave directly to his left. He watched the cave for several minutes. When he was confident the bear was not lying in wait near its mouth, he jumped off the boulder.

As Man-with-no-hair explained what he had seen, Scott noticed a subtle change in his friend's demeanor. He was tense, of course, but there was something else.

Together they cautiously approached the cave.

There were fresh bear tracks in the coarse dirt of the cave mouth. There was no blood in the tracks. They had reached the home of the great bear. Here, he would be stronger. Here, he would be more difficult to kill. Here, he would fight harder.

The two men stood at the mouth of the cave, staring into impenetrable darkness.

Scott glanced at Man-with-no-hair and the look on his face sent a shiver down his back. His eyes were dark and cold, his jaw was set, the muscles flexing. Scott almost felt sorry for the bear because he knew he was looking into the eyes of a stone-cold killer.

Afraid Man-with-no-hair was going to charge into the cave, Scott picked up a fist-sized rock and chucked it into the lair. The rock echoed hollowly as it bounced off the rock wall and fell to the floor. The bear made no sound. Scott glanced at Man-with-no-hair, picked up another rock, took a few steps into the cave and threw it, too. Again, the bear made no sound.

Man-with-no-hair's features began to relax, as though he already knew what the outcome would be. He touched Scott's arm to get his attention and together they backed away from the cave.

Man-with-no-hair located a pitch snag and by pulling and jerking, he broke off large pieces of the resinous material. Fortunately, the wood was straight grained and was easy to split into long slender pieces. Man-with-no-hair took several of the pieces and tied them together. They returned to the cave. Scott lighted one end of the pitch slivers. When the torch was burning well, they walked into the bear's den.

The cave was large enough to allow the men to stand erect and walk side by side. Scott had an arrow nocked and Man-with-no-hair carried his knife in his right hand, the torch in his left.

The bottom of the cave was covered with fine dirt and sand; they made no sound as they crept into the lair of the giant bear.

The passage into the cave made an abrupt right turn. Man-with-no-hair poked his head around the corner. He motioned for Scott to follow. The corner led to a chamber that was the end of the cave. The bear was lying on the floor of the chamber, dead.

"Make fire. Skin bear." Man-with-no-hair said, as he knelt down and began to break the torch into kindling.

Relieved, Scott quickly left the cave and went in search of wood. When he returned, Man-with-no-hair had already begun the task of skinning the massive beast. Scott added the wood to the kindling and then went to assist Man-with-no-hair.

From the right turn, to the back of the chamber, the roof of the cave began to slope down and Scott had to duck to get into position to grasp a leg. He hit his head in the process. As he rubbed his head, he looked at the roof of the cave and was shocked at what he saw.

The roof of the cave was reflecting the firelight; upon closer examination, he saw that it was solid gold.

"Gold! GOLD! Man-with-no-hair, this is gold. Do you know what that means?" he asked, barely able to contain his excitement.

"Skin bear now," Man-with-no-hair said.

"Man-with-no-hair, you don't understand! You don't know what we can do with this gold! We're rich! We will never want for anything again as long as we live. We will have more money than we..."

"Skin bear now," Man-with-no-hair interrupted softly.

Scott looked at Man-with-no-hair and the look on his face told him that his friend was interested in one thing – skinning the bear.

"Yes. Yes, let's skin the bear."

The inside of the cave soon became filled with smoke and both men had to make several trips outside, into the fresh air, before the bear was skinned.

Coughing and eyes watering, they finally dragged the hide to the mouth of the cave. There, in the dwindling light of the day, Scott built another fire, while Man-with-no-hair went after the horses.

After they had eaten, the men lay on opposite sides of the fire, each with his own thoughts.

Scott was thinking about elegant carriages, castles and owning thousands of acres of land. He had already figured that he would use all of the horses to transport the gold to the East Coast.

"Scott," Man-with-no-hair said, startling him out of his daydreams.

"Yes," Scott answered, surprised that Man-with-no-hair was still awake.

"What is rich? What that mean?" Man-with-no-hair asked, truly puzzled.

"Why, rich is when you have enough money to buy anything you want. Rich is when you live…"

"What is money?" Man-with-no-hair interrupted.

"Money is what you use to buy things."

"What are things you would *buy* with money?" Man-with-no-hair interrupted again.

"We could buy a home and clothes. We could buy horses and catt—"

"Why you need money? Why *buy* what you have now?" Man-with-no-hair asked. He had seen the greed in his friend's face, and though he didn't know what it meant or what had caused it, he had seen the look on other faces in the past and knew it was not a good thing. He did not know what Scott's intentions were and he would not ask. He would not tell his friend what to do, he would only offer advice if he were asked, or subtly point things out to make those around him aware of the path they were taking.

Scott jerked into a sitting position. He ran his hands through his hair. "What was I thinking?" he asked himself aloud. He had everything he could possibly ever want. He had two of the best friends he could ever hope to have. The tepee was not a castle but it was their home, a good home where friends lived together in peace. They did not have cattle but they had a horse herd that was growing rapidly. Life here was difficult and challenging, but considering the rewards, he realized he was already rich, and had been for quite some time.

As Scott remembered what they had been through together, he felt a stab of guilt. Embarrassed, he looked toward Man-with-no-hair. His friend was facing away from him, making no sound. He was glad his friend could not read his mind. Or could he? He was very perceptive, after all.

That night Scott dreamed of castles, fine clothing and attending court. When he awoke, he had no memory of the dream. He was glad to be away from the cave and the temptation of greed.

It was late afternoon when Scott and Man-with-no-hair rode into their camp. Scott could see Dew-on-the-grass-in-the-moon-when-the-leaves-fall standing between the fire and the tepee. He didn't – couldn't – wait until his horse was cared for. He slid off the horse's back and ran to her. She didn't know quite what to expect but she was smiling. Scott took her into his arms and held her close. His behavior was unusual and he wasn't sure what she thought of it, but she returned his embrace and he was thankful. The greed and guilt washed away in one loving embrace.

Scott released his hold on her before he injured her. He put his hands on her shoulders and held her at arm's length, looking at her. She returned his gaze and in that moment he felt an inner warmth that could not be purchased with all the gold in the world. He kissed her cheek and turned to take his horse to the corral.

"Scott," Dew-on-the-grass-in-the-moon-when-the-leaves-fall said softly.

He stopped in his tracks and turned to her.

She put both hands over her heart. "Dew-on-the-grass-in-the-moon-when-the-leaves-fall has love for you," she said with a voice that made the strength go out of his knees.

"I have love for you, too," he said.

He went back to her and took her in his arms. He heard Man-with-no-hair grunt as he led Scott's horse to the corral.

Chapter Eleven

With the arrival of spring, came a series of new tasks to be performed. The horses were no longer threatened with hunger and were often left unattended in the meadow. All three people worked on the hides that had been rolled all winter. Dew-on-the-grass-in-the-moon-when-the-leaves-fall used the hides to replace articles of clothing and the various paraphernalia she used around the camp. Man-with-no-hair often worked on a necklace made from the claws and canine teeth of the two bears they had killed. Also, his other mare had foaled and he now had two fillies to train. Scott spent as much time as he could with the spotted Indian pony – *his* horse.

The new horse was a superb animal. He was truly a mountain horse. He was sure footed, had good wind, and was extremely tough.

The horse was tentative about his new master at first, so Scott worked slowly, until he had the animal's trust. With trust came acceptance.

Three weeks after the death of the young Indian, Scott swung onto the back of the new horse. The animal took his weight well, as Scott walked him around the meadow. Cautiously, Scott touched his heels to the horse's ribs and was nearly unseated as the horse sprang into a gallop and raced across the valley floor.

Scott tried to use the reins to turn the horse but the animal seemed to be confused by the tugging and pulling. Man-with-no-hair, who was watching closely, suggested he try to guide the horse with his legs and by shifting his body weight. Scott tried that approach and the horse responded well. Scott on the other hand, struggled with his co-ordination but with practice, the horse soon had him trained.

Scott worked the horse in an area of the meadow that was near the camp and free of debris, in case he instructed the animal improperly and ended up on his backside.

As Scott reached the eastern end of his working area, he turned the horse around and saw Man-with-no-hair riding out of camp on his fastest horse. When Scott reached the western end of his working area, Man-with-no-hair was waiting for him.

"You got fast pony, uh," Man-with-no-hair said with a wry grin and a twinkle in his eye.

"I think this horse will outrun any horse in the valley," said Scott smugly.

Man-with-no-hair laughed openly. "We see, my friend."

Scott rode around Man-with-no-hair and came alongside of him. "How far?" he asked.

"To the big rock in the stream," Man-with-no-hair answered.

"I'm ready when you…"

"IIIIIIEEEE!" screamed Man-with-no-hair, and they were away.

The rock in the stream was about half a mile downstream from the camp. It was a large rock that seemed to have come from nowhere. There were no other rocks around and it was too far into the valley floor to have rolled from the canyon walls. Man-with-no-hair and Scott had ridden by the rock on many occasions and rarely failed to look upon it with curiosity.

The horse that Man-with-no-hair was riding was his personal favorite. It was a large, powerful stallion.

With the sudden start of the race, Scott was once again nearly unseated. If he had not heard Man-with-no-hair laughing at him, which made him hold on tighter, he probably would have fallen off. By the time he had regained a sitting position, Man-with-no-hair was two lengths ahead of him. When Scott reached a natural riding position, he started gaining on Man-with-no-hair at a rate that would overtake him long before they reached the rock.

Man-with-no-hair noticed Scott gaining on him. He whooped and *ki-yied*, attempting to get more speed from his mount. Man-with-no-hair's antics seemed to have more affect on Scott's horse than on his own.

Scott leaned forward until his head was just above the base of the horse's neck. The horse stretched out until it appeared to be but a few feet above the ground. Scott passed Man-with-no-hair as if he were standing still. Scott glanced back to see if Man-with-no-hair was still running his horse. Man-with-no-hair's mouth was agape as if he could not believe what he had just seen.

Scott flashed by the rock, easily six lengths ahead of Man-with-no-hair. What a ride! What a feeling! The horse's gait was so smooth, Scott felt as if he were riding on the wind.

Scott slowed the horse to a walk. Man-with-no-hair came alongside of him. They walked the horses for about a quarter of a mile before they turned back toward camp.

"You have fastest horse in the valley," Man-with-no-hair admitted as they neared the camp.

Scott had an opportunity to have some fun at his friend's expense, but decided to pass. He knew how proud Man-with-no-hair was of his horses and he wished he hadn't beaten him so badly.

"I may have the fastest, but you have the most," said Scott, hoping to placate Man-with-no-hair's injured pride.

The wry grin returned and Man-with-no-hair said, "Today, you were lucky."

2

When Scott was not working with his horse, he was busy constructing a lean-to. They were accumulating more items than could be stored in the tepee. Also, they were all tired of smelling the green hides all winter. If the hides were left unprotected they would rot or the rodents would attack them.

The lean-to was a simple construction, much like the cabins of the colony. He used dry deadfalls that ranged from six to eight inches in diameter at the small end. The two sides and the back wall were about six feet in length; it would eventually be about six feet high in front and five feet high in the back.

He went to great pains to flatten two sides of each timber to ensure a tight fit. It would have been an easier task with an adze but all he had was the hand axe and it was getting dull. The blade had several deep nicks. He was going to have to find a way to sharpen it or it would soon become useless.

Man-with-no-hair and Dew-on-the-grass-in-the-moon-when-the-leaves-fall watched his progress with curiosity. It was obvious they had never seen accommodations constructed from wood.

Man-with-no-hair and Scott did very little hunting except for small game such as rabbits and grouse. They had no need for large amounts of meat; besides, the deer were still lean from winter. "Watch horses," Man-with-no-hair told him. "When horses get fat, deer get fat."

Dew-on-the-grass-in-the-moon-when-the-leaves-fall was beginning to show signs of the life that was growing within her. One day, it occurred to Scott that there was no one there to help her with the delivery of the child.

Scott left the lean-to and joined Dew-on-the-grass-in-the-moon-when-the-leaves-fall at the fire. He squatted beside her. "I don't know how to help you when the baby is born."

"Dew-on-the-grass-in-the-moon-when-the-leaves-fall not need help," she replied, giving him a strange look.

"What do you mean you don't need help? How will you do it alone?" Scott asked, puzzled and concerned.

"Do it Indian way," she stated matter-of-factly.

"How is that?" Scott asked, now genuinely concerned.

She gave him a mock look of exasperation and said, "When the time is here, I will go into the forest and have the baby."

"What? You will go into the forest to give birth – by yourself? With no help? Why would…"

"Yes, I will go alone," she interrupted. "Why would someone go with me?"

"What about the baby? What if something goes wrong? What if you need help? What about you?" he asked, with unconcealed anxiety.

"If baby not right, baby die. If Dew-on-the-grass-in-the-moon-when-the-leaves-fall not right, Dew-on-the-grass-in-the-moon-when-the-leaves-fall and baby die," she stated flatly.

Her statement overwhelmed Scott with emotion. He was suddenly stricken with guilt, for he was the cause of her condition.

"I don't want you to die. I don't want the baby to die either," he said quietly.

Dew-on-the-grass-in-the-moon-when-the-leaves-fall put down her tools and looked at Scott. "I do not want to die. I do not want baby to die. If baby is weak, it will die. If Dew-on-the-grass-in-the-moon-when-the-leaves-fall is weak, she will die. That is the way of life here. Only strong live, the weak die. If not so, soon all Indians be weak. Men not hunt in the cold, people get sick. People die for no reason. This way is best."

She picked up her knife and returned to preparing the meal.

Scott could not believe what he was hearing. It seemed strange that she was willing to accept the possibility of death without question. Upon reflection, he realized she didn't take death lightly; she simply accepted the existence of the threat of death. He had been raised by the white settlers and had been taught what they believed, such as the fear of death. No matter how much time he spent among peoples who did not fear death, it was ingrained in him and would not be easily overcome.

Scott left the campfire trying to think positive thoughts, after all, children were born every day. Being pregnant was not an automatic death sentence. However, if she did die, how much of the responsibility was his and how would he respond to losing her?

When Scott reached the lean-to, he was unable to concentrate on his work.

All he could picture in his mind was Dew-on-the-grass-in-the-moon-when-the-leaves-fall, alone in the forest, trying to force a child out of her body.

Scott left the lean-to, picked up his bow and quiver and strode out of the camp.

When he reached the other side of the valley, he turned west, staying close to the edge of the timber. As he walked, his thoughts were focused on Dew-on-the-grass-in-the-moon-when-the-leaves-fall and not his environs. After he had walked about a half mile, a large grouse sprang up at his feet and flew into a nearby tree. Scott was startled out of his thoughts by the sudden flapping of the grouse's wings. He was temporarily disoriented and wasn't certain where he was. He had no recollection of walking the distance he had covered. He ducked into the darkness of the timber and watched the surrounding area for several long minutes. When he was certain he was alone, he went to the tree in which the grouse had landed.

Grouse are not known for their intelligence when it comes to outwitting predators; this particular bird was no exception. Fifteen feet up the tree, it huddled next to the trunk in an attempt to conceal itself, yet it clucked at him like a barnyard chicken.

Scott moved around the base of the tree until he located a shooting lane that offered an unobstructed shot at the bird. He took careful aim and shot the grouse out of the tree. The bird came out of the tree with a commotion of flapping wings and breaking branches. Scott ended the birds suffering the instant it fell to the ground.

Scott took cover at the base of the tree and scanned the valley floor and the timbered hillside behind him. Again, he wanted to make sure the noisy bird had not attracted other hunters. After several minutes of carefully scrutinizing the area around him, Scott once again concluded that he was alone and not in danger.

He left the tree to search for another grouse or a rabbit. He made up his mind to pay closer attention to what he was doing. Daydreaming could be a fatal pastime in this country.

His skill was much improved when he concentrated on what he was doing. He soon came upon a fat rabbit that he would not have had a chance to bag if he had been thinking about anything but hunting. As it was, the rabbit presented an easy target and Scott was soon on his way back to camp with food for the next meal.

Dew-on-the-grass-in-the-moon-when-the-leaves-fall was still working over the fire and Man-with-no-hair was working with the fillies when Scott walked into camp.

Dew-on-the-grass-in-the-moon-when-the-leaves-fall smiled when he approached with the fresh game. She did not smile because he had food in his hands, but because his nearness made her happy. Her love for him made her smile when she looked upon him.

Dew-on-the-grass-in-the-moon-when-the-leaves-fall's smile increased her beauty, if that were possible. When she smiled her whole face seemed to light up. It was impossible to look at that smile and not return it with a smile of his own, which Scott did.

Scott was not angry with Dew-on-the-grass-in-the-moon-when-the-leaves-fall; he simply had difficulty accepting some of her customs. He was certain the customs of the inhabitants of James Fort would seem strange to her. There were things he would have to learn to accept, and hope for the best in situations that were beyond his control.

Scott dressed out the rabbit and grouse. By the time he finished, Dew-on-the-grass-in-the-moon-when-the-leaves-fall had finished preparing the meal. She called to Man-with-no-hair and he joined Dew-on-the-grass-in-the-moon-when-the-leaves-fall and Scott at the fire.

"You see deer?" Man-with-no-hair asked, as he sat down.

"No," Scott answered. "Many tracks, but no deer."

"Elk signs?"

"No, only deer signs."

"How far you go?"

"About a mile west on the north edge of the valley," Scott answered.

"If I had deer skin, I make moccasins," Dew-on-the-grass-in-the-moon-when-the-leaves-fall stated.

Man-with-no-hair glanced at his moccasins and then looked toward Scott. "Tomorrow we get a deer?" he asked.

"Yes, we will," Scott confirmed cheerfully.

3

The next morning, Man-with-no-hair and Scott rode out of the camp shortly after sunrise. Man-with-no-hair rode a horse and led another. Scott rode his spotted horse. They rode to the north edge of the valley and then turned east. There were plenty of signs but Man-with-no-hair refused to hunt larger game near their camp.

When they had ridden about five miles, they spotted a small herd of deer feeding in the tall grass of the valley floor.

Man-with-no-hair watched the herd for several minutes before he indicated a fat, barren doe. "We will take her," he said.

"What difference does it make?" Scott asked.

"She has no fawn. Fawn too young now, die without doe."

Scott knew Man-with-no-hair was concerned about exhausting the food supply in the valley in which they lived; if game was scarce in the winter, starvation could become a reality.

The deer were about a quarter of a mile away. The intermittent breeze was in favor of Scott and Man-with-no-hair.

"Wait here," said Man-with-no-hair. "Give me time to get closer. Ride horse across meadow. Ride to timber. Ride slow. Let deer see you."

With that said, Man-with-no-hair slipped off his horse and stepped into the tall grass. A shiver ran up and down Scott's back as he witnessed the ease with which Man-with-no-hair silently disappeared from sight.

Scott waited about ten minutes. He gathered the reins of Man-with-no-hair's horse and the pack-horse and slowly rode across the valley floor. Before he was half way across, one of the deer (there were fifteen in the herd) raised its head and watched him. Within a few seconds, all of the deer were watching him. Two big bucks took tentative steps toward the timber, never taking their eyes from Scott. The fawns seemed content to let the adults do the worrying and continued to eat. As Scott neared the southern edge of the valley floor, he turned to the east, toward the deer.

Suddenly, the doe that Man-with-no-hair had chosen leaped into the air and fell into a heap where she landed. She jumped back to her feet, took two steps and fell back to the ground.

Scott loped the horses toward the fallen doe. The rest of the herd scattered as he approached. Scott was shocked when Man-with-no-hair stood up; he was less than ten feet from the fallen doe. His stalking ability was uncanny.

"If you had gotten any closer, you could have jumped on her and ridden her back to camp," Scott joked, as he dismounted near the fallen deer.

Man-with-no-hair's response was one of his wry grins.

Together, the two men made short work of butchering the deer. They soon had the doe secured on the back of the pack-horse and were on their way home. They returned to camp before noon. They took the doe off the pack-horse and carried her to a meat pole they had tied into a tree specifically for skinning larger game. The flesh was still warm and the hide slipped off the carcass with little effort.

Dew-on-the-grass-in-the-moon-when-the-leaves-fall, who was obviously pleased with their success, immediately took the hide away and staked it out.

Man-with-no-hair spent the rest of the day working with the fillies. Scott worked on the lean-to. Dew-on-the-grass-in-the-moon-when-the-leaves-fall began to smoke the meat from the doe.

That night, as Man-with-no-hair and Scott went to the meadow to bring the horses in for the night, Scott noticed one of Man-with-no-hair's mares acting strangely. Man-with-no-hair was very attuned to his horses and he noticed it too. Man-with-no-hair handed Scott the lead ropes of the two horses he was leading and went to the mare.

Talking softly, Man-with-no-hair slowly approached the mare. When he reached her, he placed his hand on her shoulder and walked around her, talking as he went. He placed a lead rope around her neck and lead her to where Scott stood waiting. He smiled as he walked and Scott knew that what troubled the mare was not serious, but he was concerned, nonetheless.

"She ready to take a mate," said Man-with-no-hair. "You want another spotted pony?"

Scott was touched. Man-with-no-hair was very proud of his horses and Scott assumed he would continue breeding the mares with his stallions. He also knew Man-with-no-hair was impressed with the spotted horse. He had an eye for a good horse.

"Yes, I would like another horse like mine," Scott answered.

Man-with-no-hair became serious as he said, "We cannot put mare in corral. Stallions will fight for her."

They returned the horses to the corral and tied the mare near the tepee. The stallions were aware of the mare's condition, however, and the occupants of the tepee got little sleep as the horses neighed and nickered at each other throughout the night.

The next morning, Man-with-no-hair led the horses out of the corral and into the meadow. He then led the mare into the corral with Scott's stallion. The mare was just coming into heat and was not ready for the advances of the stallion. She kicked him several times and tried to elude him within the confines of the corral. The other two stallions were more interested in romance than food and soon returned from the meadow and pranced around the corral gate.

Man-with-no-hair laughed. "Maybe tomorrow she be ready." He laughed again. "If Dew-on-the-grass-in-the-moon-when-the-leaves-fall kick like that, you not soon be father." Dew-on-the-grass-in-the-moon-when-the-leaves-fall blushed but she laughed with Man-with-no-hair and Scott.

The mare and the spotted horse battled throughout the night, making it the second night in a row Man-with-no-hair, Dew-on-the-grass-in-the-moon-when-the-leaves-fall and Scott got little or no sleep.

"Why you not teach your horse to be quiet at night?" Man-with-no-hair grumbled, good humored, the next morning.

"Why don't you teach your horse to be quick about taking a mate?" Scott retorted.

The laughter started again.

The laughter stirred emotions deep within Scott. It brought a feeling of unspoken closeness. A need, if you will, of the people he shared his life with. His heart was happy, for he knew love.

4

As the weeks slipped by, spring became summer. The buds turned into leaves, the valley became green and even more beautiful. Scott had finished the lean-to and they stored much of their gear and belongings in it, giving them much more room in the tepee. Man-with-no-hair worked with the fillies every day. They were no longer the spindly- legged creatures they had once been. It was a pleasure to watch them race across the valley floor. There had been several days of rain but now the sky was blue and cloudless; the temperature rose with each passing day. Dew-on-the-grass-in-the-moon-when-the-leaves-fall's stomach had become quite swollen and it was becoming difficult for her to accomplish all of the tasks she had previously performed. Scott stayed closer to camp. When he was away, it was seldom longer than half a day. He helped her with the chores as much as she would allow. Man-with-no-hair was becoming more and more distant.

5

The doe hide had cured and Dew-on-the-grass-in-the-moon-when-the-leaves-fall had begun to make moccasins. Scott was standing on the soft hide and Dew-on-the-grass-in-the-moon-when-the-leaves-fall was tracing the outline of his foot with a piece of charcoal from the fire. They had made a pair for Man-with-no-hair that morning. Scott had helped by punching the holes and stitching the pieces together, under Dew-on-the-grass-in-the-moon-when-the-leaves-fall's watchful eye, of course.

As Scott was standing on the hide, having his foot traced, he saw Man-with-no-hair race across the mouth of the finger in which they lived. He had given no warning cry and was not carrying his weapons. Scott was not alarmed but he felt he should make certain there was not a problem; besides, he was curious.

"What is he doing now?" Scott asked, as much to himself as Dew-on-the-grass-in-the-moon-when-the-leaves-fall.

Scott had been fussing over Dew-on-the-grass-in-the-moon-when-the-leaves-fall all morning and she had about had all the "help" from him she could stand for one day. She looked up from her work but Man-with-no-hair had already passed by the mouth of the small meadow. "You should go see," she said, with mock concern.

"Yes. Yes, I should," said Scott, not quite sure what to make of her tone.

"Go, go, go," she said with a smile, as she shoved him off the hide.

Scott slipped his feet into his old moccasins, picked up his bow and quiver and raced to the meadow. He turned to the left, which was the way Man-with-no-hair had been going, and ran until he saw his friend standing at the edge of the timber. Scott quickly knelt down in the tall grass and watched until he knew everything was all right.

Man-with-no-hair was slowly turning in circles, looking into the sky. He looked as though he were lost. Scott was about to get to his feet when Man-with-no-hair dashed into the forest, at full speed. Scott had no idea what was going on, but he sprang to his feet and followed him.

Scott dodged around a tree and nearly ran into Man-with-no-hair. He skidded to a stop and looked at Man-with-no-hair, who was once again looking around as though lost.

"What are you doing?" Scott whispered.

"Honey bee," Man-with-no-hair whispered as he kept his eyes focused on the upper reaches of the forest canopy.

"I thought…"

"SSSHHH!"

Scott tried to follow Man-with-no-hair's gaze and he thought he saw the bee too. Man-with-no-hair ran in the direction the bee had gone, Scott at his heels. They kept up with the bee for about fifty yards but finally had to stop and wait for another one to pass by.

They had to follow four more bees before they located the hive, which was in a standing, dead cedar tree. The entrance to the hive was a four-inch hole about five feet up the base of the tree. The tree itself was about two feet in diameter and fifty feet tall.

Several bees buzzed around as the two men drew nearer to examine the cedar tree.

"We come at night," Man-with-no-hair said, as he began to slowly back away from the hive.

On the way back to the camp, they discussed various ways to get the honey out of the tree; ways that would cause them the least amount of pain and discomfort.

Dew-on-the-grass-in-the-moon-when-the-leaves-fall was excited at the prospect of having honey in camp. She stopped working on the moccasins and began to construct a hide container for the honey. It was a large container and Scott wondered with despair if they were expected to fill it completely.

After the sun had set, they waited for the full moon to rise. The light of the moon lighted the way for them as they made their way through the dense forest. They had not been able to come up with a viable plan to extract the honey. They decided to take a closer look at the tree at night to determine if it offered a weak spot on which they could concentrate.

When they reached the hive, Scott put the empty honey container down and slowly approached the tree. He looked into the hole but could see nothing. He put his hands on the outside of the tree; it felt solid. But, if the bees had made a home on the inside, how solid could it be? He put his right hand into the hole, grasped the wood and pulled. He heard the wood give. He pulled harder. The wood gave slightly and then he heard the buzz of angry bees. Man-with-no-hair was watching him closely and did not need to be told twice to get out of there as Scott reefed on the wood with all of his strength. A massive slab of wood tore loose from the tree and the two men were forced to race away from the swarming bees.

Scott could feel several bees on his face. He closed his eyes and swatted at the bees. With his eyes closed, he ran headlong into a standing tree. He hit the tree so hard he ricocheted off and landed on his back. The impact nearly knocked him unconscious, but the thought of the swarming bees and the sound of Man-with-no-hair laughing at him, as he ran through the forest, were enough to make him get back to his feet and get back to camp as quickly as possible.

When Scott finally stumbled into camp, he found Man-with-no-hair on his knees by the fire laughing so hard tears were streaming down the side of his face. Dew-on-the-grass-in-the-moon-when-the-leaves-fall had a concerned look on her face but she was laughing too. Despite himself, Scott laughed with them.

They had managed to elude most of the bees but both men had been stung several times. Scott's face hurt, but that was as much from running into the tree, as from the bees.

The next morning, Dew-on-the-grass-in-the-moon-when-the-leaves-fall was not in the tepee when Scott and Man-with-no-hair awoke. They thought nothing of it until they stepped out of the tepee and she was not outside either. Scott's first thought was she had gone into the forest to deliver the baby.

In a voice that was uncustomarily gruff, Man-with-no-hair told him it was too soon for that.

Scott looked at his friend curiously and was about to ask what was troubling him when they saw Dew-on-the-grass-in-the-moon-when-the-leaves-fall walk into the finger. She was carrying the heavy container and it was full of honey.

Scott ran to her and relieved her of her burden.

"How did you do this?" Scott asked her, when he noticed she had no visible stings.

"Did it," she said, shrugging her shoulders.

"How?" he asked

"Put hand in tree, take honey out," she answered nearing exasperation.

"Did you get stung?"

"No."

"Why?"

"I didn't make bees mad," she stated, matter-of-factly.

Chapter Twelve

With the advent of summer, the inhabitants of the valley found that there were few demands on their time. Game was plentiful and easily obtainable. Once the horses were delivered to the meadow, they cared for themselves. They had many hides tanned and ready to be made into clothing or shelter, when the need arose. If it were not for Dew-on-the-grass-in-the-moon-when-the-leaves-fall's condition, Scott would have been exploring the nearby mountains and valleys. Man-with-no-hair, on the other hand, was ready to move on.

One day Scott sat down next to Dew-on-the-grass-in-the-moon-when-the-leaves-fall. He had just finished gathering wood for the fire.

"Do you know what is the matter with Man-with-no-hair?" he asked her.

"He not tell you?"

"He has said nothing to me."

Dew-on-the-grass-in-the-moon-when-the-leaves-fall frowned but made no response.

"What has he said to you?" Scott asked, worriedly.

"He not say to me, but I know. I watch him. Man-with-no-hair will go away soon."

Scott's jaw fell open as a look of disbelief crossed over his face. Dew-on-the-grass-in-the-moon-when-the-leaves-fall saw the injured look and tried to comfort him, but the shock was too deep, and her attempts failed.

"It Dew-on-the-grass-in-the-moon-when-the-leaves-fall's fault Man-with-no-hair will go away," she said flatly.

"What do you mean it's your fault?" he asked, incredulously.

"Man-with-no-hair say before, his woman die. Baby die too. Man-with-no-hair and Dew-on-the-grass-in-the-moon-when-the-leaves-fall are from same people. Dew-on-the-grass-in-the-moon-when-the-leaves-fall care for Man-with-no-hair, Man-with-no-hair care for Dew-on-the-grass-in-the-moon-when-the-leaves-fall. Man-with-no-hair not want to be here if Dew-on-the-grass-in-the-moon-when-the-leaves-fall does not live when baby comes."

As Scott was absorbing what he was hearing, Dew-on-the-grass-in-the-moon-when-the-leaves-fall continued, "Man-with-no-hair like to go see. He climb one hill...see another...go see over the other one. Sometimes men need to go see."

"Do you think he will come back?" Scott asked, trying to disguise his disappointment.

"Dew-on-the-grass-in-the-moon-when-the-leaves-fall not know. I know we are his people now. We are family. I think someday he will come back."

Scott got to his feet and turned toward the meadow. He turned back and knelt down beside Dew-on-the-grass-in-the-moon-when-the-leaves-fall. "It is not your fault if he chooses to go away," he said, as he held her closely.

When she released him, he got to his feet and walked to the meadow in search of Man-with-no-hair.

Scott spotted him on the north side of the valley. He was sitting on a root wad talking to the fillies. They were feeding a few feet away. As Scott drew near, he noticed a sullen look in his friend's face.

"My friend is troubled," Scott said, as he sat down beside Man-with-no-hair.

"Augh!" Man-with-no-hair grunted as he looked across the valley floor.

As Scott watched Man-with-no-hair's face, he knew his friend was trying to find the words to tell him how he felt and what he wanted to do.

"If I didn't have to stay here to be with Dew-on-the-grass-in-the-moon-when-the-leaves-fall, I would like to ride out to see those mountains," Scott said, indicating the towering peaks to the west. "As it is, I have to stay, but you do not. This is your home too, and you can come back whenever you want. If you want to go see, then go see."

Man-with-no-hair looked at Scott with renewed respect. He thought Scott knew why he had to go away, but it was difficult for him to say. Scott had put him in a position where he didn't have to say anything. "I will be back before the snow comes," Man-with-no-hair said as he slid off the root.

Scott joined him, and, as the two men walked across the meadow, Man-with-no-hair asked, "You be safe?"

"We will be safe," Scott answered, confidently.

"You will work with the fillies?"

"Yes. Yes, I will," Scott answered, surprised by the request. Man-with-no-hair had spent a great deal of time working with the fillies; not necessarily training them, but getting them used to human hands and the sounds of their voices. Scott never suspected that job would fall to him.

Man-with-no-hair spent the rest of the day preparing to leave. He finally decided to take a spare horse and use it as a pack-animal. He preferred to travel light, but he was still unaccustomed to this new country and was unsure of what to expect. He felt, and Scott concurred, he would be better off if he had too much than not enough. He packed extra clothing and enough food to allow freedom from hunting for several weeks.

That evening, Scott, Dew-on-the-grass-in-the-moon-when-the-leaves-fall and Man-with-no-hair sat around the fire in the gathering dusk. They usually turned in shortly after dark for there was little they could do in the absence of sunlight. Tonight, however, all three of them continued to sit around the fire. They spoke very little; there was nothing that needed to be said. They each drew comfort from the presence of the other. A camaraderie existed between them that could only be shared by people who had sat around the same campfire – had risked or would risk everything for the safety of the other, and could be counted on to do whatever was best for the group. A closeness existed that was so strong it was palpable. They did not need to speak to convey their feelings.

When, at last, they had to retire for the night, they did so with reluctance. This would be the last campfire they would share for quite sometime. Possibly forever.

2

As sunlight penetrated through the dense forest and filtered into the camp of the three wanderers, Man-with-no-hair loaded his belongings onto the pack-horse. Scott's horse was tied near the one Man-with-no-hair would ride; the two friends would ride together for a while.

When the pack was securely in place, Man-with-no-hair turned from the horse and walked to Dew-on-the-grass-in-the-moon-when-the-leaves-fall. They spoke in low voices that Scott could barely discern. He was certain they were speaking in Shawnee. He promised himself he would work harder at learning their language; not so he would know what they were saying, but so they could communicate more effectively and more comfortably.

Man-with-no-hair and Dew-on-the-grass-in-the-moon-when-the-leaves-fall clasped hands and then he turned away and mounted his horse. Scott swung onto the back of his horse and together, he and Man-with-no-hair rode out of the camp.

When they were out of the finger and on the main valley floor, Man-with-no-hair began to speak. Scott was amazed for he had never heard Man-with-no-hair speak more than half a dozen words at a time, until now. Man-with-no-hair warned him of things to beware of and things to look out for and things he probably should not attempt to do.

Scott raised his eyebrows and grinned as he listened to Man-with-no-hair, who sounded more like a scolding old hen than a fierce warrior. When Man-with-no-hair saw the look on Scott's face, he realized what he had been doing and immediately stopped.

"My heart is sad today," Man-with-no-hair said, as if the statement would explain his behavior. "I think Dew-on-the-grass-in-the-moon-when-the-leaves-fall and baby will live. I cannot be here if she does not."

The thought sobered Scott. "I understand," he said quietly.

They rode in silence for a time, listening to the swish of the tall grass and the dull thud of hooves falling on the soft valley floor.

When at last Man-with-no-hair stopped, Scott knew it was time to turn back.

"Ride with care, my friend," said Man-with-no-hair.

It was the first time Man-with-no-hair had ever spoken to Scott without looking at him. The implication was not lost on Scott.

Scott clapped Man-with-no-hair on the back and turned his horse around. After the horse had taken a few steps and Scott thought he could trust his voice not to break, he repeated, "Ride with care."

When Scott had gone a hundred yards, he heard his name called as it echoed across the valley. He spun his horse around and saw Man-with-no-hair on top of a small rise.

"SCOTT WALKER!" he shouted. "I WILL RETURN BEFORE THE SNOW FALLS!"

Scott raised his arm to signify that he understood and then watched as Man-with-no-hair turned and rode away.

As Scott rode back to the camp, he reminisced about the time he had spent with Man-with-no-hair and the things they had learned from each other. Scott was certainly not a tenderfoot and though he could probably survive comfortably, he still had much to learn and Man-with-no-hair was as good a teacher as he could ever hope to find.

When Scott returned to the camp, he went to the corral and released the horses. They had been taken to the main valley so many times, he didn't have to do anything but release them and they would make their own way to the feed and water.

Dew-on-the-grass-in-the-moon-when-the-leaves-fall was half-heartedly working on a hide. "Do you need help?" he asked, looking for something to occupy his mind for awhile.

"No. There not much more to do," Dew-on-the-grass-in-the-moon-when-the-leaves-fall answered.

Scott turned to go. He was going to wander into the woods in search of firewood.

"Scott."

He turned to see that Dew-on-the-grass-in-the-moon-when-the-leaves-fall had risen from the hide and was holding a hand out to him. He went to her and took her hand into his, and allowed her to lead him away from the camp and out to the main valley floor. Neither of them spoke, they just walked and listened to the birds and watched the grazing horses.

Dew-on-the-grass-in-the-moon-when-the-leaves-fall suddenly noticed some small red berries growing close to the ground. She bent over and picked one, and tasted it. It was tart but tasty. After a quick survey, she noticed the valley floor was covered with the small berries. She sent Scott back to the camp to fetch a container. She told him exactly which container she wanted, not wanting him to bring one that contained herbs or spices.

Scott hurried back to the camp and soon returned with the container she had requested. He knelt down and helped her pick berries but they were small and demanded all of his attention. Dew, despite her condition, knelt down and worked quickly. Soon the container was full and Scott carried it back to the camp.

On their way back to the camp, Scott had noticed one of the horses had drifted away from the rest of the herd. He decided to retrieve the wandering horse before it got too far away.

While Scott was away, Dew-on-the-grass-in-the-moon-when-the-leaves-fall searched through her supplies until she found some nuts she had gathered the last fall. She cracked the nuts and then ground them into a coarse meal. She then smashed the berries and added them to the nuts. She added enough honey to thicken the berry juice. She was adding the honey to her creation when Scott returned from the meadow.

Scott sat down beside her and watched with anticipation as she divided the concoction into two bowls and handed one of them to him.

The snack was very good but it was also very sweet and rich. Scott had difficulty eating his half but would not chance offending her and cleaned his bowl.

3

The warm days of summer passed slowly, but they were far from boring. There was always something to do; the completion of an insignificant task now, could make a crucial difference during the winter. Man-with-no-hair had been gone for a month and the tasks that he would have performed now fell to Scott.

Scott devoted a few hours each day to gathering wood. He also spent time with the fillies and his horse. He shared as much time with Dew-on-the-grass-in-the-moon-when-the-leaves-fall as he could.

Summer had progressed to the point that the days were very hot. Every creature seemed to become listless in the heat.

Dew-on-the-grass-in-the-moon-when-the-leaves-fall, with her swollen belly, was obviously uncomfortable. She tried to conceal her discomfort, but Scott saw through her attempts. She was fine in the early morning and at night, but she could not bear the heat. Finally, Scott insisted that she rest in the shade during the hottest time of the day.

Late one afternoon, as Scott walked across the meadow to round up the horses, he saw a dark, thick cloud of smoke towering over the western peaks. The fire was very far away and Scott felt no immediate threat, however, he was in awe of the magnitude of a fire that could send such a plume of smoke into the sky.

Scott herded the horses into the corral and then told Dew-on-the-grass-in-the-moon-when-the-leaves-fall about the fire. Together, they walked to the meadow and looked at the awesome cloud.

Scott thought of Man-with-no-hair and he hoped his friend was nowhere near the fire.

Dew-on-the-grass-in-the-moon-when-the-leaves-fall mumbled some words in Shawnee. Scott turned to her and saw the fear on her face. Suddenly, he realized the predicament she faced: she could not run and was limited to how far she could walk in a day. If she rode a horse for any length of time, she could lose the baby.

The thought of being chased by a roaring fire, even in his peak condition, caused a shudder to run up his spine. He turned to Dew-on-the-grass-in-the-moon-when-the-leaves-fall and tried to comfort her. "The fire is very far away."

"We should watch it," she said, without looking away from the towering cloud of smoke.

They went back to camp to eat. After the meal, they returned to the meadow and beheld a spectacular view. Though the sun had been down for an hour, the entire western sky was lighted in red and yellow. Scott made a silent promise to himself that he would be more careful with fire in the future.

Dew-on-the-grass-in-the-moon-when-the-leaves-fall was also in awe of the fire, but she was frightened, too. She would not be placated simply because of the apparent distance.

"Tomorrow I will ride west. I will find out how far away it is." He told her, hoping to make her feel better.

His words did little to lessen her fears, but she nodded her head in understanding.

Minutes turned into an hour as they stood, captivated by the spectacular view before them. At last, they realized that they were standing in the darkness and returned to camp. There was no way to determine the direction of the fire from their location; Scott would have to make that determination tomorrow.

Sunrise found Scott two miles west of the camp. He had been riding slowly until there was enough light to safely increase his speed. When there was sufficient light, he kicked the spotted pony into a faster pace.

When he approached the fork in the valley, where he and Man-with-no-hair had tracked the Indians last winter, Scott slowed his pace. He watched for tracks and other signs, but saw nothing to cause concern.

This time, Scott went into the southwestern fork of the valley; neither he nor Man-with-no-hair had ever explored this area. Scott moved cautiously, though there was no sign of human movement. If something happened to him, Dew-on-the-grass-in-the-moon-when-the-leaves-fall would be in jeopardy.

Scott became irritated because he was unable to locate a place that offered a view to the west, which would allow him to determine the scope and direction of the fire.

Late that afternoon, Scott followed a trail that led him to an open hillside. From his vantage point, he looked into a deep, wide, timbered valley. The valley was easily twenty miles wide. The foothills and long sweeping ridges of the majestic mountains formed the western edge of the huge valley. The fire was a long way beyond the foothills.

The fire still raged, and though the wind sent ashes into the valley in which Scott and Dew-on-the-grass-in-the-moon-when-the-leaves-fall lived, the blaze was too far away to be an immediate threat to them.

As soon as Scott saw how far away the fire was, he decided to head back to camp. He didn't have time to get back today but he had enough daylight left to cover a considerable amount of ground.

He turned his horse and found himself face to face with a dozen mounted Indians.

Chapter Thirteen

As Man-with-no-hair rode away from Scott, he found himself regretting his decision to leave. He was an independent individual; since the death of his wife, he had had no one to worry about but himself. Now, he had an adopted family that he had learned to care very much for.

He did not regret his decision to come west with them; quite the contrary, for he had been ready for a new adventure. He had quickly recognized Scott's strength, as well as his survival skills. And, despite the treatment he had received at the hands of his own people, it was good to hear Dew-on-the-grass-in-the-moon-when-the-leaves-fall speak the Shawnee tongue.

He was concerned about the welfare of his friends. Scott was skillful and learned quickly and displayed sound judgment, but he still had much to learn to survive the day-to-day challenges and life threatening situations that continuously presented themselves. Alone, he would survive; with Dew-on-the-grass-in-the-moon-when-the-leaves-fall to worry about, he would die. He would return...He must return.

Man-with-no-hair had traveled in the company of Scott for so long, it felt strange to ride alone. After several days of travel, he shook off the feelings of loneliness and once again became one with his surroundings.

2

Man-with-no-hair had never given much thought to his abilities. In his youth, however, he had noticed he had always been able to bring meat into the village, even when older, more experienced hunters were unable to do so. There had been no one to teach him the skills of survival. He had secretly listened to the older hunters as they bragged about their exploits and the methods they employed. He would then rush into the forest and practice what he had heard. He practiced over and over again. While the other boys his age were playing, he was practicing. The other boys would not have played with him had he wanted them to, so he was content to be alone in the forest.

When he reached the age of fifteen, the practice began to pay off. He was the best hunter in the village. Regretfully, he was the only one who was aware of his ability, though he did receive questioning glances from other hunters when he was the only one to bring meat into a hungry village.

His skill had gotten greater than even he could have hoped. He had grown bored with simply sneaking close enough to the game to kill them with an arrow. He welcomed any challenge his mind could conceive. Eventually, he was able to get close enough to the deer to touch them before he shot them. The first time he attempted that feat, the reaction of the startled deer caused him to break out in uncontrollable laughter and he was unable to get a shot off.

After a time, he realized, though touching a wild animal required stealth and skill, it was not the challenge he longed for. The men of the village – the great hunters and warriors – they were going to become the targets of his skills.

He finally lost count of the times he approached a hunter in the forest, touched him, and departed without being detected.

He took special pleasure in causing his tribesmen irritation or discomfort when possible. On one occasion, he found one of the better hunters of the village sitting in the forest, leaning against a tree. Man-with-no-hair approached the hunter from the front, circled around him, and using a twig, touched his ear. With great difficulty, Man-with-no-hair kept from laughing as the brave swatted at the imaginary insect.

Not one time was he ever detected.

As Man-with-no-hair grew older, he came to realize the stories the hunters told about their skill and prowess were more fabrication than truth. They recounted their exploits, claiming skills they wished they possessed rather than what they were actually capable of accomplishing. Many of the hunters were very skillful, but there was not a warrior in the village who could match Man-with-no-hair's skills. He soon became contemptuous of the braggarts and stopped listening to their stories.

A neighboring Shawnee village was attacked and the call for vengeance was sent out. All of the warriors of Man-with-no-hair's village prepared to respond to the call. Man-with-no-hair spent much of the evening preparing himself and his weapons. As dawn drew near he painted his face, shaved his head and left his lodge. He approached a group of gathering warriors and was scoffed at and told to remain behind – for his own good. A war chief stepped out of the crowd and took him aside. He told Man-with-no-hair he would not be needed on this foray and he should remain in the village until he had been taught the ways of war.

Man-with-no-hair had jerked away from the war chief and returned to his lodge. He was seething, not only because his services had been rejected, but also because he could hear the snickers and laughter of the young men his own age who were going into battle.

Man-with-no-hair had been losing respect for his tribesmen for sometime, this final episode was all he could bear. The war chief who had taken him aside was one of the warriors he had encountered in the forest.

When the war party left the village, they went to the southeast. Man-with-no-hair went west and never looked back.

3

After he left the village, he traveled at a pace that was determined by his surroundings. Some days he was able to cover a great distance, others he covered much less. There was no pressure to be at a certain place at a certain time; he went where he wished. If there was an indication of something special or exciting to see, he went that way until he was taken by a new whim.

It was his random, zig-zagging course that brought him to the outskirts of a strange village.

Unsure of the reception he would receive, he surveyed the village from concealment throughout the remainder of the day. He saw nothing to give him an indication how these people would treat him.

He withdrew to the grassy plains and spent the night formulating a plan.

Before there was a hint of dawn on the eastern horizon, he walked among the cone-shaped tents and seated himself at a fire, near the center of the village.

As dawn approached, he heard people moving about in the tepees. Soon he heard muffled voices talking rapidly and knew he had been discovered. He heard several people moving slowly toward him but he did not move. When he looked up he expected to see armed warriors, prepared to pounce on him. Instead, what he saw came as quite a relief, for though the warriors were armed, they were more curious that hostile.

An older man made his way through the group of warriors and addressed Man-with-no-hair. Man-with-no-hair was unable to understand the older man's words so he responded in Shawnee. The old man raised his eyebrows at the sound of the Shawnee language. The old man was able to speak in broken Shawnee and soon Man-with-no-hair explained that he had been shunned by his people and was searching for a new place to call home. When the old man was sure the Shawnee were not going to come in search of him, he offered Man-with-no-hair a place in his village.

No one had ever entered Bull Calf's village unobserved; he found the fact that it had been done by a young Shawnee a bit disquieting. He made sure the young man knew they were not a warring people and violence would not be tolerated unless they were attacked and were acting in self defense.

To make sure the young man's heart was pure and he had not been sent to spy on his people, the old chief told the young man he would be expected to hunt for the women who were without husbands.

Man-with-no-hair quickly agreed to all of the old man's demands. He learned there were eight women he would have to hunt for. That was a formidable task, but one he was capable of accomplishing.

Fortunately, the weather was pleasant, for there were no vacant tepees in the village. None of the villagers were prepared to invite this ghost-like stranger into their homes. Man-with-no-hair had slept under the stars since he had left his village and to continue to do so was not an inconvenience for him.

The day after his arrival, Man-with-no-hair hunted. He was unfamiliar with the terrain and he hunted alone, but he brought meat into the village, nonetheless.

Bull Calf watched, thoughtfully, as Man-with-no-hair delivered meat to the designated tepees.

Each day, Man-with-no-hair hunted and delivered meat. Three old women told him they had enough meat for a while. They were getting old and slow and could not care for the meat as rapidly as he brought it to them. This gave Man-with-no-hair more time for exploring and learning the country surrounding the village.

One aspect of the surrounding area that fascinated Man-with-no-hair was the absence of trees. The forests had given way to rolling hills covered in tall, thick grass. Man-with-no-hair was also captivated by the animals that inhabited the plains. He had seen buffalo and elk before, but never in such vast numbers. He had never encountered antelope until now and found them to be a very worthy quarry. But the animals he was most interested in were the horses. He had seen a few horses but they did not roam freely in the eastern forests.

The first time Man-with-no-hair came upon a small herd of horses he did not pursue them because he thought they must belong to someone else. When he returned to the village he asked Bull Calf about them and was told that they belonged to whomever could catch them.

The members of the tribe who had horses, kept them together and guarded them closely on the outskirts of the village. There were about twenty heads in the herd. They used the horses of the herd to capture more horses.

A half-moon after he had entered the village, Man-with-no-hair returned from hunting to find two old Squaws in his sleeping area. They were in the process of wrapping sewn buffalo hides around erected tepee poles.

Man-with-no-hair was about to ask what they were doing. He thought they were giving his spot to someone else and he would have to leave the village. He could not imagine what he had done to make them want him to leave. Dejected, he turned and saw Bull Calf coming toward him. Now, he knew he would be asked to leave.

Man-with-no-hair was overcome with relief when the old man told him he thought he was a great hunter and was pleased he had come into his village. The tepee was to be his new home and he was welcome to stay as long as he liked.

Man-with-no-hair thanked the chief and promised him he would never be sorry for allowing him to live in his village.

The chief started to leave but turned and asked Man-with-no-hair to come to his fire that night.

Man-with-no-hair was unsure what the chief wanted but he would be there as asked.

Man-with-no-hair watched the women until the tepee was completed. He went inside and sat down; it felt good to have a place to call home.

As evening approached, Man-with-no-hair went to the fire of the chief. He sat down, cross-legged, and waited quietly for the chief to appear. Man-with-no-hair became somewhat uncomfortable when the people of the village began to come and stand around. When the entire population of the village was gathered around the chief's tepee, the old man stepped outside. Man-with-no-hair got to his feet and waited.

"You have been in our village only a short time," Man-with-no-hair would never forget the words of the old man. "But you have proven yourself to be a very good hunter and a man with a good heart. You have told me you do not have a man to call Father. My sons have gone on to the home of the Master of All Life. So, I no longer have sons. I would adopt you as my son, if you would like to have a man to call Father."

Man-with-no-hair was taken by surprise and was almost too emotionally overwhelmed to speak. At last, he would have a father. And, from what he had seen of the old man, he couldn't have asked for a better person to fill that role.

"I would be proud to be your son," Man-with-no-hair said as clearly as he could. Though he spoke in Shawnee, the entire tribe seemed to understand what he had said.

There was gleeful shouting as the old man stepped forward and put his hands on Man-with-no-hair's shoulders. "From now on your name will be Man-with-no-hair. Your name will remind you of where you came from. Any other part of your past will not be spoken of again. Today is the first day of your new life."

That night there was a celebration. Man-with-no-hair was overwhelmed by the generosity of these plains people. It was a happy time for him, but he was curious why these people were as quick to accept him as his people were to shun him. He decided then he would never judge another person by any means other than that person's actions and deeds.

That night, Bull Calf relieved Man-with-no-hair of his singular responsibility of supplying meat to the eight squaws. That responsibility would once again be shared by the entire village. This was especially good news for Man-with-no-hair; he needed the extra time to devise a method of capturing one of the wild horses. He was also becoming interested in one of the squaws whom he had supplied with fresh meat. Her name had been Spotted Fawn and her man had been gored by a wounded buffalo. Man-with-no-hair viewed himself as the lowest ranking brave in the village; he had only a tepee that had been given to him. When he had some horses, he would approach Spotted Fawn.

4

Capturing a horse became Man-with-no-hair's primary goal. He was gone from the village from dawn to dusk and often spent the night on the plains. Several braves offered to help him or loan him a horse but he preferred to do this thing on his own.

Finally, his persistence paid off and he located a small herd of horses. He watched the horses for several days to learn their habits. When he was comfortable with the location of the herd, he made his move on them.

The horses were in a small draw and the breeze was steady from the west. Man-with-no-hair approached from the east. He had targeted a young horse that was not more than one-moon-old. He was a student of nature and he knew if he caught the foal, he would have a good chance of catching its mother, as well.

He carried two braided ropes. The ropes were gifts from some of the old squaws he had supplied with meat.

He crawled slowly through the tall, thick grass, taking more time than he normally would have. He wanted a horse very badly and did not wish to frighten them.

The herd was guarded by a stocky, reddish-brown stallion. At one point, Man-with-no-hair had to stop and wait for the stallion to move away from the foal and its mother. He had no intention of trying to catch the stallion on his first horse-capturing foray.

When Man-with-no-hair was very close to the foal, he reconsidered his options. Originally, he had planned to get close enough to throw the rope over the foal's head; however, the grass was too tall to allow him to make an accurate toss. His only recourse was to physically grab the foal and then drop the rope over its head.

Man-with-no-hair worked his way nearer to the foal. The young horse acted as if it sensed his presence, but was too young to recognize him as a threat. Man-with-no-hair lay prone upon the ground; the foal unknowingly took a step closer to him.

Man-with-no-hair's hand streaked through the grass and grasped onto the foal's fore leg. The foal shrieked with panic and tried to jerk away from whatever had it by the leg.

When the foal jerked, the action helped pull Man-with-no-hair to his feet. When he had his feet beneath him, he dropped the loop over the foal's head and released its leg. The shrieking foal raced to its mother's side. Man-with-no-hair followed, wrapping the other end of the rope around his wrist as he ran. The foal stopped when it reached its mother, but the rest of the herd was now alerted to the danger. The stallion immediately began to round them up and move them away.

The foal tried to keep up with its mother but was unable to do so while dragging Man-with-no-hair. Man-with-no-hair ran as fast as he could, trying to keep up with the foal, not wishing to cause it injury. When he could no longer maintain the fast pace, he began to slow down. Fortunately, the foal was beginning to tire. Man-with-no-hair had little difficulty holding the young horse to a slower pace. The mare circled continuously, whinnying at Man-with-no-hair and her foal.

The stallion led the herd into a long, steep ravine that was choked with scrub oak and other brush. Man-with-no-hair wrapped the rope around the first tree that was big enough to hold the foal. The rest of the herd moved on, but the foal was unable to follow. The foal's mother continued to circle.

Man-with-no-hair made a loop in the second rope and went after the mare. She moved away, watching him closely. When they got too far away from the foal, Man-with-no-hair stopped and went back to the young horse. The mare followed. Man-with-no-hair repeated that procedure three more times until he finally got the wind in his favor. While walking back to the foal for the fourth time, he suddenly seemed to disappear.

The mare stopped in her tracks and stomped her hooves. She knew danger was nearby but she could no longer see from where it came. She took two steps toward her foal. Nothing happened. She took another step. Nothing. She wondered what had frightened her in the first place. What she wanted was her foal back by her side. She took several steps closer to the foal. The stallion shrieked at her from the ridge top. She looked at him and nickered softly. Suddenly, there was a rope around her neck. She screamed in panic and raced toward the stallion.

Man-with-no-hair was barely able to dodge around several trees as the mare dragged him through the dense thicket. When she started up the far side of the ravine, Man-with-no-hair lost his footing and fell to the ground. He had wrapped the other end of the rope around his hand before he had looped the mare; there was no danger of him losing the rope. There was however, a danger of being dragged to death if the mare did not tire soon. When the mare reached the top of the ridge, the stallion raced off toward the rest of the herd. The mare stopped and looked back toward the foal. Man-with-no-hair quickly got to his feet as soon as the mare stopped.

The sudden appearance of Man-with-no-hair behind her caused the mare to begin to run again. She did not panic as badly as she had before, nor did she follow the stallion; instead, she circled her foal. Man-with-no-hair was able to keep his feet under him until she reached top speed, at which time, he fell headlong onto the prairie floor.

The mare ran until she could run no more. Man-with-no-hair, though battered and bruised, was able to get to his feet. His buckskins were torn and dirty but he still held the rope.

Man-with-no-hair tried to lead the mare but she balked. He tried to walk toward her but she backed away. He suddenly realized that if he couldn't find a way to restrict the mare's movement, he was in a situation he could not possibly hope to win. Sooner or later he would have to eat and drink; in order to do so, he would have to release the rope. In the distance, he heard the foal whinny. The mare raised her head and nickered softly. Man-with-no-hair gave the mare slack and she moved toward the foal. When he moved to follow, she stopped. He gave her slack and she moved. A short time later, the mare nuzzled the foal. Man-with-no-hair tied the rope around a tree that was large enough to hold her and close enough to allow her contact with her foal. When the rope was securely tied, Man-with-no-hair stepped away and fell to the ground, exhausted.

Man-with-no-hair lay on the ground until his strength returned. Rested, he got to his feet and went in search of a game trail. When he located a path that was frequented by rabbits, he set a snare and returned to the horses.

He approached the mare slowly, not getting too close. He talked to her softly. She was uncomfortable with his presence but did not panic as before. He did not crowd her. He backed away and sat down. His entire body was sore from being dragged across the prairie and he did not feel like confronting the horse now. He sat there and talked to her and the foal until it was too dark to see them.

A half-moon later, Man-with-no-hair led the mare and foal into the village.

The people looked at him strangely as he passed by on his way to his tepee. He assumed it was because his clothing was torn and dirty and his arms and face were covered with scratches. When he tied the mare near his tepee, he noticed many people had followed him. The mare was becoming nervous and he had to ask the people to move back.

Bull Calf came shuffling through the crowd. "We were worried about you," he said, with obvious relief on his face.

"The mare would not lead until today," Man-with-no-hair said.

"Who helped you catch the horses?" Bull Calf asked, looking around at the mare and foal.

"No one," Man-with-no-hair answered.

"You did this by yourself?" Bull Calf asked, incredulously. A murmur went through the crowd.

Man-with-no-hair looked into the crowd; he was beginning to wonder if he had done something wrong. "I did this alone," he answered. "Have I done something to offend my new father?" he asked.

Bull Calf's jaw dropped open as he looked at Man-with-no-hair. The old man shook his head slightly, as if unsure of what to say. Finally, he managed to form the words he had been trying to get out of his mouth.

"You do not shame me. You honor me more each passing day. You have taken us by surprise. It usually takes several mounted men to catch just one horse. You have come home with two. We knew you were a great hunter, but we did not know you were this skillful. Will you teach your skill to our hunters?"

"I will teach those who want to learn," Man-with-no-hair told him.

"That is good, my son," said Bull Calf, before he nodded and turned away, to shuffling back to his own tepee.

5

Most of the crowd followed the old man, eventually going their own way. Several young women remained near Man-with-no-hair's tepee. They were gathered in a tight group pointing and giggling. Man-with-no-hair tried to ignore them, but after all of the lonely hours he had spent, it felt good to have someone pay attention to him.

He was more interested in Spotted Fawn, but she was not in the group of young women. He scanned the village and quickly spotted her. She was watching him from a distance. When she saw him looking at her, she ducked into her tepee.

That night, as Man-with-no-hair was about to doze off, he heard a scuffling sound outside the tepee. He thought he detected the sound of a giggle. He was about to get out of his robes and investigate when the back of the tepee lifted up. One of the young women from earlier in the day crawled into the tepee. Other hands pulled the wall of the tepee back into place and then disappeared. There was more giggling and the sound of receding footsteps. The young woman who had crawled into the tepee got to her feet and dusted off her clothing. Man-with-no-hair was about to speak when she stepped beside his sleeping robes, let her clothing fall to her feet and quickly got into the robes with him.

Once again, Man-with-no-hair tried to speak but she put a finger across his lips and shook her head. Slowly she took control of the situation and Man-with-no-hair soon found himself enjoying her company very much.

Man-with-no-hair had never been with a woman and he found the experience to be fascinating as well as very enjoyable.

Late in the night, Man-with-no-hair felt the young woman leave the robes. His eyes were filled with sleep and he was vaguely aware of the side of the tepee rolling up and down. Much to his surprise the young woman had left and another had taken her place.

It was long after dawn before Man-with-no-hair walked out of his tepee the next day. He had never slept so late and was somewhat angry with himself for doing so now.

He glanced around the village. No one seemed to be looking at him, but he felt eyes upon him, nonetheless. He did not know who his visitors had been but he was sure they were watching him. He did not see Spotted Fawn so he turned and went to his horses.

Man-with-no-hair sat down a short distance from his horses. He talked softly for some time before he tried to get closer. With ultimate patience and understanding, he was able to put his hand on the mare by late afternoon. After he touched her, he slowly backed away and left them alone for the rest of the day

That night, Man-with-no-hair was visited again. He was beginning to wonder if he would ever get another good night's sleep…He also wondered if he cared.

The next day, Man-with-no-hair was able to get close to the mare more quickly. Once again, after he touched her, he left her alone for the rest of the day. When he left her, he also left the village and hunted.

Soon after leaving the village, he saw a yearling antelope on a distant slope. He quickly began his stalk. A short time later, the antelope was slung over his shoulder and he was on his way back to the village.

People shook their heads in amazement when he passed by them. Man-with-no-hair dropped the antelope by the door of Spotted Fawn's tepee. She did not appear to be at home so he turned to leave.

"Why do you bring this to my door?" a soft voice asked from behind him.

Man-with-no-hair turned to see Spotted Fawn standing in the flap door of her tepee. "Once, Bull Calf asked me to do this. He then told me I no longer had to do this. He did not tell me not to do this," answered Man-with-no-hair.

"You did not answer my question," said Spotted Fawn.

"I wanted to do this, so I did it," Man-with-no-hair explained.

"I will not sneak into your tepee late at night," she said, raising her head slightly, defiantly.

"I did not ask you to do that. That is not what this is for," Man-with-no-hair responded, indicating the antelope carcass.

"You know I was spoken for once," she said, less defiantly.

"That does not concern me," Man-with-no-hair replied.

"You are young, but your prowess is well known in the village. I do not have a father. If you wish to see me, you would have to speak to my mother's brother."

Man-with-no-hair was taken by surprise at her sudden change in attitude. It took him a moment to compose himself. "Point him out to me and I will speak to him."

Spotted Fawn pointed to a middle-aged man sitting in front of a tepee, three tepees away from hers.

Man-with-no-hair looked toward the man. When he turned back, Spotted Fawn was gone.

Man-with-no-hair walked to the uncle's fire. "I would speak to you about your niece," he said in an even voice.

The man looked up from his meal, "Your hands are empty. Do not come to me with talk of my niece with empty hands."

Man-with-no-hair was taken aback by the uncle's abruptness. The uncle did not speak bitterly, just bluntly. "I will be back," said Man-with-no-hair as he turned and walked away.

Man-with-no-hair strode to his tepee. He did not know what the uncle required to allow him to talk to him about Spotted Fawn. He knew he could ask Bull Calf but some things were better done if you figured them out yourself. He did not want to offend the uncle by offering too little. All he had was two horses, but he was not prepared to offer them at this time. He could eventually use them to capture more horses.

He decided he would do what he did best: he would hunt. There were enough people in the village to share the meat with and he would give the hides to the uncle.

Hunt is what he did. He hunted elk, buffalo, deer, bear and antelope. He had hides staked out all around his tepee. The smoking racks of all the fires in the village were covered with meat supplied by Man-with-no-hair.

When he was not hunting or caring for the hides and meat, he was working with his horses. The foal was no longer afraid of him and the mare was becoming more receptive to his advances with the passing of each day.

By the time the hides were cured, the mare nickered for his attention as he approached. He still did not consider trying to ride her, but he could handle her without fear of being kicked or bitten.

At last, Man-with-no-hair gathered the hides and tied them into two packs. The packs were heavy and he carried them to the uncle's fire with great effort.

The uncle looked up as Man-with-no-hair dropped the packs, causing dust to fly up in all directions.

"I would speak with you about your niece," Man-with-no-hair stated flatly.

The uncle looked from Man-with-no-hair to the two large stacks of hides. He was not an evil man, but he was suddenly struck by the wealth he had just received and the wealth that could be made available to him by this Shawnee.

"I see you have not come with empty hands again, Shawnee," said the uncle. "But you seem to have forgotten how beautiful my niece is and how much she means to me. You have brought many hides but..."

Suddenly the uncle's wife burst from the tepee and began scolding him very seriously. The uncle tried to get the upper hand, when he regained his composure, but she grabbed a piece of firewood and began to wield it over his head.

With arms raised to fend off the impending blows, the uncle said, "You have brought much more than was necessary. You may speak to me about my niece." The wife dropped the wood into the fire and seated herself near enough to hear what was being said.

When the talking was done, Man-with-no-hair got up and left the fire. When he delivered two horses and two buffalo hides to the uncle, he would be able to claim Spotted Fawn. Man-with-no-hair would not necessarily have to use a horse to capture more horses but it would save a lot of wear and tear on his body if he did. He decided it was time to see if the mare would let him ride her.

He was thinking of what he had to do and did not see Spotted Fawn smiling happily from behind the flap that covered the door to her tepee.

Without wasting time, Man-with-no-hair went directly to his horses. He still wasn't prepared to let them run with the horses of the villagers; he was afraid they would return to the wild, so he kept them tied near his tepee.

He approached the mare slowly, as usual, talking as he drew nearer. She nickered softly as he put his hands on her neck. He untied her and led her a short distance away from the foal. He petted the mare and rubbed her with a handful of grass. As always, the mare was soothed by his touch and she was soon completely at ease. He dropped the grass and grasped the mare's mane, continuing to talk to her as he leaned toward her. He suddenly jumped up and put his weight on her back. The mare whinnied as she nervously sidestepped, unsure of what was happening to her. Man-with-no-hair dropped off her and stood beside her. Slowly, she began to settle down. When she was no longer nervous, he repeated the process. After two days of this procedure, he finally swung onto the mare's back and rode her around the perimeter of the village.

Man-with-no-hair had spent almost as much time with the foal, which was a filly, as he had with mare. It would be a long time before he was able to ride the filly but he wanted her to be ready when the time came.

He did not know if Spotted Fawn owned a horse so he decided he would give the filly to her. To him, it seemed a gesture of his feelings for her; they would soon be together anyway, so the mare and the filly would be reunited. Man-with-no-hair led the filly through the village. She probably would have followed him without the lead rope, but he didn't trust her around other people or their belongings; which were scattered around their tepees.

When Man-with-no-hair approached Spotted Fawn's tepee, he saw her slicing meat and placing it on a drying rack. She looked up as he drew near. When he looked into her face he began to get a strange feeling and knew he was in trouble.

"This horse is for you," Man-with-no-hair said evenly, though his palms were sweating and his stomach was in a turmoil.

"Why?" Spotted Fawn asked, with mock curiosity. "You are supposed to give two horses to my uncle, not to me."

"I will, but I want you to have the filly," he stated, simply.

"What will I do with a horse?" Spotted Fawn asked, pointedly.

"Ride her," he said as he began to feel the blood rising to his cheeks and beads of perspiration breaking out on his forehead. There were several young women seated nearby and they were paying closer attention to the discussion than the tasks they were performing. He had not expected this kind of response from Spotted Fawn.

"Where would I ride a horse?" asked Spotted Fawn, concealing her amusement at his discomfort.

"On the prairie. Wherever you want," answered Man-with-no-hair, with a trace of frustration in his voice. He asked himself why this woman couldn't just accept the horse and be done with it.

"That horse is too young to ride," Spotted Fawn pointed out.

"Someday she will be able to carry you," Man-with-no-hair stated. "Do you want her or not?" he asked, looking for a way to escape from the situation.

"What will I do with her until then?" Spotted Fawn asked, serious for the first time since the conversation began.

"You will learn her. She will learn you," Man-with-no-hair began to speak with the passion of a person much older than himself. "You will learn to trust her and she will trust you. She will be your friend when all others may turn away from you. She will take you where you wish to go. She will take you away from danger and help keep you safe. All she will ask in return is that you love her and care for her."

Man-with-no-hair had been looking at the filly as he spoke. Now he looked at Spotted Fawn and she saw the depth of his feelings written upon his face. She was immediately sorry for teasing him. She was immensely impressed by the way he spoke and the thoughts he had. "Yes, I want her," she said, thankfully. "I have never had a horse before. I do not know how to care for her. Will you show me?" she asked, coyly.

"I will teach you what I know," said Man-with-no-hair, as he began to feel his confidence returning.

Spotted Fawn got to her feet and approached the filly with an outstretched hand. The filly shied away from the unfamiliar hand. Spotted Fawn gave Man-with-no-hair a hurt look.

"You must move slowly," he informed her.

"I think she doesn't like me," said Spotted Fawn.

"It will take time for her to get to know you," Man-with-no-hair told her.

"How long?" Spotted Fawn asked, genuinely concerned.

"Not long," he answered hopefully. "Walk with me and the filly will see us together. As we walk you can speak to her and touch her. Soon she will know you are her friend."

Spotted Fawn was attracted to Man-with-no-hair, both by his physical appearance and an invisible aura that she attributed to his great prowess. He moved with a quiet grace she had never seen before. She had never been this close to him, and now, she found that she was the one with the jitters. She wanted to stand closer to him but she did not want to seem too anxious. She needed to get back to work, but she couldn't make herself leave his side. Her eyes glazed over and she did not respond when he asked her to walk with him. He was turning away, looking at her strangely. She dropped her knife and grasped the back of his shirt. She felt dizzy and almost fell. He grabbed her gently and held her until she was able to stand. She was afraid she looked too willing, but decided she didn't really care.

"I'm fine," she said, in response to his unspoken question.

"Will you walk with me?" he asked again.

"Yes," she answered, in a quiet voice.

Together, they walked through the village, the filly following behind them. When they reached the edge of the village, they circled around until they came to the place where the mare was tied. She nickered loudly at the sight of her filly. The filly answered and became excited at the sight of her mother.

She does not like to get too far from her mother," Man-with-no-hair said in a voice that was made happy by the actions of the horses.

He gave the filly's lead rope to Spotted Fawn and then went to the mare and untied her. He rejoined Spotted Fawn and together they led the horses onto the prairie.

"I hear you can sneak close enough to wild animals to touch them. Is that true?" Spotted Fawn asked, knowing he would deny it because it was an impossible feat to accomplish.

"It is true," Man-with-no-hair replied honestly.

"Can you sneak up on people too?" she asked with disbelief.

"I have," he answered evenly.

"Do you think you could sneak up on me?" she asked, hoping for a first hand demonstration of his abilities.

"Yes," he answered.

"Even if I were looking for you," she asked, incredulously.

"Yes," Man-with-no-hair replied, in a tone of boredom with the direction of the conversation.

"Do it," she challenged.

"Now?" he asked.

"Now. I must see this."

"Don't you believe me?" Man-with-no-hair asked her.

"Yes, I do. You do not have to do this. I'm sorry…"

He handed her the mare's lead rope and turned away from her. He turned back and instructed her not to release either one of the ropes. He turned and walked into the tall buffalo grass.

They were on the top of a gentle slope. Man-with-no-hair walked to the bottom of the slope and up the other side. When he went over the crest of the next hill, Spotted Fawn could no longer see him.

Where Spotted Fawn stood, the grass was only knee high and she was confident she would see him coming long before he could reach her.

After several minutes, Spotted Fawn began to get concerned. She should have been able to see him trying to sneak back over the hill, but could not. A gentle breeze began to blow across the top of the grass, making it impossible for her to distinguish the movement of Man-with-no-hair from that of the wind. With frustration, she tried to look in all directions at once.

She was so intent upon searching for Man-with-no-hair that she was unable to suppress the yelp of surprise that escaped her when he wrapped his hand around her ankle.

Chills ran up and down her spine; her eyes bulged and her heart hammered in her chest. How could this be? He had not had enough time to get back to her. Was he a man or a spirit?

Man-with-no-hair quickly got to his feet and took her in his arms. "I did not mean to frighten you," he said, genuinely concerned.

"How…?"

"I taught myself. It took many years."

"If Bull Calf had seen that, he would change your name to Smoke."

"I am not smoke. I am a man."

Spotted Fawn was overwhelmed with mixed feelings and troubled by the fact that she didn't know how to sort them out. She had been interested in Man-with-no-hair from the first time she had seen him. She didn't know why she became aloof when he was near. She had been thankful for the advances he had made toward her and had been angry with herself for the way she had responded to them. She had been pleased with his persistence but wondered why he continued when she was so short with him. She had heard the young women talking about slipping into his tepee and found it difficult to control her anger and hurt feelings. Now, when she thought she finally had her feelings and temperament in order, she found herself at her wit's end, trying to discern whether he was a man or a spirit.

Man-with-no-hair could see that Spotted Fawn was upset. He took the lead ropes from her hands, as she stared at him with a blank look on her face. He gently touched her shoulder and turned her toward the village. He was frustrated by her reaction. He had done as she had asked and now she was acting distant again.

They returned to the village without speaking. Man-with-no-hair left Spotted Fawn at her tepee and staked the mare and filly near his. He tried to work on some arrows but found he couldn't concentrate and soon put them aside. He went inside his tepee and crawled into his robes. He tossed and turned for a long time before he fell asleep.

Man-with-no-hair woke with a start. Someone was in the tepee with him. There was no sound from the village, he assumed it was late at night.

"Who is there?" he asked, as he drew his knife from its sheath.

"It is Dancing Flower," a voice answered softly from somewhere in the darkness.

"What do you want?" Man-with-no-hair asked gruffly, already knowing the answer.

"I want to be with you," she said in a purring voice.

"Go away! Leave me alone! I do not want you here," Man-with-no-hair said in a voice that left no room for doubt.

"You liked me before. Why…?"

"Go away, now!" Man-with-no-hair's voice boomed in the confines of the tepee.

He heard the girl gasp with shock and surprise and was immediately sorry he had raised his voice toward her. He was about to apologize but she bounded to her feet and rushed through the door of the tepee.

6

The light of dawn had yet to touch the eastern horizon when Man-with-no-hair left his tepee and walked to his horses. He released the filly and swung onto the mare's back. He spent the entire day riding on the prairie. The filly was exhausted when they returned to the village that night.

He staked the mare and walked to his tepee.

Spotted Fawn was sitting in front of his tepee. She got to her feet when she saw him coming.

"Once again, I have acted badly toward you," she apologized. "I have come to tell you that I want to be your wife, if you still want me."

"Why do you act the way you do?" Man-with-no-hair asked, truly puzzled.

"I don't know," she answered honestly. "I thought I knew what I wanted until you caught me on the prairie yesterday. I was shocked by your ability. I wondered if you were a man or a spirit. Now, I know you are a man and I want to be your woman."

"Are you sure?" he asked.

"When my man went away, my heart was sad. It was a long time before my heart was happy again. It is hard to be friendly when your heart is sad. It is hard to speak from your heart when your heart is sad. My heart is happy now. I have spoken from my heart."

"Tomorrow I will catch two horses and kill two buffalo for your uncle," Man-with-no-hair said, with no doubt about his ability to do as he had said.

Chapter Fourteen

Scott looked into the faces of the braves, hoping to determine their intent by the way they looked at him. He could detect no hostility.

One of the braves touched the flanks of his horse with his heels and approached slowly, cautiously. When the Indian was a few yards away, he stopped his horse and spoke to Scott.

Scott was unable to understand what the brave had said. He tried sign language and found there were enough similarities between the sign language he knew and that of these Indians to allow for a certain amount of communication.

The Indian asked Scott what he was doing on their hunting grounds.

Scott pointed to the cloud of smoke and signed that he had come to see how far away the fire was.

The Indian asked if he had also come to hunt.

Scott told him there was plenty of game where he lived and he did not need to come here to find food.

The Indian asked Scott where he hunted.

"One day to the east," Scott signed.

He asked where he lived and how many people were in his village.

Reluctantly, Scott told him where he lived and that his village consisted of two other people. One of the people was his woman and she was heavy with child, and he should be getting back to her.

The Indian asked Scott if the other people were like him.

"No," he signed, adding, "They are like you, but from far to the east."

The Indian asked, "Why you have hair all over his face?"

Scott signed, "My people come from another land, across the great water."

The Indian gave no sign he knew what Scott was talking about.

The brave signed that he would send a scout to Scott's village to make sure things were as Scott had said.

Scott informed the brave that he, or any of his people, were welcome in his village.

The brave nodded and turned away. The rest of the Indians followed him and they were soon out of sight.

Scott exhaled loudly. He had not felt threatened, but he had been uncomfortable because he had not known what to expect. He touched his heels to his horse and they began to make their way home. Scott did not push the horse as he had originally planned. He felt it would be better to move slowly and be a bit more cautious.

In the fast, fading light of day, Scott kicked the pony into a gallop. When there was no longer enough light to travel at that speed, he slowed the pony to a walk. He considered dismounting and spending the night where he was, which he ordinarily would have done. But, under the circumstances, he decided to give the pony its head and let it take him home; he wanted to get back to Dew-on-the-grass-in-the-moon-when-the-leaves-fall without further delay.

Scott rode into the finger just before dawn. He was sleepy but awake. The pony nickered as they approached the tepee. Scott rode to the corral and dismounted. He heard Dew-on-the-grass-in-the-moon-when-the-leaves-fall moving about as he rode past the tepee.

Scott put the horse into the corral and walked to the tepee. Dew-on-the-grass-in-the-moon-when-the-leaves-fall was stirring the coals of the outside fire when he arrived.

"You rode all night. The fire is near," she said without looking up, fear in her voice.

"No. The fire will not reach us," he said as he squatted beside her, poking a stick at the glowing embers.   Dew-on-the-grass-in-the-moon-when-the-leaves-fall looked at him and he felt her dark eyes piercing into him. She had detected something in his voice that told her everything was not right. In many ways, she was as perceptive as Man-with-no-hair.

She looked into the softly glowing coals and asked, "What is it that troubles you so?" in a dusky voice that he barely recognized.

He knew she feared the worst. She was not a pessimist but in her present condition, she had to view any unknown as a threat.

Scott explained what had happened and that they should expect a visit from one of the Indians at any time.

A gush of air escaped from Dew-on-the-grass-in-the-moon-when-the-leaves-fall – a sigh of relief. She had not known what to expect, but obviously, the news was not as bad as she has thought it might have been.

Not knowing what to expect from other people made Dew-on-the-grass-in-the-moon-when-the-leaves-fall defensive. She would not openly display hostility unless she were threatened, but she decided if someone was going to be intimidated, it would not be Scott and herself.

Dew-on-the-grass-in-the-moon-when-the-leaves-fall prepared a meal in the pre-dawn light, which was her favorite time of day. "We should make the camp ready for a visitor," she said. "When he rides in, he will know that you and Man-with-no-hair are great hunters with much skill and prowess. He will know that you are powerful and not to be taken lightly."

"How will we do that?" Scott asked, amazed at her ability to grasp a situation and find a way to turn it to their favor.

"What do you fear more than anything?" she asked, smiling. She was not laughing at Scott's fear, she was happy with the plan that was formulating in her mind.

Scott thought for a moment and then said, "Why, the great bears, but…"

"Yes, the bears. Do you think you are alone in your fear of those giants? I do not think so. How many bear skins do we have?"

"We have two," Scott answered, with a smile that told her he saw where she was going.

"When the sun rises, we will move the bear skins outside. We will make it look like we are working on them."

Scott was impressed with the idea and readily agreed.

Shortly after sunrise, they had the bear skins arranged where they wanted them. Scott released the horses and herded them toward the meadow. Then they waited.

There was not a vantage point on their side of the valley from which they could watch for an approaching rider from the west. Scott would not consider crossing the valley and ascending the other slope to keep a look out. He did not want to leave Dew-on-the-grass-in-the-moon-when-the-leaves-fall alone for that long.

They waited all day but no one came to their camp. Dew-on-the-grass-in-the-moon-when-the-leaves-fall, though apprehensive, waited patiently. Scott, on the other hand, acted as if he were about to lose his mind. He did not wait well. He was bored and nervous. He could not concentrate on anything he tried to do. Dew-on-the-grass-in-the-moon-when-the-leaves-fall hoped the stranger showed up soon, for Scott's sake.

That night they retired earlier than usual. Scott had not slept the night before and was very tired. Dew-on-the-grass-in-the-moon-when-the-leaves-fall had started having sharp pains in the afternoon. Dealing with the pains and keeping them from Scott had worn her out, as well.

Dew-on-the-grass-in-the-moon-when-the-leaves-fall fought the pains throughout the night. She thought she had kept them from Scott but when she opened her eyes, she saw him sitting cross-legged across the tepee, watching her.

"What is happening?" he asked, concerned.

"I do not know," she answered. "It is the baby but I do not know what it wants."

"I do not like to see you in pain," he told her.

"The pain is not so bad," she lied. "How long before sunup?" she asked, trying to change the subject.

"I don't know." Scott answered, "I haven't been outside yet."

Overwhelmed by a sudden urge to relieve himself, Scott got to his feet and stepped out of the tepee. Quietly, he hurried into the forest. On his way back to the tepee, he heard the sound of a horse walking toward the camp. He took cover behind a tree and watched as a stranger rode into the finger.

2

The light of dawn was just beginning to color the eastern horizon, yet there was not enough light for the brave to recognize the bear skins for what they were. He could however, determine the shape of the tepee and knew he was in the right place.

Scott watched from concealment as the brave dismounted and walked to the fire. He knew Dew-on-the-grass-in-the-moon-when-the-leaves-fall would have heard the approaching horse and would be expecting some kind of response from him soon.

The brave seated himself near the fire and remained motionless. It suddenly occurred to Scott that the brave was attempting to display his own form of intimidation, like Scott and Dew-on-the-grass-in-the-moon-when-the-leaves-fall had done by displaying the bear skins. This brave hoped to use the element of surprise to get the upper hand before their initial conversation.

As the day grew lighter, the brave became aware of the two bear skins, one on either side of the door to the tepee. He slowly got to his feet and moved closer to the skins. He was obviously in awe of what he saw.

Scott made his move. Though he was nowhere near as proficient as Man-with-no-hair, he had learned from a master and he *was skillful*. When the brave turned to examine the other skin, Scott was standing there, too.

"AUGH!" The shocked brave issued as he stepped backwards. The brave had obviously not been with the group of warriors Scott had encountered and now he got a double shock – a man with hair on his face and a man who appeared from nowhere.

As the brave stepped back, he tripped over a piece of wood and fell heavily to his back.

From inside the tepee, the occurrences outside sounded like a fight breaking out. Dew-on-the-grass-in-the-moon-when-the-leaves-fall burst out of the tepee with a knife in either hand.

The brave rolled over and came to his feet, open hands raised in front of his face. It was immediately obvious he had not come to fight. Scott moved to Dew-on-the-grass-in-the-moon-when-the-leaves-fall's side and she looked to him for insight on how to proceed. When he was standing beside her, he gently placed his hand on her right arm and pushed down until the knife was at her side.

When the brave realized he was not going to be attacked, relief washed over his face.

Scott motioned for him to be seated by the fire. Slowly, the brave came forward and seated himself where he had been earlier.

Scott helped Dew-on-the-grass-in-the-moon-when-the-leaves-fall sit down and then he sat beside her. Scott pointed to a piece of meat that was spitted over the fire pit. The brave nodded his head, leaned forward and sliced off a thin piece of meat.

Scott spoke a few words in Powhaten. The brave did not understand the words. Scott tried a few words in Shawnee, the results were the same. They had not been in the village at the edge of the prairie long enough to learn that language and as yet, Man-with-no-hair had not taught it to them. Scott used sign language and the brave responded.

The brave asked where the bear skins had come from. Scott explained that his friend had killed one and he had killed the other. The brave looked into the forest that surrounded the camp. Scott signed that his friend had gone away.

When the brave was satisfied that there was no danger, he got to his feet and motioned that he would be right back.

Scott and Dew-on-the-grass-in-the-moon-when-the-leaves-fall watched curiously as the brave walked out of the finger. A short time later they saw him returning, leading a woman and a boy toward the camp.

Scott immediately realized that Dew-on-the-grass-in-the-moon-when-the-leaves-fall would have help when the baby came. He was more grateful than he could say.

The brave reseated himself by the fire pit. He signed that his name was Three-legged Wolf. The woman's name was Meadow Flower and the boy was Hawk-that-soars.

Scott signed greetings to them but they remained motionless, standing behind Three-legged Wolf.

Three-legged Wolf felt he had made a less than favorable impression on Scott and Dew-on-the-grass-in-the-moon-when-the-leaves-fall. He felt that the only way to change their impression of him was to let them know what a great hunter and warrior he was.

The truth of the matter was, Three-legged Wolf had less than adequate skills. The fault was not his however, for his father had taken a bad fall, which left him crippled. The father had not been able to teach Three-legged Wolf all he needed to know. Sadly, no one else cared to share the responsibility, resulting in an improperly trained young man. The reason Three-legged Wolf had been sent to investigate the hairy-faced man was this: if he failed to return, he would not be missed.

"Three-legged Wolf hunts the great bear too," he signed. He made the words sound like a challenge rather than a statement.

Meadow Flower looked at him sharply but quickly resumed her former position.

Scott had the uneasy feeling that it was very fortunate for Meadow Flower that Three-legged Wolf had not seen her response to his statement. Her response convinced Scott to watch this man very closely.

When Scott did not respond to his statement, Three-legged Wolf thought it was due to fear. Thinking he had the upper hand, he took the challenge one step farther. "You and me, we go hunt the great bear," he signed.

Scott looked at Dew-on-the-grass-in-the-moon-when-the-leaves-fall. He was astonished that someone would hunt the bear if they didn't have to. Dew-on-the-grass-in-the-moon-when-the-leaves-fall's face was darkened and Scott felt that a rage was building in her, the like of which he had never seen.

"I do not hunt the bear unless they threaten us. If they come to this valley, I will kill them. If they stay away, they are safe from me."

"Bold words," signed Three-legged Wolf.

"True words," signed Scott, indicating the two bear skins.

Three-legged Wolf was beginning to realize perhaps this man was not frightened and maybe it would be a good idea for him to change the subject.

"I was sent to see where you hunt. My woman will stay with your woman.

My son will watch the horses while we are away."

Scott was reluctant to accept his proposal but he was so thankful to have someone nearby for Dew-on-the-grass-in-the-moon-when-the-leaves-fall sake, he would have agreed to almost anything.

Scott noticed a travois attached to Meadow Flower's horse. He was immediately aware of its purpose. "You can camp where ever you choose," Scott signed.

Three-legged Wolf turned to Meadow Flower and spoke to her for several seconds. When he finished, she took the boy and they led the horses near the lean-to and began to set up their tepee.

The fact that Three-legged Wolf was not going to help them erect the tepee was not lost on Scott and Dew-on-the-grass-in-the-moon-when-the-leaves-fall.

Three-legged Wolf sliced off another piece of meat. As he ate, he looked at Dew-on-the-grass-in-the-moon-when-the-leaves-fall in a manner that made her very uncomfortable. When she could stand it no longer, she got to her feet and went to assist Meadow Flower and Hawk-that-soars.

After Dew-on-the-grass-in-the-moon-when-the-leaves-fall had moved away, Three-legged Wolf signed, "Good woman," and gave Scott a look that he did not appreciate.

Scott was more convinced than ever that he was going to keep a close eye on this new *friend*.

When Three-legged Wolf had eaten his fill, he suggested that Scott show him where he hunted.

Becoming more annoyed by the minute and resentful of his presence, Scott had to bite his tongue to keep from lashing out at Three-legged Wolf for his inconsiderate behavior. However, he knew he would have to get along with him in order to be allowed to remain in the valley.

Scott got up from the fire pit and went to the corral. Three-legged Wolf followed him and was obviously impressed when he saw the corral and its contents.

"You have many horses," he signed. But Scott was busy trying to catch the spotted horse and did not respond.

When he had a rope around his horse's neck, he herded the rest of the horses out of the corral. Three-legged Wolf watched the horses run by with a greedy look on his face.

Scott saw the look and knew he should do something to change the way Three-legged Wolf was thinking. Scott didn't like to lie; generally, there was no reason to do so. He decided now was a good time to lie and it would be a good one.

As he stepped through the corral gate, Scott turned to Three-legged Wolf and signed, "We have many horses because we take care of them. What is ours is ours. Someone took two horses from us before we lived here. Man-with-no-hair and I hunted him down. We staked him on an anthill. He has not come back to take more horses from us."

Three-legged Wolf swallowed hard and Scott noticed his apparent discomfort. "That would stop most people from taking what is not theirs," he signed.

Scott led the horse to the tepee Meadow Flower and Dew-on-the-grass-in-the-moon-when-the-leaves-fall were erecting. Hawk-that-soars had followed the horses out of the finger and into the meadow.

Dew-on-the-grass-in-the-moon-when-the-leaves-fall was equally upset about the recent turn of events. However, she was glad for the company of Meadow Flower, and she knew her presence would make Scott feel better too. Scott's displeasure was obvious as he drew near.

Dew-on-the-grass-in-the-moon-when-the-leaves-fall started to get to her feet but Scott ran to her and told her to stay down. "I don't know when we'll be back," he said.

"I know. Ride with care." Scott nodded his head and started to turn away. "When he sees what he has been sent to see, he will go away."

Scott nodded again and then swung onto the horse's back. He turned away and saw Three-legged Wolf mounting his own horse. Together, they rode out of the finger. Scott turned east and gave the pony enough rein to allow it to travel at a fast walk. He wanted to cover some ground but he didn't want to go so fast it would be difficult to converse with Three-legged Wolf.

As they rode, Three-legged Wolf seemed to be impressed by the amount of game signs near the camp. Scott tried to explain that they didn't hunt nearby except out of necessity. He either didn't understand or couldn't fathom the concept.

When they reached the fork in the valley, they stopped and Scott told Three-legged Wolf about what the bear had done to the young Indian boy. He also told him about the lay of the land and the amount of game signs he and Man-with-no-hair had seen there.

Three-legged Wolf asked about the eastern fork and Scott told him they had not had an opportunity to explore that area as of yet.

"Let's go there now," Three-legged Wolf signed.

"If you wanted to explore, you should have said so earlier," Scott signed. "I don't want to be away from Dew-on-the-grass-in-the-moon-when-the-leaves-fall too long."

"She's just a woman."

"She's my woman, and I will care for her," Scott signed angrily.

Three-legged Wolf shrugged his shoulders and followed Scott back to the camp. As they turned into the finger, Three-legged Wolf signed, "If we leave earlier tomorrow we will have time to go into the eastern fork of the valley."

Scott was anxious to explore the unseen land but his first priority was to Dew-on-the-grass-in-the-moon-when-the-leaves-fall. He would not leave if she needed him nearby.

When they rode into the camp, Dew-on-the-grass-in-the-moon-when-the-leaves-fall and Meadow Flower were working together near the fire pit of Three-legged Wolf's tepee. Both women were smiling and seemed to be getting along very well. Scott was happy for Dew-on-the-grass-in-the-moon-when-the-leaves-fall; it had been a long time since she had had female companionship.

Dew-on-the-grass-in-the-moon-when-the-leaves-fall was kneeling by the fire. When she saw Scott, she got to her feet, with great effort.

Scott jumped from the horse's back and ran to her. The pain and discomfort were written on her face, though she continued to smile.

"Meadow Flower thinks the baby will come soon," she said excitedly.

Scott wrapped his arm around her as they walked toward their own tepee. When they were half way there, she doubled over in pain. Scott was about to shout for Meadow Flower to come and help but the pain passed as quickly as it had come and Dew-on-the-grass-in-the-moon-when-the-leaves-fall stopped him from saying anything.

"Will she help you when the time is here?" Scott asked Dew-on-the-grass-in-the-moon-when-the-leaves-fall.

"There is little she can do. If I need help, she will be here."

"Three-legged Wolf wants to go out again tomorrow. I have shown him where we hunt but he is not satisfied with what he has seen. He wants something else. I don't know..."

"Beware of that one," Dew-on-the-grass-in-the-moon-when-the-leaves-fall whispered quietly, though they were too far from their visitor's tepee to be overheard.

"Oh, I assure you, I will watch him closely."

"As long as Meadow Flower is here, you do not have to be here to look after me."

"I don't mind looking after you," Scott said, as they reached the tepee and he helped her to sit down.

Dew-on-the-grass-in-the-moon-when-the-leaves-fall gave him an affectionate look that he had come to love. "I want you to go with him tomorrow," she said, through poorly masked pain.

"I will go with him, but he wants to go to the eastern fork of the valley. We have not been there. I do not know what we will find. I do not know that we would be able to get back before nightfall."

"I think you should be here before dark tomorrow. I think you should get back," she groaned, her eyes pleaded more than her words ever would.

"I will return before dark," he promised.

3

Just before dawn, Scott and Three-legged Wolf rode out of the finger, turned east and rode hard for the forks of the valley.

Scott had not wanted to leave; Dew-on-the-grass-in-the-moon-when-the-leaves-fall had tossed and turned all night. She was frightened and in pain, but she insisted, very firmly, that he go with Three-legged Wolf.

When they reached the forks of the valley, Scott insisted they slow their pace. This was new country to him and he was too cautious to ride into it recklessly.

As mid-day approached, Scott found himself fascinated with the change in the lay of the land. The farther east they went, the rougher the ground became; not steeper, but broken up with low plateaus and shallow, but steep ravines. The timber had been replaced by sagebrush and juniper. One could see for great distances in all directions but there were also thousands of hiding places all around them.

They stopped on every ridge or high place they crossed and looked about very carefully. The lay of the land had affected Three-legged Wolf also and, much to Scott's relief, he too finally seemed concerned about being cautious.

The appearance of the land had drawn them farther than Scott had intended to go. If they turned back now, they wouldn't have to push the horses too hard to reach camp by nightfall.

"It's late. We'll turn back now," Scott signed.

"We have many hours of daylight left," Three-legged Wolf signed back.

"It will be dark by the time we get back," Scott motioned, as he turned his horse around and touched his heels to its flanks.

Scott did not wish to argue with Three-legged Wolf. He felt the best way to avoid an argument was to start back and let his companion do as he wished. Scott kicked the spotted pony into a gentle gallop that would enable him to cover many miles without exhausting the horse. He felt Three-legged Wolf would follow, which he did.

When Scott had covered a considerable distance, he slowed the horse to a walk, allowing it to blow. Three-legged Wolf pulled alongside Scott and slowed his horse too. When they had allowed the horses to walk for about a mile, Three-legged Wolf violently kicked his horse and held on tightly as it burst into a full gallop. Scott thought he was being challenged but he already knew how fast his pony was and felt no compunction to enter into a race this far from camp. The spotted pony wanted to run but Scott held him to the same pace they had been traveling. Three-legged Wolf was soon out of sight.

Scott rode by the fork of the southern valley before he realized where he was. He felt more at ease now, than he had since they had left familiar territory that morning. It pleased him to know he would have an hour of daylight left when he rode into camp.

Scott topped out on a small rise and saw Three-legged Wolf ahead of him. Three-legged Wolf was on the ground, beside his horse. He had the reins in his hands but the horse was raring up; Three-legged Wolf seemed to be limping. He was unable to remount the horse.

Scott tore his eyes away from Three-legged Wolf and scanned the valley. He saw nothing. He scanned again, more slowly. Nothing. He let the horse walk forward, slowly. The horse had taken but a few steps when the wind changed and he felt a shudder run through the animal. He knew then what was wrong. He looked into the wind...nothing. He looked toward Three-legged Wolf...Nothing. He looked into the wind and detected movement out of the corner of his eye.

A giant bear was loping over a ridge, heading directly toward Three-legged Wolf.

Three-legged Wolf's horse sensed the bear and screamed in panic but Scott barely heard it, for he had kicked the spotted pony into a full gallop, on a course to intercept the bear.

The bear had no idea Three-legged Wolf had ridden within two hundred yards of him; the wind had been wrong. When he loped over the ridge, he had not been in pursuit. But, when he heard the shouts of the man and the screams of the frightened horse, he stopped and stood on his hind legs to see what all the commotion was about. When he stood up, the man saw him and let go of the horse. The horse was too fast for him to catch anyway. The man seemed unsure of what to do. He knew he could catch the man; he had done it before. He was about to drop onto all fours and go eat the man when he became aware of the sound of another running horse. There was a blur as the horse raced by, and suddenly there was something stuck in his throat, it wasn't very big but it hurt. The man on the ground was running away; there was another man on the other horse. The other man had made his throat hurt and he was coming back. Maybe...catch the horse...kill the man...

Scott raced the spotted horse directly at the standing bear. As he drew near, the bear dropped to all four and charged toward him. Scott gave the horse its head and readied his next arrow. The horse should have turned away from the bear the instant he was free of guidance but it maintained a course that would bring Scott close enough for a shot. As the horse and bear came closer together, the horse took a course that would make it next to impossible for the bear to catch them.

Scott released his second arrow, hitting the charging bear between the shoulder blades. The bear fell, rolled over and came to its feet, roaring ferociously.

Scott turned the horse and pulled him to a stop. The horse was trembling with nervous anticipation; it was more lathered now, than from all the running it had done previously.

The bear rose up onto its hind legs. Scott walked the horse, slowly, toward the bear. Fifty yards away, the bear roared again. The horse was trembling so badly it was a wonder it could walk. Forty yards, the bear shook its massive head and swatted at the air with its huge paws. Scott nocked an arrow. Thirty yards, Scott drew back on the bow and released the arrow just as the bear began to drop onto all fours. The arrow had been aimed at the bear's throat; as it lowered itself down, the arrow struck it in the eye.

The bear fell to the ground writhing in pain, trying to dislodge the arrow with its large, seemingly clumsy paws.

Incredulously, Scott felt sympathy for the wounded bear. Despite his feelings, he knew the bear was a threat to him and his family. The best way to end the bear's suffering was to kill it; and do so quickly.

Scott circled and came at the bear from its blind side. The bear was so intent upon the arrow in its eye, Scott was able to get within twenty yards.

His next shot penetrated deeply into the bear's rib cage, puncturing a lung and grazing the heart. The bear spun toward Scott with amazing speed and dexterity. Thankfully, the spotted pony was equally quick and it dodged safely away from the attacking bear.

The bear did not give chase, instead, it returned to the task of trying to remove the arrows from its body. Scott watched the bear until he was certain its attention was focused on the arrows and not him. Slowly, he began to approach the bear again. When he was close enough, he found once again that the writhing, twisting body made a poor target. He drew back on the bow and waited. When the bear stopped moving for a moment, Scott released the arrow. The shot was good: it entered the bear's neck and stopped abruptly. Scott thought, hoped, he had hit the spinal column.

Once again, the bear whirled in the direction the pain had come from. When he was unable to catch his tormenter, he shook his head with rage. When he shook his head, the movement finished the work the arrow had begun. The bear's neck snapped and he fell to the ground in a lifeless heap.

Scott turned the horse in time to see the bear fall. He watched for several minutes. When the bear did not move, he rode closer to it. From horseback, he looked down on the fallen brute. He felt no particular pride or satisfaction in his accomplishment. He was glad that a threat had been removed before anyone had been injured or killed. The meat of the bear was not that good; they did provide a very good hide, but this was a poor time of year to be gathering hides.

Scott turned away from the bear and continued to ride slowly toward the camp. He would return tomorrow and skin the bear; he would barely get back to camp before dark as it was.

As he rode, Scott saw no sign of Three-legged Wolf or his horse. When he reached the meadow outside the hidden finger, he was dismayed to see the horses still in the meadow; Hawk-that-soars should have rounded them up by now. When he turned into the finger, the camp was deserted. No one came running out to welcome him home.

Chapter Fifteen

Spotted Fawn's village had no particular ceremony to announce the fact that two people had been wed. In the case of Man-with-no-hair and Spotted Fawn, however, the entire village turned out and danced throughout the night.

Spotted Fawn's father had died of natural causes several years earlier. Her mother was alive and well. Man-with-no-hair promised her she would never have to worry about food or shelter as long as she lived. She was aware of Man-with-no-hair's reputation as a hunter and gladly welcomed him as her daughter's husband.

Several summers passed before a new life began to grow within Spotted Fawn. They had known much happiness despite the concern they shared at Spotted Fawn's inability to conceive. Man-with-no-hair was ecstatic when he learned Spotted Fawn was with child.

In the time since he had wed, Man-with-no-hair's mare had mated twice and had thrown a colt and another filly. The filly he had given to Spotted Fawn was heavy with her first foal.

As the changing moons passed, Man-with-no-hair proudly watched Spotted Fawn's stomach grow larger. Everything was normal until the last moon of her pregnancy. Spotted Fawn began to experience sharp, stabbing pains.

Spotted Fawn was a strong woman with an iron will. Man-with-no-hair could barely comprehend the amount of pain required to make tears well up and run down her cheeks. He knew she considered the tears a sign of weakness. To protect her from embarrassment, he pretended not to see them.

One night Spotted Fawn awoke, issuing ear-piercing screams of pain. Man-with-no-hair sprang to his feet and ran to get Spotted Fawn's mother. He had gone but a short distance when he saw her hurrying toward the tepee. She, too, had heard the screams.

Spotted Fawn's mother sent Man-with-no-hair to a tepee on the outskirts of the village. His mind was nearing a state of panic but he did as she asked. The tepee was shared by three old squaws. Man-with-no-hair had provided them with much meat in the past. The old squaws grumbled at being awakened in the middle of the night; and though it took them only a few moments to respond to Man-with-no-hair's plea for help, it seemed to him it took far too long. They hustled to Man-with-no-hair's tepee with him prodding them all the way. He tried to enter the tepee behind the squaws but he was rudely pushed back and told to stay outside.

The sounds of pain that were emitted from within the tepee were almost more than Man-with-no-hair could bear. He stalked back and forth in front of the tepee, walking faster, stepping harder, when he heard a cry of pain. He kicked at the dirt and threw his arms into the air. He had never felt so powerless in all his life. He shouldered the responsibility for the pain Spotted Fawn was enduring and prayed to any god who would listen to stop her suffering.

In the early morning twilight, just a few moments before the sun broke over the horizon and spread its face on a new day, Man-with-no-hair sat awaiting the quiet cry of his child. The cry he heard instead, made his heart sink. Spotted Fawn's mother began to wail the death song.

Unwilling to believe, Man-with-no-hair rushed to the tepee. He tore the hide flap away and stepped inside. The sight he witnessed caused a revulsion that stayed with him for many years. Spotted Fawn was still swollen with a child that was improperly turned and unable to exit her body. Both were dead.

Man-with-no-hair stepped out of the tepee and fell to his knees. He raised his arms to the heavens and emitted a piercing wail of agony that sent a shiver of pain through the heart of every member of the village. He never looked upon the face of Spotted Fawn again.

Man-with-no-hair got to his feet and walked to his horses. He approached the filly he had given to Spotted Fawn. She nickered as he drew near. Silently, he withdrew his knife and quickly cut the filly's throat. He dropped the knife to the ground, turned away from the dying horse and walked out of the village. He had no concept of time. He walked until exhaustion overtook him and he fell face down upon the plains. When he awoke, his mind was still numb with pain and anguish. He knew only that he had been walking. He got to his feet and continued to walk, impervious to his surroundings. He remembered nothing he saw, he had no thoughts, he simply walked...and walked.

One moon after the death of Spotted Fawn and her child, a gaunt figure staggered into the village. His clothing was dirty and torn. His cheeks were sunken and sallow. Had it not been for his clothing, many of the villagers may not have recognized Man-with-no-hair for who he was.

He had not eaten the entire time he had been gone from the village. As he was nursed back to health by Spotted Fawn's mother, he was haunted by one question: Why had Spotted Fawn died and he had not?

2

Man-with-no-hair remained bitter for many years. With the exception of an occasional loss of temper, the villagers were unaware of the depth of his bitterness.

He took little pleasure from hunting, though he never failed to provide for Spotted Fawn's mother as he had promised. He refused to consider taking another mate. The young women, tired of being shunned, stopped coming to his tepee in the night. He had no ambitions, no desires, no reason to exist until the strange, hairy-faced man and the Shawnee-speaking woman were found on the plains.

The tongue of the Shawnee revived his spirits. It was because of their treatment of him that he had become the man he was. When he heard the young woman speak his native language, it renewed the spark of his existence and drew him from the depths of the depression in which he had been residing. He felt he owed her more than he could ever repay.

Spotted Fawn's mother had died the winter before Scott and Dew-on-the-grass-in-the-moon-when-the-leaves-fall arrived in the village. Bull Calf was old and probably would not see another summer. There would soon be nothing holding Man-with-no-hair in the village. When Scott and Dew-on-the-grass-in-the-moon-when-the-leaves-fall decided to leave, he was anxious to go with them.

Chapter Sixteen

Scott slid off of his horse and walked to his tepee. He opened the flap: Dew-on-the-grass-in-the-moon-when-the-leaves-fall was not there. He looked toward Three-legged Wolf's camp and saw that no one was there either.

He was beginning to feel equal amounts of fear and anger.

He ran to his horse and swung onto its back. As soon as he was mounted, he saw Dew-on-the-grass-in-the-moon-when-the-leaves-fall step out of the forest. Scott jumped off the horse and raced to her. In his haste, and in the gathering gloom, he was upon her before he realized she was carrying a small bundle. He nearly knocked the bundle from her arms in his attempt pull her close to him.

Dew-on-the-grass-in-the-moon-when-the-leaves-fall stepped away in time to prevent the bundle from falling to the ground. "Be careful," she chided him softly. "It is your son you are trying to knock out of my arms."

Scott had been so glad to see her, he hadn't noticed how pale she was or how tired she looked. His senses were dulled with shock as her words were absorbed by his brain. He had a son…Dew-on-the-grass-in-the-moon-when-the-leaves-fall was safe…She had done it…

"Are you…?"

"I am well. I need rest. I need your help," she said.

Scott bent and swept her off her feet and into his arms. He carried mother and son to the tepee. He thought he heard a sound from the other camp but he gave them no notice. He had a wife and child to care for.

"Where are Meadow Flower and Hawk-that-soars?" Scott asked, as he gently lowered Dew-on-the-grass-in-the-moon-when-the-leaves-fall to the buffalo robes.

"I do not know. They were not here when I went into the forest."

"You did this by yourself?" Scott asked in amazement, as he parted the furs and looked upon the face of his son.

"It was nothing," Dew-on-the-grass-in-the-moon-when-the-leaves-fall said in a tired voice. "Where is Three-legged Wolf?" she asked, remembering that he had not been with Scott.

"I don't know. His horse threw him when he rode by the bear. The horse ran away…so did Three-legged Wolf…I guess." Scott was so engrossed in the baby he was barely aware that he had been speaking.

"What bear?" Dew-on-the-grass-in-the-moon-when-the-leaves-fall almost shouted. "Did he talk you into going after one of the giant bears?"

"What…What? No! There was a bear between here and the forks. It is dead. It will not be a threat to us."

"Did you kill the bear?" she asked in a quiet, even voice. She stared at him with her large dark eyes; eyes that were glistening with pride…and fear.

"Yes, I killed it. I had to. It was too close to here. It would have killed Three-legged Wolf if I hadn't."

"We can talk later," she said softly. "I need to rest." She lay on the furs, the child at her breast. "He has your eyes. His eyes are blue; like the sky," she mumbled as she drifted off to sleep.

Scott sat beside her and watched the baby nurse as Dew-on-the-grass-in-the-moon-when-the-leaves-fall went to sleep. His heart was bursting with pride and happiness. He wished Man-with-no-hair were here to share this moment with them.

2

The next morning Scott prepared a meal for Dew-on-the-grass-in-the-moon-when-the-leaves-fall. He was a bit out of practice but the meal was edible nonetheless. As he worked around the outside fire, he saw Three-legged Wolf step out of his tepee and walk toward him. He walked with a slight limp.

"Where did you go?" Scott signed, after the Indian had seated himself by the small fire.

"I went after my horse," Three-legged Wolf signed defensively. "By the time I caught him I could not find you. Today we can go back and find that bear. We will kill him."

"The bear is dead," signed Scott. "If you had gone back to look for me, you would know the bear was dead," Scott signed before he realized what he was implying.

Three-legged Wolf's demeanor went from defensive to anger in a heartbeat. He jumped to his feet and signed violently, "I did go back. You were not there."

Scott shrugged his shoulders and turned to take the food into the tepee.

Three-legged Wolf was enraged when Scott turned away from him. A few seconds later, Scott stepped out of the tepee. "When you are ready, we will go skin the bear," signed Scott.

Three-legged Wolf's jaw dropped open at Scott's suggestion. "I do not skin," he signed. "That is work for women and children."

"In this camp we share the work," signed Scott.

"I see you do woman's work," Three-legged Wolf signed, indicating the meal he had prepared for Dew-on-the-grass-in-the-moon-when-the-leaves-fall. "Do you let your woman hunt," he added, a sneer beginning to appear on his face.

Scott dropped his bowl of food and stepped across the fire pit. For the first time in a long, long time he was angry...Angry enough to strike another person, something he had never done in his life.

Scott was broad in the shoulders and deep in the chest. His physical strength was obvious and could be very intimidating. He easily outweighed Three-legged Wolf by forty pounds.

Three-legged Wolf involuntarily took three steps backward. Scott's fists were clenching and unclenching as he stepped across the fire.

"My woman is with child. I would not send her to do work that I could do. That makes no sense to me. You are lazy and do not care about your woman or you would not treat her the way you do. You do not tell the truth. You say words to make you sound better than you are. You are not the kind of man I wish to spend time with. I want you to pack up and go away. I have shown you what you came to see. There is nothing else for you here. I will not speak to you again." With that said, Scott turned away and saw Dew-on-the-grass-in-the-moon-when-the-leaves-fall standing outside the tepee. She smiled and ducked into the tepee; Scott followed.

Three-legged Wolf had made people angry before, though it usually took a little longer than this had. He turned away from the fire pit and walked to his own tepee. He was somewhat thankful his woman and son had not seen the confrontation between himself and the hairy-faced man, but it really didn't matter that much. When he got to his tepee, he sat down and leaned against a tree and shouted at Meadow Flower to get out of the tepee and take it down. It was time for them to return to their own village.

From within his tepee Scott heard Three-legged Wolf barking instructions to Meadow Flower and Hawk-that-soars. He was afraid of what he might do if he went outside, so he sat in the tepee with Dew-on-the-grass-in-the-moon-when-the-leaves-fall and the baby until they were gone.

"I am sad that Meadow Flower is going away too," Scott said. "It looked like you two were getting along well."

"We were. I will be sad when she is gone. I will be happy when Three-legged Wolf is gone," she added flatly. "You should name your son soon," she said, intentionally changing the subject.

"*I* should name him?" Scott asked.

"It is a father's right to name his child," she informed.

"What do you think *we* should name him?" Scott asked.

"It is not for me to say," she said, with a bright smile. "I will not speak of it again. This is for you to do alone."

Scott was suddenly very nervous. He had never thought about the seriousness of naming someone. That person would carry their given name for the rest of their life. This was serious indeed.

"How long do I have?" he asked.

Dew-on-the-grass-in-the-moon-when-the-leaves-fall laughed openly, filling the tepee with a melodic ring. "There is no time. But you should do it soon so he will know who he is."

"I must go skin the bear. I will have a name for him when I return."

Dew-on-the-grass-in-the-moon-when-the-leaves-fall raised her eyebrows as if surprised by his statement. What he had said sounded like a statement a Shawnee would have made. His words pleased her very much. Scott knelt beside her and kissed her softly on the forehead. He had kissed her like that many times before, not an Indian way of showing affection, but something she had grown to like very much. She enjoyed his closeness and found herself craving his next show of affection.

After Scott kissed her on the forehead and drew away, he thought her eyes seemed to be glazed over and wondered if he should stay with her. He was about to ask when she favored him with a smile that made him want to stay where he was. Unfortunately, he had a bear to skin and if he waited much longer, neither the hide nor the meat would be of any worth. He stood up and walked out of the tepee on shaky legs.

Scott walked to the meadow, caught the spotted pony and rode to the fallen bear. As he rode, he tried to think of a name for his son. He immediately decided his son would not have an English name; that life was a part of his past he would never embrace again. He knew the boy's name would have the ring of an Indian name. He knew how Man-with-no-hair and Dew-on-the-grass-in-the-moon-when-the-leaves-fall had gotten their names; he had not thought to ask Falling Feather how he had been named. The thought of his former friend saddened him and he briefly considered naming his son after him. After some thought, however, he decided not to name the boy Falling Feather; he would feel sadness every time he spoke the name. He had killed the bear on the day the boy had been born; perhaps he should think along those lines. He had respect for the giant bears and the boy would be able to draw strength from a name with "bear" in it, but names like: Bear-rolls-in-the-grass, Bear-dies-with-an-arrow-in-the-throat or even Bear-stands-on-two-legs, did not appeal to him. He was beginning to wish he had not told Dew-on-the-grass-in-the-moon-when-the-leaves-fall he would have a name by the time he returned. He thought of her...What was it she had said when he had looked upon the boy for the first time? She said the boy had his eyes...eyes like the sky. Scott had seen his reflection in pools of water but he had not paid particular attention to his eyes. He was told they were blue; it was one of those things that just didn't matter to him. Now it mattered. The boy had blue eyes...Eyes like the sky...Sky Eyes. Scott reined the horse to a stop. Sky Eyes. He had it. He wanted to return to the camp and tell Dew-on-the-grass-in-the-moon-when-the-leaves-fall. Sky Eyes. It had a ring he liked. Dew-on-the-grass-in-the-moon-when-the-leaves-fall had said the words too; the name had come from both of them.

With renewed happiness he galloped toward the bear. He would make short work of this task and quickly return to Dew-on-the-grass-in-the-moon-when-the-leaves-fall. He had a name for their son. Sky Eyes.

Chapter Seventeen

When Man-with-no-hair reached the forks in the valley he turned south. He passed the wallow where the Indian boy had been killed. He had the uncanny ability to let his mind wander as he rode through new country, without missing anything.

Thinking of Spotted Fawn made him sad, as always. On the other hand, his memories of her were all good. He still missed her very much, even after all this time.

He rode by the canyon that held the cave where the bear had died. He rode into country he had never seen before. His keen, shifting eyes missed nothing. Without thinking about it, he appreciated the beauty the Great Spirit had put upon the land for his children to enjoy. The crest of each rise offered a new panorama, as the next one drew him on.

After riding south for half a moon, Man-with-no-hair came upon a small river. He had wanted to explore the towering mountains for some time; the river would provide an accessible route to that end. He turned west and followed the river upstream.

The river offered a winding course to follow, but there were game trails and the yearly floods kept the under brush to a minimum. Man-with-no-hair had no trouble picking his way along the watercourse.

He followed the stream for less than half a moon. Several times he came upon smaller feeder streams, but he always kept to the main river. Now, he was at the confluence of two streams that were of equal size. Both streams were divided by a long, steep ridge. From where Man-with-no-hair sat on his horse, he could see the way the ridge wound its way up the mountain until it joined with another ridge. He had known he would eventually come upon steep terrain; this is where it would start.

Man-with-no-hair rode his horse to the base of the ridge, dismounted and led both horses up a series of switchbacks until they gained the top of the ridge.

Once on top of the ridge, he remounted and rode toward the top of the mountain. The top of the ridge varied in width from a narrow, hazardous trail to being wide enough for a small village to camp on. In places, it was nearly level, in others it was so steep, he had to dismount and lead the horses. There were areas where solid rock jutted out of the earth like the backbone of some giant, prehistoric creature.

The animals that lived in the mountains or valleys had been using this ridge for countless ages and the signs of their passage, a winding trail, would remain forever, regardless of the fate of the animals.

Man-with-no-hair now traveled on the path they had created. By late afternoon, he reached a saddle where the two ridges joined. The climb had been long and hard and he had gotten no sympathy from the hot sun that had beaten relentlessly upon his back.

After Man-with-no-hair reached the saddle in the ridge, he rested for a while. He had the stamina to go farther but after a brief inspection he saw the mountain would not offer another level spot to camp for quite some time.

He took the pack from the second horse and turned both animals loose to graze on the grass in the saddle. When his camp was established, he went exploring; he still had a short time before dark. Following one of the game trails that crossed the saddle, he came upon a large solid rock bluff. A small trickle of water ran down the face of the bluff. He walked toward the freshet.

Over the eons, the falling water had rinsed all of the top soil and small gravel away. After that, it had attacked the face of the solid rock itself. Eventually, even the rock began to give way, and now Man-with-no-hair looked into a declivity that held enough water to satisfy his needs as well as the needs of the horses. He drank deeply then returned to the saddle. He took the horses, one at a time, to the natural tank and let them drink. He repeated the process the next morning before he continued up the ridge.

On the morning of the second sunrise since leaving the water hole, Man-with-no-hair rode above the timberline. He had never witnessed terrain like this before and was overwhelmed by its splendor. A feeling of insignificance passed through him as he compared himself to the awesome mass of the mountains.

One afternoon, Man-with-no-hair came upon a wide bench. The bench wound its way around the mountain in a southerly direction and varied in width from distance he could see, to that which was too wide to determine. He and the horses were growing weary of the constant climbing; the bench was a welcome sight.

Man-with-no-hair followed the bench for several sunrises. He passed several alpine lakes that held his attention for quite some time; he was impressed with their ability to reflect the deep blue sky and the gray-brown slopes of the mountains.

Eventually, the bench began to sweep, ever so gently, around and down the mountain, growing narrower as it did so. Finally, the bench led him so far around the mountain that he was facing northwest. That night, he camped on the last remnants of the bench.

The next morning, Man-with-no-hair rode a narrow, winding trail into a massive timbered valley.

The trail split at the mouth of the valley, one contouring its way up the side of the mountain, while the other entered the valley. Man-with-no-hair was certain he would miss the grandeur of the high-up mountains, but the days were hot and the nights were cold and he had climbed enough; it was time for a change. He rode into the valley.

Game was abundant in the valley. Even in the thick timber, the trail was covered with fresh deer and elk tracks. Many times during the day he heard deer jumping away, as he and the horses spooked them from their beds with their passing.

After riding half of the day in the dense timber, the trees finally gave way to a long, winding meadow. The meadow reminded him of the two friends he had left behind. This valley was similar in looks only, for it was much larger and there was much more timber. There was a small stream in the center of the meadow. Man-with-no-hair went to the stream and allowed the horses to drink. He drank, too. When they had their fill of water, he led them to a small grove of trees, stripped the pack, and turned them both loose. He knew they would not wander far, but if they did, they would come when he called.

The next morning, Man-with-no-hair was underway before daylight, as usual. When the sun was directly overhead, the valley began to spread out and the timber on the valley floor became more sparse. He could see the towering boundaries on either side of the valley.

He was about to ride out of the last of the trees on the valley floor when he suddenly reined his horse to a stop. There were horse tracks in the trail ahead of him. He looked around but saw no movement. Cautiously, he slid from the horse's back and crept to the tracks. He let out his breath when he discovered the tracks were very old.

Man-with-no-hair was excited by the prospect of meeting new people but he knew that there could be dangers involved with doing so. From now on he would have to be more cautious.

He mounted the horse and directed it toward the timber at the edge of the clearing. He rode slowly, for he was not in a hurry and he hoped he would be less visible. A short time later, he saw the tip of a tepee. Slowly, cautiously, he moved closer. When he was close enough to see the entire tepee, he could also tell that it was the only tepee in the camp. There were no others.

Himself, Scott and Dew-on-the-grass-in-the-moon-when-the-leaves-fall lived in a single tepee. He did not think that was strange. But, for some unknown reason, there was something about the single tepee ahead of him that seemed unusual.

He watched the tepee for a long time. He was a very patient man and he saw no reason to put himself at risk by moving too hastily. He saw no movement, but there was a wisp of smoke coming from the campfire. He touched his heels to the horse and began to move closer. Very slowly.

As he rode, he caught a flash of movement out of the corner of his eye. Instinctively, he rolled from the horse's back, putting the animal between himself and the movement. As his feet touched the ground he heard an arrow whiz over where his head had been. He disappeared into the thick grass.

Man-with-no-hair quickly circled and waited. He was in front of his horse, close enough that he could see it. The horse suddenly nickered and side stepped. Man-with-no-hair knew someone was moving toward his animals. He crept forward, thankful for the gentle breeze that touched the top of the grass.

Man-with-no-hair heard soft footsteps coming in his direction. Suddenly a young boy appeared between him and the horses. He had an arrow nocked. He was looking on the ground for the person who had fallen from the horse.

Moving quickly and silently, Man-with-no-hair sprang ahead and grasped the boy's ankle. A startled gasp escaped from the boy before Man-with-no-hair jerked his foot out from under him, sending him crashing to the ground. The boy landed on his back, which knocked the wind out of him in a gush. Man-with-no-hair was on top of him before he could recover. The boy dropped his weapon as he struggled to get free. He squirmed and wiggled as he swung his arms and kicked his legs.

Man-with-no-hair judged the boy to be in his tenth summer. When the youth became exhausted by his efforts, Man-with-no-hair got off him, rolled him onto his stomach and picked him up by the nape of his shirt. In his other hand, Man-with-no-hair took the reins of his horse and walked toward the tepee.

Under the present circumstances, he would be hard put to defend himself if he were attacked again; however, if this boy had been guarding the tepee, there probably weren't any other men around.

When they reached the tepee, Man-with-no-hair dropped the boy to the ground. The boy rolled over once and was immediately on his feet. He crouched slightly and looked as if he were going to attack. Man-with-no-hair admired the boy's tenacity and, also, he knew better than to think the boy could not do him physical harm.

Man-with-no-hair was prepared to take the boy's rush when a woman's voice stopped him. The voice had come from inside the tepee.

The boy hissed an answer to the voice.

The voice spoke again, almost harshly. Reluctantly, the boy changed his defensive posture to one of acceptance.

The boy motioned for Man-with-no-hair to wait where he was. When he was satisfied that Man-with-no-hair was not going to move, he ducked into the tepee.

Man-with-no-hair looked around for cover, in case the boy came out of the tepee with a weapon in his hands. There was no cover nearby.

A few moments later, the flap was lifted and the boy stepped into the sunlight. He was leading a woman by the hand. The woman appeared to be about the same age as Scott and Dew-on-the-grass-in-the-moon-when-the-leaves-fall. Though she was young, Man-with-no-hair could tell there was something wrong with her eyes.

The boy turned to face Man-with-no-hair and the woman did likewise. Man-with-no-hair had made no sound and the woman turned her head slowly from left to right as she attempted to determine where he was standing.

The boy spoke to the woman in a low, muffled voice and the woman turned her head and looked with unseeing eyes into the eyes of Man-with-no-hair.

Man-with-no-hair signed to the boy, asking what had happened to his mother.

The boy signed back, explaining she was his sister, not his mother. She had fallen from a horse in the spring. She had hit the ground hard and her eyes had gone away.

Man-with-no-hair signed, asking if she was completely blind. She was an attractive woman and his heart was sad for her loss.

The boy signed that sometimes she could see outlines, other times she could see nothing.

"Why are you alone? Where are your people?" Man-with-no-hair asked with his hands.

The boy spat upon the ground. He signed, "They left her behind because

192

she could not keep up when they traveled. I stayed behind to care for her. I will kill you if you harm her."

Man-with-no-hair involuntarily raised his eyebrows at the boy's threat. His respect for the boy continued to grow.

"I will not harm your sister," signed Man-with-no-hair. "You are a brave boy. You will be a good warrior."

The boy was pleased to here the praise but he was not ready to relinquish anything to a complete stranger. "Here, I am a warrior."

Man-with-no-hair nodded his head at the boy's statement, stifling a grin that threatened to spread across his face.

"I am Man-with-no-hair. I am Shawnee."

The boy looked at Man-with-no-hair and wondered why someone with hair to their waist would be called Man-with-no-hair; but was too polite to ask, now.

"I am Runs-Like-An-Antelope. My sister is Morning Fawn. We are Arapaho," he said proudly. "What is Shawnee?"

The woman's name sent a shiver of pain through Man-with-no-hair's heart. His face gave no indication of the pain he felt. As he looked at the woman, he wondered if this were an omen; perhaps the spirits were trying to tell him something.

"What is Shawnee?" the boy repeated.

"We are from the east," Man-with-no-hair signed, when he realized he had been caught wandering in the past. "Four, maybe five, moon's walk to the east."

The boy's jaw dropped open as he tried to comprehend the distance Man-with-no-hair was referring to.

Man-with-no-hair noticed that Morning Fawn was terribly thin. He wondered if they had been eating regularly since they had been left behind.

"Have you hunted well, Runs-Like-An-Antelope?"

The boy blushed deeply and looked at the ground, unable to look Man-with-no-hair in the eye. "My arrows are not true," he signed at last. "I have caught a few rabbits but they are not enough."

Man-with-no-hair glanced at the sun and determined there was plenty of time to make a hunt.

"Come, Little Warrior, we will hunt now."

"Why would you hunt for us?" asked the boy.

"Because I am hungry too," answered Man-with-no-hair.

The boy spoke to his sister and then took her back inside the tepee. Man-with-no-hair staked the two horses near the camp. When Runs-Like-An-Antelope came out of the tepee, he and Man-with-no-hair walked to where the boy had dropped his bow and arrows earlier.

"Your arrow was true when you shot at me," signed Man-with-no-hair.

The boy blushed again. "That was the best shot I ever made; I still missed."

"Not by much," Man-with-no-hair signed with a wry grin.

When the boy had gathered his weapons they walked farther up the valley. A short distance from camp Man-with-no-hair spotted a fat doe drinking from the stream.

"There is our next meal," Man-with-no-hair signed. "You move off to the left and keep low."

The boy nodded and moved off as he had been instructed. Man-with-no-hair disappeared into the grass.

The doe had been far, too far away for a shot when Man-with-no-hair spotted her. He very quickly closed the distance on her and was about to move closer when the boy, who was still too far away, sprang to his feet, gave a whoop, and charged the deer. The startled doe leaped across the stream and raced along the edge of the forest. The boy launched an arrow that fell pitifully short of the running deer.

In disbelief, Man-with-no-hair got to his feet and walked to the boy.

"Why did you do that?" he signed patiently, without anger.

"We could get no closer on our bellies," answered the boy. "The Arapaho hunt from horseback. My arrows are not true when I hunt from my belly."

"Your arrows are true and I will show you what can be done when you hunt well on your belly," Man-with-no-hair signed in curt motions that commanded the boy's attention. "You wait here and I will go kill the deer you scared away."

Though he was young, Runs-Like-An-Antelope knew it was impossible to get close to a jumped deer. As he considered this information, he remembered how Man-with-no-hair had caught him by the ankle a short time ago. He suddenly realized he should pay very close attention to what this Shawnee did next.

The doe had run for a long way. For some reason she did not enter the timber. She watched as the two, two-legged creatures stood in the meadow. She sniffed the air but the wind was coming from the wrong direction. She blew through her nose, making a whistling sound; she still could not smell them. As she watched, one walked away from the other, jumped the stream and disappeared in the knee-high grass. They were strange creatures, but now there was only one to watch, and it was not threatening her. She lowered her head and bit a mouthful of the sweet, green grass. She raised her head; the two-legged creature had not moved. She didn't like being this close to it, but it was not threatening her and the grass was very good...

She lowered her head for another bite of grass. She felt a sharp pain in her chest. Just before she jumped, her ears detected the sound of a bowstring, and she wondered what had made the sound. Her chest hurt but she was fast and could run away from danger. Right now, though, she was tired and needed to rest. She would rest for a moment and then jump up and run away. There, under that bush was a nice place to rest, just for a moment. She lay down. She was confused because she was panting heavily, as though she had run a great distance. It felt so good to lie down, but she should be on her way. She couldn't get up...but that was all right because it felt so good to lie there and rest. Maybe she would run away later, now she wanted to sleep...rest and sleep...it had never felt so good to rest...her chest didn't hurt anymore...the rest must have helped...more rest...

Man-with-no-hair knew his shot was a good one. He did not move until the deer had run away. He knew she would not go far, especially if he didn't push her. When he could no longer hear her as she jumped, he slowly stood up.

Runs-like-an-antelope was standing where he had been told to stay. Man-with-no-hair waved an arm, motioning for the boy to join him. Runs-like-an-antelope jumped the stream and raced to Man-with-no-hair's side.

"I have never seen anything like that before," he signed excitedly. "Will you teach me how to do that?"

"I will teach you only if you want to learn," Man-with-no-hair said evenly. "Just because you want to do something does not make it so. It will take much practice. You will fail many times before you are able to do it as well as I do. If you do not fear failure or hard work, I will teach you."

Without realizing what he had done, Man-with-no-hair had committed himself to Runs-like-an-antelope for a very long time.

"I would like to learn," signed Runs-like-an-antelope. Man-with-no-hair's words had sobered him and he suddenly realized what he was asking of a complete stranger.

Man-with-no-hair nodded his head, then turned and walked to where the deer had been standing when he shot her. He looked about until he saw blood on the grass. Runs-like-an-antelope saw the blood too, and looked expectantly at Man-with-no-hair for an indication of when they should go after her.

Man-with-no-hair saw the look on the boy's face and signed, "Give her time to die. The shot was good but if she is not dead when we get to her, she will run away and will be harder to find. With each step she takes, she gets farther from your camp."

When they had waited long enough, Man-with-no-hair signed for Runs-like-an-antelope to lead the way to the doe. The boy was surprised at the opportunity but readily accepted.

"Move slowly," Man-with-no-hair signed. "Do not let your excitement cloud your judgment. If she is still alive she may kick you and a kick from those hooves can break a leg, or kill you, if she hits you in the right place."

The boy nodded his head, indicating he understood.

2

Man-with-no-hair and Runs-like-an-antelope dragged the deer to the tepee. There, they hung and skinned it. Man-with-no-hair sliced off enough meat for the evening meal.

"Tomorrow we will cut up and cure the rest of the meat," Man-with-no-hair signed to Runs-like-an-antelope.

The next morning, Man-with-no-hair was up before the sun. He had slept outside the tepee; he always woke up early when he slept outside.

In the early light of dawn, he walked to the stream and cut some willow branches from which he would fashion a drying rack.

Runs-like-an-antelope came out of the tepee as Man-with-no-hair finished making the drying rack. Together they began to butcher the doe.

Whenever Man-with-no-hair used a knife, or any other cutting tool, he was especially careful. In the past, he had seen squaws with missing fingers or thumbs; it caused him to shudder when he thought of the effect a missing finger would have on his hunting ability.

Man-with-no-hair suddenly turned from the hanging deer and looked toward the timbered slope across the meadow floor. His attention had been focused on butchering, but his senses had alerted him...Telling him they were being watched. Though he saw no movement on the slope, he would continue to watch it very closely.

3

A pair of hungry, yellow eyes looked at the camp from the shadows of the thick timber. The smell of venison and horse dung filled the old cougar's nostrils and its stomach rumbled in protest of the lack of nourishment it had received of late. The cougar followed a game trail down the slope and then it padded softly into the open timber, closer to the camp.

When the big, old cat reached the edge of the meadow, he sat on his haunches in the shade of a pine tree and licked his chops as he watched the activity around the camp.

He didn't like the idea of having to encounter the two-legged creatures to get a meal, but he was running out of options. He had barely survived last winter and he was yet to recover from the starving times he had suffered through. But, at his age, that had become a fact of life. He was nowhere near as swift or as strong as he had once been and the deer seemed to have become more fleet-footed. Some of his teeth were missing and most of those that remained were no longer sharp. He had difficulty killing anything but the smallest of creatures. On the bright side though, he was becoming a very good thief.

4

Runs-like-an-antelope placed a long slender log on the fire. They had no tools with which to chop wood. When the log burned in two, he would place both halves on the fire and so on until the log was completely burned up.

Man-with-no-hair glanced at the boy as he struggled with the long log. When he was satisfied the boy was not going to burn himself or knock the drying rack over, he continued slicing the meat.

It occurred to Man-with-no-hair that perhaps Morning Fawn would prefer to sit in the sun rather than in the dark, gloomy tepee. He rose to his feet and put his knife in its sheath at his waist. He walked to the flap of the tepee but before he could push it aside the boy was at his side.

"What do you want?" Runs-like-an-antelope signed.

Man-with-no-hair had to smile respectfully at the boy's tenacity. "Would your sister rather sit in the sun than in the tepee?" he asked.

"I'll ask her."

Runs-like-an-antelope crowded in front of Man-with-no-hair and entered the tepee. Man-with-no-hair waited a moment and then followed him.

5

The cougar was not one to miss an opportunity. When the two-legged creatures entered the tepee, he rose to his feet and trotted across the meadow. His growling stomach urged him on and he began to lope. He was drawing near and he began to salivate as he saw all of the meat standing before him.

One of the horses saw a movement in the tall grass and turned its head in that direction. The horse shrieked when it saw the cougar racing toward the camp. The horse tried to turn and run but the stake held it tight. The horse panicked and the terror spread to the other horse.

The cougar could not believe what it was seeing. He loved horse meat but they were usually much too fast for him to catch. These horses were frightened but they didn't run away. The great cat's adrenaline seemed to feed on the fear his presence created. He was close now. With a feeling of dominance he had not felt in a long, long time, he leaped through the air and landed on the back of a horse.

Chapter Eighteen

Two days after the birth of Sky Eyes, Dew-on-the-grass-in-the-moon-when-the-leaves-fall tried to resume her duties around the camp. She was visibly weak and Scott insisted she rest for at least one more day.

He prepared a broth for her that tasted better than he had a right to expect. Dew-on-the-grass-in-the-moon-when-the-leaves-fall must have liked it too for she drank until it was gone.

Scott had staked out the bear hide and he fleshed it when he was not caring for Dew-on-the-grass-in-the-moon-when-the-leaves-fall. He would not venture from the camp until he knew she had regained her strength.

He smiled as he remembered how pleased Dew-on-the-grass-in-the-moon-when-the-leaves-fall had been with the name he had given their son.

Scott knew his responsibility had increased with the birth of Sky Eyes. He felt his level of awareness had increased as well; he felt closer to his environment. When he herded the horses to the meadow and heard the chirp of the birds, he not only heard, he listened. It was as though they were singing their song just for him. All of his senses were becoming more alert to the small things he had taken for granted before the birth of Sky Eyes, such as the smell of the pines and the chuckle of the stream. The silent flight of a high-soaring bird filled his senses and made him feel at peace.

2

Working together, Scott and Dew-on-the-grass-in-the-moon-when-the-leaves-fall made a cradle board in which she could carry Sky Eyes while she worked. Scott was apprehensive about the device but he had seen similar objects in the past and reasoned that they were safe to use.

When Sky Eyes was three days old, Dew-on-the-grass-in-the-moon-when-the-leaves-fall put him in the cradle board and carried him to the meadow as she went with Scott to round up the horses.

By the time the horses were in the corral, Dew-on-the-grass-in-the-moon-when-the-leaves-fall was exhausted. The exercise had felt good, and in a way, the exhaustion felt good too; she was healthy and soon her strength would return.

As Scott watched Dew-on-the-grass-in-the-moon-when-the-leaves-fall trotting across the meadow, shooing the horses toward the finger, he once again realized how wonderful his life was. Food was plentiful, there were no threats from outside forces and he had Dew-on-the-grass-in-the-moon-when-the-leaves-fall and Sky Eyes. The only thing missing was Man-with-no-hair. Scott hoped his friend was safe and would return soon. Perhaps if Man-with-no-hair were here, together, they could put up with the behavior of Three-legged Wolf and Dew-on-the-grass-in-the-moon-when-the-leaves-fall would be able to have the company of Meadow Flower. Perhaps.

Chapter Nineteen

When Man-with-no-hair heard the horse scream, he froze in his tracks. Runs-like-an-antelope's objection to Man-with-no-hair's entry into the tepee never got out of his mouth. Morning Fawn gasped and began to tremble.

Man-with-no-hair had to fight the urge to rush out of the tepee. He did not know what the threat was and did not want to rush headlong into unknown danger. He listened carefully, feeling sick every time the horse screamed. Finally, he heard the cat growl and knew instantly what it was, though he was shocked that the cat would attack so near the camp.

Man-with-no-hair stepped out of the tepee just as the cat landed on the back of the pack-horse. He reached for his bow and quiver, but the bucking, pitching horse afforded him no shot at the cat.

With strength derived from sheer panic, the horse broke the braided rope that had held him fast. Kicking and bucking, the horse tried to throw the cat from its back. As it attempted to shake the cat loose, the horse straddled the fire and stepped on the long log Runs-like-an-antelope had placed there. The log broke, but as the horse moved away from the fire it kicked one end of the log, sending sparks and embers far into the meadow.

The old cat could do little damage with his worn out teeth, but his claws were still sharp and proved their worth as he raked the horse's neck.

The smell of its own blood caused the horse's panic to increase. Speed had been the horse's ally in the past; perhaps if it ran away, it could outrun the danger on its back. Screaming, the horse raced away from the camp, across the meadow and into the forest at a breakneck pace.

A deep anger burned in Man-with-no-hair as he ran across the meadow in pursuit of the horse and cat. To him, his horses were more like friends than beasts of burden. It would give him great pleasure to kill this cat.

When Man-with-no-hair was deep in the forest he slowed to a walk. Ahead of him, beyond a wall of thick timber, he could hear the dying screams of his horse. The horse had died hard and that made his heart sad. The cat screamed, triumphantly.

With an arrow nocked, Man-with-no-hair slipped through the forest. He still had not spotted the cat when he was distracted by screams from Runs-like-an-antelope. For a moment Man-with-no-hair considered ignoring the boy until the cat was dead. Screams from Morning Fawn changed his mind and he turned from the cat and raced back to the meadow.

Man-with-no-hair was shocked when he ran out of the timber. A fire was spreading across the meadow. There was so much smoke that he could not see the tepee. He turned and ran up wind and circled behind the fire.

The heat of the flames caused the wind to whip around; the fire seemed to be burning in all directions at once.

Morning Fawn was standing outside the tepee when Man-with-no-hair got to her. Runs-like-an-antelope was not in sight. Man-with-no-hair knew he would not have left his sister behind. Man-with-no-hair took Morning Fawn's wrist and led her toward the remaining horse. He looked for the boy as he led her away from the tepee. Man-with-no-hair released the woman's hand for a moment. He took out his knife and cut the rope that held the frightened horse. As frightened as the horse was, it would not run away from him. He put his hands around Morning Fawn's waist and easily lifted her onto the horse's back.

Morning Fawn was speaking excitedly in her language. Man-with-no-hair could not understand her words but he knew she was asking about her brother. She could not understand him, though he tried to reassure her.

Man-with-no-hair turned to the tepee one last time. He saw the boy rushing toward them with as many of their possessions as he could carry. Man-with-no-hair waved his arm signaling the boy to hurry as he wrapped the lead rope around his hand. Leading the horse, he began to run toward the distant, high peaks.

When they were far enough from the fire to determine the direction of the wind, Man-with-no-hair adjusted their course to the northeast. He knew if the wind changed the fire would overtake them. Their only hope was to move away as quickly as possible. Runs-like-an-antelope was still too young to run like an antelope and soon grew too weary to maintain the grueling pace set by Man-with-no-hair.

Man-with-no-hair gave half of Runs-like-an-antelope's burden to Morning Fawn and then lifted the protesting boy onto the horse, behind his sister. Man-with-no-hair ignored his objections and gathered the lead rope and led the horse on at an even faster pace.

2

Man-with-no-hair ran, leading the horse, until well after dark. The moon rose early and though it was not full, it provided enough light to allow him to continue the escape.

By the next dawn, Man-with-no-hair was still running. He had run throughout the night. He was beginning to tire but even at this point, he had not begun to tap the limit of his endurance.

After leaving the meadow, they had crossed a ridge. From that ridge, they had followed a long gentle slope to the bottom of a large timbered valley. The slope on the other side of the valley was equally gentle, which was good, for Man-with-no-hair, who had already run a long way, was now running uphill. They crossed out of that valley and dropped into terrain that was much more rugged. Rather than fight the broken ground, Man-with-no-hair led them to a ridge, on which they traveled up, toward the high, silhouetted peaks. The next dawn found them high enough up on the ridge to see the smoke, but they were still under the timberline. However, it appeared that the wind near the fire had changed in the night, for the fire was now sweeping to the north.

Man-with-no-hair was relieved but unwilling to stop. If the wind changed again the fire could overtake them very quickly.

Unable to maintain the fast pace in the steeper ground, Man-with-no-hair was forced to walk rather than run. When he finally stopped to catch his breath, he turned back to check the fire. He also looked at the two people on the back of the horse...Morning Fawn was squinting at the morning sun.

"Can she see?" Man-with-no-hair signed to Runs-like-an-antelope.

Surprised, the boy spoke to his sister and then signed to Man-with-no-hair. "She can see more now than she has seen for a long time!"

Man-with-no-hair considered this information and then returned his attention to the fire. There was an incredible cloud of smoke far to the north. There was also some smoke coming from the wake of the fire. At last, Man-with-no-hair began to relax. They had eluded the fire; they would be safe.

Man-with-no-hair continued up the ridge. By late afternoon, he discovered that the ridge led to a bald knob. The only way to go was down; they had climbed the ridge for nothing. From their vantage point, he picked another ridge that would take them into the higher peaks. By dusk, they were in the bottom of a small, steep canyon, almost to the ridge Man-with-no-hair had chosen to follow.

By nightfall, Man-with-no-hair and the horse were exhausted. There was water where they stopped, but Man-with-no-hair had to roll some river rocks aside to make enough room for the horse to drink. He instructed Runs-like-an-antelope to care for his sister and then he rolled into one of the robes and was immediately asleep.

The late morning sun was shining brightly old when Man-with-no-hair was awakened by the smell of cooking meat. He rolled over and saw a small cooking fire burning. After the forest fire, his first instinct was to jump up and stomp the fire out. He quickly realized the absurdity of the thought. He saw a medium sized bird spitted over the fire and as the aroma drifted to his nostrils he remembered how long it had been since he had eaten.

When he rolled out of the robes, he saw Morning Fawn sitting across the fire, looking at him.

"Can you see?" Man-with-no-hair signed to her. Runs-like-an-antelope was not in sight.

"I can see better today than yesterday. My sight is returning."

"My heart is happy for you," said Man-with-no-hair.

"I do not understand your tongue," Morning Fawn signed.

Man-with-no-hair repeated what he had said in sign language.

Morning Fawn smiled briefly and then signed, "You are younger than I thought."

Man-with-no-hair thought it was a strange statement and didn't know how to respond. He simply nodded his head and then indicated the bird spitted over the fire.

"It will be ready soon," Morning Fawn signed.

Man-with-no-hair stood up and saw the horse feeding on the grass that grew in the damp earth, near the stream. He still did not see Runs-like-an-antelope.

"Where is your brother?" he signed.

"He has gone to look for a way out of the canyon," she answered.

Man-with-no-hair nodded his head again. He realized he hadn't told the boy about the ridge he had seen; nonetheless, he was impressed by the boy's attempt to help them out of their situation. As he squatted near the fire, waiting for the bird to cook, he found himself daydreaming about raising the boy as his son. He could picture the two of them slipping through the forest, on the track of fresh meat for the camp.

Man-with-no-hair was pulled away from his thoughts when Morning Fawn rose to her feet and removed the bird from the fire. She handed the entire bird to him. Man-with-no-hair frowned slightly at the gesture and then tore the bird in half and gave her an equal portion.

"There were two birds. Runs-like-an-antelope and I have already eaten," she signed.

"Eat this too," Man-with-no-hair insisted, remembering how thin she was.

"The meat should be for you, but I will do as you say."

Man-with-no-hair thought that was a curious statement too but was well aware of the fact that the customs of Indians varied from one village to another. Besides, he had more pressing things to worry about and gave it little more thought.

When he finished eating, Man-with-no-hair went to the horse and took it to water. The horse lowered its head and sniffed at the water but did not drink. Man-with-no-hair suddenly realized that Runs-like-an-antelope had probably watered the horse before he had gone in search of a way out of the canyon.

Man-with-no-hair heard a limb snap. He released the horse and disappeared into the underbrush as if he were no more than a wisp of smoke.

Runs-like-an-antelope came through the brush and saw the untied horse. His sister was sitting near the fire, mouth agape, staring across the small stream.

Suddenly, Man-with-no-hair appeared a short distance downstream, directly behind Runs-like-an-antelope. He took two steps forward and put his hand on the boy's shoulder.

"HIIII-YEEE!" the boy shouted, as he whirled around and made ready to defend himself. "Why did you sneak up behind me like that?" Runs-like-an-antelope signed rapidly.

"I didn't mean to startle you," signed Man-with-no-hair. "I heard a sound. I thought it was you but I wasn't sure. What did you find, Little Warrior?"

"I am Runs-like-an-antelope," signed the boy, as he struggled to regain his composure.

"I meant no disrespect," Man-with-no-hair signed with a broad smile.

"I found a ridge that will take us out of this canyon. I do not know if it will take us over the high mountains."

Runs-like-an-antelope turned to his sister who was still staring at Man-with-no-hair as if he were some sort of a spirit. Having recovered from being surprised, Runs-like-an-antelope had to smile at the look on her face.

"I told you he moved like smoke," he said to her in Arapaho.

Morning Fawn looked from the boy to Man-with-no-hair. "You are a man?

You are not a spirit?" she signed.

"I am a man with a gift. You will suffer no harm from me."

"You may wish to leave the horse behind," Runs-like-an-antelope signed.

"Where I go, the horse goes."

"The way is hard. He may be killed."

"Then we will find another way."

"There is no other way."

"The fire is far to the north. If we have to, we will go back the way we came."

"There is nothing for us back there," signed Morning Fawn.

"Do you want me to take you to your people?" Man-with-no-hair asked with his hands.

Runs-like-an-antelope spat at the suggestion. "We have no people! I hope they were in the fire," he signed angrily, immediately sorry for his words. He loathed his people for their treatment of his sister, but he did not wish death upon them.

"My brother speaks from his head and not from his heart," signed Morning Fawn, as she recognized the boy's apologetic look. "But he is right, we no longer have people. We have no place to go."

"I have friends over the mountains," signed Man-with-no-hair. "They would welcome you."

"I thought you were from far away," signed Runs-like-an-antelope.

"I am. We came to the mountains together."

"Your whole tribe came with you?" asked Runs-like-an-antelope.

"No," Man-with-no-hair signed, laughing. "There are just two of them." For a moment, a look of despair crossed his face as he remembered Dew-on-the-grass-in-the-moon-when-the-leaves-fall and the condition she had been in. "There *were* two of them," he signed with sadness.

Man-with-no-hair was suddenly overcome with an extreme case of homesickness. "Come, let's go," he said, forcing a smile. "I want you to meet my friends."

3

Runs-like-an-antelope led the way down the stream bed. After a bit, he turned onto an ancient game trail that led up the slope.

When they had climbed a short distance, Man-with-no-hair recognized that they were, in fact, on the ridge he had seen the day before. He saw no reason to share that information with the others; he would let the boy think he had discovered a way over the mountains.

"Slides have covered the trail up ahead," Runs-like-an-antelope signed to Man-with-no-hair.

"Lead the way, Runs-like-an-antelope. We will figure out what to do when we get there," he signed back to him.

Man-with-no-hair smiled to himself as the boy proudly led the way up the trail. He then turned to Morning Fawn. He knew she was still weak from much hunger and he was worried about her.

"Are you strong enough to walk?" he signed to her. "If not, you can ride, for a while."

Morning Fawn looked from Man-with-no-hair to the horse and the pack that it carried, which they had rigged to carry their few remaining possessions. She knew the horse had grown weary during their escape from the fire and that it may soon face the struggle of its life, as they attempted to cross the mountains.

"I will walk," she signed back to him.

Man-with-no-hair nodded his head and turned to follow the boy up the trail. He would keep a close eye on Morning Fawn. Her will was stronger than her actual strength; if they had to wait for her, they would do so. They were going home, and if it took longer because of her, so be it.

When they left the stream bed, they also left the cover of foliage. The trail contoured up the ridge, across the open hillside. The hot, late-morning sun beat down on them as they climbed higher and higher. They followed the trail into a small draw. There, the trail intersected with another trail that would take them to the crest of the ridge.

It was on this trail that they came upon the first slide. Man-with-no-hair was surprised at the distance Runs-like-an-antelope had already covered that morning.

The trail had not caved off, rather, detritus had slid down the hill and covered it completely. It was easy enough to determine the course of the trail, but Man-with-no-hair was concerned about the loose shale rock that lay knee-deep ahead of them.

The slide was very wide and would take them quite some time to cross. Man-with-no-hair couldn't help his two companions and lead the horse at the same time. He staked the horse and took Morning Fawn by the left arm. Runs-like-an-antelope was about to object, but thought better of it and turned to lead the way across the slide.

Man-with-no-hair walked on the downhill side of Morning Fawn; if she fell, he would be able to catch her.

Slowly, they made their way across the loose rock. The way was made more difficult and tiring because each time they put a foot down, it threatened to slide down the hill.

Halfway across, they stopped to rest. Morning Fawn sat on a large boulder. Man-with-no-hair turned around to check on the horse. The horse was fine but when Morning Fawn stood up she stepped on a large, flat piece of shale. The shale slipped and she lost her balance and slid past Man-with-no-hair and down the hill before he could respond. If he had not been looking at the horse, he may have been able to reach out and grab her.

As she slid, she rolled over and dug in with her feet and fingers. She looked up and saw Man-with-no-hair rushing down the hill toward her. He moved like a cat, barely losing his footing as he jumped and ran, moving closer to her. She knew he was putting himself at risk to help her and she felt bad for her clumsiness.

Man-with-no-hair reached her just as she finally stopped sliding. He instructed Morning Fawn to get on his back. She looked at him with disbelief but when he repeated himself, she did as he asked. It was a difficult maneuver because she felt that any movement would cause her to slide farther down the hill. Finally, she quickly reached out with her right arm and grasped Man-with-no-hair's shirt. When he did not slide away from her, she moved closer until she was able to get onto his back.

Man-with-no-hair could run for a long distance with a full-grown deer on his back. The weight of Morning Fawn was inconsequential. She held on tightly because movement could throw him off balance. Slowly, with great caution, Man-with-no-hair worked his way back up the slope. When he reached Runs-like-an-antelope he continued to carry Morning Fawn until they reached the other side of the slide.

When Morning Fawn released him and dropped to the ground, Man-with-no-hair turned to go after the horse. When he turned, Morning Fawn was looking at him. Her sad eyes told him she was sorry for the trouble she had caused. She put her arms around his waist and held him closely. Man-with-no-hair and Runs-like-an-antelope exchanged a glance that expressed their mutual confusion.

When she finally released him, Man-with-no-hair hurried back across the slide, to the horse. The slide, though loose and dangerous, was not a threat to someone with his skills and abilities. He knew the horse could cross also, though not with his confidence.

He pulled the stake and led the horse forward. The rope became taut as the horse balked. He gave a few gentle tugs on the rope and the horse reluctantly followed. Man-with-no-hair picked his way carefully, considering the horse's footing more than his own. It soon became apparent that Man-with-no-hair was not going to be able to continue picking the way because the horse slid a few inches down the slope with each step.

The horse was trembling with fear and Man-with-no-hair was trying to console it by talking softly as they walked.

When they neared the halfway point, the ground gave way from under the horse. Man-with-no-hair was on the uphill side of the animal but was unable to release the lead rope in time to prevent being pulled down the hill. The horse managed to keep its feet under it but the slide caused it to panic. As Man-with-no-hair slid down the hill he narrowly missed being struck by the flying hooves as the horse made its own way up and across the loose slope. Shaken, but not hurt, Man-with-no-hair got to his feet and continued on until he reached the other side.

Morning Fawn was waiting nervously. She had a worried look on her face, so he smiled briefly to show he was not hurt. He looked from her to the horse. Runs-like-an-antelope had run down the hill and caught the animal when it came out of the slide area. He was leading it on a contour that would intersect with the game trail up the hill from where they stood.

Man-with-no-hair looked at Morning Fawn and the relief on both of their faces was apparent.

"Are you hurt?" asked Morning Fawn, as Man-with-no-hair drew near.

"No," signed Man-with-no-hair as he brushed gravel out of his clothing.

Man-with-no-hair led the way as they continued up the trail. Runs-like-an-antelope was waiting for them. When they reached the boy and the horse, Man-with-no-hair checked the animal for injuries. He found some scraped hide on the legs but there were no deep cuts or bleeding wounds. He patted the horse on the rump, relieved he had not lost another animal.

"Thank you for catching the horse. Runs-like-an-antelope is a good warrior."

The praise made the boy feel good. He proudly signed, "Follow me, I will lead you over the mountains."

Before the sun was directly overhead, Morning Fawn began to lag behind.

"Will you ride now?" Man-with-no-hair asked.

"I do not wish to fall from another horse," she signed.

"You will not fall from this horse," Man-with-no-hair promised. "I will not release the lead rope. The horse will not run away or fall down. You will be safe."

A little embarrassed, she nodded her head and averted her eyes.

With the location of the pack on the horse's back, even Man-with-no-hair would have had difficulty mounting the horse. He had to help her onto the horse's back. He put his hands around her waist with only that thought in mind. When he looked into those large, dark eyes that were looking back at him, he felt a stirring within himself he had not felt for a very long time. He relished the closeness of the woman yet, strangely, it made him feel uncomfortable too. He had known but one love in his life and her memory was still strong in his mind.

Morning Fawn perceived much from the touch of Man-with-no-hair. She knew he was a good man; she knew he wanted to be near her. She could also see in his eyes that there was, or had been, someone else.

"Thank you for being kind to Runs-like-an-antelope," she signed, breaking the spell that had overcome them.

Man-with-no-hair lifted her onto the back of the horse and then signed, "He is a good warrior."

The boy was ahead of them, interested only in leading the way up the hill. He had not seen what had passed between Man-with-no-hair and his sister. Man-with-no-hair took up the lead rope and followed him up the trail.

As the sun began to stretch toward the western horizon, they found themselves in a long, sweeping saddle between two towering peaks. Behind them lay a maze of deep canyons and up-thrust ridges and knobs. The air was cool, even in the afternoon sun. Ahead of them, the ground was broken, yet more gently. The way out of the saddle would be steep for a while, but once they were down, the going would be much easier than it had been for quite some time. In the far distance, Man-with-no-hair thought he recognized the knobbed mountain that overlooked the valley in which his friends awaited his return.

There was no water in the saddle and it was too late in the day to attempt a descent. It would take at least a day to get off the steep slope.

Man-with-no-hair helped Morning Fawn from the horse and then began to prepare the camp. There was a gentle breeze that felt good but would become very cold when the sun went down.

He sent Runs-like-an-antelope to look for wood while he went the other way in search of something for dinner.

Shortly before sunset, Man-with-no-hair returned with two grouse. He found a small fire burning and a pile of wood that would last throughout the night. Runs-like-an-antelope had gone after another load of limbs. Morning Fawn had used some of the limbs and their largest robe to erect an effective windbreak. When Runs-like-an-antelope returned with his last load of wood, both birds had been spitted and were beginning to cook.

Runs-like-an-antelope hunkered down near the small fire and sniffed the aroma hungrily.

"My friend is not one of the People," signed Man-with-no-hair, wishing to prepare his new friends for the meeting with Scott and Dew-on-the-grass-in-the-moon-when-the-leaves-fall.

"What is 'Not one of the People'? What does that mean?" signed Runs-like-an-antelope.

Morning Fawn spoke sharply to Runs-like-an-antelope in Arapaho. Man-with-no-hair looked questioningly at both of them.

"My sister says I should be more polite. I did not mean to be discourteous. I do not understand."

"His people come from far away. They live in this land now, but before that they came from across a big water…Like a lake…A lake it would take three or four moons to row across."

Amazed, both Morning Fawn and Runs-like-an-antelope began to sign questions at him so fast he could not tell what they had asked. Smiling, Man-with-no-hair indicated they should take turns with their questions.

"Have you seen such a lake…Water?" asked Runs-like-an-antelope before his sister could pose her question.

"I have not seen it, but I believe my friend when he tells me. He tells of other strange things too. He told me his father came to this land in a canoe that could carry more men than there are in most villages."

"There were very many men in our village," signed Morning Fawn.

"It is difficult to believe but my friend would not tell these things if they were not true."

"You said your friend was not one of 'the People.' Does he look different from us?" signed Morning Fawn.

"That is why I wanted to talk to both of you about him. He is a strange-looking man. His hair is yellow. He has hair on his face. Sometimes he skins the hair off his face with a knife."

"He is a man?" asked Morning Fawn.

"He is a man," Man-with-no-hair answered, laughing.

"Why is his hair yellow?" asked Runs-like-an-antelope.

"He and I have talked about such things many times. He told me he has seen people with red hair. Others have brown hair. It seems to me they are a mixed race. I used to think that was a bad thing but his woman is with child. The child will be of mixed race. Maybe it is not such a bad thing."

"What of his woman? What is she like?" signed Morning Fawn.

"Her name is Dew-on-the-grass-in-the-moon-when-the-leaves-fall. She is Shawnee, like me. She came from a different village."

"What is the man's name? How did he meet Dew-on-the-grass-in-the-moon-when-the-leaves-fall?" asked Runs-like-an-antelope.

"His name is Scott Walker (he had to say the name for there was no way to sign such a name). Dew-on-the-grass-in-the-moon-when-the-leaves-fall's village was attacked by the Seneca. Most of the men were killed. Women and children were taken prisoner. Dew-on-the-grass-in-the-moon-when-the-leaves-fall escaped but she was wounded. Scott found her and cared for her. She would have died if not for him. They traveled together for a time and Dew-on-the-grass-in-the-moon-when-the-leaves-fall decided she wanted to stay with him. We found them at the edge of the prairie and took them to our village. They stayed for a time and decided to move on. There was nothing for me in the village so I came with them."

Morning Fawn detected a change in the tone of Man-with-no-hair's voice when he said there was nothing in the village for him. "There once was someone for you in the village. What happened?" she asked, signing in a manner that depicted courtesy, though she thought she already knew the answer.

"I had a woman but she died while giving birth. The baby died too. That is why I left my friends behind. I did not want to be there when the baby came. Dew-on-the-grass-in-the-moon-when-the-leaves-fall is like a sister to me and I did not want to be there if she did not live. Now, I must know they are both safe."

"How long will it take to get where your friends live?" asked Runs-like-an-antelope.

"If it was their valley I saw earlier, the sun will rise on us (Man-with-no-hair opened his hand and spread his fingers apart, indicating five fingers) this many times before we reach my home," Man-with-no-hair answered the boy, though his eyes were locked into the eyes of Morning Fawn. They communicated with each other without the use of their hands or voices.

Runs-like-an-antelope was about to ask another question when he saw the way Man-with-no-hair and his sister were looking at each other. He rolled his eyes and shook his head. He pulled a drumstick off one of the grouse. As he ate he wondered what it was that made adults act the way they did. Eventually he stopped worrying about that; the grouse was good and he was tired. It had been a long day.

4

The next morning, they were all up before dawn. The breeze from the night before had turn into a cold wind. They hastily broke camp and loaded the horse. They started down the long slope without eating; most of the grouse had been eaten anyway.

As they made their way down the slope, Man-with-no-hair continued to look at the tops of the smaller mountain range to the east. He was certain he could see the mountaintop on the north side of the valley where Scott and Dew-on-the-grass-in-the-moon-when-the-leaves-fall waited.

Around mid-day, they came upon a spring and stopped to rest. As is often the case, it was as difficult going downhill as it was going up, though less tiring. It was harder to keep your feet under yourself; each step had to be made with care.

Morning Fawn had to walk, too. The ground was too steep and loose for her to ride the horse. Man-with-no-hair looked at her and wished he could take time to hunt. She needed nourishment, but mid-day was not a good time to hunt, even for him. There was little game on the steep, open slope anyway. He also wished they could hurry so he would have more time to hunt when they reached the bottom, but he didn't think she could go much faster than they were traveling now.

"I will carry you," Man-with-no-hair said as they prepared to leave the spring.

"No. I know you are strong, but I will walk," she signed back to him.

"The way is hard and we must hurry if we are to get to the bottom before nightfall."

"Do you think I am weak and unable to keep up?" she asked with a hurt look.

"I think it has been too long since you have eaten regularly and your strength has gone away. When times are better, it will return. For now, you need help. I am here to help you. I do not wish to hurt you or offend you. You need to eat. I need to get us to the bottom in time to hunt so you can eat. Do you understand?"

"I understand. I will do as you say. I am sorry for the way I am," she signed, embarrassed.

"There is no need to apologize, the fault is not yours." He turned to Runs-like-an-antelope, "I will go first and carry your sister. You follow and lead the horse. What I am asking is a hard thing. It is something for a warrior to do, are you ready for that kind of thing?"

Runs-like-an-antelope swallowed hard. He knew the trail ahead was treacherous and he knew how much Man-with-no-hair cared for the horse. He did not want to fail – he did not want to let Man-with-no-hair down. "I am ready. I will lead your horse safely down the hill."

Man-with-no-hair smiled and put a hand on the boy's shoulder. "I am sure you will," he said. "If I get ahead of you, do not worry, I will come back for you. I will not leave you behind."

Man-with-no-hair turned and helped Morning Fawn get onto his back. She wrapped her legs around his waist and her arms around his neck. He was about to start down the hill when he felt a tug on his shirt. He turned back to Runs-like-an-antelope.

"I do not know who sent you to us," signed the boy. "But I am glad you are here."

Unable to sign back to the boy, Man-with-no-hair put his arm around his shoulders and drew the boy to him. "I am glad I am here too, Little Friend," he said in Shawnee.

Man-with-no-hair released the boy and started down the slope. He made good time and was soon far ahead of the boy and the horse. The weight of Morning Flower did not slow him down, though he was more careful than he ordinarily would have been. To take a fall under these circumstances could result in more than just Morning Fawn being hurt. Several times he felt her breath on his ear and cheek, which made it more difficult to concentrate on the trail.

At last, Man-with-no-hair and Morning Fawn reached the bottom. When they reached flat ground, they came into a small glade of mixed conifers and hardwoods. A small stream gurgled through the glade. Man-with-no-hair stopped and let Morning Fawn down when they came upon an old fire pit.

"If you can gather some wood, I will go back for the boy," signed Man-with-no-hair.

"I will have a fire going when you return. I will find some edible roots and greens too."

"I will be back as soon as I can," signed Man-with-no-hair before he turned and raced up the slope.

5

The sunset and darkness spread over the mountains and valleys. Firelight flickered, happily lighting the faces of Man-with-no-hair, Morning Fawn and Runs-like-an-antelope. They ate hungrily of the fresh venison from the young buck Man-with-no-hair had killed after he had gotten the boy and horse off the steep slope.

Once again Runs-like-an-antelope was very tired. It was all he could do to keep his eyes open long enough to feed himself. When at last he could eat no more, he wiped his hands and rolled into his robe. Man-with-no-hair was already asleep and so was his sister – he thought. He heard her get out of her robes and walk across the camp. He glanced at her through sleep-blurred eyes and thought it strange that she did not have her clothes on. She was standing where Man-with-no-hair was sleeping. That's a good thing he thought as he drifted off to sleep and dreamed dreams of hunting with his brother – Man-with-no-hair.

Chapter Twenty

Scott had not worked with Man-with-no-hair's fillies as often as he should have. There had been too many interruptions. Dew-on-the-grass-in-the-moon-when-the-leaves-fall required a lot of his time. He did not mind caring for her but he had promised Man-with-no-hair he would work with the young horses.

Three-legged Wolf had been gone for seven days, or was it eight? One day was the same as the next in the valley and it really didn't matter, anyway.

Now, as Scott waited for Dew-on-the-grass-in-the-moon-when-the-leaves-fall to join him, he rubbed one of the filly's back with dry grass. The filly liked the attention and she leaned against him, asleep on her feet.

The filly's mother was standing a few yards away. Suddenly the mare jerked her head up and looked to the west.

The motion was not lost on Scott. He knew someone or something was coming. He dropped the grass and picked up his bow. He was prepared to face any danger that threatened their lives. He would have preferred to ride the spotted pony, but it was too far away. Instead, he leapt onto the back of the mare and with the added height, searched desperately for the oncoming danger. He saw nothing.

Dew-on-the-grass-in-the-moon-when-the-leaves-fall stepped out of the finger. She had Sky Eyes on her back. She saw Scott on the back of the horse. Something about his demeanor told her that the possibility of danger loomed over them.

Scott waved Dew-on-the-grass-in-the-moon-when-the-leaves-fall back into the finger. Reluctantly, she did as he instructed.

Turning the horse with leg pressure, Scott kicked the mare into a slow trot as they moved away from the finger, always looking west.

Scott did not know what to expect. If it was another bear he could be in serious trouble; he was not familiar enough with the mare to know how she would act under such extreme pressure. If it were Three-legged Wolf or his people...

It was not a bear. He could see a horse. There were three people; a woman was riding the horse, a man was leading and a small boy followed behind. It must be Three-legged Wolf. Where were his other horses? He didn't walk like Three-legged Wolf. He looked like Man-with-no-hair. The horse looked like Man-with-no-hair's horse. Where was the other horse? Who were those people?

It was Man-with-no-hair!

"Dew-on-the-grass-in-the-moon-when-the-leaves-fall! Dew-on-the-grass-in-the-moon-when-the-leaves-fall, it's Man-with-no-hair! Man-with-no-hair is back! I see him, he's coming now!" Scott shouted as he slid from the horse's back and ran toward his friend.

Scott and Man-with-no-hair seldom shouted. The noise of their voice would give away their position or frighten away a potential meal. Now, for the first time in nearly nine months, Scott's voice echoed across the valley.

Scott saw Dew-on-the-grass-in-the-moon-when-the-leaves-fall hustling out of the finger. He turned back to wait for her but she waved him on. He turned again and ran toward his friend.

Runs-like-an-antelope had tried to prepare himself for the meeting with the hairy-faced man Man-with-no-hair had described to him. What he saw now was almost beyond his comprehension. He saw the hairy-faced man and he could accept that, but the hairy-faced man was running in circles in the meadow, shouting at people who were not there. When the hairy-faced man turned and ran toward them, Runs-like-an-antelope wondered why Man-with-no-hair called this crazy man friend? He, himself, was preparing to dive into the underbrush.

Man-with-no-hair saw the apprehension on the boy's face. He stopped the horse and signed that he had nothing to fear. Man-with-no-hair had heard Scott shout Dew-on-the-grass-in-the-moon-when-the-leaves-fall's name and then he saw her trotting out of the finger. The relief that washed over him was visible and unmistakable

Scott was so overjoyed, he stopped and roared as if he were one of the great bears. He pounded his fists on his chest and roared again before he started running toward Man-with-no-hair and his companions.

Man-with-no-hair would have responded in kind but he started laughing at Scott's behavior and was unable to do so. He saw Runs-like-an-antelope dart into the forest and stopped Morning Fawn just as she was getting an arrow nocked.

"He is my friend. He will not harm you. He is showing me his heart is happy that I am home," said Man-with-no-hair, forgetting they could not understand his words.

Morning Fawn poked Man-with-no-hair in the back. When he turned from Scott to her, she signed, "I thought you said he was a man. He acts like an animal. He has frightened Runs-like-an-antelope. Why does he behave so strangely?"

"He is my friend and he is glad to see me," signed Man-with-no-hair.

By the time Man-with-no-hair finished signing to Morning Fawn, Scott was just a few yards away. Man-with-no-hair turned back and faced his friend as he came to a stop in front of the horse. Man-with-no-hair stepped forward and extended his hand to Scott. Scott clasped Man-with-no-hair's forearm and Man-with-no-hair clasped Scott's. The firmness of their grip and the look that passed between them spoke volumes about how they felt and how glad they were to be reunited.

"How is it with you, Scott Walker?" Man-with-no-hair asked.

"I am well, Man-with-no-hair. Welcome home, my friend."

Man-with-no-hair was about to say he was glad to be back in the valley when he saw Dew-on-the-grass-in-the-moon-when-the-leaves-fall making her way toward them. He released Scott's arm and walked toward her. He could see she was no longer heavy with child, and then he saw the backboard she carried.

"Dew-on-the-grass-in-the-moon-when-the-leaves-fall, it does my heart good to see that you are well. I thought about you when I was gone. How is your child?"

"The child is well. He will be better now that his uncle has returned."

"Thank you. You make my heart smile. Come, I want you meet my friends."

Together, Man-with-no-hair and Dew-on-the-grass-in-the-moon-when-the-leaves-fall walked back to where Morning Fawn and Scott waited. Runs-like-an-antelope was yet to come out of the underbrush.

"Tell your brother to come out and meet my friends. They will not harm him," signed Man-with-no-hair to Morning Fawn.

Morning Fawn spoke to Runs-like-an-antelope. A few moments later there was a rustle in the brush and the boy stepped out and came forward. Man-with-no-hair helped Morning Fawn off the horse. She stood beside him as he made introductions.

When everyone had greeted everyone else, Morning Fawn stepped forward and signed that she would like to see the baby.

Dew-on-the-grass-in-the-moon-when-the-leaves-fall met Man-with-no-hair's eyes and knew it would be all right. She took the backboard off and handed it to Morning Fawn.

"He has eyes like the sky," she said, as she cooed to the baby. She was unable to sign, so she spoke the words in Arapaho. Everyone looked to Runs-like-an-antelope for an interpretation. When he had signed his sister's words, he stepped forward to satisfy his curiosity. He had never seen a blue-eyed baby before.

Everyone looked at Sky Eyes. They smiled when he smiled and laughed when he cooed and gurgled. Watching the baby seemed to make the tension dissipate.

After a few minutes, Dew-on-the-grass-in-the-moon-when-the-leaves-fall said, "Come to the camp. There is a stew on the fire." She had noticed how thin Morning Fawn was and was curious to hear her story. She had also noticed how close she stayed to Man-with-no-hair and was curious to hear *that* story, as well.

As they walked toward the camp, Scott asked, "What happened to the other horse?"

"She was killed by a mountain lion," answered Man-with-no-hair. "Did you see the smoke from the fire?"

"Yes I did. We thought we might have to leave the valley, but it went to the north."

"The cat started the fire when it jumped on the mare's back. We were almost killed in the fire," Man-with-no-hair said.

"I thought of you when I saw the smoke. I hoped you were not in its path."

When they reached the camp, Man-with-no-hair stripped the pack from the horse and turned it loose. It quickly found its way back to the meadow and the rest of the horses.

Everyone sat around the small fire and waited patiently as Dew-on-the-grass-in-the-moon-when-the-leaves-fall served up the stew. She had to sort through her belongings to come up with enough bowls to feed everyone at once. Morning Fawn held Sky Eyes as Dew-on-the-grass-in-the-moon-when-the-leaves-fall busied herself.

"Where will we stay?" Runs-like-an-antelope signed to Man-with-no-hair.

"We will make another tepee," Man-with-no-hair answered.

"They do not speak our language. We should teach them so they do not have to talk with their hands," said Scott in Shawnee.

"Your Shawnee has improved," said Man-with-no-hair, looking from Scott to Dew-on-the-grass-in-the-moon-when-the-leaves-fall.

"I had a good teacher," said Scott proudly.

"I think you are right. They should learn to speak Shawnee, but we should learn to speak Arapaho, too. This is far north for them but sometimes they come near here. We should be ready to talk to them when they come. We should all learn to speak Scott's language too. You are here, someday others like you may come, too," said Man-with-no-hair.

Man-with-no-hair gulped some of the stew. When he took the bowl away from his mouth, he saw the new bear hide. "You hunted one of the bears while I was away."

Scott told him about the encounter with the other Indians and the brush with Three-legged Wolf. He explained why he had challenged the bear and why he had asked the other Indian to leave the camp. "I am glad there is another woman in the camp. I know Dew-on-the-grass-in-the-moon-when-the-leaves-fall is lonely," said Scott, as he looked from Man-with-no-hair to Dew-on-the-grass-in-the-moon-when-the-leaves-fall.

Dew-on-the-grass-in-the-moon-when-the-leaves-fall gave him an appreciative look and then returned her attention to trying to communicate with Morning Fawn.

"How much meat do we have?" asked Man-with-no-hair, as he finished the last of the stew in his bowl.

"There is enough for three days, with this many people," Scott answered.

"We should hunt tomorrow," Man-with-no-hair suggested. "Are the buffalo still nearby?"

"I saw their signs the last time I was at the forks of the valley," Scott told him.

"We will need buffalo hides to make another tepee. There would be too much meat to care for if we killed that many buffalo at one time. If we kill two tomorrow and two more later, we won't risk losing the meat," Man-with-no-hair explained.

"I agree," said Scott. "Two buffalo will be much meat."

Man-with-no-hair saw Runs-like-an-antelope watching him and Scott. "You will hunt buffalo with us tomorrow," signed Man-with-no-hair.

"I can hunt buffalo," the boy signed back proudly.

Scott gave Man-with-no-hair a curious look, thinking the boy was too young to go along.

"He is very brave," Man-with-no-hair said in response to the unasked question.

"He is welcome to hunt with us," Scott signed so Runs-like-an-antelope would know what he had said.

2

The small camp was alive with activity long before dawn the next morning. Runs-like-an-antelope was beside himself with anticipation.

Man-with-no-hair was shocked at the profound effect Dew-on-the-grass-in-the-moon-when-the-leaves-fall had had on Scott during his absence. When he stepped out of the tepee, he looked more Indian than white. If it had not been for his hair, it would have been difficult to tell what race he belonged to. Dew-on-the-grass-in-the-moon-when-the-leaves-fall had attached an eagle feather to his hair. He wore a new shirt that had shells and bear claws and teeth sewn into the fabric. He had painted a streak across his forehead and another down his nose that forked at the nostril and spread across each cheek.

Scott felt a bit foolish as he stepped out of the tepee. He had never gone to so much trouble just to get ready to hunt. He was proud of the new shirt Dew-on-the-grass-in-the-moon-when-the-leaves-fall had made for him and he painted his face because she asked him to. He caught Man-with-no-hair's look and was encouraged when his friend nodded his head in approval. Runs-like-an-antelope was in awe of the way Scott looked.

Man-with-no-hair led three horses to the tepee. Scott took the lead rope of the spotted pony and swung onto its back. When he was seated he saw Runs-like-an-antelope signing to Man-with-no-hair. He was unable to tell what the boy had said but he saw enough to know that the spotted horse had been the subject of the conversation.

"Runs-like-an-antelope said he has heard of horses like yours but has never seen one. He said it comes from the land of the 'Nez Perce,' from the other side of the mountains."

Scott considered this information and was curious if anyone would ever come in search of the young man the bear had killed.

When Runs-like-an-antelope was mounted, they turned and rode out of the finger. The boy continued to marvel at Scott's horse, but he seemed equally impressed to be on the back of one of Man-with-no-hair's mares.

They saw several deer and a small band of elk as they rode toward the forks. Had their intent been to simply bring in fresh meat, they would have been on their way back to camp very soon.

When they reached the forks, they could not see any buffalo but there were plenty of fresh signs. For some reason, the buffalo liked to stay around the forks of the valleys, though not in great numbers. Perhaps there was water or salt nearby.

The tracks were scattered signs of milling and feeding animals and it was difficult to tell where they had gone, for they had knocked down the tall dry grass in all directions.

"We should split up until we find them," Man-with-no-hair suggested.

"I'll go this way," said Scott, indicating the southern valley.

"The boy and I will circle around here. Do not go too far," he warned. "We should hunt them together."

Scott agreed and then turned his horse around and rode into the southern fork of the valley. He usually watched his surroundings very closely, but now he rode slowly and watched even more carefully, not wishing to spook the buffalo before they were ready to hunt them.

Scott heard a whoop, and as he turned, he heard the drumming of hooves on the valley floor. Two-dozen buffalo came crashing out of the forest, on the north side of the valley. They entered the southern valley and thundered toward Scott. Man-with-no-hair and Runs-like-an-antelope came out of the timber in close pursuit.

Scott's heart hammered in his chest, not out of fear, but from excitement: the hunt was on and the game was at hand. He knew the spotted horse was fast enough to take him out of harm's way and then catch up with the herd again.

The lead buffalo saw Scott and turned enough to sweep around him. Scott on the other hand, moved to intercept.

Man-with-no-hair got close to a yearling calf and shot an arrow into its lungs. The calf separated from the herd and was soon lost in a cloud of dust.

Scott closed in on a large cow and shot an arrow behind her front shoulder. The hit was good but the cow was large and she did not go down. Scott nocked another arrow. He was about to shoot the cow again but she faltered and stopped running. Scott rode by her an instant later and hit her with another arrow. The cow went down as the spotted pony pranced about, anxious to give chase to the herd. Scott turned his horse and saw Man-with-no-hair shoot and kill a young bull. Runs-like-an-antelope had stuck three arrows in another young bull but his bow was too weak to drive the arrows deep enough to kill the animal quickly.

When Man-with-no-hair saw the bull he shot fall, he raced to help Runs-like-an-antelope. When he caught up with him, he did not interfere. His intention was to make sure no harm came to the boy, not to kill his game for him.

Scott stepped off the spotted pony and walked to the dying cow. She was still alive but unable to move. He drew his hand axe and moved around behind her to avoid her hooves. A final blow from the hand axe put an end to her suffering. Scott tied his horse to a foreleg of the cow and went to check on the other two buffalo. They were both dead when he got to them. He returned to the cow and began to butcher her.

Scott had the entrails removed and was half finished skinning the cow when Man-with-no-hair and Runs-like-an-antelope returned. The boy had blood smeared all over his upper body. To Scott, it seemed a strange custom, but he was aware of the emotions that were invoked when a young hunter made his first kill.

"We have killed too many," said Man-with-no-hair, with a wry grin.

"We should send Runs-like-an-antelope back for Dew-on-the-grass-in-the-moon-when-the-leaves-fall and Morning Fawn," said Scott, as he looked at the rapidly rising sun. "Soon it will be hot. It will help to get the hides off but there will be flies too. I do not think you and I can save all of this meat without help."

Man-with-no-hair nodded. Runs-like-an-antelope was euphoric about his accomplishment and Man-with-no-hair hated to ruin that by sending him after the women, but he was the only clear choice.

Runs-like-an-antelope was a child of the wilderness. The ways, or rules, of the wilderness dictated what you had to do to survive. If you broke the rules, you would perish. You may get lucky once or twice, but the rules were strict and eventually you would have to pay the price, which was your life or the lives of others around you. Today, he would have to learn a new rule: sometimes you had to do things that you did not want to do – for the good of the others. It was the unspoken rule of the camp in which Man-with-no-hair, Scott and Dew-on-the-grass-in-the-moon-when-the-leaves-fall lived. It was a rule Three-legged Wolf had been unwilling to accept and for that, he was no longer welcome. It would be awhile before he completely understood the importance of the rule and Man-with-no-hair expected an argument when he asked the boy to go after the women.

"There is much meat to care for," he signed back to Man-with-no-hair. "I would like to stay and help but I can see that we will need the help of Dew-on-the-grass-in-the-moon-when-the-leaves-fall and Morning Fawn. I will bring them here."

The boy's response both surprised Man-with-no-hair and made him very proud. "What you do is a good thing. Scott and I are happy to have you in our camp."

Man-with-no-hair's words made the boy feel proud – and useful. He had felt needed and useful when he had been taking care of his sister; however, he had had no one to share that accomplishment with. Now, there were people to be proud of him and he was anxious to please them.

"Ride quickly, there is much meat to care for," signed Man-with-no-hair as he slapped the boy's mare on the rump and watched her burst into a gallop.

It was early afternoon when Runs-like-an-antelope returned, leading Dew-on-the-grass-in-the-moon-when-the-leaves-fall and Morning Fawn. Each of the women rode a horse and carried tools for butchering. Scott and Man-with-no-hair had gutted and skinned all of the fallen animals. They were in the process of boning out the second carcass when help arrived.

Dew-on-the-grass-in-the-moon-when-the-leaves-fall and Morning Fawn immediately sized up the situation and began to bone out one of the other buffalo.

By late afternoon, all of the meat had been cut from the carcasses. Man-with-no-hair and Scott had made two travois with which to transport the meat. They had discussed curing the meat where they were but decided they did not wish to be away from camp that long. It would take several days to cure the amount of meat they had.

Ordinarily, they would not have prepared to move so late in the afternoon, but for the last few days, the moon had been approaching full. On this night, the last night before it was completely full, there would be enough light to allow them to move safely through the valley. The moon would light their way until dawn, but they would arrive in camp long before that.

It was late when they got back to camp. It had been a long, hard day for everyone and they were tired. Sky Eyes cried for attention and Dew-on-the-grass-in-the-moon-when-the-leaves-fall immediately saw to his needs. Though the moonlight was bright, the finger was timbered on either side, and little light shone into the camp. Thus, there was little to be done in way of preserving the meat until morning. When the horses were seen to and the travois propped up, everyone turned in.

The next morning, everyone was up early and they worked throughout the day. That evening, all six people sat around one fire. They had just eaten and were all feeling good about what they had done together.

"I have seen these men do things that only women do in an Arapaho village," Morning Fawn signed to Dew-on-the-grass-in-the-moon-when-the-leaves-fall. "It is good that they help us, but why do they do it?"

"It is the way it has always been in this camp," Dew-on-the-grass-in-the-moon-when-the-leaves-fall answered. "There are too few of us for most of the tasks to fall to one person. There are things I do not let them do, but if it weren't for their help, some of us would not be alive now."

"They don't seem to mind doing things most warriors would not do."

"I am sure," Dew-on-the-grass-in-the-moon-when-the-leaves-fall signed back, "there are things they do not like doing nor do they want to. But if they didn't do them, someone else would have to or it would not get done. If enough things do not get done, we would die in the winter. To survive the winter here, we must all work together."

"You spent the winter up here?" signed Morning Fawn incredulously.

"Yes," Dew-on-the-grass-in-the-moon-when-the-leaves-fall answered, confused by Morning Fawn's sudden response.

Man-with-no-hair and Scott had been busy discussing how many more buffalo hides would be needed to complete the new tepee. Now, they turned their attention to the two women, sensing they were about to learn something new about the country in which they lived.

"No one stays this high in the mountains in the winter," said Morning Fawn, less adamantly now that she had an audience.

"Why do you say that?" Man-with-no-hair asked, trying to understand the point she was trying to make.

"There is too much snow. It gets too cold. The horses will starve. Old people and babies freeze to death. No one stays this high in the winter. It is a bad thing to do."

"We have no place to go," signed Man-with-no-hair. "We do not know where to go where we will be safe. We could go where the Arapaho go in the winter."

Runs-like-an-antelope spat upon the ground near the fire. Everyone looked at him curiously, wondering just how deeply his hatred for his former people ran.

Embarrassed by his display, the boy blushed, but signed, "I will not live in the camp of the Arapaho. They treat their dogs better than they treated my sister. I will not forgive them."

Man-with-no-hair was concerned about the boy's hatred but now it was more important to learn what they should do in the winter. "We had a hard time last winter but we lost no horses. No one here froze to death."

"Last winter was mild," signed Morning Fawn. "From the signs I have seen, this winter will be mild too. In a normal winter, the snow would be over your head...when you are on your horse."

Man-with-no-hair's jaw dropped open in total shock from what he had just learned. He looked at Scott who was showing equal signs of disbelief. All they could think of was how lucky they had been last winter. If they had gotten normal snowfall, they would all be dead now.

3

A few weeks later, the camp contained a second tepee. It was smaller than the tepee they had brought with them. Scott, Dew-on-the-grass-in-the-moon-when-the-leaves-fall and Sky Eyes needed less room than Man-with-no-hair, Morning Fawn and Runs-like-an-antelope, so they decided to move into the new, smaller tepee. They could enlarge the tepee when the need arose, or when they decided to hunt the buffalo again.

The new tepee was completed just in time, for the seasons were beginning to change. The nights were cool and there were fewer hours of daylight. The hardwood leaves were beginning to change color and drop from their trees. The needles of the tamarack were turning yellow.

Morning Fawn convinced them they would be safe another winter in their mountain home. They would stay, but the following summer would be devoted to locating a place for them to live in the winter. They would have to find a place that was lower in elevation but had enough wood for fires and enough game to keep their bellies full.

The mare that had been bred to Scott's horse was beginning to show the first signs that she was with foal. Always curious about the ways of animals, Man-with-no-hair decided to keep track of the time that passed between the time the mare was bred and the when the foal was born.

In the dim, cold hours of early morning, Morning Fawn slipped from the tepee and stole into the forest. There, alone, she could be sick without the others knowing. Man-with-no-hair had told her about Spotted Fawn and the agony he had gone through when she and their baby died. Morning Fawn did not wish to be a cause for concern until it was unavoidable.

4

Late the following spring, Morning Fawn gave birth to a fine, healthy girl. Though it was her first child, it was an easy birth and Morning Fawn recovered very quickly. Man-with-no-hair was beside himself with pleasure and pride. The month before the birth had been very difficult for him. He had known Morning Fawn and the baby would die. He did not know what to do with himself and not even Scott could get him to relax. He would pace about the camp, talking to himself. He would walk to the meadow, get on a horse, get back off and return to the camp, where he would continue his incessant pacing. He had no desire to hunt or explore. He felt a burning need to be away from the camp but was unable to leave, and not know what was happening with Morning Fawn. Everyone in the camp was relieved when the child was finally born.

Man-with-no-hair named the baby girl Fawn out of respect for the two women who had meant so much to him in his life.

Two weeks later Man-with-no-hair's mare threw her foal. It was a colt and it had a spotted blanket, though smaller than its father's blanket.

5

The camp was growing and there was much happiness. There were hard times, too, but because they worked together, they always managed to overcome all obstacles before them.

The weeks turned into months and the months turned into years, and the years began to slip by. Scott and Man-with-no-hair spent many hours teaching Runs-like-an-antelope and Sky Eyes the secrets of survival. When she could escape from the camp, Fawn joined in the lessons, as well.

Over the years, Three-legged Wolf returned to the camp several times. He was very uncomfortable around Man-with-no-hair and he never stayed long. No one missed him when he was gone.

During the long, dark days of deep winter, the members of the small village spent many hours together. They taught each other their native languages. They were soon tri-lingual. This was important, because they never knew when they would meet someone who would speak one of the languages. More important, was the fact that they would not have to rely on sign language and they would be able to share their histories with each other. When Scott talked about great boats and massive homes built of stone across the giant, salty lake, they always wanted to hear more. He was equally impressed with the stories they had to tell of their heritage.

Chapter Twenty-one

Ten years had passed since the birth of Sky Eyes. There was peace in the camp and all was good. Unfortunately, all was not good in the world that surrounded the camp.

2

In some areas, the previous winter had been exceptionally severe. Anticipating the severity of the winter, Man-with-no-hair and Scott had moved the camp to a lower elevation. They had discovered the area while scouting. Though still cold, they didn't have to worry about the enormous amounts of snowfall. There was ample wood and game.

Far to the north of the snow-buried, hidden finger, a Crow village was facing starvation. The migrating animals had left early and there was very little to eat.

Several years earlier, at a summer gathering of Crow villages, there had been a dispute over the ownership of about twenty-five horses. The chiefs of all of the other villages accused the members of the village that was starving of the crime. A fierce argument ensued, which ultimately left the village all but excluded from the Crow nation. The summer and fall before the harsh winter, the hunters of the village had suffered much bad luck. It seemed that no matter which direction they hunted in, they ran into hunting parties of other Crow villages, as well as Sioux and Northern Cheyenne. Singularly, their numbers were too small to defend their hunting grounds.

Worse than the infringements on their hunting grounds, was the predation their horse herd suffered at the hands of other villages and nations. In the past, there had always been enough horsemeat to ensure their survival through a particularly tough time. Now, there were not enough horses to mount all of the warriors.

In an act of desperation, a group of warriors rode out of the village. They were the best and strongest warriors of the village. The importance of their mission was not lost on a single warrior: if they did not succeed, the village would starve.

The plan was to raid the horse herd of a nearby Sioux village.

When the Crow left their village the sky was overcast and threatening. The temperature was far below freezing. They hoped the weather conditions would help them catch the Sioux unsuspecting.

Two days later, the Crow approached the Sioux village at dusk. They waited at a distance until the village settled down for the night. When there was no longer visible movement in the village, the Crow moved in to surround the Sioux horse herd.

Though it was cold, the Sioux did not leave their horses unattended. The horses were simply too valuable to them. One of the guards became suspicious when the horses he was watching began to move away. He ran into the meadow and saw two Crow leaning over their horses, hoping to avoid detection. The sentry sounded the alarm and then had to make a run for the village, for he was being chased by two more mounted Crow.

Half-naked warriors left the warmth of their tepees with weapons in hand. They rushed forth to protect their village. A bloody battle ensued in which the warmly dressed Crow released their pent up anger on the ill-clad Sioux.

The Crow indiscriminately killed every Sioux who crossed their path. They stole food from unoccupied tepees and when they had what they wanted, they destroyed the homes.

What the Crow left behind that night, was a village that was in much worse condition than their own.

As the Crow pushed the stolen horses toward their own village, they were soon overcome by the gravity of what they had done. Indians very seldom killed other Indians. They stole horses from one another and there were various ways of counting coup on other peoples. Actions, though sometimes violent, were seldom fatal. Even stealing women and children was considered acceptable – slaughtering and pillaging an entire village on a cold winter night, was not. The Crow knew this, and though their village would soon eat again, they did not celebrate their victory.

When the Crow warriors returned to their village, they slaughtered ten horses and divided the meat among the villagers. The next day they killed five more horses. Within a few sunrises, the strength of the villagers had returned.

A half moon after the warriors returned with the Sioux horses, the Crow chief made a difficult, but necessary, decision. The village would move out of the area. He knew the Sioux would not forget what they had done and forgiveness was out of the question. Their only hope was to go far away and stay away. The next day, the only sign that remained of the village were travois tracks in the snow.

3

The Sioux who survived the Crow attack made their way to the nearest Sioux village. Soon the details of the attack spread throughout the Sioux nation. Word also reached other Crow villages and though they sent emissaries to the Sioux explaining their non-participation, they spent many sleepless nights fearing retribution.

The Sioux decided against a hasty retaliation. The winter was just too severe. They would wait until the summer gathering and then send a thousand warriors against the Crow village.

4

The fleeing Crow moved far to the south. They endured many hardships along the way. Several squaws bore children in the night only to find themselves on the trail again the next morning. Game was scarce and they continued to eat the horses. They encountered villages of various nations but always gave them a wide berth, without making contact.

When at last, the bitter winter began to loosen its grip on the land, the Crow hunters began to bring meat into the village. However, along with the longer, warmer days, came the knowledge that the Sioux would also soon be coming.

The Crow chief was crafty. He knew his people were exhausted from traveling throughout the winter. It would take more than a few warm days for them to fully recover from the ordeal. He felt his best hope was to take his people into rough terrain where they would not be susceptible to the Sioux numbers that surely would come against them. The trick would be to find such a place that also had an adequate food supply.

At last, in late spring, the Crow came into a large hanging valley that was surrounded by jagged peaks. The valley contained deer, elk and various smaller game. There were also several small streams, so water would not be a problem.

The chief sent warriors out to learn the lay of the land. They were also to look for escape routes in all directions. He also sent warriors to the surrounding peaks in search of vantage points from which to watch for the Sioux.

5

When the Sioux came together for their summer gathering, there was much happiness. The winter had been long and hard and it was good to see old friends who had pulled through the difficult time, too. Oftentimes, family members married people from other villages. The summer gatherings were an opportunity to visit with these seldom seen offspring and siblings. This particular year, there was also much sadness.

The survivors of the raided village recounted their story around the campfires at the gathering. Within a few days, the Sioux had worked themselves into a frenzy, wanting nothing but revenge. Young warriors, anxious to prove themselves in battle, pleaded with the elders to be quick about organizing a war party to go against the Crow.

In their infinite wisdom, the assembled chiefs waited until the time was right. They waited until they knew all of the snow was gone out of the passes and the migrating herds, which would sustain the war party, had returned to the higher elevations. They were also patient because they knew an entire Crow village could not escape them.

At last, the chiefs sent the word that the time had come. Waves of excitement ran through the encampment. Each chief was asked to supply a certain number of warriors. An unlucky few would have to stay behind to hunt for and protect the collection of villages.

Finally, one morning, as the sun was beginning to show itself over the eastern horizon, four hundred Sioux warriors rode out of the encampment.

Though the Crow had traveled in the deep snow, the signs of their passing were still upon the land. There were horse droppings, and an occasional travois mark or a partially covered campfire. For the Sioux, the trail was easy to follow.

6

A Crow sentinel raced his horse into the village. He quickly spread the word that the Sioux were coming.

The Crow villagers quickly disassembled their tepees and stashed them in pre-determined locations in the forest. The Sioux war party was too large for them to fight, so they would run into the mountains. When the village was dismantled, the villagers divided into three groups. Each group went in a different direction and soon the entire village had disappeared into the forest.

7

Two days later, the Sioux rode into the abandoned village. It took little time to learn what had taken place. The Sioux, too, divided into three groups and continued to pursue the Crow.

The Crow had studied the land well and they led the Sioux on a wild chase. The Crow managed to elude the Sioux at every turn. The Sioux were becoming frustrated with the maneuvering capabilities of the Crow.

Chapter Twenty-two

Summer was a favorite time for the members of Scott and Man-with-no-hair's *village*. It was the only time of the year they could totally relax. It was the best time to work with the young horses, as well as the young warriors.

"It is time to see if Sky Eyes and Fawn have learned what they have been taught," Man-with-no-hair said to Scott, one bright, sunny morning.

"I agree," said Scott. "It's time for a test to see what areas they need help in. What do you think would be the best way to test them?"

"We will give each of them a horse. We will give them a two-day head start. At the end of two days, we will begin to track them. When ten days have gone by, if they return to camp without being captured and they are not starving, they will have learned well.

"It is a good test," said Scott, smiling. Secretly, he wished he could have traded places with Sky Eyes and devised methods with which to confuse whomever tracked him.

Sky Eyes knew the time for testing his abilities was at hand but he was surprised to learn that his first test would begin that very day. He was disappointed when he learned Fawn would accompany him but she was a good friend and his disappointment was short lived.

A short time after Man-with-no-hair and Scott had discussed the test, Sky Eyes and Fawn rode out of the camp. Sky Eyes rode the spotted pony Scott had had for so many years. Age had taken its toll on the animal but he still had many good years left in him.

Dew-on-the-grass-in-the-moon-when-the-leaves-fall and Morning Fawn watched proudly as their children rode out of the finger. They each had a three-year-old child playing in the dust near the fire pit. Their village was indeed growing.

When Sky Eyes and Fawn disappeared into the timber on the other side of the meadow, Scott and Man-with-no-hair went to the meadow to work with the horses. Every summer there were new foals to train. The horse herd was growing too.

Some time later, Scott saw Dew-on-the-grass-in-the-moon-when-the-leaves-fall and Morning Fawn walking toward him. Man-with-no-hair was going to ride a three-year-old filly for the first time and everyone wanted to watch. Dew-on-the-grass-in-the-moon-when-the-leaves-fall was carrying their second son, Son-of-bear-killer, a name Man-with-no-hair had suggested. Morning Fawn was carrying her son, Sneaks-quietly-through-the-grass, a name Scott had suggested.

When Dew-on-the-grass-in-the-moon-when-the-leaves-fall and Morning Fawn joined Scott, they watched Runs-like-an-antelope lead the filly to Man-with-no-hair.

Man-with-no-hair stroked the filly gently and talked to her in a soothing voice. He slowly walked around the horse, talking and stroking her as he walked. When he was once again standing in front of the horse, he scratched her between the ears. The filly seemed to thoroughly enjoy the special attention she was receiving.

Man-with-no-hair stepped to the side of the horse, taking the lead rope from Runs-like-an-antelope. With one fluid movement, he swung on top of the horse's back. This was the time when the hours of gentle, caring treatment paid off. The filly did not pitch and buck as everyone feared she might. She was obviously nervous with the unaccustomed weight on her back, but she displayed no signs of fear or panic.

"You won't see me thrown from a horse today," Man-with-no-hair said with an exultant smile.

In a way, everyone was relieved; being thrown from a horse could result in a serious injury. However, they were somewhat disappointed that the filly did not attempt to dislodge its rider. They all watched patiently as Man-with-no-hair began to teach the filly to respond to his body movements.

After a while, Dew-on-the-grass-in-the-moon-when-the-leaves-fall and Morning Fawn decided to return to the camp.

Runs-like-an-antelope mounted one of his horses in case the filly tried to run off with Man-with-no-hair on her back.

Scott returned to work, cleaning the hooves of a mare.

Sky Eyes and Fawn were high above the meadow, climbing the ridge Man-with-no-hair, Scott and Dew-on-the-grass-in-the-moon-when-the-leaves-fall had come down when they first came to the valley.

One-hundred-fifty Sioux curiously watched the inhabitants of the valley from the cover of the thick timber.

2

"They are not Crow. We will not attack them," said Running Elk, the senior warrior of the party.

"They are evil. They have probably already helped the Crow," said Buffalo-stands-in-the-river.

Running Elk eyed the younger warrior closely. He did not like Buffalo-stands-in-the-river; he was quick to talk but slow to back up his sharp words. The older man wondered what caused a man to turn out the way Buffalo-stands-in-the-river had.

Running Elk would have dismissed the younger man completely, except his father and uncle were both powerful medicine men. Running Elk feared nothing he could see; he could not see spirits however, and he feared them and the people who consorted with them.

"How can you say they are evil?" asked Running Elk.

"Look at that one," said Buffalo-stands-in-the-river, indicating Scott. "I have never seen a *man with* hair on his face. Have you? Look at the color of his hair. Have you ever seen a *man with* that color of hair. He looks like a coyote or a wolf. Have you ever seen a coyote or wolf walk on two legs? This is a strange place and the people who live here are strange. If they are strange – they are evil! The good spirits that protect us sent the Crow against us so we would come here and rub out these evil creatures."

Running Elk didn't like it, but the arguments of Buffalo-stands-in-the-river were beginning to make sense. The situation was worsened by Running Elk's dread of offending the spirits.

"We should send someone to talk to them," said Running Elk. "If they have not helped the Crow, we will leave them in peace. If they have helped the Crow we will kill them and move on."

"Who will you send to talk to them?" Buffalo-stands-in-the-river asked sarcastically. "Will you go? Will you send a young man against a spirit? What will you tell his mother when he is dead?"

"Enough," said Running Elk. "Spread the warriors out. Attack when I give the word."

Smiling humorlessly, Buffalo-stands-in-the-river turned to the warriors and spread the word.

Two squaws were walking across the meadow; they each had a young child at their side. Two braves were mounted. The evil one was cleaning the hooves of a horse.

Running Elk gave the signal.

3

Scott heard the hoof beats of running horses. He thought it was Man-with-no-hair and Runs-like-an-antelope. It was too late when he realized the sound was too loud for just two horses. He was dropping the hoof and preparing to stand and look about when he heard Man-with-no-hair issue a blood-curdling war cry. His blood seemed to freeze in his veins when he saw a large number of Indians swarm around Man-with-no-hair. Man-with-no-hair would have stood a chance had he been on any horse other than the inexperienced filly.

"MAAAAAAAAN," Scott screamed as the swarming horde overtook his friend. As soon as the word was out of Scott's mouth he saw a least a dozen arrows penetrate his friend's body.

Runs-like-an-antelope drew his knife and charged the attackers. He slashed and cut as he rode through their ranks. He killed two warriors outright and wounded three more before two arrows in the back knocked him from his horse. Three warriors jumped from their horses and stabbed and cut the fallen body.

Scott had been running toward Dew-on-the-grass-in-the-moon-when-the-leaves-fall and Morning Fawn and the children without realizing he had been moving. He watched the unbelievable scene as he ran. Dew-on-the-grass-in-the-moon-when-the-leaves-fall and the others had only gone a short distance when the attack began. Scott had closed that distance considerably, but the attackers were going to get to Dew-on-the-grass-in-the-moon-when-the-leaves-fall before he did.

"Run, Dew-on-the-grass-in-the-moon-when-the-leaves-fall," he shouted "RUUUUN…"

His words were a wasted effort. They were running. There was no hope. Scott stopped running when the women and children became surrounded. He could no longer see them but he could see the attackers shooting their bows and swinging their tomahawks.

Scott's stomach retched when he thought of his beloved Dew-on-the-grass-in-the-moon-when-the-leaves-fall falling to the ground spilling her life's blood on the meadow she had loved so. His body went into shock. He was unaware of what he said or did. He knew he was going to die…Without Dew-on-the-grass-in-the-moon-when-the-leaves-fall he was already dead.

"YOU..." he tried to curse but it had been so long since he had heard someone curse, he couldn't remember how. He had to say something to them...damn them to hell...somehow...

"YOU BLOODY, MURDERING SONS-OF-WHORES!" he screamed at the top of a broken, harsh voice.

They no longer ran their horses. There was no need. There was no one left but Scott and he was not running from them.

Scott was facing them as they turned their attention from the dead women and children to him. At the sound of his voice they all began to move toward him, forming a semi-circle around him.

A foolish young warrior kicked his horse into a gallop and charged, intending to drive a buffalo spear into Scott.

Scott drew his knife and waited. When the young warrior was close, he parried the spear and disemboweled the warrior as he rode by.

Scott's action caused a stir among attackers. Before he turned back to face them he felt a sharp pain in his side. He looked down and saw an arrow protruding through his new doe-skin shirt.

His brow furrowed slightly as he looked at the arrow. Strangely, his mind seemed to say, *So this is what it feels like to get shot with an arrow. It's not as bad as I thought it would be.*

His mind was in shock. He did not feel the pain of the arrow. He laughed at the Sioux warriors. He couldn't help himself, he knew this was a sad time. He should not be laughing.

"Ha Ha. You can't hurt me, you pieces of buffalo dung," he said as he defiantly faced the Indians, looking from one face to the next.

Scott watched as a brave drew back his bow and released an arrow. He watched the arrow fly through the air as if it were moving in slow motion.

The arrow hit Scott in the stomach and despite his best efforts he could not conceal all of the pain he felt. He doubled over but managed to stand erect after the initial impact. He looked at the attackers defiantly.

"You cowardly sons-of-whores," he said. He tried to say it louder and more bitterly, but it was becoming more and more difficult to speak.

"Your squaws have more courage than you," Scott said to them as another arrow struck his body. The third arrow struck him in the breast bone and knocked him to the ground. He landed hard on his back but managed to roll to his hands and knees. He coughed and saw a spray of blood fly out of his mouth. He still felt little pain and was thankful for that. He slowly got to his feet and found that his knees were getting wobbly. He turned and faced his attackers again. He tried to throw his knife at one of the closest Sioux but he had unknowingly dropped the weapon when the first arrow had struck him. He simply swung an empty arm at the astonished Indian.

Feeling a desperate need to retaliate in some way, Scott spat blood at them. He had no weapon. He knew he could not walk to them, though they were very near. If he could put his powerful hands on one of them…they would know his strength. The ridiculous act of spitting at them made Scott laugh. He laughed and spat until another arrow knocked him down again.

"I hope all of your unborn children die before they are born," he said so quietly that none of the Sioux heard the words.

Scott got to his hands and knees but could not get to his feet. His vision was becoming clouded. He thought he saw a small rock in front of him. He reached for the rock and threw it at the Indians. The throw was too weak to harm a child much less a full-grown warrior. There were no more rocks…he threw dirt at them.

He raised his head high enough to see legs walking toward him. *Oh, dear God in heaven, here it comes*, he thought as he recognized a tomahawk swinging beside the approaching legs.

"Be strong," he mumbled. "Do not let them see weakness. Think about good things. I love this meadow. I love this land. I love Dew-on-the-grass-in-the-moon-when-the-leaves-fall, oh yes, I love Dew-on-the-grass-in-the-moon-when-the-leaves-fall. I love Man-with-no-hair. Does that sound strange? I've never said that before. I love Sky Eyes. I love…"

The attack had no more than begun and Running Elk was sorry he had let himself get talked into it. They had no right to attack these people. They had caused the Sioux no grief.

His warriors had seemingly gone berserk once the bloodletting had begun. The quick death of the two Sioux seemed to increase their frenzy. His braves attacked the two woman and children as if they hoped to gain some prestige from the act. By that time, it was too late for Running Elk to stop them.

After the women and children had fallen, they became aware of someone yelling at them in a strange tongue. All of the Sioux turned in unison. The man before them truly was a strange looking man, but he was a man. Running Elk and his warriors slowly rode toward the hairy-faced man. The warrior chief was so intent upon looking at the hairy-faced man, he didn't see the young warrior charge him until it was too late. It happened too quickly. Everything was happening too quickly.

Running Elk's shock turned to respect when the hairy-faced man continued to defy them, even with an arrow sticking out of his side. Respect turned to awe as the strange looking man defied them with laughter. Respect and awe turned to pity when the dying man spat blood at them and threw dirt at them. Pity turned to disgust when Buffalo-stands-in-the-river dismounted, walked forward, and drove his tomahawk into the man's head. Disgust turned to disgrace when Buffalo-stands-in-the-river issued a triumphant war cry as he turned to face his fellow warriors.

Running Elk slowly dismounted and walked to Buffalo-stands-in-the-river. He looked from the fallen man to the triumphant warrior.

"We have done a bad thing here today," said Running Elk.

"We have killed the evil ones," said Buffalo-stands-in-the-river, incredulously.

"We have done a bad thing here today," repeated Running Elk as he drew his knife and cut Buffalo-stands-in-the-river's throat.

"We have done a bad thing here today," Running Elk said for the third time. This time he said it more loudly, so all could hear. "We are Sioux," he continued. "We are a proud and powerful people. Not only have I shamed myself today, I have shamed my people. I am not fit to lead you. I am not fit to live. I will not eat. I will not drink. I will walk upon the earth until the spirits take me away. You return to our people and tell them what has happened here."

With that said, Running Elk dropped his knife and walked across the meadow. He was never seen again.

Part Two

Chapter Twenty-three

Sky Eyes and Fawn watched the attack with wide-eyed horror. The same question raced through their minds at the same time: *why...why...why?*

They were safely away from the bloody scene, and in no danger; but they no longer had a home to return to at the end of their test.

No tears were shed. They had not learned to cry; they had learned to survive.

"What will happen now?" asked Fawn, as she looked from the carnage to Sky Eyes and then back to the valley floor.

"No one will come to look for us," answered Sky Eyes, as the weight of their aloneness swept over him.

Fawn looked at him strangely as she considered his statement. "What will we do?"

"We will survive," Sky Eyes answered, matter-of-factly.

"I know," she said. "But I will miss them. I loved them."

"I did, too, Little One. I did, too."

Sky Eyes turned from the bloody scene of his family's death. He led the spotted pony up the steep hill. Fawn remained where she was, staring into the valley.

"We must go," Sky Eyes warned, when he noticed she was not following him.

"I want my mother," she said so quietly he barely heard her words.

"I know, but your mother is no more. Our families are no more." Sky Eyes told her softly, patiently.

"Why did they come? Why did they kill our families?" asked Fawn, as she turned and faced up hill, looking at Sky Eyes.

"I do not know, but what is done is done. There is nothing we can do for them. We must take care of ourselves now," Sky Eyes explained.

"Can we go back to the valley? That is our home. We can live there," she said, hopefully.

"We will never go into that valley again!" Sky Eyes said with such bitterness it shook the young girl.

"Where will we go?" she asked.

"I do not know, but we must find a safe place to make our camp. We have much to do before winter."

Once again, Sky Eyes started up the hill. This time Fawn followed him. As he struggled up the slope, he considered the situation he and Fawn were faced with. Though he was young, he was very confident in his abilities to provide for and protect himself and Fawn. He had been taught by masters of survival. He had seen Man-with-no-hair get close enough to a deer to touch it before it knew he was there. Sky Eyes had not touched a living deer yet, but he had come very close. The problems that faced him, however, were not necessarily centered on his ability to be stealthy. He must be able to recognize a suitable and safe place to live. There must be adequate food and water.

Several times in the past few years, when the signs indicated the winter would be hard, they had gone to another camp. Sky Eyes considered going there, but he was afraid the people who had killed his family would go there looking for him and Fawn. He also didn't know if there would be game there at this time of the year. He would have to spend the rest of the summer, if necessary, looking for a new place to live.

Food was not as serious a problem for Sky Eyes as was shelter. If game was at hand, he would be successful. He would need buffalo hides to make a tepee. He had never killed a buffalo. If Man-with-no-hair and his father had not been killed, they would have taken him on their annual buffalo hunt. Fortunately, they had shared their techniques and strategies with him. Unfortunately, his bow was not strong enough to drive a fatal arrow into a full-grown buffalo.

Sky Eyes found that if he concentrated on the survival of Fawn and himself, he had little time to think about their dead family members, lying on the valley floor. He was bitter about the unprovoked attack, but there was nothing he could have done. He had been too far away to retaliate, but such an act would have been little more than suicide. He had briefly considered following the marauding Indians and killing them one at a time, but he knew he would have eventually been caught. Fawn would suffer whatever fate befell him.

"Elk hide!" he said out loud.

His thoughts had remained on their survival. He couldn't kill a buffalo but he could kill an elk. They could use elk hides to make their tepee. Fawn was only in her ninth summer; they would not need a great deal of room inside a tepee. They may not need more than three elk hides to make their tepee. The meat from three elk would last them for a long time.

Sky Eyes began to feel better now that a survival plan was beginning to formulate. The time factor was still a serious consideration. He had to find a safe place to live that had elk in the vicinity. They had at least two more moons of summer, but it would take at least a week to finish each hide, once it had dried.

Sky Eyes suddenly became aware that he had reached the top of the slope. He was ashamed that he had been so deep in thought that he had not been watching where he was going. That was a very good way to get killed and he vowed to be more alert in the future.

"Where do we go now?" asked Fawn, from behind him.

"This is the ridge our fathers and my mother followed on their way to the valley," said Sky Eyes. "There is a village many days to the east. I do not know what people live there. We will not go there. We will go east until we find a ridge that will take us north."

Fawn seemed satisfied with his decision.

She was numb with shock from witnessing the slaughter of her friends and family. She was not able to see or feel. She simply followed Sky Eyes. She wanted to go back to the meadow to be with her mother but Sky Eyes had said "No." She knew her mother was safe and was waiting for her to come and help her. She couldn't understand why Sky Eyes wouldn't let her go back. He had said they were "no more" but how did he know? She had seen the attack, too, and she knew her mother was safe. She would talk to him about going back when they stopped to camp for the night. She would make him understand that her mother needed her and she must go back.

Time passed very slowly for Fawn. Her mind told her she was in the meadow, but this did not look like their meadow. She was confused and the confusion was frightening. She was thankful for Sky Eyes. He had always been a good friend to her and she knew he would take care of her.

They came into a saddle as dusk was approaching. There was a small group of trees on the eastern slope of the saddle. Sky Eyes decided to camp near the trees.

Sky Eyes tied the spotted pony to a low limb on one of the pine trees. He expected Fawn to do the same with her horse, but she just stood there with the lead rope in her hand.

Fawn's mind had been able to accept the fact that she had to follow Sky Eyes; however, she was unable to adjust quickly to a different situation.

"Fawn...Fawn. Tie your horse to the tree."

She shook her head slightly and looked at Sky Eyes with a lost look that told him she did not understand what he wanted her to do.

"Tie your horse to the tree," he repeated gently.

Fawn looked over her shoulder at the horse as if she were seeing it for the first time. She looked questioningly at Sky Eyes.

Sky Eyes' brow furrowed into a frown when he saw the look on Fawn's face. She had never acted like this before. He did not know what to do for her.

"Tomorrow we can go back to the meadow. We have to go back to the meadow. My mother needs me. I have chores to do."

Sky Eyes took two steps toward the girl and took the lead rope from her hand. He led the horse to a tree and tied it off. He returned to Fawn and put both hands on her shoulders.

"Fawn, your mother is dead. She is no more. All of them are dead. We can never go back. That is a valley of death, if we go back we will die, and then we will be no more."

Sky Eyes had been raised in a strange way for one of his blood and the time in which he lived. He had been taught the skills of survival and the ways of a man, but he also been taught compassion for people and animals. He was respectful of the wishes of his elders. He had learned that if he did as he was told, even though he didn't understand why, there was usually a lesson forthcoming. He was raised in an environment that demanded a contribution from everyone, for the good of the group. Now, he was impatient to get underway and begin a new life. His burden would be great without the help of Fawn. Difficult as it was, now was the time for patience and compassion.

"I am sad that our people are no more. My heart is heavy with the pain of our loss. I had much more to learn and now there is no one to teach me. I must now teach myself, and you. I must take care of both of us and I will need your help. Man-with-no-hair and my father are watching from the heavens, I must make them proud. Your mother is watching from the heavens, you must make her proud."

Fawn's face suddenly brightened as if she had not a care in the world. "Can I see my mother in the sky?"

Neither of the children had ever seen a person die, nor had they ever seen a dead person. In an attempt to placate Fawn's feelings, Sky Eyes had to broach a subject of which he knew nothing.

"I have never seen a face in the sky," said Sky Eyes honestly. "But I feel in my heart that we are being watched over." He looked to the setting sun, hating to change the subject but unable to wait any longer. "You prepare the camp and I will go in search of something to eat."

With that said, Sky Eyes gathered up his bow and quiver. He was about to leave when Fawn said, "I am not hungry."

"I am not hungry either, but we must eat. We have much hardship ahead of us and we must be strong," said Sky Eyes, before he turned and walked away from Fawn and the horses.

Fawn watched as he contoured out of the saddle and disappeared into a thick stand of timber. She stepped away from the horses and looked at the sky. She could see no face looking back at her. "Are you up there, Mother?" she asked, softly. "If you can hear me, Mother, I will try to be strong. I will try to make you proud. I...I miss you, Mother."

Fawn turned her attention from the sky to the two horses. She took the packs from the animals and began to arrange the camp.

Sky Eyes returned a short time later with a plump rabbit. He was glad to see that Fawn seemed to be getting over the shock and was contributing to the well being of the camp. The camp was nicely arranged and she had even gone to the trouble of removing the larger rocks from the places where they would sleep. She had also gathered wood and cut two forked sticks to use to spit a small animal.

"You have done well, Fawn," Sky Eyes praised her, hoping to keep her spirits up.

"I will make them proud," is all she said.

As Fawn turned the rabbit over the flames of the small fire, she had another thought concerning her mother. The first stars of evening were beginning to twinkle and she wondered if she would be able to see her mother's face in the night sky? With childish expectation, her spirit lightened even more, much to Sky Eyes' approval.

When they finished eating, they crawled into their sleeping furs. There was much sadness in their hearts, but they were weary from the long, hard climb. Fawn fell asleep the instant she laid her head down. When Sky Eyes was certain she was asleep, he rolled over in his furs and was soon asleep, himself.

Just before dawn, Sky Eyes awoke with a start. The kind of start that often comes when waking in a strange place. His eyes opened slowly and when he became aware that he didn't recognize his surroundings, he sat bolt upright in his furs. He looked around until he saw Fawn sleeping across the ashes of last night's fire. That's when he realized where he was and how he had gotten here.

He had dreamed of hunting with Man-with-no-hair and his father. He had also dreamed that he had seen them die. With awakening came the realization that their deaths had not been a dream.

A deep sadness washed over him. He was lost without the guidance of Man-with-no-hair and his father. What did they expect from him? What was he to do?

He heard Fawn stir in her sleep. The stirring of the girl evoked his *knowing* of what was expected of him and what he had to do. He was suddenly angry with himself for the weakness that had allowed him to feel sorry for himself.

Sky Eyes got out of his furs and knelt by the dead fire. He took half of the remaining rabbit meat and went to Fawn's side. He gently touched her shoulder to awaken her. Fawn, too, awoke with a start but she was quickly reassured by Sky Eyes' presence.

"I am going to check our back trail. You eat and then load the packs. I will put them on the horses when I get back."

Fawn nodded her head as she rubbed the sleep from her eyes.

Sky Eyes walked back through the saddle and up the other side. From a rise in the ridge, he could see a long way in the direction they had come. He sat on a protruding rock, under a bushy, overhanging limb and watched their back trail for an hour. He saw nothing to indicate they were being followed. From his vantage point, he could also see Fawn as she packed their belongings. When she had all of the bundles tied and ready to load, she sat on one of them and looked into the heavens. When Sky Eyes was certain there was no immediate danger from the people who had killed his friends and family, he returned to the camp and Fawn.

"What are you looking for?" asked Sky Eyes, as he quietly walked into the camp.

Sky Eyes' words startled Fawn out of her daydreams as she jumped and gasped.

"I didn't hear you coming," she said.

"You should be more aware of what is happening around you," Sky Eyes chided gently.

"I was talking to mother. I was apologizing to her," Fawn explained.

"Apologizing for what?" asked Sky Eyes.

"For not looking for her last night. You said they were watching us. I looked for her in the sky yesterday, but I did not see her. When I saw the twinkling stars last night, I thought I would be able to see her in the night sky. But I was so tired I went right to sleep and did not look for her. I don't want her to get angry. I don't want her to think I don't care…"

"You can look tonight. I will help you stay awake. I am sure your mother is not angry with you," said Sky Eyes, as some of his concern for the girl returned.

Fawn smiled broadly with the knowledge that Sky Eyes was going to help her. She knew she would not fail if he helped her.

Suddenly, the smile disappeared. "They left us yesterday. What if they only had one day and I missed them?"

Once again, Sky Eyes was caught without an answer to Fawn's difficult questions. He looked into a sad face that was pleading for understanding. He considered what the girl had asked and suddenly struck upon an answer.

"The first twinkling star you saw was your mother," he said to her. "She came out first to make sure you were safe. Then, she stayed out all night to watch over you."

"Are all of the stars in the sky the spirits of people who have died?"

"People have lived on the land for a long time. Many of them have died. I think the stars are the spirits of those who are no more. They are watching over the ones they left behind."

"I hope you are right, Sky Eyes. I would like to think you are right," she said, with a trace of her smile returning.

"We must be on our way," said Sky Eyes, as he took the first pack and secured it on the back of his horse.

Soon both horses had been loaded and they were underway. They continued to follow the main ridge, searching for a feeder ridge that would take them to the north.

Around mid-day they found just such a ridge. It was not as large as Sky Eyes would have liked, thus it would be steeper, but it would have to do. They would have to be more cautious. The slope from the main ridge to the head of the feeder ridge was very steep.

"Don't get on the downhill side of the horse," said Sky Eyes. "If he falls, he will crush you."

"I will try," said Fawn, as she moved around in front of the horse.

The slope was too steep for them to go straight down. They had to contour across the face of the slope and switchback several times. The feeder ridge was rather steep itself and their progress was considerably impaired.

Late in the afternoon, Sky Eyes saw a grouse dusting itself on the crest of the ridge, some distance ahead of them. He stopped his horse and motioned for Fawn to bring her horse alongside his. When she did so, he handed her the lead rope and told her he was going after the grouse.

The ground was steep and covered with loose rock that made silent travel difficult. There was very little cover. The stealth required to get close to the grouse under those conditions would have deterred many, more experienced hunters. Sky Eyes, on the other hand, had been taught by Man-with-no-hair, and to him, this would be a relatively simple stalk.

Sky Eyes did not have very many arrows and decided not to risk losing or damaging one in the rocky ground. He had seen his father throw rocks at grouse in the past. Often times, you could throw several rocks before the birds decided they would live longer if they flew away. He left his bow with Fawn and began to work his way down the ridge.

There was a large, jutting rock on the left side of the ridge-top that would allow Sky Eyes to throw his stone from concealment. It took him over an hour to reach the rock. On the way, he had gathered a few stones that fit his hand, as he crawled.

As he began to scale the jutting rock, he heard the grouse fly away. He was disappointed but not angry. He had invested a lot of time in the stalk and had nothing to show for his effort. He turned his head and looked up the hill, expecting to see disappointment on Fawn's face. Instead, her mouth was gaping as she looked down the hill, in wide-eyed terror. It suddenly occurred to Sky Eyes that someone or something else had startled the grouse.

Sky Eyes quietly climbed to the crest of the jutting rock and looked upon the trail. He could see where the grouse had been dusting itself. He looked down the trail a few yards and saw a crouching mountain lion. The cat's golden tail twitched as if it hadn't realized the bird had flown away.

What concerned Sky Eyes more than the loss of a meal was that the cat was less than twenty yards away and he had no weapon other than a handful of stones.

Sky Eyes was nervous but he did not panic. He tried to remember if his father or Man-with-no-hair had ever said anything about a predicament such as this, but could remember nothing.

The cat rose up on its feet and walked to where the grouse had been. It sniffed the soft dust and looked in the direction the bird had flown. The wind suddenly changed and blew from Sky Eyes to the lion, filling the cat's nostrils with the boy's scent. The cat crouched and snarled as it turned slightly and faced the rock outcropping.

If the cat had been able to see the boy, perhaps it would have acted differently. As it was, the boy's scent was strong and the cat knew he was close, but it didn't know *where*. The uncertainty caused the cat to lose its nerve. It turned in the direction the grouse had flown and loped down the side of the ridge.

Sky Eyes waved his arm, signaling Fawn to come down the ridge. He was relieved the cat had not seen her or the horses; they would have been easy prey.

"I thought I was going to lose you, too," said Fawn, when she stopped near the jutting rock.

"When the wind changed, the cat smelled a great hunter and decided it wanted to live another day," Sky Eyes managed to say, without his voice breaking.

Fawn looked at him closely but she could detect no signs of deception and was satisfied that the boy was as brave as he sounded. The acceptance of his bravery gave her more security than even she realized.

"There may be no meal tonight," said Sky Eyes.

"I would rather we both be alive and hungry than one of us not be alive," answered Fawn.

Sky Eyes' brow furrowed as he considered the profoundness of her statement. What would happen to her if he were killed? How long would she survive? Could she survive? How much suffering would she have to endure?

As he contemplated these questions, he decided that when they found a place to live, he would teach her what he had learned about survival. When he was through with her, she would be able to survive on her own, if the need arose.

They watched the cat until it was out of sight and they were certain it no longer posed a threat. When it disappeared at the bottom of the long, steep slope, they continued along the ridge top.

Dusk caught them in a poor place to camp. The ground was steep and there was no water. The horses had not had water for two days and Sky Eyes was becoming concerned about them. They had come a long way down the ridge but he doubted they would make it to the bottom by the end of the next day. He couldn't even count on there being water when they reached the bottom, for that matter.

Sky Eyes tied the horses to brush growing in the rock outcroppings on the most level ground he could find, before dark. The grass that grew on the ridge was sparse and dry but he and Fawn pulled what they could find and put it before the horses.

"Tomorrow we will eat again," Sky Eyes promised, as they settled down into their furs. They had made their beds between two large rocks to keep from sliding down the slope in the night.

"I know," said Fawn as positively as she could, hoping the upbeat sound of her voice would dissipate any feelings of failure he might be feeling.

"LOOK! There's mother!" said Fawn, as she spotted a twinkling star on the eastern horizon.

Her sudden loud voice startled Sky Eyes but he quickly recovered. He felt better when he saw a peaceful look cross the girl's face. He looked at the distant star and wondered if there really was something to what he had told Fawn. There was a certain amount of contentment to be derived from feeling that you were being watched over.

"Look, there's my mother. And beside her is my father," said Sky Eyes, as he too, became overwhelmed by the need to believe that they still existed, somewhere.

Soon, the stars became too numerous to identify with their deceased family members and they contented themselves by watching the sky fill up with the twinkling past-life forms. They both fell asleep looking into the heavens.

Dawn was a faint light in the eastern sky when Sky Eyes woke up. He rolled over and looked at Fawn. She was already awake. She was still looking into the dark sky.

"My mother is the first one to go away," she said, sadly.

"She is the first one to show herself at night," Sky Eyes reminded her. "She has been watching over you all night. She must rest too," he added.

Fawn considered what Sky Eyes had said and her mood improved quickly when she realized he was probably right.

"If we hurry, we may reach the bottom of the ridge today," said Sky Eyes, as he rolled out of the furs.

Fawn quickly rolled out too and together, they soon had the horses reloaded. The sun was peeking over the eastern horizon as they resumed their trek down the long, steep ridge.

2

By late afternoon, Sky Eyes could smell water in the valley below. The horses could smell it too and the children had to hurry to keep from being stepped on by the thirsty animals. They were still high on the ridge when the small, winding stream became visible. The sun was hot and the children were becoming weary from lack of nourishment.

"There is water in the valley," said Sky Eyes, as he pointed the stream out to Fawn. "We must hurry or it will be dark before we get there," he continued, as he looked at the girl.

He was immediately shocked by her appearance. She had been behind him all day. She had kept pace with him, so he had given his undivided attention to his surroundings and where he was going. He had not looked back or asked the girl how she was faring. Her face was drawn and her color was not good. She looked exhausted.

Sky Eyes was infuriated with himself for not paying closer attention to Fawn. He knew there was little he could have done to alleviate her suffering, but an occasional rest stop would have helped considerably. On the other hand, he was proud of her for not complaining.

"I know you are weary," Sky Eyes said to her. "But, if you can make it a little farther, we can get to the bottom and water, before dark."

"I will do my best," she said tiredly. She had seen the shocked look on Sky Eyes' face and was embarrassed that her fatigue was that apparent. Her throat was dry and her stomach was growling for food but she knew Sky Eyes was suffering the same symptoms. He had offered no excuses, nor would she.

When they had rested a few minutes, Fawn said, "We should be on our way."

"Are you ready?" Sky Eyes asked, suspiciously.

"I am ready. I want to drink from that stream tonight," Fawn said, as bravely as she could.

Sky Eyes got to his feet and started down the ridge. Fawn followed, a short distance behind him.

Dusk gathered around the young travelers as they worked their way down the ridge. The way had become less steep, but they were now surrounded by thick timber and were forced to slow their pace in the gloomy, gray-light of pre-darkness. When, at last, they reached the bottom of the long, steep ridge, they found their situation had not improved a great deal. The ground was broken with narrow deep gouges that were impassable for the horses. There were wind-felled trees and jagged rock outcroppings. All of this was surrounded by timber that was so thick, the light of the brightest day was not allowed to penetrate to the forest floor.

Sky Eyes appraised the situation with young, knowing eyes. He knew he would be risking one or both of the horses if he tried to make the stream in the dark.

"We can not take the horses through this in the dark," he said to Fawn. "We will have to wait until morning to go the stream."

"There is grass at the base of the ridge. Can we leave the horses there and go to the stream?" Fawn asked meekly.

Sky Eyes considered her request. He didn't like leaving the horses unguarded, but he knew Fawn would not have asked if she were not desperate.

"Yes, we can do that," Sky Eyes said hesitantly. "But we will have to hurry. I do not want to leave the horses alone any longer than necessary."

Fawn agreed. After the packs were removed from the horses, the youngsters slipped into the eerie forest. The moon had been in the sky before the sun had gone down but its bright light offered no assistance to the children. Fawn stayed very close to Sky Eyes so they would not become separated in the almost total darkness. Sky Eyes continuously waved his hand in front of his face to avoid being stabbed in the face by a sharp limb.

An hour later, the timber thinned enough to allow moonlight to filter into the forest. Shortly thereafter, they walked into the small meadow they had seen from the ridge.

Fawn attempted to run by Sky Eyes to get to the water. He grabbed her roughly, by the shoulder, and pulled her back.

"We must take care," he whispered hoarsely into her ear.

"I'm sorry. I'm so thirsty," Fawn whimpered

"I am thirsty too, but we must be careful, Little One," warned Sky Eyes.

He took her hand into his and they slowly walked across the meadow. Despite his need for water, Sky Eyes would not allow himself to become careless. He stopped several times to listen to the night. Each time he heard nothing to indicate they might be in danger. Finally, they reached the stream. Sky Eyes released Fawn's hand and allowed her to drink. He knelt beside her and cautioned her not to drink too much, too quickly. Reluctantly, Fawn obeyed him. Sky Eyes drank a little and looked around, always on the alert, and then drank more.

"We must get back to the horses," Sky Eyes whispered nervously, when they had drunk their fill.

Fawn detected the anxiety in his voice. "Is there something wrong? Have you seen something you didn't tell me about?" she asked, apprehensively.

"I have seen nothing, but there is something about this place. It doesn't feel right. I think there is danger here."

Fawn began to look about more closely now that her need for water had been sated. Her eyes became wide with fear when she recalled the attack on their families. She stepped close enough to Sky Eyes to touch his body. His closeness was reassuring to her.

"Let's hurry back to the horses," said Sky Eyes. "Keep low and stay with me," he instructed.

As the two children ran, crouching, away from the small stream and toward the thick timber, and their horses, a twelve-hundred-pound grizzly bear lumbered away from the same stream. Fortunately for the children, the bear went in the opposite direction. The bear had lived near the small meadow all summer; he had come to think of it as his domain and he was prepared to defend his domain against all foes. All foes, that is, except the ones who had entered his valley on this night. He had smelled the scent of those strange two-legged creatures before, and when their scent was present, it was usually followed by the scent of death. Odd as it may seem, the largest grizzly bear in a five-hundred-mile radius surrendered its domain to the two small children without so much as a warning growl.

Sky Eyes felt safer and less vulnerable when they were within the shelter of the forest. They carefully picked their way back to the horses. Once there, they immediately rolled into their furs and were soon fast asleep.

Sky Eyes slipped from his furs in the dim light of dawn and went in search of a safe route for the horses to follow to the stream. He thought Fawn was sleeping, but she had heard him stirring and arose shortly after he left. She prepared the horses for travel while he was gone.

In the light of day, Sky Eyes had no trouble locating a game trail that led through the timber and to the stream. When he returned to the camp a few minutes later, he was surprised to find the horses ready to travel.

"You've done well," he said, thanking her.

Fawn accepted his compliment without comment as she untied her horse and followed Sky Eyes on the route he had chosen. Soon the horses were drinking water from the cool, clear stream.

"We will be able to ride now," said Sky Eyes when the horses had drunk their fill.

"Which way will we go?" asked Fawn, in a concerned tone.

"I don't know," said Sky Eyes, as he looked about nervously. "But I want to be away from here as soon as possible."

Though Fawn didn't say it, she was disappointed. The meadow was small, but it was lovely and peaceful. She would have been content to stay for a while.

When the horses finished drinking, they began to eat the lush, green grass that was growing along the edge of the stream. Sky Eyes was so intent on watching for danger he didn't realize the horses were no longer drinking. A sudden movement by his horse broke his concentration and he led the way across the stream.

After crossing the stream, Sky Eyes located a game trail that led them to the northeast corner of the meadow. The trail created a narrow passage through the thick timber. Sky Eyes followed the trail until it was joined by a more distinct trail from the north. He followed the trails until they became dim, at which time he searched for a trail that was being used more often. This method of travel kept them on trails that were more apt to be open and passable, and it kept them in the proximity of game.

3

By late afternoon, after traveling through dense forests that were broken by occasional small meadows, they came upon a large meadow that was divided by a small river. The trail they were on was joined by two other trails. The combined trails led to the river.

The beauty of the meadow was breathtaking. The prospects for good hunting were encouraging.

"We will rest here for a few days," said Sky Eyes, matter-of-factly.

"Can we not stay here?" asked Fawn, tiredly.

"If there are elk. It's too soon to know," he answered.

"I like it here," Fawn said, doggedly.

"You have just gotten here. How do you know what you like? You are weary. Your weariness is clouding your judgment."

"All I meant was it looks peaceful," she responded, with a hurt look.

"We will see," said Sky Eyes as he led the way across the meadow, to a coppice near the bank of the river.

Sky Eyes dismounted near the trees and tied his horse to a stout bush. A quick scan of the area told him this was indeed a good location. Water was plentiful, there was abundant feed for the horses, the trees would provide shelter from storms and there was an endless supply of firewood. If there were elk nearby, this could become their new home.

Sky Eyes turned to Fawn's horse and helped her from its back. Ordinarily, she would not have required assistance, but the awkward packs made mounting and dismounting difficult. After securely tying Fawn's horse, the two youngsters began to clear dead limbs and debris from under the trees where they would make their temporary camp. When an adequate area had been cleared, Sky Eyes removed the packs from the horses.

"We must eat tonight," said Sky Eyes solemnly. "I will hunt while you arrange the camp. When the horses can no longer reach grass, you will have to move them. Make sure they are tied well."

Fawn nodded her head as he spoke. "I will do as you ask," she said, as he gathered his bow and quiver. "Sky Eyes," she said, as he turned to leave. He turned to face her. "Hunt well – your family is hungry."

As Sky Eyes considered her statement, he realized, once again, how much was dependant upon his abilities. Had he been of weaker spirit, he may have succumbed to the enormous burden that had been placed upon him. But, Sky Eyes was not weak, he was born of survivors and trained by survivors, and the word quit was not a word familiar to him.

"We will eat fresh meat tonight," Sky Eyes promised, before he turned from Fawn's hopeful gaze.

Sky Eyes walked quickly through the tall grass of the meadow. An observer would have thought the boy was being careless. Until, that is, they looked closer and saw how the boy's eyes darted back and forth, searching for signs. When the boy entered an area that was abundant with fresh signs, he slowed his pace and became as indefinable as the gentle, dark shadows of the nearby trees.

The boy slipped through the tall grass until he came to a well-used game trail. He studied the tracks in the trail for a few moments; when he was sure the trail was being used on a daily basis, he put himself in a position that would allow for a close, clean shot, without him being detected.

As the heat of the day began to wane, the creatures of the evening began to stir. Sky Eyes waited patiently, motionlessly, for the arrival of the deer. As he sat in the tall grass, listening for the telltale sounds of approaching deer, he heard the unmistakable sound of a hoof as a deer walked upon the winding trail. With utmost care, he readied his bow and waited for a target to present itself. He did not have long to wait, for no sooner had he gotten an arrow nocked than a young buck walked into his line of sight.

Sky Eyes had been taught too well to become careless at this juncture. He waited until the buck lowered his head to take a bite of grass before he made the necessary movement required to launch the arrow.

The boy's aim was deadly and the arrow penetrated deep into the deer's lungs. The surprised deer jumped and ran for the cover and protection of the forest.

Sky Eyes sat without moving for nearly half an hour. When he did move, he rose to his feet and walked to where the deer had been standing. He searched the ground carefully until he found the deer's tracks. Slowly, he followed the tracks until he saw small specks of blood on the green blades of grass. There was a good blood trail that was easier to follow than the tracks, but Sky Eyes continued to move slowly, with caution, in case the deer was still alive. He didn't want the wounded animal to run farther into the forest, which might result in its escape and eventual waste.

Sky Eyes took several steps along the blood trail and then he stopped and looked in the direction the deer had taken. When he saw no movement, he took several more steps and then stopped and looked about again.

At last, he came upon the deer and was relieved to find that it was quite dead. He immediately began the task of butchering. He quickly removed the entrails and then began to skin the young buck.

As he was skinning, he was struck by the thought that he was going to have a difficult time getting all of this meat back to camp before dark. The light of day was fading quickly and he wasn't sure he would have time to make two trips. The buck, though small, was too big for him to carry. If he didn't hurry, he would have to make the second trip in the dark. He wasn't afraid of the dark, but other, larger predators would be roaming the meadow after the sun went down and the scent of blood could make them a danger to him.

He thought of ways in which he could use one of the horses. The deer would be too awkward for him to place upon a horse's back and he had no means with which to drag the carcass. He would have to hurry and hope he could make two trips before another predator claimed the remainder of his kill.

When the deer was skinned, Sky Eyes used his knife as a saw and cut a groove into the backbone, just below the ribs. When the groove had encompassed the spine, he took the deer's front legs in his hands and twisted the front half of the body. At first nothing happened and Sky Eyes almost panicked. Suddenly the spine snapped and he quickly separated the front half of the deer from the back half.

Sky Eyes quickly put the hind-quarters on his shoulder, picked up his bow and trotted back to the camp.

His knees threatened to buckle and he was breathing in deep, ragged breaths when he entered the camp, but there was no time to rest. He dropped the meat on one of the packs, and without a word, turned and raced back across the meadow to the remainder of his kill. He wished he had time to save the hide and some of the internal organs but he felt he would be lucky to get back to camp with what meat he had.

Without hesitation, he picked up the front quarters of the deer and began to move toward the camp as quickly as possible. As he made his way through the meadow, the sun fell behind a distant ridge. In the gathering gloom, he saw several deer, cautiously watching him from a distance. Perhaps the threat of predation was not as imminent as he had feared. He hurried back to the camp, nonetheless.

In his absence, Fawn had fashioned a crude fire pit. She was trying, unsuccessfully, to build a fire when Sky Eyes returned with the front quarters of the young buck.

Sky Eyes dropped his burden by the hind-quarters and went to Fawn's assistance.

"I'm sorry I couldn't get the fire started," Fawn apologized. "You are breathing hard. Was there danger?" she asked shakily.

Sky Eyes made a spark in the tender and gently blew it into a small flame. As the flame grew, he carefully added small twigs until the fire was big enough to add larger pieces of wood. When the blaze was large enough to survive without his undivided attention, he turned to Fawn. "I did not expect you to have a fire going. There are tricks that you have yet to learn. I will teach you those tricks. You should know how to build a fire, but you must also learn to respect the power of the fire." Fawn's large brown eyes never left Sky Eyes as he spoke to her. "There was no danger but I know other hunters roam the meadows. I wanted to be back in camp before dark so one of them would not try to take our food away from us."

Sky Eyes cut a piece of meat from the hind-quarters. He cut the meat into thin slices and spitted them over the fire. The thin pieces of meat cooked quickly and soon the children were eating their first meal in quite some time. When they could eat no more, they rolled into their furs and were asleep almost instantly.

They slept soundly. So soundly, in fact, that they did not hear the lonesome, chilling howl of the nearby wolf, nor did they hear the response of the pack as they answered back, in preparation of the hunt.

4

The rising sun found Sky Eyes and Fawn working hastily in an effort to preserve the meat, knowing it would spoil quickly in the heat of the day.

They had constructed a crude drying rack. When the rack was full, Sky Eyes raced across the meadow to the site where he had butchered the deer. He had hoped to salvage the hide and some of the internal organs. When he returned to the camp empty-handed, Fawn looked at his face and saw that he was very troubled.

"What is it?" she asked, almost afraid to hear what he was going to tell her.

When Sky Eyes reached the remains of his kill, what he found sent a chill up and down his spine. The internal organs were gone and the hide was ripped to shreds. He was unable to see tracks in the grass so he began to circle the area until he came to a patch of bare ground. He found exactly what he had feared he would find, and more. The bare area was covered with the tracks of many wolves. One track in particular was so large he could easily fit his hand inside of it, with room left on either side.

He did not want to tell Fawn what he had found; she had enough to worry about as it was. But, she had to know, she had to know that there was a looming threat and she would be in danger if she became careless.

"There are wolves here," he said somberly.

"There are always wolves," she said. "What is it that troubles you about these wolves?"

"I think they live nearby. They can be a threat to the way we live," he expressed, intentionally not mentioning the size of the track he had seen. "We must watch the horses carefully. We must be in camp and have a fire going before it gets dark."

"We always have to watch the horses," she pointed out.

"I know, but now we have to watch them more closely. I can not hunt and watch the horses at the same time," he told her.

"I am here," Fawn reminded him. "I can watch the horses while you hunt."

"What of your chores? Who will do your work while you watch the horses?"

"You hunted yesterday. We have enough meat for many days. I can gather nuts and roots while you watch the horses. When the meat is gone I will watch the horses while you hunt."

When Sky Eyes realized the simplicity of her plan he became slightly angry with himself for not thinking of it himself. But he couldn't be too angry, because they had a plan, a plan that would work.

The following day, Sky Eyes led the horses to the river. When they had satisfied their thirst, he allowed them to feed upon the rich, green grass along the bank of the stream. Fawn had gone upstream in search of roots and greens. He was unable to see her so he swung onto the back of his horse. He saw her head bob up and down several times before she went out of sight over a small rise. Leading Fawn's horse, he began to slowly make his way upstream, allowing the horses to feed as they walked.

Quite some distance upstream from camp, Fawn was working earnestly at a root with her digging stick. A sixth sense suddenly made her aware that she was being watched. She stopped working the root and looked up, and slowly began to scan the area around her. She saw nothing, but the feeling would not leave her. Slowly, she got to her feet for a better view of her surroundings. She had just stood to her full height when a giant wolf padded softly out of a dense thicket. She was paralyzed with fright. She was barely able to see over the wolf's back, as he trotted by, far too close to her. The wolf did not look at her; in fact, it acted as if she were not there.

Fawn was still standing, motionlessly, when Sky Eyes rode to her, several minutes later.

Sky Eyes became concerned when Fawn did not respond to the sound of the approaching horses. When he stopped the horse beside her, she did not move. He leapt from the horse and stepped to her side.

"What is the matter with you?" he asked sternly. "You must pay attention when you are out alone!"

She did not respond verbally. Instead, she turned her head toward him and he knew immediately by her vacant stare that something was terribly wrong. Her eyes were wide and her mouth was open, and twitching ever so slightly.

"Fawn, what is it?" he asked, genuinely concerned.

"The wolf," she finally managed to say.

The concerned look on Sky Eyes face changed to terror.

"Where?" he asked, in a voice that croaked from sudden dryness.

Fawn pointed to where the wolf had passed. Sky Eyes closed his eyes and gulped at the nearness of the tracks. He took two steps toward them and turned back to Fawn. He had gotten close enough to tell that they were the same tracks he had seen where he had killed the young buck.

"Come," said Sky Eyes. "We must pack our things and leave this place."

"He didn't even look at me," Fawn said, as much to herself as to Sky Eyes.

Sky Eyes looked at her curiously. "This time he was not hungry. Next time he will eat you," he ventured.

"I don't think so," Fawn responded, timidly.

Sky Eyes gave her a puzzled look as he took her arm and led her back to the camp. When they reached the presumed safety of the camp, Sky Eyes relaxed, a little. But he continued to scan the surrounding meadow for movement.

"I don't want to go," said Fawn, as Sky Eyes began to roll up the sleeping furs.

"What of the wolf?" Sky Eyes asked incredulously.

"I don't think he will harm us," she muttered softly.

Sky Eyes was astonished by her misplaced trust. "That giant beast is a wild animal. He lives by killing things that are smaller and weaker than he is. HE LIVES BY KILLING!" Sky Eyes, said louder and more sternly than he intended.

Fawn flinched at the tone of Sky Eyes' voice.

"I know how he lives," she stated evenly. "I also know that we must kill to live. I know you won't understand this, but I feel safer with him out there."

Sky Eyes' mouth involuntarily dropped open.

"How can he make you feel safer?" he asked skeptically.

"I don't know," she answered shortly. "I just feel it. I don't want to go."

"Are you forgetting about me? What of the horses? What if he kills one of the horses? What if he kills…me?"

"NO, I HAVEN'T FORGOTTEN!" she screamed at him.

Sky Eyes was taken aback by the intensity of her outburst. She had never been so insistent. He carefully considered the difficulties involved with staying where they were. Remaining would increase his responsibility manifold. He would know no peace; he would get no rest.

"We will stay for a few days," he said at last. "But if there are no elk, we will move on."

5

Sky Eyes and Fawn stayed on at their camp for four more days. In that time, Fawn dried the meat of a second deer Sky Eyes had killed. Sky Eyes had intentionally left the internal organs behind, hoping the wolf would not bother him and Fawn if it had a full belly. He had also searched tirelessly for signs of elk, but found none. However, he did find that the meadow was separated from another meadow by a narrow strip of timber. And that one was separated from another and another and so on for a long, long way.

Fawn was saddened by their forthcoming departure, but she understood why they needed to do so. She accepted the need to leave, though she had not seen the wolf again.

At dawn, on the fifth day after the encounter with the wolf, Fawn sat on her horse waiting for Sky Eyes to get mounted. She listened to the birds chirping in a nearby bush. She listened to the chuckle of the stream as it wound its way through the meadow.

"When we find elk, I want to live in a place like this," she said, as Sky Eyes swung atop of his horse.

Sky Eyes looked thoughtfully at the meadow, and the river, and the copse of trees in which they had camped. "We will see," he said as he touched his heels to the flanks of the horse.

From a dense thicket, on the ridge that overlooked the meadow, a pair of large, yellow eyes watched the two children ride across the river and through the tall grass of the meadow.

Sky Eyes and Fawn rode for a week. The connecting meadows stretched farther than Sky Eyes could have imagined. At dusk, on the seventh day, Sky Eyes and Fawn stopped near one of the dissecting strips of timber. Together, they cleared an area large enough for their sleeping furs and a small fire. With that done, Sky Eyes unloaded the horses and led them in search of water. Fawn stayed behind to organize the camp.

Sky Eyes had not seen water as they had approached the strip of timber. He hoped to find a spring or a small stream in the next meadow. What he saw when he stepped out of the other side of the timber pleased him a great deal.

The meadow broadened out to a vast rolling plain to the southeast. Directly ahead of him, the meadow was divided lengthwise by a low, sharp ridge. Another, much larger ridge, and surrounding hills in the northeast were the walls that surrounded the valley. The tall hills that formed the northwest boundary of the valley consisted of timber choked draws and open ridge tops. A small winding stream reflected the glowing light of the setting sun. More impressive than the scenic beauty, to Sky Eyes, was the herd of elk feeding near the center of the valley.

The wind was blowing from behind Sky Eyes, directly toward the elk.

They were a long way off, but they detected his scent and raised their heads. They looked in his direction but did not panic and run away, for which he was thankful.

Sky Eyes turned away from the elk and led the horses along the edge of the timber. This route to the stream would take longer but he hoped to avoid frightening the elk.

"I was beginning to worry. It's getting dark," said Fawn, as Sky Eyes finally led the horses back into the camp. "Did you not find water?"

"I found water and much more," he said, as he staked the horses where they could feed throughout the night.

"You've found elk!" she said, elated by the excitement in his voice.

"And more," he said, as he stepped away from tying the second horse. "Come, I will show you."

Together, they walked through the timber to the adjoining meadow. Fawn gasped when her eyes beheld what lay before them.

"We can live here?" she asked excitedly.

"I see no reason why we cannot stay here," Sky Eyes assured her.

"What if the elk leave when the snow comes?" she asked, apprehensively.

"We will have what we need from the elk long before the snow comes," Sky Eyes stated confidently. "Even if the elk leave, we will have enough meat to last the winter."

"When will you hunt the elk?" she asked excitedly.

"I will hunt tomorrow," he said, smiling at her excitement.

Together, they turned and walked back to the camp. Sky Eyes built a small fire while Fawn finished arranging the camp.

"We will have to camp here for several days. When we have enough elk hides for a tepee we will move into the valley."

"Will I be able to hunt with you?" Fawn asked hopefully.

Sky Eyes considered the request and the ramifications.

"I would like to take you with me and teach you to hunt. I would teach you what Man-with-no-hair and my father taught me. Someday I will. But for now, there will be much for you to do here. We will need many drying racks and much wood needs to be gathered. If we don't care for the meat, it will spoil in the heat of the day. We will need the meat to survive the winter."

"I understand," she said sadly, knowing he was right.

"You learn quickly and you do things well," he said. "When we are not so pressed, I will take you," he promised.

The praise and the promise made her feel better and her cheerfulness soon returned.

Fawn warmed venison over the small fire. The children ate as they watched the stars slowly begin to appear in the sky. When Sky Eyes had eaten his fill he rolled into his sleeping furs, his mind hashing over different methods to harvest as many elk as possible, until he fell asleep.

When Fawn was sure Sky Eyes was asleep, she talked to her mother until she too, fell asleep.

Chapter Twenty-four

Dawn was yet to put its crimson stain upon the eastern horizon when Sky Eyes got up. As he rolled out of his furs, he checked the wind. It had not changed since yesterday, he would have to circle the elk herd. He ate a piece of meat Fawn had left on the rocks that surrounded the fire pit. With his mouth full, he picked up his bow and quiver and walked to the horses. After a moment's indecision he took Fawn's horse too; he would need both horses to carry a large elk. He swung onto his horse's back and led Fawn's horse.

From horseback, he surveyed the camp. Fawn was sleeping peacefully, a small wisp of smoke rose from last night's fire. The stars illuminated the meadow; Sky Eyes took advantage of the light and searched the meadow for signs of danger. All seemed well.

He touched his heels to the flanks of the horse and rode to the southeast edge of the meadow. When he got to the edge of the meadow, he came to a small rise. He crossed over the rise and then turned east and rode through the narrow strip of timber. When he exited the timber, he could not see the elk and he hoped they could not see him. He turned back to the southeast and rode toward the rolling hills until the steep, low ridge was between himself and the herd. He turned east again, intending to circle the ridge until he was east of the herd.

Midway along the ridge, he came upon a well used game trail that led up the ridge. He dismounted and tied both horses. Sky Eyes then turned and raced up the trail. When he reached the top of the ridge, he could see the bedded herd near where they had been when he had seen them last night. He could also see where he and Fawn had walked through the timber to look at the valley. The face of the ridge was too steep to traverse from where he stood, but from his vantage point he could see a tree covered flat that was nestled protectively at the base of the ridge. The flat area looked to be a good place to build a permanent home. But that would have to wait until later; now, he was after the elk.

He raced back down the slope to the horses. He quickly mounted and continued along the base of the ridge. When the ridge began to peter out, he rode over the top of it and tied the horses to some brush.

The wind had not changed; it was blowing into his face as he walked into the meadow and made his way toward the elk herd.

2

Fawn awoke shortly before the sun appeared over the eastern horizon. She looked hopefully at Sky Eyes' furs and was saddened to see that he was gone. She had hoped he would change his mind and take her along.

Dismayed, she rolled out of her furs and crawled to the fire. She gently blew upon the ashes until she saw an ember begin to glow. She probed the coal with a twig and blew on it until it burst into a small flame. The flame went out immediately, but she knew it was hot enough to rebuild the fire. She took some fine shredded bark from her wood supply and placed it on the ember. She then placed several small twigs on the bark. Once again, she began to blow on the ember. Soon a tiny tendril of smoke began to curl through the small pile of tinder. One more gentle breath and a hungry flame leapt to life and began to consume the dry fuel. As the flame grew, she added more wood until the fire was large enough to leave unattended.

She warmed enough meat for a morning meal and then began to make preparations for the forthcoming task. She dug out an area for another fire and surrounded it with stones. She then went into the timber, in search of firewood. Fuel was in abundance, but much of it was either too small or too big for her to drag back to the camp. She gathered what she could until she had a large pile outside the new fire pit.

When she had an adequate supply of firewood, she went in search of limbs for the construction of drying racks. She would have preferred willow but there was none to be found. She felt that Sky Eyes would get angry with her if she went as far as the river just for willow. She made do with green pine limbs. She cut the limbs from the nearby trees. When she had a pile of limbs she sat down and peeled the bark off them. She carried the stripped limbs into camp and began tying them together with strips of deer hide.

She was working busily, paying attention to nothing but her work. Suddenly she began to feel uneasy – her sixth sense again. She raised her head and looked across the fire into the yellow eyes of the giant wolf.

3

The grass in the valley was waist high to Sky Eyes. He crouched down as he ran, following crisscrossing game trails. Running in that position was uncomfortable and tiring, and he soon had to stop and rest. He rested on his knees, breathing as quietly as possible. When his breathing returned to normal, he slowly raised his head above the grass and looked for the elk. He did not see them but had not expected to. He was still a long way from where he had seen them earlier that morning. He resumed his tortuous method of running until he was forced to rest again. This time, after he had rested, he was able to see the herd. They were close enough that he was going to have to start taking more time and being more careful. Moving more slowly, he used the skills he had been taught since he had begun to walk.

Sky Eyes got on his belly and wormed his way through the grass. When he was half way to the elk he stopped and waited for the gentle breeze to resume. When the breeze blew, it rustled the top of the tall grass. When the grass moved, Sky Eyes moved. When the breeze stopped Sky Eyes stopped and waited patiently, listening for sounds of the herd to determine their closeness.

He heard a calf mewling to its mother and knew he was close enough. Now came the hard part, the part he always struggled with. He was close to his objective, but not close enough to make a killing shot with his bow. He now must nock an arrow and continue to crawl, with the bow extended in front of him, without making noise and alerting the elk to his presence.

With an arrow nocked and the bow in his left hand, he stretched out on the valley floor. He rolled slightly to his left side. He pushed down with his right hand and raised himself slightly and then pushed with his feet. He moved only a short distance at a time and only when the breeze was stronger than usual.

He heard footsteps ahead of him and immediately stopped moving. The footsteps were very close. When the next breeze gusted through the meadow, Sky Eyes drew his knees up to his stomach and rolled into a kneeling position. As the gentle breeze continued to blow, he parted the grass and saw the body of an elk before him. Without hesitation, he drew back on the bow and released the arrow, hitting the elk in the ribs.

The startled elk kicked its hind feet into the air twice and then raced across the meadow. The wounded elk ran away from the herd and stopped. It turned and looked in the direction it had come from and then issued two sharp, piercing warning barks. The rest of the herd became agitated when they heard the warning. A foolish young bull that was more curious than frightened, walked cautiously toward Sky Eyes. The bull never saw the warrior who shot the arrow into his throat. The arrow was well made and sharp and it penetrated deeply. The startled bull flinched and started to run away but he was mortally wounded and did not go far. The bull fell dead upon the grass of the meadow in which he had been born.

Alarm immediately spread through the herd. One of their members had fallen and not gotten back up, another had run away and was barking a warning to the rest of them. Animals were running into each other as they attempted to escape from a danger they could not see. Soon, the entire herd was well out of range.

Sky Eyes rose to his feet and looked at the herd as they huddled together on the far side of the valley. He knew he would need more than two hides for a tepee and considered going after at least one more elk. When he considered the amount of work he had before him, he decided to forego any more hunting until these two elk had been cared for – he had been taught not to waste what he had been given.

Sky Eyes now faced several dilemmas: he had to care for the fallen elk as soon as possible. Fawn was preparing the temporary camp to process the elk meat. Sky Eyes liked the looks of the campsite he had found and did not wish to move all of the elk meat twice; the elk were very big and he was going to need help butchering them. He quickly decided that he was going to need Fawn's help. He raced back to the horses and galloped them toward the temporary camp.

4

Her breath caught in her throat, nearly choking her, as fear coursed through her veins. She was too frightened to move…To think. She simply looked at the wolf, as chills ran up and down her spine.

It was as if she had been in a dream, for suddenly, the wolf was gone and Sky Eyes was kneeling before her, shaking her by the shoulders.

"Fawn! Fawn! What is the matter with you?"

She felt lightheaded and placed the back of her hand on her forehead. She blinked her eyes and wondered if the wolf had really been there at all.

"The wolf, Sky Eyes. The wolf followed us," she blurted out.

Sky Eyes looked at her incredulously. "Where?" he asked hoarsely, not wanting to believe what she had said.

"There," she said, pointing to where the wolf had been standing.

Sky Eyes stood up and slowly walked in the direction Fawn had indicated. He had taken but a few steps when he saw one of the massive tracks in a mound of dirt that had been deposited by a burrowing rodent. He was shocked by the nearness of the track and sickened by the thought of what he would have returned to, had the wolf attacked.

He turned back to Fawn. She was still kneeling, staring aimlessly across the meadow. Sky Eyes walked to her, took her hands and gently pulled her to her feet. "We must hurry," he said patiently. "We have much meat to care for."

Fawn seemed to be recovering her senses but she was still very distracted. "You killed an elk?" she asked numbly, not noticing the blood on his clothing.

"I have killed two of them," he informed her. "We must move quickly or the meat will spoil. I also found a place to camp…it won't be a camp…I think it will be our new home."

The reappearance of the wolf troubled Sky Eyes a great deal. He was also troubled by the thought of losing all of the elk meat. As much as he hated to ask, Fawn would have to be alone again. She would also have to perform some very difficult tasks by herself. Trying times such as these, often determined the survival of their kind.

"Fawn, we must hurry," he repeated. "I will put everything on your horse and you can take it to the new camp. You will have to unload it by yourself. When it is unloaded, you can go to the stream for some willow to make drying racks," he said, as he noticed the poor ones she was making with the pine limbs.

"Where is the new camp?" she asked, hearing the urgency in his voice.

"I'll show you when we get to the elk," he told her.

Sky Eyes quickly loaded all of their belongings onto Fawn's horse. Fawn was recovering from her shock and helped him break camp. Sky Eyes swung onto the back of his horse and pulled Fawn up behind him. They rode through the narrow strip of timber and into the next meadow, toward the closest of the fallen elk.

When they reached the young bull, Sky Eyes swung a leg over the horse's neck and slid to the ground. He pointed out the approximate location of the new camp. Fawn looked at him apprehensively.

"I do not wish for you to be alone, but there is nothing I can do now. Go to the camp and unload your horse and then come back. We will make drying racks tonight."

Fawn had no desire to be alone, even for a short time. She knew the importance of what they were doing however, and offered no argument.

Sky Eyes drew his knife and began to skin the elk. Fawn clucked the horse into motion and rode away, toward the new camp. As she rode, she cast her eyes continuously over the meadow, expecting the wolf to leap out at her at any moment; she was struggling to keep her imagination in check.

"Why is he following me?" she asked herself quietly. And then she struck upon a different tack: *Why hasn't he attacked me? Will he attack me? Why wouldn't he attack me? Why hasn't Sky Eyes seen him?*

Fawn was so absorbed in thought she almost rode by the new campsite. Receiving no instruction from its rider, the Appaloosa stopped and began to eat grass. Fawn was jerked away from her thoughts by the lack of movement. She looked about, puzzled for a moment, by the unfamiliar surroundings. As she looked across the stream she saw the site Sky Eyes had described to her. She gently nudged the horse ahead and into the stream.

When she reached the other side, she began to feel guilty about her slow pace. She jumped from the back of the horse and unloaded the packs as quickly as possible. She considered making the drying racks but decided Sky Eyes was right and they should butcher the elk as quickly as possible, first.

With the help of a jutting rock ledge, she swung onto the back of her horse and hurried back to Sky Eyes.

Sky Eyes heard the footfalls of the approaching horses. He looked up to make sure it was Fawn. When he saw it was she, he returned to his work.

Fawn stopped the horses nearby and slid to the ground. Sky Eyes did not look up from his work as she walked to him. She grasped the leg he was skinning and held it steady for him.

With Fawn's help, the butchering was completed in a short time. When the young bull was quartered, Sky Eyes tied two quarters together with a strip of hide. With a great deal of effort, he and Fawn were able to get one quarter over the back of the Appaloosa. They lifted the second quarter until the weight was evenly distributed. They did the same thing with the other two quarters and Fawn's horse.

When the horses were loaded, the children led them across the meadow to the new camp. The loads were unstable and difficult for the horses to carry. If they had had a long way to go, the strips of hide may have cut into the horse's backs. As it was, the trip was short and neither of the horses was injured.

271

When Sky Eyes and Fawn entered the new campsite, Sky Eyes went in search of a pole, on which to hang the meat. A few minutes later he returned, dragging a section of a dead, fallen tree. With Fawn's help, he lashed the pole between two standing trees. The children were so short, they had difficulty tying the meat pole high enough to keep the quarters from touching the ground.

Sky Eyes looked at their handiwork with chagrin. He did not have time to make it better, now. Together, they turned from the hanging meat and returned to the meadow for the second elk. The second elk had begun to bloat but the meat had not spoiled. The children worked quickly to remove the thick, protective hide, allowing the carcass to cool. They then removed the entrails and quartered the animal, and loaded it on the horses, just as they had done with the first elk.

The meat pole bowed and creaked when they hung the meat from the second elk on it, but it did not break. It was late afternoon and they still had much work to do. Sky Eyes instructed Fawn to begin work on the drying racks. He returned to the meadow to retrieve the hides of the elk.

By the time Sky Eyes returned with the hides, Fawn had constructed one drying rack and was working busily on the second one. Sky Eyes pulled the hides off the horse's back and dragged them, one at a time, to a clearing that would expose them to the sun for most of the day. As he was preparing to stake the hides, Fawn reminded him they had no firewood. He turned from the hides and went in search of fuel. By the time he had enough wood to last the night, it was too dark to continue working the hides. In the light of the fire, Sky Eyes sliced meat and placed it on the drying racks. Fawn continued to construct the racks, trying to keep ahead of Sky Eyes.

The children worked throughout the night and into the next day. The cool night air helped preserve the meat that was not yet on the drying rack. They cooked some of the meat, but most of it was dried by the sun. When the meat was completely dry, it was taken off the racks and replaced by more meat. They had enough racks and concentrated on slicing the meat so they could hang more when room was available.

Sky Eyes and Fawn sat side-by-side slicing the meat. The mid-day sun was warm and they both fell asleep as they worked. Sky Eyes awoke just before dark and quickly gathered enough fuel to keep a small fire going throughout the night. He quickly built the fire as the last rays of light faded from the sky. He carried Fawn to the fire and covered her with her sleeping fur. Taking his own fur, he covered himself and he too, was soon fast asleep.

5

The next morning, Sky Eyes awoke with a start. He was confused. He didn't know where he was or how he had gotten there. His first thought was of Fawn. When he sat up and saw her sleeping across the fire from him, he remembered where he was.

The fire had burned out during the night, for he had not awakened to add more fuel. He was somewhat angry with himself because he was responsible for their safety.

By the time Fawn finally woke up, Sky Eyes had finished slicing the meat and had tended the drying racks. When the last of the uncured meat was placed on the drying racks, they turned their attention to the hides.

"There has been much work," said Fawn, tiredly.

"I will never kill two elk in one day again," Sky Eyes swore.

They both knew the importance of the hides. Though they would need more, these two would be the start of their home, a home they would need to survive the winter. The two elk had given them almost enough meat to last the winter.

I will hunt again tomorrow," said Sky Eyes. He saw Fawn look at him expectantly and knew what she wanted. "I would take you, if you want to go," he told her.

"I would like to hunt with you," she said excitedly, already forgetting how much trouble the butchering had been.

"I will take you but you will watch and learn. If I am ever injured or sick you may have to hunt for us. I will teach you what I have learned but you must be patient and listen closely."

"Can I shoot at something with your bow?" she asked, excitedly.

"The time for shooting a bow will come, but it is not here yet. We have enough meat. With one more hide we will be able to make a tepee. When we have no work to do we will have time to explore, and then I can begin to teach you what you need to know. I will make a bow for you and you can practice with it, when you have time."

Sky Eyes was happy to see Fawn respond favorably. It was good that she was excited about hunting. He interpreted it as a willingness to learn. She would have to *want* to learn to have the patience to listen to him and do as she was told; she thought it would be easy, but it would not. If their parents were still alive or if they lived in a community, she would not be required to hunt; it might even be frowned upon. But, under the circumstances, their survival might hinge on her ability to provide food, or at least play a part in the taking of the animals the Provider had given them.

When the hides were staked out to Sky Eyes' satisfaction, he took the horses to the stream and allowed them to drink. Fawn remained in the camp and put their things in order.

Sky Eyes rode back from the stream, leading Fawn's horse. "Let's ride to the top of the ridge. We should be able to see the elk from up there."

Fawn gladly accepted the invitation. Using the same rock outcropping, she mounted her horse and followed Sky Eyes around the end of the ridge and up its gentle slope.

Sky Eyes stopped in the same place he had stopped the day before. He could see no elk. At first he was sad and then he became concerned. His first thought was that he had frightened them away.

Fawn saw the concern on his face and was about to ask what was troubling him when she saw movement in the forest on the other side of the wide meadow. "There! I see them, Sky Eyes."

Relief washed over his face as he followed her finger and saw the slow moving herd feeding in the timber.

"That is where we will hunt!" Sky Eyes said, excitedly. He was about to turn away and return to camp when he suddenly turned back toward the valley and acted as if he were smelling the wind.

"What is it?" asked Fawn, worriedly.

"The weather…it is going to change."

"It is not time for winter yet," Fawn said, as she imitated Sky Eyes and tried to pick up the scent of the weather.

"It is not winter. I think a storm is coming."

"We have seen storms before, why does this one concern you?"

"It does not concern me. I have never felt a storm coming before. We have not seen storms here, they may be different than where we lived before."

Standing beside him, on the top of the ridge, she opened her senses to her environment. Just before they mounted their horses and rode back to the camp, speaking softly, she said, "I can feel it, too."

6

When they returned to the camp, there was little that needed to be done. They both felt the affects of the butchering marathon and the warm afternoon sun made them sleepy.

"Let's gather some wood and then we can turn in early," said Sky Eyes. "Tomorrow will be another busy day for both of us," he added.

Working together, they soon had a pile of wood that would easily last for several days.

The bottom of the sun was just above the western horizon when they lay upon their furs and waited for sleep to take them away.

"This is a good camp and I like it here," said Fawn. "But with all of the trees over us, I can't see Mother when she comes out at night."

"Is it not enough to know she is up there?" Sky Eyes asked.

"I like to see her when she comes out," Fawn responded, simply, as she yawned and stretched.

"The trees will protect us from the wind," Sky Eyes explained, unnecessarily.

Fawn made no further comment. When Sky Eyes looked at her, she seemed to be already asleep. He shook his head, grinning, and then went in search of his own dreams.

The next morning, the sky was overcast and threatening rain. Fawn came wide awake the instant Sky Eyes touched her shoulder. They ate quickly in the fading darkness and were on their way as soon as there was enough light to see by. As they rode across the valley floor, large wet drops of rain began to fall. Before they reached the timber on the other side, the clouds opened up and dumped a downpour on the mountain valley. The children huddled under a bush but they were hopelessly soaked. Occasional gusts of wind whipped the rain about, but in time, the storm began to disperse and they could see blue sky between the clouds.

Sky Eyes watched the storm with concerned eyes. At this time they had no shelter, but what if this had been a month from now and this had been a snowstorm? He and Fawn both knew they would perish without adequate shelter.

The sun broke through the clouds as the children tied the horses and made their way up the slope and into the timber. The wind died down to a gentle breeze that caressed their faces as they carefully approached the elk herd.

Sky Eyes led Fawn on a meandering course, as he followed the fresh trails made by the elk. He stopped every so often to look and listen. He carefully scanned the forest floor ahead of them. Sometimes elk were difficult to see and oftentimes when you saw one, there were three or four you hadn't seen, and they would warn the others.

When they had been in the timber for a while, they came upon a ridge top that overlooked a grassy basin.

As was his practice, Sky Eyes approached the ridge top slowly and carefully. He got on his hands and knees and crawled to a small bush. From under the bush he peered over the crest of the hill.

The elk were bedded down in the grass. The cover on the slope was sparse but he knew he could get close enough for a shot, if he were careful.

He motioned for Fawn to join him. He asked her to wait under the bush until he signaled her to follow him. Sadly, she agreed. This was not a time for a discussion.

Sky Eyes scanned the timber and the fringes of the basin carefully for some time (Fawn was beginning to wonder if he ever would leave) before he made his move. When he was certain there were no elk he had not seen, he quietly slipped over the rim of the ridge and slowly crawled toward the unsuspecting herd.

Fawn watched with amazement as Sky Eyes almost seemed to disappear before her very eyes. As she watched, she became more certain than ever that she wanted him to teach her what he knew. She was very impressed with his ability.

Sky Eyes made his way toward a two-year-old cow. She was not as large as he would have liked but the way to larger animals was blocked by frolicking calves, who would alert the herd to danger.

When he was within bow range of the cow, a sixth sense made her aware that something was amiss. She got to her feet and looked about. Her eyes fell on Sky Eyes twice but he did not move and she did not recognize him as a threat. When she lowered her head to feed, Sky Eyes moved in closer. A short time later, he was close enough and he made his shot. He was unable to get up and had to shot from a half-laying, half-sitting position.

Regardless of the position, the shot was good and the cow bolted away. The rest of the herd came to their feet in an instant. They saw no threat and did not run away. Sky Eyes was tempted to go after another animal, but the last time had been a good lesson and he refrained from doing so.

Sky Eyes got slowly to his feet and walked back up the hill. The shot on the cow was good but it would be a while before she died. Fawn was smiling broadly when he got to her. "If you go after the horses, I will track the cow and start butchering her," he suggested.

Fawn's smile faded for a moment until she remembered that he had been good enough to include her in the hunting party. "I will get the horses," she said, smiling again.

"Go straight down the hill. When you get to the meadow, turn right and you will come to the horses," Sky Eyes instructed.

Sky Eyes watched her make her way quickly down the hill. He appreciated her presence and her willingness to help. When she was out of sight, he turned his attention back to the wounded cow. He could not see her but he could hear her thrashing about in the brush. When the sounds of her dying stopped, he began to work his way toward her.

7

Fawn walked down the ridge where it was steep and trotted when it was more level and free of underbrush. It didn't take long to reach the edge of the valley. When she walked out of the timber she had to squint her eyes because of the bright sunlight that filled the valley. She turned to the right and walked near the edge of the timber, where the grass was shorter and traveling was faster and easier.

Fawn had gone only a little ways when she became aware of a presence and knew the wolf was following her. She did not quicken her pace or seek a place to hide. She was frightened of the wolf but she had a deep, unexplainable feeling the beast would not harm her. She refused to look behind her however, to see how close he was. Despite her determination, she was about to break into a panic-driven run when she caught sight of the horses.

The horses nickered when they saw her, but they acted agitated, too. As she got closer to the horses, they began to whinny and fight their lead ropes.

Fawn turned around and saw that the wolf was indeed following her. He was a stone's throw away, standing in the wet trail she had made in the grass. He whimpered softly, turned, and disappeared into the tall grass.

Fawn went to the horses and talked soothingly to them, until they calmed down. The horses soon acted as if they had forgotten about the wolf and continued to graze. Fawn untied her horse and led it to a wind-felled tree that she used to get onto its back.

Leading the Appaloosa, she returned to where she had come out of the timber. She had leaned a forked stick against a tree so she would recognize the place, when she saw it. Much of the timberline looked the same and it would be easy to go up the wrong ridge. The horses were uneasy around the scent of the wolf and seemed eager to enter the forest, even if it meant going up a steep hill.

She was unable to take the horses on the trail she had made when she came down the slope. She had to contour and make a number of switchbacks before she finally returned to where Sky Eyes had shot the elk. She had no difficulty following the blood trail. Sky Eyes would have answered her had she called out, but he would have done so reluctantly; he did not like to speak loudly while in the forest.

The cow had died in an awkward position and Sky Eyes was struggling to get the hide off her. He was relieved to see Fawn.

"I am glad you're back. I need your help," he said, as she tied the horses.

Together they pushed, pulled, pried and lifted until the elk was in a more favorable position. With Fawn's help, Sky Eyes soon had the hide removed and began to quarter the carcass. He was unsure how he was going to get the quarters down the steep slope but he knew he would think of something, even if he had to bone out the meat and carry it down on his back.

When the elk was quartered, Sky Eyes tied two quarters together as he had done on the previous elk. This time, he folded the elk hide and laid it across the Appaloosa's back. With a fantastic effort from both children, they got the tied quarters on the horse's back. The folded hide protected the horse from being cut by the strip of elk hide.

Unwilling to sacrifice the hide, which they needed so badly, Sky Eyes decided to make another trip rather than load meat on both horses.

It took a long time to get to the valley floor with the meat and hide. They had to stop several times to readjust the load. Sky Eyes would liked to have left Fawn in camp, so she could begin to process the meat, but he knew he would need her help in loading the remaining two quarters on the Appaloosa. When the first load was secured on the meat pole, they immediately struck out across the valley, intent upon completing the packing before dark.

"I saw the wolf again," Fawn said, nonchalantly, as they walked across the meadow.

"When?" asked Sky Eyes.

"When I came down the hill for the horses," she answered.

"Why didn't you tell me sooner?" he asked angrily.

"I forgot. He…"

"You forgot? How could you forget? What are you thinking about?" he asked, his temper getting out of control.

"I was worried about getting up the hill in time to help you butcher the elk. What does it matter? He will not hurt me."

"Ha! And how is it you know he will not hurt you?"

"He followed me to the horses. He was close but he did not bother me. I don't…"

"He followed you?"

"Yes. Mother said it is not polite to speak when someone else is speaking."

Sky Eyes stared at her in open-mouthed wonder. He wanted to respond but only shook his head.

"Tomorrow I will hunt the wolf and kill it," he said matter-of-factly.

"I don't think so," Fawn said softly.

"We will see!" Sky Eyes retorted sharply.

Fawn flinched at his tone and Sky Eyes was immediately sorry he had spoken so sharply. It angered him to hear Fawn speak of the wolf. She seemed to be taking the side of a savage creature rather than his.

It was late afternoon by the time the children returned to the camp with the last of the elk meat. Together, they removed the meat from the horse's back and secured it to the meat pole. Sky Eyes rekindled the fire and then took the horses to water. Fawn began to cut thin slices of meat from one of the quarters. When Sky Eyes returned, he tied the horses and then staked the fresh hide near the first two.

As he was staking the hide, he became paralyzed with fear when he thought of what would happen if the wolf destroyed the hides. They would be without a home for the winter…They would die.

He had no recourse. The hides had to remain staked out or they would not cure. If they did not cure, the tepee would rot before winter was over. He had to kill the wolf…

When the hide was staked out, he went back to the camp to help Fawn with the meat. He was frowning when he approached her.

"Does the wolf still trouble you?" she asked.

"Of course he does! What happens if your wolf decides to eat the elk hides? We will be without a home. Does that not trouble you?" he asked.

"I hadn't thought of that. He is not my wolf," she said, giggling.

Her humor did nothing to improve Sky Eyes' disposition and he frowned at her angrily, before he turned his attention to slicing meat.

279

As he worked, Sky Eyes' mind was busy trying to formulate a plan for hunting the wolf. He had never hunted a wolf and he did not remember hearing his father or Man-with-no-hair talking about hunting wolves; it had never been necessary to do so. He didn't know what methods to employ. Hunting another predator was a bit unnerving.

At last, the sun settled out of sight over the western horizon, thus ending another long, trying day in the lives of the two children. Half of the meat from the third elk had been sliced from the bone; the drying racks were full again. Sky Eyes had gathered enough wood to keep the fire burning brightly throughout the night.

As the nearby forest grew darker, the flickering flames of the fire illuminated the trunks of the trees with an eerie light that made them appear to be moving. As Sky Eyes watched this optical illusion with curiosity, he heard the unmistakable howl of the great wolf. A shiver ran up and down his spine causing an involuntary shudder. Fawn glanced at him when she saw the movement out of the corner of her eye. Sky Eyes, embarrassed, tried to act as if nothing had happened. Wisely, Fawn made no comment.

Though the boy was young and in many ways, inexperienced, he was a well-trained hunter. Even at his young age, he possessed some skills that would be the envy of many full-grown warriors with fully developed hunting skills.

At last, he settled upon a plan of action to take against the wolf. It was so simple, he was angry he had not thought of it earlier.

"I will be gone when you wake up tomorrow. Keep working on the meat. I will help you when the wolf is dead," he said, as he rolled into his sleeping fur.

"It will do you no good to hunt the wolf," she stated flatly. She knew by his actions that Sky Eyes had thought of a way to get the wolf and though she wouldn't admit it, she was concerned for the wolf's safety.

Sky Eyes contained his anger without a word. He lay down in the furs and was soon asleep.

Fawn worked late into the night, slicing the meat in the light of the fire. When she became too sleepy to continue, she wiped her hands and added wood to the fire. She went to her sleeping furs and covered herself. The last thing she heard was the eerie howl of the wolf, as his song to the night echoed off the surrounding ridges.

8

Sunlight was shining brightly through the treetops when Fawn woke up the next morning. She sat up in her furs and rubbed the sleep from her eyes. She yawned as she looked at Sky Eyes' empty sleeping furs. She looked at the fire and saw that Sky Eyes had put wood on it before he had left the camp. She also noticed that both horses were gone. That seemed odd to her. She threw the top fur aside and stood up. When she turned around she saw the wolf lying in the shade of a nearby tree. He was stretched out, with his head up, looking at her. His tongue protruded from his mouth as he panted in the early morning warmth. He whined softly as Fawn looked at him.

"This is not natural," Fawn said to herself, as she watched the wolf. "He should come over here and eat me. Why is he acting this way?" She had no explanation for what was taking place. She had no explanation for the way she felt. Not understanding why she was doing it, she began to walk toward the wolf. As strange as anything else, the wolf's tail began to thump upon the ground as she approached. She did not understand the meaning of the expression and did not know how to interpret the action. Horses whinnied when someone approached them. What if...

The wolf did not become aggressive. She took another step toward him. Suddenly the wolf's head snapped around and he looked into the forest behind him. He rose quickly to his feet and trotted toward her. Fawn knew she was about to die but she was suddenly paralyzed with fear and she could only stand and watch the wolf come toward her.

9

Sky Eyes led both horses out of camp long before the sun came up. When he reached the valley, he mounted the Appaloosa and led Fawn's horse. He rode toward a bend in the stream, where he could safely leave the horses. When he reached the bend, he dismounted and let the horses feed until the sun came up. When there was adequate light, he tethered the horses and turned to make his way up the ridge and back toward the camp.

For some reason, the wolf was attracted to Fawn. He didn't understand why, he didn't even try to understand. All he knew was the wolf was a threat. He couldn't allow a threat like this to go unchecked.

If the wolf appeared today, Fawn would see him. He didn't like using

Fawn as bait; but he was unaccustomed to hunting predators and was at a loss for another solution. Besides, according to Fawn, the wolf had made no effort to harm her. It was as if the beast were looking out for her. What an inconceivable idea.

Sky Eyes quietly followed the ridge top back to the rock bluff that backed up the camp. From his elevated position he could look down through the treetops, into the camp. He found a comfortable place to sit, near the base of a bushy tree, offering him some concealment.

He had been watching the camp for less than fifteen minutes when he saw the wolf slipping through the timber. He watched as the wolf crept upon the camp as quietly as a shadow.

Fear gripped Sky Eyes' throat as he imagined the wolf trotting to Fawn's sleeping furs and devouring her as she slept. His fear was somewhat alleviated when he saw the wolf lie down on the outskirts of the camp.

With all the skill the boy possessed, with the stealth of the wolf itself, he left his vantage point and began to work his way down the slope.

As Sky Eyes silently wormed his way toward the camp, he came to a small rock outcropping. From the outcropping, he could look directly into the camp. He saw Fawn sitting in her bed. He was still too far away to hit the wolf with an arrow and he knew he had to hurry, he also knew this was not a time to make a mistake. He proceeded with care, refusing to be coerced into an error by the dangerous circumstances.

As he drew nearer to the camp, foliage and tree trunks obstructed his view, making it impossible to get a clear shot at the wolf. He was at his maximum bow range from the camp when the wolf detected his presence.

He had made *no* sound. The wind had not changed. The wolf just *knew.*

Sky Eyes did not see the wolf look at him but he did see it rise and walk toward Fawn. Once again, he was frozen in the grip of fear. He was too far away for a killing shot and he knew it; all he could do was watch.

Sky Eyes had known for some time that the wolf was big, but he did not know until now, just what a monster he was. He was appalled when the wolf walked by Fawn, close enough to brush her with his shaggy fur, and saw that its back was as high as the top of her head.

With stupid relief, Sky Eyes watched the wolf disappear into the tall grass, as quickly as smoke on a windy day. He stepped out of concealment and ran to Fawn, wishing to console her, when in fact it was he who was in need of consolation. The incident had shaken Sky Eyes but Fawn was unexplainably calm, despite the lack of color in her cheeks.

When the wolf disappeared, Fawn turned around and saw Sky Eyes coming toward her. His eyes were wide, his mouth was gaping and his skin was pale.

"I told you he wouldn't hurt me," she said quietly, in a tone that Sky Eyes had never heard her use. "I also told you, you wouldn't kill him."

Because of her tone, and because he was so shaken, Sky Eyes did not take offense, or respond to either statement.

"Are you all right?" he asked, trying to keep his voice from breaking.

"Of course I am. I was a little afraid at first, but not now. He will not harm me. That is what I know."

Sky Eyes was beginning to become annoyed at her attitude and tone of voice. "I'm going after the horses," he said, before he turned and strode from the camp.

Later, Sky Eyes led the horses into the camp. Fawn was fleshing one of the elk hides. He turned the horses loose and sat on a protruding rock to watch them. He was close enough to Fawn to converse with her without talking too loudly.

"I don't think you should hunt the wolf again," she said, without looking up from her work.

"The wolf may not harm you – but what of me? What of the horses? What would become of us if he chewed up those hides?" he asked gravely.

She had been looking at him, now she hung her head. "I don't know," she answered softly, as she reflected on the consequences of her request.

"I don't know what to do," Sky Eyes admitted painfully. "It is my responsibility to protect you and the camp. When I hunted the wolf, I made no sound. I had the wind, yet he knew I was there. I think he has powers."

Fawn was astonished by Sky Eyes' remarks: his confidence had been shaken.

"You are a great hunter," she said with conviction. "You are young but I am sure there are grown warriors who would be envious of your skills. We both know the difficulties involved with hunting predators. I know what I'm talking about, I saw you sneak up on that cow yesterday."

Sky Eyes was neither boisterous nor bashful. He accepted things as they were. He was well aware of his abilities and equally aware of his shortcomings. He accepted her praise without embarrassment, for it was true. To himself though, he had to admit that the wolf had bested him.

Chapter Twenty-five

One moon after the incident with the wolf, the children awoke to find everything covered with a white glaze of frost.

The sudden appearance of cold weather caused them to hasten their efforts to prepare for the coming winter. Sky Eyes spent several days dragging in a huge pile of firewood. They both worked feverishly on the hides.

Sky Eyes dragged a log into camp that outweighed him by fifty pounds. He dropped the dead tree near the wood pile as Fawn finished stitching the hides together.

"Our tepee will be small," she said to Sky Eyes, as he rested near the fire.

Sky Eyes had known the tepee was going to be small but he was disappointed when he saw just how small it was.

"We will have to store most of our belongings and the meat outside or there won't be room for us inside," she stated.

"I will make a lean-to like we had where we lived before," said Sky Eyes.

"That would help keep things dry," she said. "We should not let the meat get wet," she added.

A lean-to was a good solution because it would be relatively easy to construct and could be done quickly. However, the meat and their belongings would be exposed to predation in the open structure.

As they discussed this problem, they made a point not to mention the wolf. They had not seen the beast since the day he came into the camp, but they had heard him howling in the hills and knew he had not gone away. They also knew that not talking about him would not keep him away, but they both had valid points concerning the wolf's presence and if they didn't talk about him, they got along better. They were about to spend much of the winter cooped-up in a tepee that was too small; neither of them wanted to spend that time angry with the other.

Sky Eyes was concerned about their wood supply. Since they had arrived at their new home, all of his time had been invested in hunting and caring for the meat and hides. They had a huge pile of wood but an extended period of cold weather would diminish the pile quickly. When he had been busy caring for the meat and hides he had used most of the wood that was close to the camp.

The next day Fawn went with Sky Eyes, as they went in search of poles for the tepee. By late afternoon, the tepee was erected and the two children looked at it with pride. It was indeed small, but it was a little bigger than either of them had expected it to be.

2

In the middle of the next moon, they endured the first snowstorm of the season. It wasn't really a storm, for only three inches of snow fell. But it was enough to tell the children that winter was upon them. Their days had been filled with hard, monotonous work; now the time had come to see if they had done enough of the right things.

The tepee was cramped, but it was warm and dry. Neither of the children could stand up inside, but if they were careful they could move about freely.

Sky Eyes had sorted the wood he had brought into the camp. When he had enough logs of the size he wanted, he constructed the lean-to. It was completed just before the snowfall. All of their meat and whatever extra belongings they had, were stored in the lean-to. Sky Eyes was concerned about not being able to close the structure, but he thought there was only one animal that would come so close to the camp to steal a free meal; that being the wolf.

Sky Eyes had noticed that the days were growing shorter. He had felt that a change in the weather was coming several days before the snowstorm hit, but the cold weather had come upon them quickly. One day, the temperature was warm and comfortable, the next it was freezing. Disquietingly, Sky Eyes realized they didn't have any winter clothing.

The consequences of being without adequate clothing were staggering.

Fawn crawled out of the warm tepee, which contained a small fire pit, and felt the bite of the autumn air. She quickly walked to the outside fire pit, where Sky Eyes was waiting.

"If it is this cold now, what will winter be like?" she asked, as she huddled over the fire.

"It will be cold," Sky Eyes answered, with a disgruntled look on his face.

"What troubles you this morning?" she asked softly. "Not the…"

"No. We have been so busy making a place to live and making sure we had protection and enough to eat, we didn't make any winter clothes," he said bitterly.

The thought of making new clothing had crossed Fawn's mind. But, she had been so busy preserving meat, and Sky Eyes had been away from the camp. By the time he had returned, the thought had slipped from her mind.

"The blame is mine, too," she said. "I thought about it but forgot to say anything to you."

Sky Eyes ignored what she had said. It was his place to foresee such things and in this case, he had failed miserably.

"I will hunt today," he informed her, "Maybe it's not too late."

"Can I hunt with you?" Fawn asked eagerly.

Sky Eyes considered the question for several minutes before he answered. He was aware of her desire to be included but he was equally aware that if the wolf followed them his chances of being successful would be scant at best.

"If it were not for the wolf, I would take you," he said. "But if he follows you, he will scare the animals away."

Fawn reluctantly accepted his decision without argument. She wanted to go with him but she realized there was some truth to what he said. She resisted the urge to inform him that the wolf had not interfered with the last elk hunt and he was a good hunter or he would have starved long ago.

Sky Eyes ate and then left the camp. As he left the timber he realized the snow was crusted and he crunched with every step. It would be impossible, even for him, to walk quietly upon the snow. He considered returning to camp but he wanted to locate the elk herd. If the elk were feeding, they would crunch too, increasing his chances of getting close without being detected.

He crossed the meadow and spent the day wandering through the hills. He saw no sign of the elk herd but he learned more about the terrain surrounding their new home.

Mid-way through the afternoon, he decided to return to camp. He was disturbed because he had found no elk signs. Tracks should have been plentiful and easy to see in the fresh snow. He knew elk migrated, but it usually took more snow than this to drive them out of the higher elevations.

When he reached the valley, he came upon the tracks he had made earlier in the day. The hair on his neck stood up and a chill ran up and down his spine when he saw the tracks of the wolf beside his tracks. The wolf had followed him...without his knowledge.

He felt that he had been careless and was very angry with himself. If he had known how to curse, he would have cursed himself then. The closest he could come, was to say, "A horse should step on your foot."

He turned and trotted along his morning trail, curious to learn how long the wolf had followed him. As he did so, it occurred to him to be thankful the wolf was not hanging around the camp, posing a threat to Fawn. After running along his own tracks for a long way, he found that the wolf's tracks never left his tracks. Another thought occurred to him: If the wolf was tracking him, he could hide and ambush the beast when it came to him.

He made a small circle to a wind-felled tree. He climbed onto the trunk of the tree and walked toward the exposed roots. The roots, and the grasses and shrubs that were up-rooted with them provided good cover and he still had an open shooting lane to his trail.

Sky Eyes sat in concealment until he got so cold he started to shiver but the wolf did not track him. Shivering uncontrollably, he left his hiding place and walked back to his trail. He made his way quickly down the slope. Once active again, he began to warm up. He was chilled again when he saw that the wolf had followed him again and had stopped just out of sight from where he was going to conduct the ambush. Shaking his head angrily, he hurried on to the camp.

Fawn was heating some meat over the fire when he walked through the trees and into the camp. "I thought you would be back sooner," she said, in a relieved voice. "It's almost dark."

"I would have been back much sooner but your wolf was following me. I tried to ambush him but he was too smart."

"When will you realize that it is not meant for you hunt the wolf? Not this wolf. You were never taught to hunt meat-eaters. It is different from hunting grass-eaters."

"If I can hunt one well, I should be able to hunt the other just as well," he retorted.

"They are different," she said, shaking her head, realizing the futility of the argument.

Sky Eyes squatted beside the fire and accepted the meat she offered him. "Did you find the elk?" she asked.

"I did not. They may be gone. I don't know."

"Where do they go when they go away?" she asked.

"I do not know. All I know is, they leave the mountains; maybe there is less snow where they go."

"Odd," she said, as she considered the complex way of nature and the effect it had on the people and animals of their world.

Sky Eyes heard her speak but saw that she was lost in her own thoughts and made no comment.

The light faded from the sky and darkness surrounded the tiny camp in the grove of pines trees. Sky Eyes dropped a large knotty piece of wood on the fire. Fawn walked beside him to the tepee. Sky Eyes went in first. Just before she ducked into the shelter she asked herself, "I wonder if the elk know something we do not?"

3

The next morning, they awoke to knee-deep snow that had fallen in the night, and it was still falling.

Sky Eyes looked gravely at the dark, heavy clouds.

"You are concerned about warmer clothing, but if we don't go far from camp, we will not need them. Everything we need is here, there is no need to go far from here." Fawn said to him, hoping to get him to stop worrying so much.

"What will we do when we need more wood?" he asked, pointedly.

"Go after wood when it is not so cold," she said, shrugging her shoulders.

Sky Eyes looked at her without making a comment. He wished survival was as simple as she seemed to think it was.

They spent the day in camp. Sky Eyes had to dig the snow away from the outside fire. The fire had not gone out but it had not burned hot enough to melt the snow away from its perimeter. Fawn worked on various projects from sewing some tattered clothing to concocting a stew. Sky Eyes tried his hand at making some arrowheads from likely looking stones he had found shortly after their arrival. Both children were surprised at how quickly the day passed.

Once again, they ate at dusk and turned in shortly after dark.

The snow continued to fall, off and on, for the next three days. Now, it was waist-deep to Sky Eyes and there appeared to be no relief in sight.

One night, Sky Eyes and Fawn were awakened by snarling sounds coming from the lean-to.

Sky Eyes sprang from his bed and leaped through the tepee door. His bow and arrows were by the outside fire pit. Bright moonlight shined into the camp from a partially cloudy sky. He glanced toward the lean-to as he ran to the fire pit but he saw nothing. His bow was where he had left it and when he picked it up, he turned toward the lean-to.

What he saw made him grit his teeth in anger. A wolverine was in the lean-to. The devil was ripping and tearing at the meat they had stored in there.

Sky Eyes drew back on the bow and released an arrow. His aim was good but the wolverine moved and what would have been a fatal hit was merely a wound as the arrow struck it near the tail.

The wolverine squalled in pain and surprise. It jumped out of the lean-to and tried to run away. It took several bounds before it saw Fawn standing just outside the tepee door. Sky Eyes was trying desperately to nock another arrow. The wolverine leaped at Fawn just as Sky Eyes reached full draw. His guts retched as he realized he was too late. He dropped the bow and while he was reaching for his knife, the wolverine appeared to freeze in mid-air.

Sky Eyes blinked his eyes and when he opened them, he saw the wolf trot between him and Fawn with a writhing wolverine between his massive jaws. Sky Eyes heard a snap and the wolverine became limp. The wolf disappeared into the night.

Sky Eyes shuffled to Fawn's side. She was standing stock still, mouth agape.

"Fawn," he said, worriedly.

She looked at him and he knew she was all right. "I didn't know he was here," she mumbled as he led her back to the tepee. "He saved my life," she said. "Sky Eyes…"

"I will not hunt the wolf again," he promised, as he pulled the flap aside for her.

"Thank you," she said quietly, as she ducked into the tepee.

The next morning, Sky Eyes examined the damage the wolverine had done. Some of the meat had received a direct shot of spray and was unusable, some small hides and leather scraps had been completely destroyed. Sky Eyes and Fawn sorted through the meat supply and discarded what had been ruined. They cleaned what they could, trying to salvage as much as possible. They did not see the wolf.

4

After the arrival of the next full moon, a warm breeze began to blow through the valley and most of the snow melted away.

Sky Eyes killed a doe when the ground was free of snow. He built a drying rack for the hide near the outside fire. He hoped the fire would work as well as the sun. The venison was a welcome treat from the steady diet of elk meat.

They saw the wolf almost daily. He was always near the camp. Sky Eyes was wary of the beast but he remembered his promise and did not threaten the wolf when it was nearby.

One day, Fawn voiced her thoughts about the wolf. "Have you seen signs of other people since we came off the mountain?" she asked.

"No," answered Sky Eyes, surprised that she had asked such a question. "Why do you ask?" he queried.

"I think the wolf has lived with people before," she answered.

Sky Eyes was shocked when he heard what she said. Why hadn't he considered that possibility? Perhaps he had been so anxious to kill the wolf that he had thought of nothing else. Fawn's words made sense. He would have to have lived with people to come near them the way he did. Now, Sky Eyes wondered what had become of the people who had shared their lives with the wolf.

The rest of the winter passed without incident. There were times when the snow was very deep and other times when their entire world seemed to be frozen. When the weather was too severe, they remained in the camp or even in the tepee all day. When the Chinooks blew and melted the snow, they gathered as much wood as they could find. Sky Eyes hunted when the weather permitted. His success rate was lower than normal but that was related to the season. He did manage to bag several snowshoe hares. The furs of the hares were thick and warm. Working together, they made a vest from the hides. Sky Eyes wore the vest when he hunted on colder days.

Finally, winter loosened its icy grip on the mountain valley. The spring rains washed the last of the snow away and all of the hardwood trees began to bud out. The world was green once again. Sky Eyes felt as though he had been released from captivity. He raced the Appaloosa up and down the meadow, feeling the warm air wash over his body, feeling free at last.

He saw movement out of the corner of his eye and saw the wolf running with him. He had to look again for the wolf too, looked as if he were happy.

He was at the far end of the meadow when he found that he and Fawn were no longer alone in the valley.

He reined the horse to a stop as he neared the narrow strip of timber that separated the meadows. He turned the horse around and was about to kick him into a run when he saw four mounted warriors leading Fawn's horse out of the camp. He did not see Fawn. He saw a flash in front of him and knew the wolf was on his way to help Fawn. Sky Eyes kicked the horse violently. The horse responded immediately, surprised at the rider's sudden behavior.

The Appaloosa raced across the meadow with speed that the boy had not yet tapped into. Sky Eyes leaning forward, almost flat on the horse's back, wishing his bow was in his hand, instead of in the camp.

As he drew nearer, he saw Fawn in front of the warriors. They were prodding her along with the butts of their buffalo spears. One of them had a long scratch on the side of his face and Sky Eyes knew why they didn't want to get too close to her.

The warriors heard the Appaloosa coming but when they looked toward Sky Eyes, the wolf sprang from the tall grass and dislodged the warrior who was closest to him. The warrior screamed in agony but Sky Eyes felt no compassion for him. Now, Fawn was his immediate concern.

"FAWN!" he screamed at her, as he came in close.

Fawn turned from the screaming warrior when she heard her name called. She saw Sky Eyes racing the Appaloosa toward her. She ran forward. Sky Eyes extended his hand to her. She raised her arm. Sky Eyes grasped her tiny hand as he rode by, without slowing down. He was trying to pull her onto the horse with him but something was wrong with his leg. He looked and was shocked to see an arrow protruding from his thigh. Even worse, there was also an arrow in the side of the Appaloosa. Sky Eyes struggled to get Fawn onto the back of the horse but she must have fallen while crossing the stream for her arm was wet and slippery. Her hand was slipping out of his grasp. He heard the wolf yelp and knew what had happened to him. He looked into Fawn's desperate eyes and was sickened when her hand slipped out of his and she fell heavily to the ground. Sky Eyes wheeled the Appaloosa and saw three of the warriors bearing down on him. He saw an arrow coming toward him and moved his leg just in time to keep from being hit. The Appaloosa was not so lucky. There was no time to get to Fawn. Grief stricken, Sky Eyes wheeled the Appaloosa again and raced across the valley. He reached down and pulled the arrow out of his leg. Once again, the Appaloosa was not so lucky, the arrows began to do their work and the wounded horse began to tire. He tried to urge more speed from the horse but it was useless. The strangers were gaining on him.

Blowing blood from both nostrils, the Appaloosa collapsed on the valley floor.

"This was my father's horse," Sky Eyes reminded himself as he fell from the falling horse and rolled into the tall grass. "Someone will pay for this outrage and the price will be high," he promised himself as he used stealth skills; this time in an effort to escape, rather than capture a meal.

His leg was bleeding and he knew they would try to follow the blood trail to find him.

Two warriors dismounted a few moments after Sky Eyes. They began to search for him. They didn't think he would get far and looked for him instead of following the blood trail.

Sky Eyes had thought they might try this and had moved quickly away from the fallen horse. Now, as they searched for him he circled them, crossing his trail and theirs.

When the warriors finally realized they weren't going to find a body or a helpless boy lying on the ground, they returned to where he had fallen off the horse and began to look for blood. While they were doing so, Sky Eyes crossed their trail again.

When the two braves left the fallen horse, they spread out a few yards apart. This maneuver just about cost Sky Eyes his life, or at least his freedom. One brave walked close enough for Sky Eyes to touch had he wished to do so, while the other one worked the blood trail. Had Sky Eyes not been wounded, he probably would have knifed the warrior in the back when he walked by; he was tempted to do so anyway, but he knew the other one would certainly kill him if he did.

As the warriors attempted to sort out the trail, Sky Eyes managed to stop the blood flowing from his leg long enough to get away. The warriors had walked on the trail, which made it more difficult to follow, coupled with the crisscross pattern Sky Eyes had laid down for them. They were unable to straighten it out. Angrily, they gave up in frustration.

Sky Eyes continued to crawl farther away. He had considered trying to get back to Fawn but he was no match for the warrior who guarded her. He reasoned that if they had been prodding her from the beginning, they probably would not harm her.

He continued to crawl. He crawled until the pain from the wound, coupled with the loss of blood caused him to lose consciousness.

5

Two frogs croaked back and forth to each other. Meadow birds warbled their soft, happy trills. A large insect buzzed as it flew lazily about the meadow grass and overhead, a red-tailed hawk screeched a warning to the rodents below.

Sky Eyes opened his eyes and listened to these sounds. He looked into the azure sky and felt the gentle breeze touch his face, but he did not move. He wasn't sure he could move. His right leg ached from hip to toe. He listened for a moment longer. When he was certain that no one was moving nearby, he raised his head. The grass was too tall and he was unable to see anything. He raised himself up onto his elbows and could see over the top of the grass. A slow, careful scan of the area assured him that he was alone.

He was about to look at his leg to assess the damage when he saw the wolf lying at his feet. The beast had an arrow in its left shoulder and another through its jaw, but it was breathing.

The fact that the wolf had risked its life trying to save Fawn was not lost on Sky Eyes. However, he had to attend to his wounds before seeing to the wolf.

He untied the drawstring of his leather trousers and gingerly took them off. The movement caused the wound to reopen and a moan escaped his lips.

Hearing the sound, the wolf raised its head and whined softly. The wolf was panting heavily and Sky Eyes could tell by the look in its eyes that it had a fever and was in great pain.

"Be strong my large, wild friend and I will help you as soon as I can."

The wolf wagged its tail at the sound of his voice. He couldn't understand the words but the soothing tone told him that he was with a friend.

Sky Eyes looked at his wound and felt his stomach roll over. He felt lightheaded and had to struggle not to lose consciousness. When the wave passed, he raised himself back up on his elbows and tried to figure out where he was. When he got his bearings, he rolled over and began to drag himself toward the stream. The wolf whined as he got farther away, but it was unable to follow him. Oddly enough, considering his past feelings for the wolf, Sky Eyes felt badly having to leave him behind. He knew of no way to tell the wolf he would be back when he could.

At last, Sky Eyes reached the stream. He parted the grass on the bank and slid onto a small gravel bar. The water rushed rapidly over the bar but it was not deep. Sky Eyes lay in the water and let it wash some of his pain away.

After a while, he began to shiver so he pulled himself onto the bar. The gravel was warm and soon he stopped shivering.

He looked at the wound again and realized it needed to be cleaned. He washed the dried blood away and looked at the wound more closely. There was a ragged hole in his thigh and he knew that was partly his fault for the way he had ripped the arrow out of his flesh. The good news was, the bone didn't seem to be damaged.

He saw a plant with long, broad leaves growing near the bank of the stream. He made his way to the plant and ripped the leaves off, one at a time. He wrapped the leaves around his thigh and tied them with the drawstring from his waist. He did not know if the plant was medicinal or not; he felt that the wound should be covered and that was all he wanted to accomplish.

He considered returning to the wolf but felt an urge to go to the camp. He had to find out if Fawn was still there, or if she were even still alive.

Crawling, he crossed the stream and made his way upstream, toward the camp. He had gone a short distance when he found a short, sturdy stick. He was tiring of crawling around on the ground, so he took the stick in his hand and stood up. He was wobbly and it was difficult to keep the weight off of his wounded leg. However, he did make better time and he could see his surroundings better.

When he reached the camp, he found it empty, as he feared he would. He was sickened to see that they had destroyed the tepee and the lean-to. He was in too much pain to worry about getting angry, but he was at a loss to understand why anyone would do something like this to another person.

6

The eyes of three, solemn young men stared at the red, glowing embers of the small fire. They all knew that by doing so they would have no night vision, if the need arose. But, night vision was the last thing on their minds on this night. When they left their village there had been four of them. Now, Otter lay outside the reaches of the light shed by the campfire, with his throat ripped out.

"What are we going to tell Otter's father?" asked Buck-that-fights-in-the-fall.

"How are we going to explain the girl?" asked Tracks-in-the-snow, who had been Otter's best friend.

Diving Eagle said nothing. He was the oldest of the young men and it had been his idea to harass the little girl. They had meant no harm and would have done nothing more than tease her. But, when she ripped his face open with her nails, he had gotten very angry. He still would not have hurt her, very much, but he had intended to take her to his village where she would have become his property and he would have taught her some manners. Then they saw the boy charging them. Before they could react, the wolf…the wolf! He had been the size of a small horse, and had come from nowhere and ripped Otter's throat out. How could things have gone so badly? Otter's death was his responsibility and things would not go well for him when he returned to the village. Otter's father was one of the village elders and a very respected man. Diving Eagle's father was a respected man too, but he had not attained the status of Otter's father.

"Diving Eagle. Diving Eagle…what are we going to do?" asked Buck-that-fights-in-the-fall.

"We are going to go back to the village," Diving Eagle answered in a tone that expressed his distaste for having to answer stupid questions. He was deep in his own thoughts, trying to imagine what the future held for him. He didn't have the patience to listen to the others whine now. He fully expected to be expelled from the village and that thought was very troubling for him.

Diving Eagle looked across the fire to where the girl was bound. He could see her eyes glimmering in the firelight. He had to admire her tenacity. She had taken him on without hesitation when he dragged her out of the tepee. The tepee…He had never seen such a small tepee. He had wondered what sort of people would live in such a small tepee.

When he pulled her from the tepee, he realized she was nine or ten, the same age as his sister, Dove. But this girl was much stronger than Dove. She was like a wild animal as she squirmed and writhed, trying to escape his grasp. He had released her when she scratched his face but the others had quickly surrounded her before she escaped. Now, he wished she had gotten away. As the others held her, he clubbed her on the head with his forearm. The blow had knocked her sprawling; he had done as much damage to his arm as he had done to her head. He had never struck another person in anger in his life. He was thinking now that evil spirits had entered his body and were making him do things he didn't want to do.

Diving Eagle got to his feet and walked to the other side of the fire. He squatted down in front of Fawn.

"Who are your people?" he asked in Cheyenne.

"He will kill you," she said, in Arapaho.

"You speak Arapaho?" he said, surprised. "What are you doing in this country?"

She was surprised to find that he spoke Arapaho but she was not willing to become his friend simply because they could speak a same language.

"He will kill you for what you have done," she repeated.

"The boy? I don't think so. I doubt he is still alive. Even if he is not dead…"

"Did you find his body?" she hissed, knowing full well they had not. "If you did not find his body, he lives. And if he lives, he will come for me and he will kill you…All of you."

"We did not mean for anyone to get hurt. Things got out of hand. We are sorry, but it is too late to make it go away. And, I do not fear little boys," said Diving Eagle as he tried to apologize and assert his bravery at the same time.

"One on one, you would probably be able to kill him," she said with a sneer. "But that is not how it will happen. You will not see him, you will not hear him. You will not know he is near until it is too late. He is like smoke when he mov—"

Unsettled by her words and the enormous guilt he bore, he reached out and clubbed her with his forearm again. He had acted without thought and was shocked by what he had done. Now, he was angry with her and himself.

"No half-grown whelp will sneak up on me," he said, through clenched teeth.

She realized she had gotten to him and she was not about to stop. She sucked blood into her mouth from the cut on her lip and spat it into his face.

"Even if he does not come, the wolf will come. You have seen what the wolf can do," she said, indicating the body of Otter.

Diving Eagle wiped the blood and spittle from his face and then raised his arm to strike her again. This time the response was premeditated and he was able to stop himself before he struck her. That she did not flinch or cower down was not lost on him.

"You are now my property. You will do as I tell you to do, when I tell you to do it. The sooner you accept the ways of the Cheyenne, the sooner you will have some of your freedom back."

"What is 'property'?" she asked, repulsively, thinking she knew exactly what he meant.

"This is my knife, it is my property. That is my horse, it is my property. You are my…"

"NO!" she said, so vehemently her upper lip curled away from her teeth. "I will die before I belong to the likes of you!"

"If you are not careful, you may get your wish," he said, in Cheyenne, as he got up to return to the fire. She spat at him again as he turned away.

7

Sky Eyes found a large scrap of deerskin Fawn had put aside for some unknown project. He carried it to the meadow. He moved slowly, not wanting to fall and make his injury worse than it was.

He intended to use the deerskin to drag the wolf to the camp. He wasn't sure he could do it, but he didn't want to leave the wolf alone in the meadow, nor did he want to move his camp into the open – it wouldn't be safe.

Vultures were circling high over the wolf when Sky Eyes returned. Some of them had already begun feasting on the Appaloosa. The wolf thumped its tail weakly when Sky Eyes knelt beside him.

"This is not natural," said Sky Eyes, as he reached out and stroked the coat of the prone beast. The wolf whimpered at the sound of his voice.

"Be easy, wolf. I'm going to move you and I don't want you to bite my arm off," he said, as he prepared to roll the wolf onto the deerskin. "We will both have to be healthy in order to save Fawn," he added, as an afterthought.

Sky Eyes had to get on his knees but he didn't have enough strength to move the wolf. Even if he had not been wounded, he would have been unable to move the wolf, which weighed more than twice as much as he did. Unwilling to give up, he tried until he was exhausted. When, at last, he had to admit to himself that what he was trying to do was impossible, he decided to move what was left of the camp to the wolf.

Slowly, he hobbled back to the camp and began to go through what was left of their belongings. When he had as much as he could carry, he returned to the wolf. The shadows were growing long but he made one more trip before nightfall.

In the gathering darkness, he kindled a fire and warmed a piece of meat. He offered meat to the wolf but the animal only sniffed at the food. It occurred to Sky Eyes that the wolf might be thirsty. It wasn't far to the stream but it was almost dark. He decided to chance the trip after water – what animal would attack when there was a wolf in his camp?

He dug around until he found a bowl and then made his way to the stream as quickly as possible; wolf or no, he didn't like being away from the fire at night. It was difficult to carry the water as he walked with the aid of the stick, but it was still over half full when he reached the camp. Unfortunately, the wolf lapped the water quickly and Sky Eyes knew he would have to go after more.

"You'll be the death of me yet, wolf," he said, as he prepared to enter the darkness again. The wolf thumped his tail.

Alone for the first time in his life, Sky Eyes stepped into the darkness. He was not afraid of the dark, but in his condition, he had a fear of those that hunted and fed in the darkness. Thus, he was not completely at ease either. He had found that he was susceptible to predation – and he didn't like it.

"My name is Sky Eyes," he said, as he shuffled toward the stream. "My father was Scott Walker. My teacher was Man-with-no-hair, a Shawnee. My mother was Dew-on-the-grass-in-the-moon-when-the-leaves-fall, she too was Shawnee. I have a wolf in my camp. He is a very big wolf and he is my friend. He would not take it well if the creatures of the night came to visit me on my way to get him a drink."

8

The next morning, Diving Eagle left the fire and walked to where Fawn slept. He reached out with his foot to kick her, to wake her up, but she had been awake for some time. She rolled away from the kick and Diving Eagle lost his balance and nearly fell down. He heard a couple of snickers from his camp and was instantly angry. Fawn had come to the end of her rope and was unable to move farther away. He kicked again. This time his foot connected with Fawn's stomach, forcing the air from her lungs in a "whoosh." Diving Eagle smiled as she writhed in pain. However, as he walked back to his fire, he wondered again what was happening to him.

The three young warriors ate but did not offer to share their food with Fawn. A short time later, they began to break camp. They loaded Otter on one of the horses. The heat was beginning to have an affect on their late friend and they grimaced when they tied him on the back of the horse.

Fawn smirked at their discomfort but when she saw the steely look she was getting from Diving Eagle, her smile went away.

The thong was removed from Fawn's ankles but they left her wrists bound. "You'll have a hard time scratching someone with your hands tied together,"

Diving Eagle pointed out.

With that said, Fawn promptly kicked him in the knee. Had she been bigger, the blow surely would have snapped the joint. As it was, Diving Eagle grimaced and backed away. He raised his arm and was advancing on her when Buck-that-fights-in-the-fall and Tracks-in-the-snow grabbed him and pulled him back.

"What are you doing? Let me go! Did you see what she did to me? I will teach her some manners and I will start now."

"Not now," said Tracks-in-the-snow. "We have a long way to go. We do not want to have to wait for her because you have hurt her so much she can't keep up. If you want to beat her, do it when we camp tonight."

"Hit me all you want," said Fawn, "But when he gets here, you will be sorry."

"What is she talking about?" asked Buck-that-fights-in-the-fall.

"It is nothing," said Diving Eagle.

"I know some Arapaho," said Buck-that-fights-in-the-fall. "Is someone following us? Was someone else living in her camp? What is she talking about?"

"She told me the boy and the wolf will came after her. I told her they were both dead. And I am sure they are dead. Have you ever been followed by a dead person?" he asked, as he fixed them both with piercing stares.

"No," they mumbled simultaneously. They didn't sound very convinced. They had tried to track a wounded boy and were unable to do so. He had attacked them, openly taking on four-to-one odds. He was young and not very big but he had the heart and courage of a seasoned warrior.

"Are you afraid of a boy?" asked Diving Eagle. He could tell what they were thinking by the way they looked.

Fawn realized that her words had had an affect on the other two warriors. "You will not see him. You will not hear him. You will not know he is here until it is too late. He is like smoke on the wind," she repeated the warning from the night before, this time to all three of the young men.

Diving Eagle took a step toward her with his arm raised. Once again, his two friends held him back. Fawn stood her ground, defying him to strike her.

"Let us be away from here before the sun rises any higher," said Tracks-in-the-snow.

Diving Eagle shook loose from his companions and walked to his horse. He was mumbling to himself as he swung onto the horse's back. When he was mounted, he gave Fawn a look that convinced her that he would not forget about her insolence. The look encouraged her to be more careful what she said to him and how she said it.

By the time they camped late that afternoon, her back had been severely bruised by prodding jabs of Diving Eagle's buffalo spear. Fawn had fought hard not to show weakness but she was in a great deal of pain. She had not had food or drink since she had been taken from her camp. Unknowingly, she asked the same question Sky Eyes had asked himself: "Why would anyone treat another person like this?"

9

The wolf finally ate a small piece of meat. Sky Eyes was elated. He had feared the wolf was going to die. The water seemed to make him feel better but he would not get stronger without eating.

Sky Eyes was recovering rapidly. Though he would not be ready to take up the trail of Fawn's captors for a few more days, he was improving faster than the wolf.

Sky Eyes had pulled the arrows out of the wolf and his wounds were healing well. He had done what he could to stop the bleeding, but he had no idea how much damage had been done. Apparently, the arrow that had gone through his jaw had not broken any bones, for the wolf was able to eat and drink.

After eating a small piece of meat, the wolf wanted more. Sky Eyes returned to the lean-to and salvaged what meat he could find. He still didn't have the strength to lift a lot of weight and was unable to move the roof logs that had fallen in when the lean-to had been destroyed.

By sharing the meat, they both began to regain their strength. The wolf was finally able to get up and walk to the stream, though he had a noticeable limp. Sky Eyes was finally able to move about freely, without the use of the walking stick, but he too, had a noticeable limp.

One day, Sky Eyes snared a rabbit. He shared the bounty with the wolf. The fresh meat seemed to have a more profound affect on them than all of the preserved meat they had eaten.

On the fifth day after Fawn had been taken, Sky Eyes was abruptly awakened by the wolf as he howled at the sinking moon. The wolf was not looking at the moon, he was looking in the direction Fawn had been taken.

"Are you ready to go after her?" asked Sky Eyes, hopefully.

The wolf thumped his tail on the ground.

Fortunately, the intruders had not found Sky Eyes' bow and quiver. As he waited for himself and the wolf to heal, Sky Eyes chipped arrowheads and made more arrows. The arrows and arrowheads were crude but they flew straight and far.

The next rising sun found two hunters, limping, side by side, on the trail of the people who had taken their friend.

Pulling logs and lifting heavy pieces of wood, along with carrying heavy loads had made Sky Eyes very strong. The more he walked, the more his strength returned. His recovery was still ahead of that of the wolf. Sky Eyes had been ready to jog when they found the horse tracks leading away, but the wolf had been unable to do so.

Patiently, Sky Eyes slowed to a pace that was more acceptable to the wolf. He remembered what the wolf had done to one of the intruders and knew he would probably need the wolf's help when they caught up with the people who had taken Fawn away. He didn't know how far the thieves had gone, but they had made no effort to cover their trail. Sky Eyes could have trailed them from the back of a running horse.

Chapter Twenty-six

Streaks of flashing lightning walked about the ridge tops surrounding a tiny valley. Distant rain clouds dumped their cargo on needy blades of grass and thirsty trees and shrubs.

Diving Eagle watched the storm clouds with dull interest. They would be back in their village tomorrow and he would have some explaining to do.

The girl was drawn and pale. He had given her only a few scraps of meat and she was very weak; but she didn't fight him anymore. She was learning manners. But the people of his village would be angry with him when they saw they way he had treated her. Buck-that-fights-in-the-fall and Tracks-in-the-snow would no longer talk to him. Even worse, they looked at him with disgust. What had happened to him?

2

From a low ridge top, Sky Eyes and the wolf watched the same storm. They had regained more and more strength with each passing day. They had hunted together, each sharing his catch with the other. Sky Eyes no longer considered a wolf for a companion as an oddity. He and the wolf walked side by side on the trail. They had become a very effective team. One night, Sky Eyes had been awakened by the howling wolf. Rather than getting angry, he sat up and howled at the night sky with his furry friend. The wolf looked at him curiously then turned back to the moon and howled again.

They had been on the trail long before dawn, everyday. They traveled well into the night. They hunted when the need arose. Sky Eyes carried what he could from their larger kills; the rest was left behind. They had no home, so it mattered not where they stopped to rest or sleep.

Now, they were close to those who had taken Fawn. Sky Eyes could smell the fresh horse dung and knew they would be on them before long.

For the first time, he tried to think of a plan to get Fawn back. He knew there were three warriors and he was concerned about what the wolf would do. He did not wish to let the warriors know he was near until at least one of them had one of his arrows sticking out of his body. The wolf was a hunter and Sky Eyes sensed that no matter what he decided to do, the wolf would do his share to help get Fawn back.

Sky Eyes turned away from the distant storm and returned to the trail. In the gathering dusk, he saw the red glow of a small fire at the far end of the small valley.

A smiled crossed his lips when he saw the fire. Fawn would be safe before this night was over. The smile turned to a sneer as his lip curled up to expose his teeth. He had not known deep hatred until they had done what they had done. Those who had killed his family had been distant and there had been far too many, thus, unreachable. Now, he was prepared to kill these people for what they had done. Sky Eyes was standing beside the wolf, his hand on the beast's back. The wolf looked toward the fire too. Sky Eyes felt the rumbling deep in the wolf's chest, though the growl was barely perceptible. Sky Eyes growled too. Sky Eyes was one with the wolf and together they were one with the land – creatures of their environment.

To kill another person was a concept Sky Eyes had never heard or thought about until his friends and family had been slaughtered in their valley. He had seen Runs-like-an-antelope kill several attackers. His father had killed at least one. He had heard the story about how his father had gotten the spotted horse, he knew people died; he hadn't known that they killed each other. He had heard the stories about Man-with-no-hair and his father killing the great bears with their bows and arrows. He now reasoned that if a bow and arrow could kill a bear, it would surely kill a man. Kill a man...? The thought sent chills racing up and down his spine. They were not chills of happiness or anticipation – they were chills of dread.

3

Fawn smiled an empty smile when she saw Diving Eagle looking at her. Her face was filthy and her hair was a tangled mess. The smile gave her a haunting appearance. Diving Eagle shuddered and her smile broadened. He picked up a willow switch and walked toward her.

Tracks-in-the-snow and Buck-that-fights-in-the-fall jumped to their feet and stood between Fawn and Diving Eagle. "You have hit her enough," said Tracks-in-the-snow. "You will hit her no more. When we get to the village and the elders have heard what has happened, you can do whatever they will

303

allow. But for now, there has been enough."

"He is near," Fawn said, in Arapaho. All three warriors turned to look at her. "You two should leave now," she said to Buck-that-fights-in-the-fall and Tracks-in-the-snow. "You have tried to help me but he does not know that. When he comes he will kill whoever is here. Go now and you will be alive tomorrow. Stay, and you will probably die before morning."

"How do you know he is near?" Diving Eagle asked with a sneer. "What powers do you have that enable you to tell when someone is near?"

"Perhaps I have seen him," Fawn responded immediately.

Tracks-in-the-snow and Buck-that-fights-in-the-fall believed what she had said and began to look around their camp. They could not see much for the sun had set and the light was fading quickly.

Diving Eagle shoved them both roughly. "She is not telling the truth. She is trying to make you afraid as if you were the child and she the warrior. Besides, I am not afraid of a little boy. Are you?"

"We didn't get a very good look at him. He may be older than we thought. He has some good skills. We weren't able to find him and he was hit hard."

"If he was hit so hard, how could he have caught up with us?" asked Diving Eagle.

"I don't know," said Tracks-in-the-snow. "But I know what we did was bad and that we will have to pay, one way or another."

"Do you think a small boy will make you pay?" asked Diving Eagle.

"I know I do not wish to die for a mistake. I do not wish to die in a place my mother cannot find when she wants to wail over my bones," said Buck-that-fights-in-the-fall.

"Go away then! When I return to the village I will tell everyone that Tracks-in-the-snow and Buck-that-fights-in-the-fall are afraid of children. You will not be asked to join in hunting and war parties. You will be left behind so the women can protect you."

Diving Eagle's words bit deeply into the souls of his two companions. Their faces blushed deeply from embarrassment and shame.

"We didn't say we were..."

The lonesome, bone-chilling howl of a wolf interrupted Tracks-in-the-snow. The sound echoed across the narrow valley, causing the warriors' imaginations to conjure up all sorts of thoughts of evil spirits.

Fawn laughed out loud.

Another howl. The sound was of a different quality...It sounded different...It didn't sound quite right...What? THE BOY.

"He is here!" said Diving Eagle.

"Do you see hi— Uh!"

Before Tracks-in-the-snow could finish his question an arrow penetrated his sternum, knocking the wind out of him. Diving Eagle and Buck-that-fights-in-the-fall turned to their friend and were shocked to see what had happened to him. When the arrow struck Tracks-in-the-snow he spun around, attempting to get away from the source of the pain. When he turned, he made it impossible for his friends to determine where the arrow had come from. They caught him in their arms and laid him gently on the ground. Blood was running from his mouth and they both knew he was going to die.

"I do not like the way this feels. You should go before it happens to you," Tracks-in-the-snow said, spitting blood as he spoke.

"We will not leave you be—"

An arrow struck Buck-that-fights-in-the-fall in the back before he could finish his promise to Tracks-in-the-snow.

Mouth agape with shock, Diving Eagle watched Buck-that-fights-in-the-fall fall across the body of Tracks-in-the-snow. Without hesitation Diving Eagle sprinted for his horse. He ripped the lead rope from the shrub it had been tied to. He sprang onto the horse's back and galloped into the night, lying as close to the horse's back as possible, hoping to avoid the fate that had befallen his companions.

Sky Eyes stepped cautiously into the light of the fire. A crouching, snarling wolf by his side. The boy looked from the fallen warriors to Fawn. He looked back at the warriors. He had just killed two full-grown men…He didn't know how to feel – or what to feel. He felt some elation, but only because he had won and Fawn was safe. He felt a great deal of anger – anger that was not sated by the death of two of those who had caused the anger. They had killed a horse his father had given him. They had taken Fawn away from him. They had shot him and the wolf with their arrows. They had destroyed his home and his food stores.

Remembering what they had done caused his anger to seethe. He dropped his bow and drew his knife. He straddled the fallen warriors and began to hack away at their motionless bodies. As he hacked and stabbed, he remembered his friends and family as they fell prey to a far superior force and he hacked for that hurt, too.

He hacked…And he hacked. He hacked until tears streamed down his face and snot bubbled from his nose. He hacked until his arms were too weary to raise the knife again. He heard someone calling his name but he could not tell where the sound was coming from. Slick with blood, he slid off of the bodies and thumped to the ground, to weak to slow his fall.

After several minutes, he realized it had been Fawn calling his name. Dropping the knife, he got to his hands and knees and crawled to her.

"Take me away from here," she sobbed.

"Are you well?" he asked, without looking at her.

"I am tired and hungry, but I am well. Please take me away from here," she begged. "Why did you do that to them?" she asked, horrified by his actions.

"They hurt you, they hurt me. They took what was not theirs to take. They killed what was not theirs to kill. They deserved more than just dying."

"But to do what you did...?"

"I was grieving for our families. I made them pay for that too. I know now that what I did was not good. I will never do a thing like that again."

"I grieve, too, but now I want to be away from here. Their village is one day from here and I think the one who escaped will be back with more of their people."

"When his friends see what happened to those two, they may decide they don't want to be his friend anymore," said Sky Eyes.

Chapter Twenty-seven

Sky Eyes shared some rabbit meat with Fawn. She ate ravenously. He had been shocked when he saw the condition she was in. He regretted the act of desecration he had committed upon the bodies of the two fallen warriors, but most of the guilt washed away when he looked upon Fawn's emaciated body.

Fawn had been bewildered when she saw the wolf walk into the camp beside Sky Eyes. She was still taken aback by the shear size of the animal and it took her some time before she was able to approach him without some trepidation.

Sky Eyes added wood to the fire and waited for the moon to rise. He didn't like to ride at night but the moon was full and the sky was cloudless; there would be ample light to see by.

Tracks-in-the-snow had been leading Otter's horse and Buck-that-fights-in-the-fall had been leading Fawn's mare. Diving Eagle had not taken any of the extra horses. Sky Eyes now claimed those horses as his.

When the moon rose, Sky Eyes helped Fawn onto her horse. He then swung onto the horse that had belonged to Tracks-in-the-snow, which looked like the best mount. He carried the lead rope of the extra horse as he led them out of the camp toward an unknown destination.

The horses were uncomfortable when the wolf was nearby but he seemed to sense that and stayed well away from them.

Fawn rode in silence until daylight, at which time, she rode alongside Sky Eyes and said, "I didn't know if you were dead or alive. I was afraid." Sky Eyes looked at her as she spoke. "I didn't let them know I was afraid. I told them you were coming and they wouldn't know you were there until it was too late." A smile touched her lips as she said, "It made them afraid when I told them you were coming. On the outside they were men but I think they were boys on the inside. The one who ran away was not a good person. He hurt me. He should have been the one who died in the camp. I am not sorry the other two are dead because they helped do what was done, but they were not bad. Once, they stopped him from hitting me. I think he will come for us again. I don't know if he will have more friends, but I know he will come."

Fawn had spoken slowly and deliberately. Sky Eyes had listened without interruption, until she was finished speaking.

"If I were alone, I would track him until one of us were dead. It is out of my hands that the one who deserved to die was the one who ran away. I have killed *people* and I don't like the way that feels. I do not want to do it again, but if he follows us, I will kill him. I will kill him first and if his friends want to stay with him, I will kill them. If they leave, I will let them go."

"Can we go back to our valley?" asked Fawn.

"There is anger and death in that place. It was a good place but we will not go back. I do not know where we will go. We will ride until we find another place."

2

Diving Eagle pushed his horse hard throughout the night. Several times the horse tried to slow down but he wouldn't allow it to do so.

At dawn, Diving Eagle ran the horse to death on the ridge above his village.

Many people had seen him riding down the ridge and they were aghast when they saw the horse fall. They were a people who knew horses and they knew that the horse had not stumbled. They knew the rider had ridden the horse to death and to them, which was a very serious thing. They mumbled their own thoughts as the rider rolled down the hill, gathered his feet and then ran the rest of the way to the village, without so much as a backward glance at his fallen mount.

They were even more aghast when they recognized Diving Eagle, for that was not the type of thing they would have expected to see him do.

A woman wailed. When people looked in the direction of the sound, they saw Otter's mother. As comprehension soaked in, the mothers of Tracks-in-the-snow and Buck-that-fights-in-the-fall fell to their knees and began to wail.

Warriors gathered their weapons and began to move toward Diving Eagle. The people left their tepees and followed the warriors.

Diving Eagle was no longer worried about losing face. He had been scared to the core of his soul and was very close to going completely insane. When he had been racing the horse through the night, his imagination had gotten out of hand and he pictured demons over his shoulder, wolves ahead of him and the small boy shooting arrows from behind every bush.

Now, as he sprinted into the camp and fell to his knees in front of the chief's tepee, his eyes were wide and his skin was ashen. His sides were heaving and he spoke incoherently.

Bear-scratching-a-tree, the chief of the village, sent a young boy after Diving Eagle's father. The youth didn't have far to go, for the man was making his way through the crowd, with a worried look on his face.

Diving Eagle's father stopped beside his son, touching him on the shoulder, letting him know he was no longer alone. Diving Eagle looked up and his father helped him to his feet.

Bear-scratching-a-tree knew Diving Eagle had left the village with three companions and that he had returned alone. The actions of Diving Eagle made him uneasy. He knew he had to find out what had happened but he wasn't sure he wanted to know. Bolstering himself, he finally began, "I can see that something terrible has happened. We are glad to see you are safe. What has become of the young men who were traveling with you?"

"WOLFBOY!" Diving Eagle blurted. Then he continued, unable to compose himself long enough to make sense. "Boy...Powers...Took a girl...Small tepee...Couldn't see him coming...Powers...Just a boy..."

"Diving Eagle," his father said sternly.

"Powers...Shot him, couldn't find him...Small tepee..."

"Diving Eagle," his father repeated. This time the young man looked at him but he continued to babble.

"Wolf...Big wolf...Powers..."

"My son," wailed Otter's mother, "What has become of my son?"

Otter's father looked at her sternly for she was about to shame him and he wanted it stopped before it was too late. She saw his look and backed away from the crowd, fell to her knees and wailed to herself.

Bear-scratching-a-tree was becoming more uncomfortable with the situation. He was overly superstitious and it was beginning to sound like the spirits had been involved with what had happened to Diving Eagle and his friends.

"Perhaps we should give the boy time to recover before we ask him more questions," suggested Bear-scratching-a-tree.

Otter's father stepped forward and addressed the chief. "We can all see that Diving Eagle is troubled. We are sure that he has had a bad time, but I would like to know where my son is and what has happened to him. It is my right to know these things."

"I too, would like to know what has happened," said Tracks-in-the-snow's father.

Buck-that-fights-in-the-fall's father grunted, signifying his need to know as well.

Bear-scratching-a-tree had missed his chance to postpone this unwelcome business and he knew it. He turned to Diving Eagle and motioned for him to sit by his fire. He motioned for the boy's father to join him. He then invited the fathers of the three missing youths to sit at the fire, also. When everyone was seated, the chief seated himself and asked Diving Eagle if he was ready to tell them what had happened.

Listening to the people of his village speak had helped Diving Eagle compose himself.

Riding throughout the night, his mind had been in shock and he had been unable to work on his story – to lessen the severity of his punishment. He would not – could not – tell a lie. He could have, however, told the story from a different perspective, making his actions sound more acceptable. Now, he would have to tell it the way it had happened and he was afraid.

"We rode into a camp. There was only one tepee and it was very small..."

3

The fire was built against the solid rock wall of a short, but steep rock outcropping. Sky Eyes dropped a few small pieces of wood on the fire and listened carefully, trying to hear the words Fawn was speaking. She was sitting on top of the outcropping and he couldn't make out the words, for she was speaking softly, but he knew she was speaking to her mother.

At last, she came down from her perch and sat close to the fire. She had to sit close because she no longer had her sleeping furs. She gave Sky Eyes a sideways glance, as she sat down. She knew he had been trying to listen to her and he had watched her as she climbed down the rock. "I feel better after I talk to my mother. You should talk to Dew-on-the-grass-in-the-moon-when-the-leaves-fall. I see her up there. She is near my mother. You would feel better if you talked to her. If you are too proud to talk to her, you could talk with your father or Man-with-no-hair, my father."

"You think I am too proud to talk to my mother?" he asked, shocked by her statement.

"No," she answered. "But I never see you talking to them. You were the one who told me they were up there, yet you never talk to them."

"Have they ever answered you?" he asked.

"No. But that doesn't mean they don't hear me. Does it?"

Sky Eyes quickly realized he had nearly dissolved her belief that her friends and family were watching over them. He was afraid she would become unstable without that belief.

"I am sure they hear your words," he reassured her. He could see the relief wash over her face as she heard his words.

"Why did they let a bad thing happen to us?" she asked.

Sky Eyes was unprepared for the question and had to think for a moment before he answered. "I think they can hear us and they can see us, at night when there are no clouds, but they can not reach down and help us. We have to learn to help ourselves. They can hear our problems, and if we learn to listen, I think we can hear them speak. But what we do and how we do it is up to us. If we do not do as we have been taught, or what we know is right, they may turn away and will not help us."

Fawn shuddered involuntarily at the thought of her mother turning her back on her. "They are still up there. That must mean we are doing what they expect," she said, hopefully.

"I am sure we have done nothing to cause them to turn away from us," Sky Eyes said, secretly hoping his words were true.

His words caused Fawn to smile, for she was content with her thoughts and dreams. She moved a little closer to the fire and lay down. She was soon fast asleep.

As she slept, Sky Eyes worried about their future. He got up, and as he walked away from the fire, he worried about where they would spend the winter. Though it was early summer, winter was always a major concern. They had no food stores, no extra clothing and no safe place to live. These thoughts were troubling, but they were secondary thoughts to the troubled young man who bore them alone. His recent deeds were what troubled him the most and he didn't know what to do about the way he felt.

From the top of a small rise, standing beside a lightning struck pine, the boy looked into the night sky. He didn't know which stars Fawn thought were his mother and father so he opened his heart to all of them. "Father...Father, are you there? Father help me. I have killed men. I don't have a place to live." His voice began to break and he couldn't make it stop. Tears gathered at the corners of his eyes as he continued, "I have to care for Fawn. Father, I don't know what to do...I try very hard but..."

He was suddenly aware of a presence near him and he turned to see Fawn standing a few feet away. She walked to him and put her arms around his waist and held him tightly. "I will help you, Sky Eyes. I will do better," she promised, as their tears joined together and ran down his bare chest.

4

When Diving Eagle finished telling his story, his father got up and walked away. He was concerned for his son's well being, but a multitude of emotions were flowing through him. He was ashamed and repulsed, yet he had been young once and knew how things could get out of hand, at times. Bear-scratching-a-tree had some difficult decisions to make and he did not wish to be there when they were made. It would cause him more shame to influence the chief's decisions. He wanted to help his son but the boy had made some poor choices and would have to pay whatever price Bear-scratching-a-tree decided was fair. Lives had been lost. His heart was heavy, for he was sure he would never see his son again.

Otter's father did not get up and walk away. He fixed Diving Eagle with a look that made the boy's skin crawl. He knew he had shamed his father and for that he was sorry, but he knew Otter's father wanted to kill him and that made him afraid. He didn't have the courage to look into the man's eyes.

Bear-scratching-a-tree saw the look Otter's father was giving Diving Eagle and knew the punishment would have to be severe. If it were not, he could lose his position and he did not want that to happen.

Bear-scratching-a-tree was as shocked as the other villagers at the things the young men had done. It was not difficult to discern that what they had done was cowardice and uncharacteristic of the Cheyenne People.

When Diving Eagle finished speaking, Bear-scratching-a-tree had formulated a plan of punishment.

"No man should tell another what to do, but you have done many bad things. You have brought shame upon your father and the Cheyenne People. You will go after the boy and girl. You may kill the wolf; men and wolves should not walk side-by-side down the same trail. You will bring the boy and the girl back to this village and they will take the place of those who did not come back with you. When the two children are in this village you will go away from the territory of the Cheyenne and never return. If you return you will be put to death."

Diving Eagle's mother wailed, piercing the silence and Diving Eagle's heart.

Diving Eagle got to his feet and walked out of the village without a word. He kept his eyes on the ground, too ashamed to look at anyone.

When he was well away from the village, he heard horse hooves pounding the ground, racing toward him. He fully expected to get a buffalo lance in the back and was too afraid to turn around. As the horse neared, he closed his eyes to the pain he knew he was going to feel.

The horse ran by him and he was not killed. Surprised, he opened his eyes. His father was sitting on the horse. He was looking at a far away mountain and would not look at his son. The older man slid off the horse, dropped the reins, turned and walked away without a look or a word.

Thankful for the horse, he swung onto the animal's back. "I'm sorry, Father," he said, before he turned and rode away. As long as he lived, he would not forget the way the muscles in his father's back had tightened when he heard the words.

5

The next morning, Sky Eyes woke early and had some time to think before Fawn woke up. He felt guilty and ashamed for his weakness. Guilt and shame were two things he could deal with, one way or another, but weakness was something else entirely. The weak did not survive and he was afraid he had doomed himself and Fawn simply by being weak. He felt inadequate to lead them but there was no one else. He felt his next decisions would surely lead to their undoing.

Fawn woke up and added wood to the fire without a word. When she had the amount of flame she wanted, she began to warm some meat.

Sky Eyes had expected her to chide him for his behavior last night but she said nothing. Perhaps she was too ashamed to speak to him.

"Fawn...I am sorry for the way I acted last night. I know I am not fit to lead..."

"You do not have to apologize to me. You have nothing to apologize for. It is I who should apologize. I have not helped you enough. I don't always know what to do. When I talked to Mother she told me that your burden was heavy and that you would need my help. She will tell me what to do when I am able to understand her words."

313

"It is not your…"

"Please. Say no more. Our parents are proud of both of us, but mostly they are proud of you. You have done more than they expected and you have done it well. You have no reason to feel shame and guilt. These are words they said to me while I slept."

Sky Eyes sat in awe of Fawn. He had certain capabilities that made him a great hunter and he had good common sense when it came to making life or death decisions. But Fawn was able to look into a person's soul and see what troubled that person. Somehow, she knew the words to say to soothe that person's heart without injuring his pride. He was amazed at the depth of her understanding.

When he looked like he had absorbed and accepted what she had said, she changed the subject, "They also said you should teach me what they have taught you."

Sky Eyes gave her a blank stare. He blinked his eyes as if he had been struck by sudden comprehension and asked, "What would you like to learn first?"

"I would like to be able to get as close to the animals as you do. But first, I would like to have a bow and some arrows."

"I will watch for the right wood. I will make a bow for you," Sky Eyes promised.

Fawn nodded her thanks and then walked to her horse.

6

Diving Eagle sat on the horse his father had given him and looked at the mutilated bodies that had once been his friends. He knew they had felt no pain from the scores of wounds, but the sight was repulsive, nonetheless. He was glad he had come alone; the other villagers would probably have killed him had they seen what his actions had caused.

What my actions have caused, he thought, as he turned his horse away to search out the trail of the boy and girl. He wanted to be angry with them for what they had done to his friends, but he knew they would never have done such a thing had he not disturbed their lives. "What will become of them if I leave them in the village?" he asked himself, out loud. "Will they be slaves? I hope not; I have seen the way people treat slaves and it is not good. They have killed members of my village, I doubt they would ever be adopted."

The horse's ears twitched as he spoke and he was glad the animal was listening. He ordinarily did not speak out loud when on the trail, but he had little to lose now. If he were overheard by marauders they could do little to him that Bear-scratching-a-tree had not already done.

The boy had not tried to cover his signs and the trail was easy to follow. Diving Eagle did not look about, scouting the horizon or searching for signs of other travelers, as was his normal procedure. It was not just a normal procedure, it was a prerequisite to life. Now, he simply followed the trail, eyes to the ground.

He had many thoughts as he rode but the one that returned time and time again was a question he had posed to himself: *Is there a difference between killing yourself and letting someone else kill you?*

7

Sky Eyes had inadvertently gathered some cedar sticks while gathering wood and now the fire snapped and crackled. The sound was pleasant but it made it more difficult to listen to the night. However, they had learned that when the wolf was nearby, they didn't have to be as alert. He would make them aware of danger.

As Sky Eyes listened to the fire, he used his knife to shape the wood he had chosen for Fawn's bow.

Fawn watched intently. They had already eaten and she was getting sleepy, but she wanted to stay awake so she could learn all there was to know without missing a step. She was determined not to be a burden to Sky Eyes. She *would* contribute to the well being of their camp.

As they traveled, the wolf roamed freely. They had no need or desire to restrict his movements. He brought in rabbits almost daily. On this day, however, he had brought in an antelope fawn. The rabbits had been satisfying and tasty but the antelope was a rare treat and they all ate ravenously.

The wolf had unknowingly destroyed most of the antelope hide but Sky Eyes skinned the fawn anyway. They had nothing but the clothes on their backs and a few rabbit hides. They knew better than to throw anything away.

Sky Eyes used sinew from the antelope to string Fawn's bow. She watched patiently as he tied the last knot.

"See if you can pull it back but do not release the string unless you have an arrow nocked," he warned.

"Why?" she asked, as she tested the weight and balance of the bow.

"It will break the bow," he answered.

"Why?" she asked, as she pulled on the string as she had seen him do.

"I do not know but I saw Runs-like-an-antelope do it once. Your father was angry with him; the bow was new."

Fawn strained but was unable to pull the bow back far enough to launch an arrow with any force, had she had an arrow to shoot.

"Do not be sad," Sky Eyes encouraged her. "If you pull on the bow several times a day, you will soon be able to pull it far enough. By the time you are ready, I will have some arrows made for you."

Fawn had been disappointed with her inability to pull the bow back, but Sky Eyes' words made her feel better.

As the evening progressed, Fawn continued to pull on the bow. When Sky Eyes awoke the next morning Fawn was standing by the fire, pulling on the bow. As they traveled, she carried the bow in her hand, trying it frequently.

They could have used the antelope hide for a more important piece of clothing but Sky Eyes was prepared to use it to make a quiver for Fawn.

He gathered limbs from dogwood and honeysuckle during the day and fletched them at night with the feathers of a dead vulture. He had no arrowheads to spare and he was still not proficient at making them, so he did not intend to put them on Fawn's arrows.

Fawn was disappointed, but she understood. She was also resolved to learn how to make arrowheads herself. She didn't know where to start but experience was a very good teacher.

Sky Eyes sharpened Fawn's arrows until they had very sharp tips. When she was able to pull the bow, she would have the tools to kill a deer, provided she hit it in the right place.

8

It was mid-day and Diving Eagle sat on his horse looking at the remains of a small campfire. He finally dismounted and walked to the fire. He bent over and put his hand near the ashes, and quickly drew it away from the hidden heat.

A crooked smile touched his lips as he realized his quarry was near.

This was the eighth day since he had left his village and Diving Eagle had had a change of heart. Actually, he had had a change of mind – he had gone completely insane from regret, shame and fear. He couldn't remember how or why, but he was convinced that the two children he trailed were responsible for his misfortune. He thought he was supposed to take them back to the village but he wasn't supposed to go there…How could he do that? Simple. He would kill them when he found them. What would it matter and who would know? Especially if he couldn't return to the village…

9

Fawn was elated when she pulled the bowstring back as far as it was intended to go. Sky Eyes praised her accomplishment and gave her the quiver and arrows. He taught her to anchor her right hand in the same place every time she drew the bow back.

A tuft of grass on a sandy hillside near their camp served as a target. The bow was stiff and she could shoot only three or four arrows before she had to stop to rest. She couldn't shoot a tight group but most of the arrows were close to the target.

Sky Eyes watched her from the fire. The horses were tied nearby and the wolf was lying on the perimeter of the camp.

A horse nickered and, always alert to the actions of animals, Sky Eyes turned to look. As he was turning, the wolf growled, leapt to its feet and disappeared in the brush. The wolf was out of sight by the time he turned back. Instantly alert, he dropped the wood he had been about to put in the pile. He had been on his knees and now he rolled to his left and into the brush on the opposite side of the camp as the wolf.

When he was in the brush, he got to his feet and ran to Fawn. He could not allow another separation. As he ran, his ankle became entangled and he fell to the ground. He kicked and twisted his foot but was unable to free himself and get to Fawn. He rolled over and saw that he was not entangled – he was caught. He looked into the lost eyes of Diving Eagle.

10

Moving with caution and deliberation, Diving Eagle made his way closer to the camp. The breeze had been prevailing all day and he had no reason to expect it to change now.

317

He had gotten off his horse and slapped it on the rump. It hadn't run very far but he was sure that it could smell the horses in the camp. As his horse approached the camp, the wolf had acted exactly as he had hoped it would.

Now, he had to kill the boy and girl before the wolf figured out what was going on.

He had seen the girl shooting the bow and knew the boy would try to get to her if he thought there was danger nearby.

Once again, things went as he had planned and the boy ran right by him. He chuckled to himself as he thought how easy this was going to be.

He grabbed the boy's ankle when he ran by and watched him fall to the ground. The boy was very strong but his grip was good and he would not let him slip away.

Diving Eagle pulled his knife. He was going to gut the boy when he rolled over.

The boy rolled over and Diving Eagle drew his arm back for a powerful stab.

The uppermost edge of the sun remained above a distant ridge. The light from the sun shone on Sky Eyes' face.

Diving Eagle's breath caught in his throat as he looked into eyes that were a deeper blue than he had ever seen. The setting sun seemed to set the eyes aflame with dancing blue lights.

Diving Eagle was enraptured by the sight and did not thrust his knife. He was so taken by the eyes, that he did not notice the girl moving toward him. He did not see her nock an arrow and draw back on the bow. He heard the *twang* of the bowstring and with the utmost difficulty ripped his eyes away from the boy in time to see the arrow before it struck him in the chest. The force of the arrow knocked him back and he lost his grip on his knife and the boy's leg. His sternum had been punctured and it was difficult to breath but, he thought, if he moved quickly he could still get the boy – the girl would die without the boy. He rolled to his hands and knees and looked up in time to see the wolf sprinting through the underbrush. "Great Creator of all life…Do not let me fall to the wolf…I will…"

Goose flesh covered Sky Eyes' body and he shivered involuntarily as he watched Diving Eagle's face disappear in the wolf's mouth. He turned away and went to Fawn; remembering the times he had hunted the wolf and what could have happened to him or Fawn.

Fawn had become well acquainted with the wolf since she and Sky Eyes had been reunited, but she was not prepared to see the great beast shake the body of the young warrior as if it were no more than that of a rabbit. She turned away and allowed Sky Eyes to lead her back to the camp.

A short time later, the wolf walked through the camp. He resumed his former position, on the outskirts of the camp.

Fawn got up and walked toward the wolf and watched his tail thump excitedly as she approached.

She petted the wolf and thanked him for his help. In the growing dusk, she continued to talk to the wolf, gesturing toward the first twinkling stars of night.

Chapter Twenty-eight

Two moons after the death of Diving Eagle, Fawn and Sky Eyes continued to roam the mountain valleys. It was now past mid-summer and Sky Eyes was concerned about where they were going to spend the winter and what they were going to do about clothing and food during those cold months.

Fawn had become very proficient with the bow and arrow and she was learning the secrets of stealth but all of this would go for naught if they died in a winter storm.

Fawn's mare had thrown a colt in the middle of the last moon; a colt with a spotted rump. Sky Eyes was pleased when he realized that the blood of the Appaloosa still lived, but it was difficult to get too excited when they didn't have a place to call home. Winter was difficult on horses, too, and he would be sad if the colt did not live to see the next spring.

One day, while on the trail, with a morning sun that was still new upon the land, Sky Eyes violently pulled his horse to a stop. The horse danced about for a few seconds, not comprehending the unusual treatment. Fawn looked at him sharply.

He had not said anything to her but he had had an uneasy feeling the night before. And now he knew what had caused the feeling.

"What is it, Sky Eyes?" asked Fawn, as she scanned the meadow ahead of them. She looked to the wolf but he had given no indication that danger was at hand. She saw the muscles in Sky Eyes' jaw flexing and she knew he was disturbed about something.

"We are home, Fawn."

The look she gave him told him she had no idea what he was talking about.

"Look about you. Have you forgotten already? This is the valley of our parents. Where they died."

"Mother…"

"Fawn, she is no more. You know that," he said sternly.

"Why are we here? You said this was a valley of death. You said we would not come here again. Why are we here?"

"I do not know. I do know that we have been drawn here. I have been following the stars that you say are our family. I think they led us here. This place was home to all of us once. I think they wanted us to come home."

"I would like to be near my mother," Fawn whispered, under her breath.

"Welcome home, Fawn," said Sky Eyes, as he led the way toward the hidden finger.